SHE HANDED ME THE paper, which I scanned in one glance. Lucy jumped up to read over my shoulder. My own face looked back at me, an inky portrait done by a police artist who had never seen me. They'd captured my eyes but the jaw was too wide, the brow too heavy, making me look like a degenerate.

I started to feel light-headed. Montgomery took the poster from me. "One thousand pound reward," he read, "for information leading to the capture of Juliet Moreau of London, wanted for murder. Age: Seventeen. Last known residence: Dumbarton Oaks . . ."

The rest of his words faded as my head started throbbing. Lucy put her hands on my shoulders, shaking me back into reason, but it was all I could do to keep breathing.

"This is impossible," Montgomery said, his voice on edge. "They've no way to prove Juliet was responsible for those deaths."

Even though I was.

Also by Megan Shepherd

THE MADMAN'S DAUGHTER
HER DARK CURIOSITY

THE CAGE

A
COLD
LEGACY

A Madman's Daughter Novel

MEGAN SHEPHERD

BALZER + BRAY

An Imprint of HarperCollinsPublishers

Balzer + Bray is an imprint of HarperCollins Publishers.

A Cold Legacy

Library of Congress Cataloging-in-Publication Data
Shepherd, Megan.
 A cold legacy : a Madman's daughter novel / Megan Shepherd. — First edition.
  pages cm
 Summary: After escaping to a remote estate on the Scottish moors, owned by the
enigmatic Elizabeth von Stein, Juliet Moreau, the product of her father's animal-
human experiments, uncovers the truth about the manor's long history of scientific
experimentation—and her own intended role in it.
 ISBN 978-0-06-212809-6
 [1. Science fiction. 2. Experiments—Fiction. 3. Identity—Fiction. 4. Love—Fiction.
5. Characters in literature—Fiction.] I. Title.
PZ7.S54374Co 2015   2014009719
[Fic]—dc23   CIP
                                                                             AC

Typography by Alison Klapthor
15 16 17 18 19 PC/RRDH 10 9 8 7 6 5 4 3 2 1
❖
First paperback edition, 2016

For Lena,
and our Scottish Highlands adventures

ONE

THE LAST TRAVELERS' INN on the road from Inverness was no place to die.

Freezing rain lashed the windowpanes as I huddled over a warm bowl of soup in a corner of the inn's ground-floor tavern. Across the table, Montgomery rubbed a scar on his arm and stared out the window, scanning the muddy road for signs that we were being pursued. In the upstairs room just over our heads, locked away from the other patrons, Edward lay dying.

I rested my hands on Montgomery's anxious ones. "We're safe here. No one would come after us this far north."

Beneath the worn canvas shirt and the pistol strapped to his side was the young man I'd agreed to marry. His silver ring circled my finger, scuffed and dented after our escape from London. For the past three days, Lucy, Edward, and I had huddled in the back of the carriage while Montgomery and Balthazar had driven us through snow and rain without complaint, north to Elizabeth von Stein's estate,

Ballentyne Manor, where we hoped to hide.

I threaded my fingers through Montgomery's. My hands were cold, as always. His were warm and solid. They belonged to a surgeon, not a servant, but I suppose it didn't matter anymore. Now, like me, he was simply a fugitive.

He turned back to the window. "I keep thinking the police will find us."

"We didn't leave any evidence for them to trace. Besides, Elizabeth stayed behind to make certain they don't suspect us. They've no reason to tie us to the . . . the deaths."

Deaths. *Murders* is what I should have said. Just days ago, in the King's College's basement laboratories, we had brought to life five of Father's water-tank creatures that had then slaughtered the most dangerous members of the King's Club. I could still picture the blood seeping from a gash on Dr. Hastings's neck.

Montgomery and I hadn't yet spoken of what had happened at King's College, though I knew the violence of it bothered him deeply. It had been terrible, but necessary—a fact we didn't quite seem to agree on.

"We were very thorough," I added in a dry voice.

A dark look crossed his face. He started to answer, but the sound of laughter drowned out his voice.

Annoyed, I turned to the inn's fireplace, where a dozen red-faced men and women in gaudy satin clothes swapped stories and pints of beer. They were part of a traveling carnival troupe following the winter fair circuit, and were the only patrons sharing the inn with us. A scraggly-haired woman finished telling a ghost story with a loud belch, and the others roared with laughter.

I didn't realize how tensely I was holding my muscles until Montgomery leaned in. "Ignore them," he said.

"It's nonsense," I muttered. "Telling ghost stories. There's enough in this world that's frightening. Only the ignorant would scare themselves on purpose."

Overhead, a floorboard creaked and I sat straighter, watching the ceiling, wondering how Edward was doing. Days had passed, and yet I hadn't come to terms with the fact that he'd poisoned himself. He had tried to end his life before—misguided attempts to kill the monster inside him— but the Beast had always been too strong. It hadn't been until the very end, when Edward and the Beast had nearly melded into one, that he'd been able to force arsenic down his own throat. He'd have been dead in hours if Montgomery hadn't stolen drugs from a chemist's shop outside of Liverpool to counterbalance the worst of the poison's effects. It wasn't a cure, but it was a chance.

Now, overcome by delirium and fever, he was caught somewhere between life and death, between being Edward and being the Beast. Lucy was up there now, tending to him at his bedside, while Balthazar stood guard outside the door.

The floorboards stopped shifting, and I relaxed. I leaned forward, letting my hair screen my face, and toyed with the ring on my finger.

"Ignorant, are we, lass?"

I tossed back my hair to see the speaker—a thin man with a potbelly gut that stretched his cheap green satin tunic. The leader of the troupe, I assumed. The room had gone silent, save the sounds of the fire popping and the barmaid cleaning glasses. None of his troupe was laughing now.

"It was a private conversation," I explained. "You shouldn't have listened in if you didn't want to hear what we had to say."

The thin man's eyebrows shot up in surprise that a young woman would speak to him so boldly. He dragged his wooden stool next to mine, leaning in so close that I could smell the sour beer on his breath. "You've a fine accent. City folk, are you? If you're smart, you'll turn back." He dropped his voice to a theatrical hush. "Strange things happen this far north. Flashes of colored light. Pools of black water. They say half the women smell of witchcraft."

He was trying to frighten me, and it wasn't working. "It's probably the smell of soap," I said. "I don't suppose you'd recognize that particular odor."

The barmaid snickered.

Montgomery's hand tightened over mine. "The last thing we need is to draw attention to ourselves," he whispered in my ear.

He was right. I started to turn away, but the thin man grabbed my stool with surprising strength and dragged me over until my face was only inches from his. "If you've a better ghost story, then by all means, lass, tell us."

Montgomery let out a sigh.

I narrowed my eyes. I should go upstairs. I should leave it be. But my nerves were agitated, and my patience was a prickly monster. If this man thought I didn't have my own horrors to tell, he was wrong.

I started to open my mouth. I could tell him about a madman banished to an island who twisted animals until they spoke and walked on two legs. Or a murderer stalking the streets of London who left behind white flowers tinged with blood. Or I could go upstairs and unlock Edward's door and let the Beast's six-inch claws *show* these carnival performers what real terror was.

"We've had a long journey," Montgomery answered for me. "Our nerves are frayed. We didn't mean to offend." His words had a finality to them that sent the man grumbling back to the fireplace, where the old woman let out another belch.

"I could have handled it on my own," I said.

He raised an eyebrow. "By dumping your soup in his lap, most likely, and starting a brawl. I told you, we need to remain unnoticed. Now I should check on the horses while there's still a bit of daylight. Eat that soup before it goes cold. You need it."

He pulled his oilskin jacket over his shirt and disappeared into the freezing rain. Alone at the table, ignoring the din from the carnival troupe, I watched the steam rise from my soup while I calculated the distance to Ballentyne Manor. We'd been riding for three days, but the rain and snow and a broken strut had slowed us, so it might be another full day before we arrived. Not much time to keep Edward's fever stabilized until we could find a cure.

Footsteps approached, and a man sank into the seat that Montgomery had vacated. I jerked out of my calculations, frowning. He wore the same gaudy green tunic as the rest of the carnival troupe, but I hadn't seen him earlier. I certainly would have remembered if I had. His skin and hair were brown, marking him as a foreigner from Africa or the Americas. I narrowed my eyes.

"I already told your leader that you won't get any stories out of me," I said.

"It isn't a story I want." His voice was deep and raspy, with traces of a faraway accent. "It's *you*, pretty girl."

I raised my eyebrow, ready to fulfill Montgomery's fears and dump the soup in the man's lap, but he only set a deck of fortune-telling cards on the table.

"Or rather, it's your fortune."

I rolled my eyes. I suppose to him I must look the perfect gullible victim: a young girl dressed in wealthy clothes far from home. "I think you meant it's my *coins* you want, but I'm sorry to say I don't believe in fortune-telling. Now, if you'll excuse me." I started to stand.

His mouth quirked in a smile. He flipped over the top card. I tried not to look at the symbol it displayed, but my curiosity won.

The Fool. It depicted a man on a journey, bag slung over one shoulder with a dog following at his heels.

I paused. The dog looked a bit like my little black mutt, Sharkey, and I *was* on a journey, though logic told me it wouldn't be difficult to infer that a girl at a travelers' inn was on a voyage. "Why did you choose that card?"

"I didn't choose it. It chose you."

I rolled my eyes again. "Does anyone actually fall for such dramatics? They certainly don't work on me." I turned to go. I should check on Edward and relieve Lucy and Balthazar of their watch. It would be a long day of travel tomorrow, and we'd all need our sleep.

"You claim not to believe in fortunes," the man said, hand hovering over the next card. "Yet you are intrigued, are you not? Come, pretty girl. One more card." Though I knew it was a trick, my feet didn't move. I jerked my head toward the deck begrudgingly.

"Go ahead, then. One more."

He flipped the card. The Emperor, an arrogant-looking man with white hair and a foppish crown. "Your thoughts are consumed with a man," the fortune-teller said. "A lover? A brother?" He studied me. "No, a father."

I sank back into the chair, every sense alert. The fire crackled while the carnival folk whispered among themselves. I could feel my own heart beating. I knew it was nonsense, but suddenly I was very curious to know what else the fortune-teller might say.

Amusement flickered over his features. "Ask me the question that is on your mind. Then you can judge for yourself if fortunes are real."

I swallowed, glancing around the room almost guiltily. I didn't believe any of it, of course. Science had long ago disproved fortune-telling. And yet I slid a coin across the table, dropped my voice, and tried to pretend I wasn't desperate to know what he would say. "Yes, it's about my father. I want to know . . ."

But I couldn't continue. Memories of Father were a hand around my throat, silencing me. The fortune-teller's gold-flecked eyes met mine, and the rest of the room dimmed. "He has some hold over you, does he not? A hold you wish broken, but it isn't that easy. A child can never escape her father."

His words struck too close to my heart, and I swallowed and looked away. "*I* can. He's dead."

The fortune-teller didn't blink. "Death, in these cases, doesn't matter."

For a moment, his words held me in a rapt silence. I thought of my father: his affection for science, his ability to focus so completely on the task at hand, his ambiguous morality, his madness. All traits I'd seen glimmers of in myself. I pictured myself at his age: a gray-haired scientist, brilliant and terrible, just like him.

One of the carnival folk let out a shrill laugh by the fireplace, and I blinked. The room came back into focus, along with my logic.

"I know how this works," I said a little too fast. "You aren't psychic at all. You're just good at reading people's appearances and mannerisms. You know it's highly likely that a girl my age would have a problem with some sort of man, so you throw out the obvious possibilities and gauge my reaction. Then you let me form my own conclusions. You've nothing to tell me except generalities that could apply to anyone."

I stood, rather satisfied with myself. I couldn't deny, however, that there was a tiny part of me that had almost wanted to believe. In a world of science, a little magic would have been welcome.

"Keep the coin," I said more softly, and turned to go.

"Silver and gold are not the only coin," he said softly. *"Virtue too passes current all over the world."*

A shiver ran through me. Instantly I was a little girl again, sitting in my father's lap as he read heavy volumes from his library. Euripides, I remembered, in the worn leather binding. I had tried to sound out the words when I'd been just learning to read, but Father had grown impatient and finished the phrase for me.

"Silver and gold are not the only coin," he had read. *"Virtue too passes current all over the world."*

It had been one of Father's favorite sayings.

I clenched my jaw. "Why did you use that phrase, in particular?"

My question was interrupted by frantic footsteps on the stairs. The barmaid and the carnival folk all turned as Lucy came stumbling breathlessly down the steps. Ever since we'd left London, a glassy dullness had settled over her eyes. She'd learned her father was a terrible man, financing my father's criminal research and plotting with the King's Club to bring his science to fruition. On top of it all, she'd found out the boy she loved was a monster. When he'd poisoned himself, she'd been inconsolable.

Her eyes locked to mine, the dullness in them replaced by a wildness that made my heart beat faster.

"Juliet," she said. "Come quickly. It's Edward—the fever is breaking."

TWO

I PULLED LUCY INTO the stairwell, out of earshot.

"He sat up," she breathed. "He looked straight at me and said my name. I saw it."

Edward had been delirious for three straight days, mumbling nonsense and thrashing in his chains. The promise—and danger—of him returning to health shot through me like a jolt of electricity. "Fetch Montgomery. He's in the stable. Hurry."

She dashed down the hallway. I climbed the stairs two at a time, tripping over my skirt, and threw open the door to Edward's room. It was a small room, with a single rope bed and old wooden dresser. Inside, a hulking man inclined over where Edward lay. To anyone else the giant would have looked a monster with his misshapen shoulders and hairy face, but to me he was like family.

"Balthazar," I said. "Is it true? Is Edward lucid?"

"I can't rightly say, miss." His big fingers knit together in hesitation. "He's delirious now, that's for certain. If he had a moment of clarity, I didn't see it."

I sat on the bed next to Edward, reaching out to touch his sweat-soaked forehead. "Edward," I whispered. "Can you hear me?"

There had been a time when Edward cared for me deeply, and I hoped that the sound of my voice might reach through his delirium. But his only response was to jerk his head away as though my touch burned him. Thick metal chains twisted around his torso and locked his hands together—a safeguard. Edward and the Beast had been a step away from melding completely in those last moments in London, and now that we'd counterbalanced the poison, we weren't certain who—or rather *what*—we'd find when the fever broke. Would one half overpower the other completely? Or would they meld into a sort of hybrid personality? Either way, Montgomery had insisted on leaving the chains securely fastened, and I hadn't argued. After all, I wasn't convinced it was truly Edward who had been in love with me as much as it had been the Beast. Though perhaps *obsessed* was the better word. To a deadly degree.

"Then you didn't see him sit up and speak?" I asked.

Balthazar's lips folded in indecision. He'd developed a sweet protective instinct for Lucy, but he also wasn't one to lie. "No, miss," he admitted. "I was just outside the door. I think Miss Lucy . . . she might have wanted it badly enough to imagine it."

Bitter disappointment twisted my heart. Of course. We all wanted Edward back so badly that it was easy to hope for miracles. This was the boy who had come back to the island to protect me, who'd understood both my dark and light sides. The only other person who had ever stood in my leaky London attic with a mangy dog and threadbare quilt and wanted nothing more out of life.

My hand hovered a few inches above Edward's shoulder. His eyes were closed, his face still as death. I felt his pulse; it was raging fast. The idea of him calmly sitting up and speaking seemed impossible. I didn't blame Lucy for imagining it, though—only moments ago I'd been nearly desperate enough to believe the words of a fortune-teller.

Lucy stumbled through the doorway with Montgomery behind her, medical bag in hand. He sank to his knees and checked Edward's vital signs with the well-practiced skill of a surgeon.

"Well?" Lucy asked anxiously.

Montgomery set down his stethoscope. He wiped a hand over his face, but not before I saw the flicker of sadness there. The two men had once been at odds, but that had changed since Edward had sacrificed himself for us. Breaking the code in Father's journals had revealed that Edward had been made with Montgomery's own blood. Now he was the closest thing Montgomery had to a brother, in spirit and in flesh. "He's still deep in the fever. His temperature is high, but it hasn't broken."

"He sat up," Lucy insisted. "He looked right at me, and it was *Edward*, I swear. It wasn't that monster."

The rest of us stood awkwardly, none of us willing to tell her what we were all thinking—that stress and sleepless nights were making her imagine things.

"I know you care for him," I said softly. "We all do. But we need to be prepared for any eventuality. The Beast was incredibly strong. The chances of Edward overpowering him aren't high."

Lucy dragged a hand through her dark curls. Her eyes were bleary with exhaustion and just a touch of madness. "I swear, Juliet. I saw it. I saw *him*."

I touched her shoulder gently as Montgomery packed away his medical bag. "Come to bed, Lucy. You need rest. Let Montgomery watch over Edward for a while."

She started to object again but broke into a frustrated sob, and I led her across the hall to the room we shared. We climbed onto the straw mattress that made my skin itch even through the layers of my dress. Through the thin walls, I heard Montgomery pacing in the room next to ours, exchanging low words with Balthazar as they discussed how much longer Edward could survive the fever. My body was heavy with worry and sleep, and with the lingering words of the fortune-teller.

I pulled the blanket tighter as the wind whistled out-side. Lucy fell asleep quickly, exhausted. I watched the faint light play on her face as she slept through nightmares. The blanket had slipped from around her shoulders, replaced by a mantle of gooseflesh. I tucked the covers around her neck. In that space between awake and asleep, fears turned over in my head.

Would we wake to find a cadaver wrapped in chains? Or would the Beast win, and Edward be lost to us forever?

The thoughts worked my insides the way a baker

kneads tough bread. Father had won in life; now he was winning in death, too. He'd created Edward and now he was the arbiter of his destruction. I sank deeper into sleep, anger and worry tangling with the uneasy feeling from my meeting with the fortune-teller. Mind reading was impossible, I knew that. But then again, many things I had once thought impossible were real—split personalities, talking animals, even the possibility of bringing back the dead.

My mind turned back to the conversation I'd had with Elizabeth in the carriage from London before she left us at Derby. I had whispered to her, low and secretive: *But that's not the end, is it? Death, I mean.* She had looked at me fearfully as she understood that I had pieced together her dark family history, which she and the professor had only alluded to. Their ancestry from Switzerland, fleeing persecution, changing their name.

What was their name? I had pressed.

Frankenstein, she'd admitted at last.

MY EYES SHOT OPEN, searching the darkness for a sense of place. A scratchy mattress below me. A single window, filled with fog. I'd slept and dreamed of impossible things.

In that carriage ride leaving London, Elizabeth had revealed that her family was descended from Victor Frankenstein, the brilliant doctor of century-old legends, but she'd insisted that his science had been forgotten and his journals lost. There was no way to replicate his procedures to bring the dead back to life.

I let out a breath I didn't even know I'd been holding

and climbed out of bed, still wearing my wrinkled lavender dress. I twisted the knob silently and slipped into the hall to look for Montgomery.

This far north the days were shorter, eaten on both ends by darkness, but now early-morning light streamed through the hallway windows. Balthazar slept on the floor outside Edward's room, keeping watch, with my little dog, Sharkey, curled against his chest. I stepped over them carefully and tiptoed to the door of Montgomery's room. When I cracked it open, I found the bed empty.

Voices came from the dining room downstairs along with the smell of freshly baked scones and coffee. My stomach reminded me that I hadn't eaten more than a bite of soup the night before. I descended the stairs, stepped into the dining room, and froze.

Four British police officers faced the bar with their backs to me, speaking with the barmaid from last night. I went rigid. A single creaking board might alert them to my presence.

"Two girls under the age of eighteen traveling with a twenty-year-old servant, a large deformed man, and possibly a young gentleman," an officer said.

I didn't dare move a step. The barmaid's eyes flickered to mine just long enough for me to read the warning written in them. It was *us* they were after and she knew it.

"You're certain they came this way, are you?" she asked.

"Clean out your ears, woman. I said we aren't certain of anything. The dispatch said they haven't been spotted since fleeing London, so all the major thoroughfares are being checked as a precaution. Train stations and the ports to the Continent and the Americas as well."

His fellow officer picked at the broken edge of the bar, bored. "I can't imagine they'd have left London for *these* parts. Not even criminals would want to hide out in muddy bogs filled with sheep's dung."

The barmaid narrowed her eyes. Relations had never been easy between the English and the Scottish, and these officers were as English as weak tea. I could practically see her face burning redder with anger as another one of the officers riffled through the ledgers on the counter.

She flipped a bar towel at him. "You can't go poking about through there."

"Keep that rag to yourself," the officer snarled. Tension crackled between them. With my breath held, I took a single step backward.

"Well?" the lead investigator pressed. "Have you seen anyone matching their description or haven't you? We've other work to do."

The barmaid glanced at me again, chewing the inside of her cheek. The woman had no loyalty to us. We were just as English as the officers. One word from her and we'd be thrown into the back of their police carriage and dragged to London to face trial for murder.

Once more, the image of Dr. Hastings's scratched-out eyes flashed in my head.

I took another step backward and the floorboard squeaked. Before the officers could think to look, the barmaid slammed her rag on the bar and said, "If they passed this way, I haven't seen 'em."

Relief flooded me, but it was short-lived. As she noisily pulled out some tankards, someone seized me from behind and dragged me into the side hallway. My heart shot to my throat as I lurched for the knife stashed in my boot until I recognized Montgomery's smell—hay and candle wax. My shoulders eased.

"They're looking for us," I whispered.

"I know. I've readied the carriage and hidden it behind the barn. Balthazar and I will get Edward. Fetch Lucy and bring our bags to the back as quickly as you can."

I dashed up the back stairs with fast, quiet steps. I had scoffed at Montgomery the previous night when he set the horses to pasture and hid the carriage behind the barn. His preparations didn't seem quite so overly cautious now.

I woke Lucy, who gasped awake, and helped her struggle into her dress.

"How did they find us?" she whispered in a fearful hush.

"They haven't found us, not yet. They're checking all the major roads. We'll have to stick to back roads from now on. It'll slow us down, but we dare not risk anything else." Together we loaded our meager belongings into carpetbags and carried them down the back steps silent as mice, with Sharkey tucked under my arm. Day was just breaking over the eastern moors, which were shrouded in a thick silver fog. If we could disappear into that fog while the police were distracted, we would have a chance.

Behind the inn, the horses stamped at the hardened earth, blowing jets of warm steam into the cold morning air as Montgomery harnessed them. "I've put Edward inside the carriage. I don't need to tell you how fragile his condition is. Balthazar will ride inside with you—his appearance is too distinctive, and we don't need anyone paying extra attention to us."

I opened the door to the carriage, where Edward lay flat on the bench-seat, moaning incomprehensibly. His eyes were closed, the chains still wrapped tight. I climbed in, pulling Lucy with me. Balthazar lumbered in behind her and held Sharkey in his lap. Quietly as he could, Montgomery drove the horses to the road, letting their soft steps get lost in the mist, until we were so swallowed up in the fog that I could no longer see the inn. He cracked the whip, and the horses bolted.

I grabbed the window for balance. Lucy sat next to Edward, his head in her lap, her fingers trailing through his sweat-soaked hair as she muttered sweet reassurances to him that he would come through the fever and be eating cinnamon cake again in no time. I didn't have the heart to tell her he likely couldn't hear her, nor would he remember anything she said. Balthazar soon nodded off. The man was able to sleep through anything.

I pushed aside the gauzy curtain every few minutes to make certain we weren't being followed. After an hour, then two, I began to relax. The fog burned off as the morning stretched into midday, but the heather was endless, a sea of rolling red hills and frozen earth, beautiful in its desolation, hypnotic in its monotony. Twice we passed small hamlets, nothing more than clusters of stone cottages with smoke rising from mossy chimneys; once a farmer, wizened and bent, riding a donkey down the dirt road.

Other than that, there was nothing but the moors, the storm clouds building to the north, and the ceaseless pounding of my heart.

THREE

THE AFTERNOON TURNED DARK as the storm grew. A sudden clap of thunder shook the carriage, making me jump. The first drops of freezing rain fell against the glass. I thought of Montgomery alone outside, hunched in his oilskin coat against the wind and the rain.

A flash of lightning lit up the dark clouds. I peered through the window, looking for bobbing lanterns on the horizon that would mean the police carriage was following us, but there was nothing.

Thunder clapped close enough to wake Lucy with a shudder. Her eyes met mine.

"Just a storm," I said softly.

Balthazar reached over and patted her hand, his dark paw engulfing her delicate fingers. There had been a time when Lucy had been terrified of the hulking man, but now she squeezed his hand in return and reached over to straighten his shirt collar, which had gone askew.

"Will the staff at Ballentyne be afraid of me?" he asked her.

She laughed. "*Everyone* is afraid of you at first sight. You look a walking terror." She brushed dust off his threadbare coat tenderly. "But once they get to know you, they'll adore you just as I do."

When I turned back to the window I saw lights ahead of us, unmoving. Another hamlet. No, larger than that. A village. After only a handful of signs of life for the past few days, the prospect of a village, tiny and crumbling though it must be, still made me anxious. Lucy's brow was knit, too.

"Surely they wouldn't have a police outpost in such a small place, would they?" She laid a protective hand on Edward's chest. His lips moved, but no sound came out.

"I can't imagine they would," I said hesitantly. "Anyway, I'm positive they'll give up the search after a few more days."

It felt like a hollow promise, and the hard look Lucy gave me confirmed it.

As we rode closer the lights took shape—candles in windows, lanterns hung outside doors. The village was nothing more than a few intersecting dirt roads, but after the desolation of the moors, it whispered of civilization.

Montgomery stopped the horses outside a tavern. He came to the carriage door, opening it just a crack to keep the rain from drenching us. "I'm going to ask for directions. We can't be far now."

We watched him saunter over the muddy street as

though he didn't even feel the bite of freezing rain. A face appeared in the tavern window. The door opened and he spoke to a woman for a few moments, then stomped back through the mud. "This village is called Quick," he told us. "The manor's only five miles from here."

"Did you hear that?" Lucy murmured to Edward, still stroking his hair. "We're almost there. Just hold on. Everything will be all right once we arrive."

Montgomery's eyes shifted to me. Neither of us wanted to remind Lucy that the prospect of Edward's fever breaking—and the Beast's reappearance—was almost more frightening than the fever itself. Delirious, he was less of a threat.

"Let's go then," I whispered to Montgomery. "And quickly."

He closed the door and in another moment we were moving again, passing through the rest of Quick. Then all too soon the village was nothing but fading lights. The storm grew and the road became rougher, and all the while Edward's eyes rolled back and forth beneath shuttered lids.

Thunder struck close by, and Lucy shrieked. Montgomery whipped the horses harder, pulling us along the uneven road impossibly fast, trying to outrun the storm. I twisted in the seat to look out the back window at the pelting rain. A stone fence ran alongside us.

"We must be getting close," I said.

"Not soon enough," Lucy breathed. "We're going to

crash if he keeps driving like this!"

The road widened, straightening, letting us travel even faster. Lightning struck close by, blinding me. The horses bolted. Lucy screamed and covered her eyes, but I couldn't tear mine away. The lightning had struck an enormous oak tree, twisted from centuries of wind. The oak took flame, blazing despite the rain. A smoking gash ran down the trunk—the lightning's death mark. I watched until the rain put out most of the flames, but it still smoldered, billowing hot ash into the night.

The horses pawed the earth, and I grabbed the window to steady myself. At this wild speed, just hitting a single rock at the wrong angle would send the carriage shattering to the ground. It was madness to go so fast. Couldn't Montgomery calm the horses?

Just when I feared the carriage would careen out of control, it stopped short, throwing me against the opposite wall. I tangled in Lucy's limbs as the chains around Edward's body clinked. Balthazar grunted, jerking awake at last. We scrambled in the bottom of the carriage until the door flew open.

Montgomery stood in the pelting rain. I feared he'd say we'd broken another strut or the horses had gone lame or we'd have to spend the night in the harsh storm.

But then I saw the lights behind him, and the night took shape into a turreted stone manor with bright lamps blazing in the windows and gargoyles on the roof vomiting rain into a stone courtyard.

Montgomery's eyes met mine beneath the low brim of his hat.

"We've arrived," he said.

THE IRON KNOCKER WAS freezing beneath my bare palm, but I pounded it again and again. Lucy huddled by my side, blanket hooded over her head, rain streaking down both our faces. In the courtyard Montgomery held the horses to keep them from bolting again. Balthazar remained in the carriage with Edward and Sharkey, hidden from view. It was one thing for strangers to arrive in the middle of a storm: quite another if they had a monster, a delirious patient wrapped in chains, and a scruffy black dog with them.

At last, the door creaked open. Knowing I must look a mess, I brushed the rain off my face and fumbled for the letter of introduction pressed safely within my dress's folds. Elizabeth had told me her housekeeper's name, Mrs. McKenna, and I expected to see a severe woman with a tight gray bun. Instead, a startlingly beautiful young woman with clover-honey skin and loose dark hair stared at us. If rain-soaked strangers arriving unannounced after dark surprised her, she didn't show it.

"I'm sorry to arrive without notice," I called over the pounding rain. "Elizabeth von Stein sent us. I'm her ward."

The young woman didn't open the door a crack wider. No expression crossed her face save one of mild suspicion. Her dress was old-fashioned and puritanical in style, covering her body from feet to chin. She wore white gloves, though whether for religious reasons or because of the cold, I wasn't sure.

Lucy gave me a questioning look, and I knew what she was thinking. The young woman, with her black hair and dark complexion, looked to be Romany. What was a Roma doing this far into Scotland, and dressed like a Puritan?

"May we come in?" I asked at the woman's sullen silence.

Her eyes flickered to Montgomery in the courtyard, and her hand went to the old-fashioned high collar around her neck, fumbling with the upper button. "Elizabeth's ward?" she asked in a flat voice. "Elizabeth has no ward."

"Her uncle, Professor von Stein, was my guardian, but he passed away recently and Elizabeth took me in. I've the papers to prove it." I glanced back at the carriage. "We'd be obliged if we could stable the horses in the barn during the storm."

The woman begrudgingly jerked her chin toward the eastern side of the house. Montgomery led the horses off, leaving us alone. She opened the door wider for us to enter, then shut it with a groan of hinges. I jumped at the sound. Lucy's eyes were wide as she stood in the center of the grand foyer, dripping rainwater onto the stone floor. The foyer was Gothic in style, ancient by the look of it. Fading tapestries collected dust on the walls. An imposing stone staircase led to an upper landing, where a chandelier flickered and dimmed. It was surprisingly bright. With a start, I realized the light wasn't coming from a flame—how on earth did Elizabeth have electricity all the way out here?

The young Romany woman stepped forward, her shoes scuffing on the floor.

I raised a frozen hand to my hair, pushing the soaked

locks out of my face. "My name is Juliet Moreau, and this is Lucy Radcliffe. Let me show you the letter of introduction from Elizabeth. . . ."

I tried to unfasten my buttons to pull out the damp letter, but my fingers were too numb. The fire in the main hall wasn't enough to chase away the chill. As I fumbled with my many layers of clothing, a clock ticked from some unseen room, highlighting the silence. I glanced at Lucy. I hadn't expected such a sullen welcome to Ballentyne, and for Lucy's part, she looked ready to run back outside and take her chances with the storm.

Another door slammed from deep within the manor and I whirled to the entryway. The Romany woman turned slowly to a back corner, where low male voices and heavy footsteps approached.

Montgomery and Balthazar entered, hands clasped behind their necks like prisoners of war. A gray-haired manservant with a thin face like a starved fox followed, pointing a rifle at the backs of their heads.

"Wait!" I cried. "We're friends of Elizabeth!"

The manservant ignored me. "I found two pistols on 'em and this rifle. They've a man wrapped in chains in the carriage. A prisoner, most like. We should alert someone in Quick to telegram the police."

My heart fluttered wildly.

"He's not a prisoner!" My words were sharp enough to shock them. The man cocked his head toward me and I saw he was missing his left ear; there was only a jagged scar in its place. Lucy shrank closer to me.

"His name is Edward Prince and he's gravely ill," I continued. "We've only chained him so he doesn't harm himself in his delirium. He isn't a threat and neither are we, so you can lower that rifle and drop this talk about sending for the police." I tore at my damp layers until I found Elizabeth's letter and thrust it at the young woman. "It's from Elizabeth. It says—"

"I can read," she said coldly, opening the letter.

Lucy clung to my side. She was normally so much bolder than I, but she was mistress of the tearoom and salon. Here, in this last bastion of civilization before the upper wilds of Scotland, was the first time I'd ever seen her rendered speechless.

The woman finished the letter and exchanged a glance with the manservant. "It is as they say it is," she said. I'd expected the letter to ease her suspicions, but if anything, her voice sounded even colder than before. Regardless, he lowered the rifle.

Montgomery took off his hat and wiped his wet hair back. "Balthazar, fetch Edward and our trunks, if you'd be so good." Balthazar shuddered like a wet dog and turned to go. Thunder crashed outside and the chandelier dimmed, plunging the foyer into low light before the howling wind let up and the chandelier flickered back to full power.

"My name is Valentina," the woman said curtly. "I'm second in charge after the housekeeper. This is Carlyle, the gamekeeper. We aren't used to Elizabeth sending guests, certainly not *wards*."

"Yes, well, here we are dripping all over your floors," I said with an uneasy laugh. "Is there a place we might dry off and warm ourselves? I think we're all nearly frozen through." I couldn't stop shivering, and it wasn't just on account of the cold.

Valentina nodded toward the roaring grand fireplace. "Wait here. I'll tell McKenna you've arrived." She exchanged another glance with Carlyle, who followed her out of the foyer.

We were left alone in the silent hall. Watery old portraits hung high above our heads, looking down on us with eyes that seemed all too real. My skin rippled as if the house had eyes and ears, and all were trained on us.

At last Lucy broke her silence to stomp off toward the fire. "Would it kill them to offer us a towel?" she hissed under her breath. "Some tea? You'd think we were lepers."

I was glad, at least, that she'd found her voice again. We huddled around the fireplace, holding our hands toward the flame. Montgomery hung his oilskin coat on a hook by the fire.

"Elizabeth warned me they were out of practice with polite society," I offered.

Lucy scoffed. Behind her, a faded threadbare boar loomed in the heavy tapestry. "Out of practice? More like they were both raised by wolves. I can't imagine, if Elizabeth were here, she'd tolerate their behavior. A rifle to Montgomery's head!"

I rubbed my hands together in front of the fire and thought of the first time I'd met Elizabeth. She'd dragged me through a kitchen window and dumped me on a hard stone floor. Perhaps I shouldn't have been surprised by our reception after all.

"Well, we are imposing on their goodwill," I said. "I'm just grateful to be out of that carriage. Besides, Elizabeth should arrive in a few days—"

A door slammed again and Valentina returned, though without any sort of towel or blanket for us to dry ourselves. If she noticed that we were all soaked to the bone and shivering, it only seemed to give her perverse satisfaction. "Carlyle will help your associate unload the carriage and carry the sick gentleman upstairs. McKenna said to bring you down to meet the rest of the staff. You've arrived at an unfortunate time. We're in the middle of a funeral."

Lucy's face went white. "Who died?"

Valentina's mouth quirked, the first flicker of emotion we'd seen other than sullenness. "The last group of strangers who came to this door."

I couldn't tell if she was joking or not.

"Follow me," she said. "The ground is frozen until spring thaw. We can't bury our bodies until then, so we hold our funerals inside."

I hesitated. "*Inside?* But where?"

Valentina met my eyes, and I realized that I wasn't certain that I wanted to know where, exactly, the bodies were kept. Nor that Ballentyne Manor was anything like the safe haven I'd expected.

"You'll see for yourself. I hope for your sake—if you truly are the mistress's ward—you have as strong a constitution as she does, Miss Moreau."

FOUR

VALENTINA LED THE WAY down the damp cellar stairs with a candle in one hand, despite the line of electric lights running alongside us.

"Best not to rely on the electricity," she explained over her shoulder. "The lights have gone out on me too many times when I'm down here alone, and it's blacker than the devil."

The farther we descended, the colder the air grew. My breath fogged in the dim lights. No wonder they stored the bodies here—the temperature and sulfuric gases released from the bogs would preserve them in near perfect condition until the spring thaw, and the stone walls would keep away the vermin.

Montgomery was close behind me, but Lucy trailed at a distance, holding her hem high so as not to drag it on the slick stones of the spiral staircase. At last we reached the bottom, where the distant sound of a droning voice came from a room ahead that glowed faintly in the electric lights.

"It was the plague," Valentina said.

"Plague?" Lucy asked.

"The ones that died. The plague killed them. Beggars following the winter fair circuit. Several women and children among them, too."

She spoke casually enough, as though dead children were as common as the sheep dotting the landscape. Lucy gasped, but Valentina's straightforward attitude didn't bother me. Back in London, it was all high tea and polished silver. Very refined, very polite. At least these people, sullen though they were, didn't deny the dangers around them.

Lucy lifted her skirts higher, as if the plague might be lurking in the damp stone underfoot, and Valentina smirked. We followed her through an open doorway into a chamber where a dozen or so servants, most of them young girls, gathered around a brass cross set on an altar.

"A chapel?" Lucy whispered to me. "In the *cellar*?"

I nodded. I'd heard about places like this. In such cold climates, when going outside was nearly impossible half the year, old households had built chapels indoors. Parts of this one, crumbled as it was, looked as though it dated back practically to the Middle Ages.

A few of the girls looked up when we slipped in, curiosity making them fidget. None were dressed as puritanically as Valentina, though all their clothes were rather dour and old-fashioned. It was a stark contrast to their bright eyes and red cheeks. Clearly they hadn't known or cared about any of the deceased, because I caught a few excited whispers exchanged about Lucy's and my elegant dresses, and Montgomery's handsome looks.

Valentina shushed them and they snapped back to attention.

At the head of the room stood an older woman with a red braid shot through with white hairs, who wore a pair of men's tweed trousers tucked into thick rubber boots. She was reading a few somber verses from a leather-bound volume in a heavy Scottish accent. She hadn't yet noticed our presence.

On closer inspection, I realized *all* the servants were women, most of them barely more than children. Where was the rest of the male staff, besides the old gamekeeper?

Montgomery stood just in the doorway, as though it would be trespassing to go any farther. When I met his eyes, he was frowning.

"What's wrong?" I asked.

He leaned down to whisper in my ear. "The bodies. I didn't expect so many of them."

The servant girls shifted, and I caught sight of the bodies he was talking about. A dozen of them were laid out on stone benches and the floor, covered with white sheets. My stomach knotted, reminding me of the King's College autopsy room, where Edward's victims had been laid out the same way. Dr. Hastings and the others I'd killed would have been laid there as well, after the massacre. Their wives and children would have come to identify the corpses. I suddenly felt sick.

Lucy drew in a breath and crossed herself.

"Don't worry," Montgomery whispered to her. "The

germs will be long gone by now. There's no danger of us catching it."

Valentina walked among the servant girls, stepping unceremoniously over one of the bodies, and whispered to the older woman, whose eyes shot to us as she said a few final words. As soon as the brief service had concluded, the red-haired woman motioned for us to follow her into the hallway.

"Goodness me," she said, pressing a hand to her chest. "Strangers during such a storm? And to arrive during these poor souls' funeral—you must never have suffered such shock. Look at you, frozen through and through. You must be starved."

The woman had a motherly way about her that made me feel safe even standing among the dead, and an enormous weight shifted off my shoulders. At least *someone* was giving us a warm reception.

"Are you Mrs. McKenna?" I asked.

"I am, my dear. My family has helped the von Steins with the management of this household for generations; you're in good hands, I promise, and if the mistress has sent you, then you're more than welcome here." She turned back toward the chapel. "Lily, Moira, you girls go make up the rooms on the second floor for our guests."

Two of the older girls skipped off into the hallway, more than glad to escape the dreary funeral. Mrs. McKenna first took my hands, then Lucy's, and even Montgomery's big ones, rubbing them and *tsk*ing at the cold as if we were children. "Come with me, little mice. We shall get you warmed."

I cast one final look back at the bodies. Mrs. McKenna pressed a hand against my shoulder, turning me away from the sight. "Aye, a shame. They took shelter here a fortnight ago—I could hardly turn them away, not with so many children among them. And the mistress would have wanted it. But they brought with them the plague, and it took all of them overnight. I doubt they have any relations who will be coming by to collect the bodies."

"None of your staff caught the plague?" I asked, as we made our way back up the spiral stairs with Valentina wordlessly trailing behind us.

"No, thank heavens. The vagrants slept in the lambing barn while they were here. I had Carlyle burn it as a precaution, though in these parts, at this time of year, it's too cold for diseases to spread easily in a house like this. We keep it well cleaned."

Her knowledge of biology impressed me, but no more so than Valentina's ability to read. It was rare for servants to be highly educated, especially in such rural parts.

We entered the kitchen, a cavernous room with a roaring fire and a pair of geese roasting on the spit. My stomach lurched with hunger. A thin girl attended to the roast, chewing her nail as she regarded us with round eyes. Mrs. McKenna opened a tin and handed Lucy, Montgomery, and me each a crusty scone.

"That'll tide you over till supper. Let's get you settled now, and tomorrow I'll show you the manor and grounds, if the storm lets up. There are times it gets so bad the levees fail and the road to Quick floods for days. We can be completely cut off. Our own little island, of sorts." She handed me the candelabrum from the table. "Take this. The electricity will likely go out if the wind continues. Follow Valentina—she'll show you to your rooms. I'll make sure my girls take care of your sickly friend. A fever, is that right?" She shook her head in sympathy. "How awful. We shall put him in a room with a fireplace to keep him warm."

"That would be lovely—" Lucy began.

"No," Montgomery interrupted. "No fire. No sharp objects either. And make sure the room has a strong lock. We'll attend to him ourselves, not your girls."

Mrs. McKenna's eyebrows raised, and she exchanged a look with Valentina, but like any good servant, she didn't probe. "No fire, then. And an extra lock on the door." She paused. "Might I see that letter of introduction?"

I handed it to her, and she read Elizabeth's letter, then looked up with a startled expression. Her gaze shifted between Montgomery and me.

"Engaged?" she asked.

Behind her, the thin little girl at the goose spit gasped.

"Yes," I said, worried. "Is . . . is it a problem?" With their high-collared dresses and sleeves down to their wrists, they might be religious types who wouldn't approve of Montgomery and me traveling together unwed.

"No, no, little mouse," Mrs. McKenna said. She glanced at the thin girl at the spit, who now wore a bright smile that seemed out of place in the gloomy manor. "It's only that, with the exception of old Carlyle, you've walked into a house of women. We haven't had much occasion to celebrate things like engagements, not in a long time. The girls would so adore helping to arrange a wedding. Perhaps in the spring, after thaw, or midsummer when the flowers are in bloom. It'll cheer them up so, especially after a harsh winter."

I smiled. "We'd love their help. And spring sounds perfect." The warm scone in my stomach, Montgomery at my side, girls tittering over wedding plans: it was starting to feel more like a home, and I told myself that the unsettled feeling I'd had when I first arrived was just nerves from the road.

I squeezed Montgomery's hand, but the troubled look he gave me said he wasn't nearly as reassured as I was.

"THERE ARE THREE FLOORS, not including the basement," Valentina said as she led us up the stairs, with Balthazar trailing behind carrying our three carpetbags over one shoulder. Two of the littlest servant girls walked alongside him with fresh linens in their arms, staring up at him. One had a limp that made her walk nearly as slowly as he did. Far from frightened, they seemed utterly transfixed by him.

"That doesn't include the towers," Valentina continued. "There's one in the southern wing and one in the north. The north tower is the biggest. It's where the mistress's observatory is. I'm the only one with a key to it, on account of the delicate equipment. She's taught me how to use most of the telescopes and refractors and star charts. In turn, I'm teaching the older girls. Education is often overlooked in female children; I'm determined to make sure the girls here have good heads on their shoulders." She cast me a cold gaze.

"Between McKenna and me, we manage quite well during Elizabeth's absences. Though we're all eager for her return, of course."

The stairs creaked as we made our way to the second floor, which Valentina explained was mostly comprised of guest bedrooms and a library they used for breakfast. The regular servants' rooms were on the third floor, and she and McKenna each had one of the larger corner rooms in the attic. Carlyle slept in an apartment above the barn.

She passed me a set of keys with her gloved hand. "One for your bedroom, and one for that of your ill friend. You're welcome in any portion of the house that isn't locked. Those are the observatory and the mistress's private chambers."

"And my dog?"

"Carlyle put him in the barn. There are plenty of rats for him to catch."

Lucy gaped. "He's supposed to eat *rats*?"

Valentina appraised Lucy's fine city clothes with a withering look. "I didn't realize he was canine royalty. Would he care for a feather bed and silver bowl, perhaps?"

Lucy drew in a sharp breath. I could practically see smoke coming from her ears. I doubt she'd ever been spoken to so boldly, by a maid or anyone else. I wrapped my arm around hers and held her back. "Rats will be fine," I said.

Valentina smiled thinly and continued up the stairs.

We reached the landing, where a long hallway stretched into darkness broken only by flickering electric lights. Heavy curtains flanked the windows, with old portraits hanging between them.

"The Ballentyne family," Valentina said, motioning to the portraits. "That one is the mistress's great-grandfather. And that woman is her great-aunt."

"But I thought the Franken—I mean, the von Stein family—owned the manor," I said.

"Victor Frankenstein, you mean? You needn't be so secretive, Miss Moreau. Elizabeth trusts us completely; she's told us all about her family's history. The Ballentynes were the original owners of the manor. The first Lord Ballentyne built it in 1663 overtop the ruins of previous structures. He was something of an eccentric. Went mad, they say."

Montgomery stopped to give Balthazar time to catch up to us. The two little girls were hanging by his side, hiding smiles behind their hands. The one with the limp skipped ahead to Valentina and tugged on her skirt. Valentina bent down to hear the girl's whisper.

"The girls say your quiet associate—Mr. Balthazar, is it?—belongs here." She pointed a gloved finger at a small portrait beneath a flickering electric lamp. "They say he's the spirit of Igor Zagoskin." The portrait portrayed a large man in an old-fashioned suit, stooped with a hunchback, face covered by a hairy beard. Balthazar blinked at the painting in surprise. The resemblance was striking.

"Who is that man?" Montgomery asked.

"One of Lord Ballentyne's most trusted servants, back in the 1660s. He was rumored to be a smart man, strong as an ox. He helped Ballentyne in his astronomical research."

Balthazar blinked a few more times in surprise, then grinned at the girl with the limp. "Thank you, little miss. I like the look of him. I shall hope to carry on in his tradition."

"Your room is through here, Miss Moreau." Valentina opened a door into a bedroom that emitted the smell of mustiness and decades of disuse, but inside I found it freshly tidied. Balthazar set my bag on the soft carpet. Valentina handed me a smaller key.

"What's this one for?" I asked. The bedroom door had only one lock.

"A welcome present from McKenna." She smirked. "I'm sure you'll figure it out soon enough. Mad Lord Ballentyne was full of surprises when he built this house."

The little girl with the limp giggled, and Valentina shushed her and swept her out of the room, leaving me alone while she showed the others to their rooms down the hall.

I went to the window, where I could make out little in the dark rain. Lightning crackled, revealing a sudden flash of ghostly white. I jumped back in surprise. It looked like enormous white sheets, spinning impossibly fast, and I threw a hand over my heart before the whirling shapes made sense.

A windmill.

At least now I knew the source of Elizabeth's electricity. Glowing lights flickered from the other exterior windows on this wing. I wondered which room was Montgomery's, and Lucy's, and which room they'd put Edward in earlier. Sorrow washed through me at the thought of him. If only Lucy's premonitions were right, and the fever would break and he'd be himself again, miraculously cured of the Beast.

Unfortunately, I wasn't nearly as optimistic as Lucy. Sometimes things *didn't* work out for the best. The King's Club massacre, for one. It had been a messy, cruel solution, even if it had saved us.

Would I take it back, if I could?

The answer eluded me, and I started to pull the drapes closed over the window, tired of the same guilty thoughts circling in my head, only to find that the curtains spanned a wider section of the wall that hid a secret door. The small key Valentina had given me was a perfect fit, and I swung it open.

I let out a soft sound of surprise when I found a second bedroom that was like a mirror to my own—except for the young man standing by the wardrobe in the process of undressing. Montgomery turned at the sound of the door. His suspenders hung by his side, his blond hair loose and still damp from the rain.

"Adjoining bedrooms," I explained, holding up the key. "This must be the welcome present Mrs. McKenna meant for us. How scandalous. I guess the household isn't as puritanical as their clothes make them seem." I tried to keep my voice light. Since fleeing London we'd barely spoken, and I didn't want our new life here to begin in sullenness. But he came to the doorway and rubbed his chin, distracted.

"What is it?" I asked.

"It doesn't feel right," he said. "Those bodies in the cellar. This place, these people, greeting us with a rifle to our heads." There was fear in his expression, which made my heart dim. Montgomery was rarely afraid of anything.

"It's better than being arrested for murder," I said.

He raised an eyebrow, unconvinced. "Well, of course. The housekeeper is kind enough, and they're good to take us in, but they're hiding something. I can smell it."

"Does it smell like musty old clothes?" I tried to lighten the mood again. "Because that's just the carpets."

He tensed, not in the mood for joking.

"This isn't London," I said, more seriously this time. "Elizabeth clearly lets them run wild, and they've no idea what to do with us. You saw the disdainful look Valentina gave Lucy, like we'd die without our tea and crumpets." I laid a hand on his chest, toying with his top button. "I suspect she's just jealous of our nice clothes and fancy address in the city."

For a moment we stood mirrored on either side of the door while the wind whistled outside. His jaw tensed, and he stepped back so my hand fell. "We don't have a fancy address anymore. We can never return to London, not since you murdered three men."

I blinked. The fire crackled, heat trying to push us even farther apart, and my heartbeat sped up. "You know I had no choice. I didn't want to do it."

"That isn't what you said at the time. I could see in your eyes how badly you wanted to kill Inspector Newcastle. You burned him *alive*." He paused, breathing heavily, arms braced on either side of the door. I could only gape, wanting to deny the accusation but not quite able to. "Sometimes you remind me so much of your father, it's frightening."

The sting in his words settled into the curtains and

bedspread like the smell of chimney smoke, and just as impossible to get rid of. "It was better than letting them use Father's research," I said in my defense. "They would have hurt so many more people. Father would have helped them, not stopped them."

He cursed under his breath. "I shouldn't have said anything."

I placed my hand on my forehead, trying to calm the blood searing in my veins. "No. Don't apologize. We said we'd always be honest with each other. And if I'm being honest with you, I think you should be thankful we have a roof over our heads and walls around us, and stop questioning Elizabeth's generosity. There's nothing wrong with these people, and there's nothing wrong with me."

I closed the door in his face, twisted the key, and leaned my back against it. He knocked and called to me, but I didn't answer. I crawled into bed and thought about Montgomery's words. It was true that I'd been obsessed with bringing the water-tank creatures to life, even knowing the bloodshed that would follow. Maybe the fortune-teller was right. Reading the future was nonsense, but there was a grain of truth in how his predictions had made me feel—as though escaping Father was impossible, even in death. Maybe, just maybe, I should stop trying so hard to fight it.

FIVE

That night, I dreamed I was in the professor's house on Dumbarton Street, in the cellar where we'd kept the Beast locked away. I descended the stairs slowly, listening for the *tap-tap-tap* of claws on the stone floor. When I faced the barred cellar door, though, no yellow eyes met mine. Tropical warmth and the smell of the sea came instead. I was back on Father's island, ankle deep in the surf, watching the volcano's plume ascend into a cloudless sky.

"You're engaged to him," a voice said from behind me. "Yet you know so little about him."

The Beast emerged from among the palms. I'd only ever seen the Beast at night, or cast in shadows. In sunlight he looked more like Edward. Just an ordinary young man—except for his golden yellow eyes.

"Montgomery and I grew up together," I said. "I know him better than anyone."

"And yet he's keeping secrets from you." The Beast stopped a few feet away from me, smelling both sweet and bitter, like the blood-soaked plumeria flowers he'd left for me in London. "I warned you about his secrets once. You like to pretend that you didn't hear, and yet here I am in your head, a voice you can't escape."

My head suddenly ached with splitting pain.

"Do you remember what I said?" he asked.

I pressed a hand to my temple.

Ask Montgomery about your father's laboratory files on the island, he had said. *About the ones you didn't see.*

MY EYES SHOT OPEN as I jerked upright. The smell of the professor's root cellar hung around me like fog. I tried to stand but the memory choked me until I realized it was only the bedspread tangled around my limbs.

Scotland, I reminded myself. *I'm in Scotland, not on the island.*

I climbed out of bed and threw open the window for fresh night air. The rain had stopped, but the smell of bogs was heavy. No matter how many deep breaths I took, I couldn't rid myself of that terrible dream.

I looked toward the door to Montgomery's room. My fingers drifted to the thin silver ring on my finger, glinting in the candlelight.

My future husband.

Had I been wrong to disregard the Beast's warning about him?

My stomach churned with worry. I didn't want to return to an empty bed, frightening dreams, and thoughts of a fiancé who might be keeping secrets. I decided to find

Edward's room and verify with my own eyes that the Beast hadn't returned.

I threw on an old dressing gown I found in the armoire. It was lacy and long, softly feminine yet old-fashioned. I lit the candelabrum and opened my door silently.

The hallway was quiet. Everyone else was sleeping soundly. I pressed the electric light button on the wall but nothing happened—the electricity must have gone off in the storm. I peered through the first keyhole I came to, at a room smaller than my own and considerably cozier. To my surprise, the bed was empty, the occupant curled on the warm hearthstones instead, his big hairy arms tucked under his heavy head, snoring softly. Balthazar. Sharkey slept in his arms, feet twitching as he chased dream rabbits. Balthazar must have snuck down to the barn to get him. The sweet scene warmed me as if I was curled by the hearth with them.

A floorboard squeaked down the hall, and I jerked upright, but it was nothing—just the manor settling. I shivered anyway as I peeked in the next keyhole. A half dozen candles burned on the table as though the room's occupant feared the dark. A soft murmur came and the figure rolled over, flashing dark curls and a pale face not so different from my own.

Lucy.

There was only one guest bedroom left, so it had to belong to Edward. I peered through the keyhole. A candle on the side table flickered there, too. Edward lay still as a corpse on the bed, not even a blink or a flicker of breath to tell me he was alive. The chains wrapped around his arms and chest glinted in the candlelight.

I shuddered. The servants must think us mad to chain a young man we claimed was a friend, but if they knew the truth, they'd be even more fearful of us. I took out the key to his room, ready to open it.

Suddenly a face blocked the keyhole. A shriek ripped through me as I stumbled backward. An eye looked back from the other side of the keyhole. It was milky white, completely devoid of color.

It blinked.

I screamed.

MONTGOMERY WAS FIRST INTO the hallway. He spotted me and rushed to my side.

"What's happened?" he asked, all tension from our fight put aside.

Another door slammed, then another, and footsteps sounded above our heads. I tried to steady my breath.

"A face," I breathed. "There's someone in Edward's room."

Uncertainty creased his forehead. He crossed to Edward's door and rattled the knob. "Still locked. Only you and Valentina have a key."

Lucy's door opened across the hall. Her sleep-dazed face peeked through the crack. "Juliet? I thought I heard a scream."

Mrs. McKenna appeared at the top of the stairs with

Valentina right behind her, both in their loose-fitting sleep shirts. "Was that you who screamed, Miss Moreau?" Mrs. McKenna asked.

"I saw someone in Edward's room. Blast it, I'm going in."

I turned the key in the lock and opened the door. We all pressed inside. Edward lay on the bed, unconscious, with sweat dripping down his brow. My heart pounded as I searched the tall curtains. Montgomery threw open the armoire, and Lucy knelt to look under the bed. They both came up empty-handed.

Had it been only my imagination?

Mrs. McKenna watched me keenly. "This person you saw," she said, throwing Valentina a wary glance. "Can you describe him or her?"

"I don't know if was a man or a woman. I only saw the person's eye looking at me through the keyhole. It was completely white, as though the iris had been drained of color."

Mrs. McKenna shared another look with Valentina, this one substantially less mysterious. I felt as though I was missing something between these two.

"Do you know the person?" Montgomery asked.

"Oh, aye, we know him." Mrs. McKenna's mouth quirked with either annoyance or amusement, I couldn't tell. She walked over to a fading oil painting in a gilded frame that stood as tall as her. To my surprise she swung it open on groaning hinges, reaching quickly into what must have been an alcove or tunnel behind the painting, and grabbed something that scrambled there.

I heard a tussle as the thing tried to get away, but then gave up with a curt little sigh and let the housekeeper pull it out.

No one was more shocked than I when her hand reemerged clutching a small child by his shirt collar's high nape. He was a tiny thing, five years old perhaps, with a shock of dark hair and a scowl that rivaled even that of the old bartender from the inn on the main road. A live white rat perched on his shoulder—a tamed pet. Lucy made a face of disgust.

When Mrs. McKenna turned him toward the light, I saw his eyes. One was a deep brown, the other milky white.

"Is this your trespasser, miss?"

"Y . . . yes," I stammered.

Mrs. McKenna let go of the boy's shirt. "This is Master Hensley. He's been missing since breakfast. He often disappears; he always comes back sooner or later, when he's hungry. I should have thought to look in the walls."

"Master Hensley?"

"Aye, Mistress Elizabeth's son." Mrs. McKenna gave me a strange look. "Didn't she mention him?"

Something curdled my blood. I'd spent a month in London with Elizabeth, sharing all our secrets, practically becoming family, and not once had she mentioned having a son.

Why not?

The housekeeper gave him a firm pat on the back in the direction of Valentina. "To bed with you, child. Leave our guests alone, else they'll think the house haunted."

Valentina held out her hand, ungloved now that she was just in her dressing gown. Her hand was surprisingly small and white beneath her long sleeve, not at all the same complexion as the rest of her body. I wondered if the pigment in her skin had been bleached in some chemical accident. That would certainly explain why she wore gloves most of the time, when she hardly acted like a Puritan.

The little boy sauntered off with her into the hallway. He barely seemed like a child in those stiff clothes, with that scowling face—more like a little man made to live in a too-small body. His scuffed shoes and the dirt under his nails spoke of frequent disappearances like this one.

"I apologize for the disturbance," Mrs. McKenna said, closing the painting. "It's an old house, filled with these tunnels. Mad Lord Ballentyne is rumored to have built them to confuse spirits that might be wandering the halls, though I think it's more likely it was to hide his distillery from the British authorities. No one uses the passages now, except Hensley. They're quite dangerous. Loose nails and uneven bricks and a few traps Lord Ballentyne set in case he was being pursued. Tomorrow I'll have Carlyle seal this painting with some nails, so you won't need to worry about anyone intruding upon your friend's slumber."

"Thank you," I said.

"As to the electricity, the girls will try their best to repair it tomorrow. Until then, you'll find more candles in your closets. Let's hope for no more disturbances this time, eh?"

I gave an uneasy nod. "Indeed."

The servants returned to their rooms, and after a few minutes Montgomery did as well, leaving Lucy and me alone with Edward. She sank onto the bed next to him, brushing an errant strand of hair from his brow.

"He's burning up," she muttered. "All the excitement must have him worried." Her hand dropped to the chain across his chest, toying with the lock almost as if she didn't realize what she was doing, but I did—she wanted those chains off him so he could sit up and be his old self. But I wasn't certain he *was* his old self, not anymore.

"Lucy," I said softly, "he's delirious. He doesn't even know we're here."

She gave me an exasperated look. "I'm the one who's been taking care of him since we left London, and I know his moods best. I swear he woke up in the traveler's inn on the way here, no matter what you say. . . ."

I'd stopped listening to her, shocked by what was happening on the bed. Before my very eyes, Edward blinked. For a moment I thought I'd imagined it. But then his eyes opened.

My lips parted in shock.

"Juliet, what's the matter?" she asked, and then followed my gaze to the bed and gasped.

Edward blinked again, wincing in pain, lucid for the first time since he'd taken the poison. "Lucy," his voice rasped.

"Edward!" She threw herself against him, running her hands through his sweat-soaked hair. "I knew you were better!"

I covered my mouth with my hand, hanging back by the door as though afraid to believe it. "Edward? Is it you?"

"Juliet." He winced in pain. "Listen to me, both of you—" He coughed, the chains rattling, and he collapsed back on the bed, overtaken with the fever again. He looked so much like the skeletal castaway we'd found on the *Curitiba* that my heart started thumping painfully hard. Back then, he'd been just a step away from death. He looked even closer now.

"Edward, can you hear me?" Lucy said. "You've been delirious for days. Montgomery gave you something to help with the poison."

I clamped a hand on her shoulder, holding her back. "Be careful, Lucy. We don't know if it's the Beast or Edward."

"Of course it's Edward!"

His eyelids fluttered and I pulled Lucy back farther, despite the chains and her insistence. "Listen to me," he said. "I can't fight him off any longer. This might be the last you hear from me."

Lucy and I both gaped at him. She shook her head. "You're recovering," she pleaded. "You'll be fine."

His eyes shifted to her. "Lucy, don't think I haven't been aware of everything you've done for me, taking care of me all this time and believing in me. Your strength gave me strength, and it was enough to keep fighting him. But even so, I can't fight forever." He swallowed hard, as though his throat was bone dry. "There was a moment, a flash, when he and I were truly one. I could see all his memories because they were *my* memories too. I know everything he knows, all his secrets—and there were many. The Beast was doing his own research. His own experiments."

His eyes shifted to mine. The tenderness in them was gone. If he still bore any love for me, it was hidden under his desperation. He needed me as a scientist now, not a former lover.

"What do you mean?" I asked, daring a step closer.

"The Beast had stolen research from the King's Men that I never knew about. He discovered his own origin. When your father created me, he made a mistake. He used a portion of the brain from a diseased jackal. It was infected with a strain of rabies that combined with the malaria in Montgomery's blood to form a hybrid disease located here...." He jerked his hand toward his head, as far as the chains would let him. "At the top of the spine. It's called the reptile brain because it controls impulse and instinct. If it's damaged, it can manifest in split personalities. It's *him*, Juliet. The Beast. If you could somehow cut it out, replace it, or drain it of the ill humors, you'd cure me of him. The Beast knew it all along. He tried to hide the knowledge from the both of us."

I couldn't speak. My head spun with the flood of information Edward was giving me. Could the Beast really be nothing more than a symptom of a diseased brain? A foe I'd fought so hard against reduced to nothing more than a hybrid strain of rabies and a botched surgery?

Lucy spun to me, eyes wide. "Can it truly be done, Juliet?"

I knew little of diseased brains, but the books I'd read did support his theory. I'd heard of men who had suffered damage to the posterior lobe suddenly speaking with a foreign accent they'd never had before. One kindhearted man had been shot through the cortex and developed a violent new personality.

"I don't know." My voice faltered. "Maybe. Montgomery is a more gifted surgeon than me." I glanced back toward the hallway, wondering what he would think of all this. Even though Edward was like a brother to him—biologically, at least—Montgomery wouldn't hesitate to kill him if he was any sort of threat.

Edward coughed. His lips moved, but I couldn't make out the sound.

"What is it, Edward?"

"Not letting me die . . ." He coughed again, and his voice hardened. "You'll come to regret that."

I jerked upright. That voice. It wasn't Edward's. It belonged to a creature with claws and glowing yellow eyes. "Lucy, get back!" I nearly wrenched her arm off as I dragged her away from the bed. "It's the Beast—he's there, too."

She stared with eyes as wide as my own. Edward coughed once more, and then his head rolled back onto the pillow. Unconscious again. I stared at his waxy face. It might not look like the Beast's, but I would know that voice anywhere.

Lucy tore away from me. "Edward?" She shook him. *"Edward?"* Her hand fell on the chain, her fingers fumbling with the lock.

"Stop!" I said, pulling her back. "You heard him—he can't keep fighting the Beast forever. If you unlock those chains, we don't know *what* you'll be setting free."

"We can't just do nothing! We have to tell Montgomery!"

I paced at the foot of Edward's bed, trying to figure out the best way to handle this.

"No. We'll wait for Elizabeth to return. She's studied surgery. She'll know if there's any truth to what he's saying. We have to keep this secret, Lucy. If Montgomery thought we were still in danger from the Beast, he might do something drastic."

She gaped. "Montgomery wouldn't hurt Edward. They're practically brothers!"

"He might not *be* Edward for much longer." I finally convinced her to come out into the hall with me and locked Edward's bedroom, testing the lock to make certain it held.

"Are you certain we can trust Elizabeth?" Lucy said. "She lied to us. She said she had no children, but there's that little boy with the strange eyes."

"Elizabeth has risked everything for us," I said. "Even now she's out there trying to keep the police off our trail. The professor trusted her, and that's good enough for me. She'll know what to do."

Lucy let out a deep breath filled with reservations. "I hope you're right."

I gave her a long hug and reassured her again, then walked her to her room. Alone in the hallway, I pressed my ear against Edward's door, listening to the sounds of him— or the Beast—breathing. My heart beat a little too fast. I tried to put Edward's cryptic few words out of my head, along with the strangeness of this place—Elizabeth had warned me, after all, to be prepared for people out of touch with normal society. I reminded myself that we weren't in danger here, and that this was also the safest place for Edward. Elizabeth had her reasons for keeping secrets from us. Despite Montgomery's fears, the greater danger by far lay out there, beyond the moors.

SIX

WE WOKE IN THE morning to find the rains from the storm had caused the bogs to overflow the levees and flood the road to Quick. I didn't mind being cut off, especially with the police searching for us, except that it might slow Elizabeth's return. I was eager to ask her about Edward's claims that the Beast had discovered a cure, as well as some of the more peculiar details of the manor—like Hensley.

Mrs. McKenna took the opportunity to lead us on a tour of the grounds that weren't flooded. Over the next few days, she showed us the goat barn and the goose pond, the glass-enclosed winter garden off the ballroom, and the vegetable cold storage in the basement, and even took us through the plain and tidy servants' floor. She explained Valentina's educational program for the younger girls: how she taught them to read and write and do sums, and how she was slowly schooling the older girls in the more sophisticated work-ings of the manor. I admired the self-sufficient nature of the estate, but the secret passages and plentiful locked doors seemed to trouble Montgomery. Likewise, Lucy found little to appreciate about the dusty manor and its pale-faced staff. The only thing she seemed to enjoy, in those rare moments when she wasn't by Edward's bedside, was Mrs. McKenna's hearty cooking.

"Mama never lets me eat like this," she said over a breakfast of bacon rashers. "She says if I don't watch my figure, men won't give me a second look."

Valentina made a disparaging noise in her throat. She hunched over the buffet table, teaching two of the girls to polish silver. "Girls weren't made to be trussed up like Christmas hens. A woman needs weight on her bones, especially in winter." She had her gloves on today, hiding those strangely pale hands. "Any man who thinks otherwise would certainly not be welcome here."

She and Mrs. McKenna looked pointedly at Montgomery. He stood by the window, surveying the moors as though he expected ghosts to rise. At our silence, he turned.

"Pardon?" he asked.

"Don't worry about him," I said. "He's as wild as the moors themselves. He certainly doesn't care if I have an extra scone or two."

He turned to us, seemingly unaware of our conversation. "There are fresh wheel ruts in the courtyard," he observed. "Does that mean the road is passable again?"

Mrs. McKenna nodded. "Carlyle took the mule to Quick as soon as the sun broke. I'd wager it's muddy as the devil's bath, but it's passable."

Montgomery forced a smile. "Juliet, you and Lucy

should take the day and walk into Quick. Some fresh air would do you both good. You could meet with the dressmaker about your wedding gown."

I gave him a hard look. He'd kept his distance the past few days since our argument, and his sudden warmth seemed out of place.

"Your wedding dress!" Lucy said. "He makes a good point, Juliet. You'd get married in a burlap sack if it were up to you. We can talk to the seamstress and . . ." Her face fell, and she bit her lip. "Oh, but we couldn't possibly leave Edward here."

She gave me a glance filled with meaning. Edward hadn't woken from his delirium again since that night three days ago, but the experience had shaken both of us.

"Balthazar and I will keep an eye on him," Montgomery answered quickly. "We'll fetch you straightaway if anything changes." He nudged my shoulder. "Go on. Think of all the girls you'd disappoint, wanting to see a real bride in a white lace dress."

Montgomery, playful? Now I was outright suspicious of his motives. I leaned in to whisper, "What about the police?"

"I asked around on the way in," he whispered back. "There aren't any police in Quick, only an old man with a telegraph. It's a tiny village. The sheep outnumber the people."

I studied him closely, wondering why he was so anxious to get me out of the house. If I had to guess, he was planning on doing some investigation into the strange happenings at the manor—and I wasn't sure I should let him, certainly not with Edward's state so precarious. On the other hand, I couldn't deny that I was curious to know what he would find. Not that I suspected Elizabeth of anything, but it was impossible to ignore that between the bodies in the cellar, a son we never knew about, and deadly secret passages, there was more than met the eye at Ballentyne.

I made a show of rolling my eyes. "Fine. For the sake of my poor taste."

But I gave Montgomery a hard look while the others weren't watching. When we returned, I'd prod him with questions until he revealed whatever he found.

WE HEADED OUT JUST after breakfast. The fresh air did brighten our spirits, particularly Lucy's. Once she got thinking about the idea of the wedding, she couldn't stop talking about dress patterns and cakes and how on earth we were going to get a proper wedding bouquet so far from London.

"I can't imagine it," she said. "You married before me. I'd have thought the world would end first. Who will give you away?"

"Carlyle, I suppose."

She made a face. "But he's so dour."

"Yes, but he's the only man on the estate."

We came over a hill, chatting lightly, but paused. The burned-out shell of the oak tree came into view, still smelling of ash. It brought back the terror from that night nearly a week ago, fleeing the police and the storm. We'd been so desperate then.

The smile fell off Lucy's face. "I do hope Elizabeth returns soon. Each day that Edward remains ill, I fear I'll fall asleep and find him dead in the morning. I keep thinking, with her medical skills, there must be something she can do."

She slipped her arm around mine, clutching it tightly. I could feel desperate hope pulsing within her. "There are medical books in the library," I said. "I'll do some research into the diseased-brain condition he described. Once Elizabeth returns, I'll speak with her straightaway."

Lucy didn't press the point, but her thoughts turned inward, unsatisfied by my answer.

We arrived in Quick in late morning and shopped around the few scattered stores, then ate a meal at the tavern and went to the dressmaker's. It was a small operation sharing the back half of the general store. The dressmaker had a few bolts of yellowing lace she was ashamed to even pull out in front of a girl as stylish as Lucy. We flipped through books of patterns and fabric samples while the seamstress took my measurements. Sometimes my eyes would catch on a beautiful dress and images would flash in my head of potentially happier times, Montgomery wearing a suit and me wearing the gown in a chapel with all our friends and family gathered. But those images soon faded. All my family was dead. Montgomery's only blood relation was a boy wrapped in chains.

I closed the pattern book, sending dust into the air. Lucy looked up from the fabric samples. "What do you think of this lace?"

The sample she held out was beautiful. A single row of scalloped edges simple enough for my taste. When I brushed my fingers over the fabric, I could practically feel it draped around me.

I'm getting married, a voice inside me said. I was happy and yet unsettled at the same time. Would things be easier once we were married? Would our secrets matter as much? Would Montgomery forget, over time, how I'd killed those three men in cold blood?

Would *I* ever forget?

"It's perfect," I said, trying to smile.

Lucy drew a handful of paper bills from her purse and exchanged a few words with the dressmaker, who stumbled over promises that I'd be the most beautiful bride north of Inverness. I'd have settled for the plainest, if it meant a peaceful future for us.

"I can hardly wait until the dress is ready," Lucy said, pulling on her coat outside. "We'll comb your hair into a chignon like that actress at the Brixton. I'm sure Elizabeth has some pins we can borrow. . . ."

Lucy kept talking, but I only half paid attention. My eyes had fallen on a stack of old newspapers in the street outside the tavern. A GENTLEMAN'S THOUGHTS ON THE CHRISTMAS DAY MASSACRE, the headline read in bold black ink, like an accusation. My thoughts went to that bloodstained room in King's College where my water-tank creatures had murdered three men. I took a step closer, read the byline, and nearly died of shock.

The article was written by John Radcliffe.

Lucy's *father.*

"There's Carlyle with the mule cart." Lucy's hand clamped onto mine, and I jumped. "He must be headed back to Ballentyne. I'm sure he'll give us a ride and save our boots the wear. That mud was something awful."

I twisted away from the newspaper so she wouldn't see her father's name. Lucy waved Carlyle down, and the old gamekeeper steered the mule toward us, pulling it to a halt.

"Not much room, but you can squeeze in there, lassies." He jerked his head at an empty place between huge baskets of vegetables.

I glanced back at that newspaper.

"You go," I said, pushing Lucy toward the cart. "There's only room for one of us to ride comfortably. I'll walk. I'd like the time alone, anyway. Getting married, you know, so much to think about."

"Are you certain?" She climbed into the cart, looking back at me, but Carlyle whipped the mule, and the cart started with a lurch. I waved to her and she settled among the baskets, waving back, until the wagon dipped over a hill and was gone.

Stooping down, I picked up the newspaper. The date was from a week ago—already old news, but it felt so immediate that I could practically smell the brine and damp fur of the water-tank creatures.

> *It was with a heavy heart that I recently attended*
> *the funeral of three colleagues who had once been*
> *highly esteemed by society,*

the article began.

I pictured John Radcliffe's pale blue eyes and shivered. As the King's Club's financier, Radcliffe was certainly not innocent, though he was hardly the worst of the bunch. Money had driven him, not science. That was why he—and the rest of the lesser King's Club members—were still alive. Not to mention that Lucy would never forgive me if I killed her father.

> *Naturally I was horrified to learn of this tragedy, and even more upset that those three colleagues, whom I had once counted as friends, were involved in a plot to bring ruin to London's lower classes. The worst of it all, however, is the loss of my daughter, Lucy, who I believe was present at the college that night. She disappeared shortly after the massacre, and her mother and I are sick with worry. . . .*

I sighed with relief. Mr. Radcliffe was formally denouncing his involvement with the King's Club, just as we had hoped he would. I had been so shocked when Lucy and I had found a preserved human brain in a hatbox in his office, never suspecting him of being more than a mere financier. Now I knew I'd been right. He was a banker at heart, not a murderer. Lucy would be pleased to hear her father had dropped his ties with that organization. Perhaps it might even lighten her spirits.

I stuffed the newspaper into my coat and looked in the direction of Ballentyne. Clouds had rolled in, thick and low, and I had five miles to walk. I started at a fast pace, hugging my arms, mind lost in the newspaper article.

The Christmas Day Massacre.

I had been obsessed with the idea of bringing the water-tank creatures to life. Feeling their bodies warm. Counting their beating hearts. Most disturbing of all, part of me had even *enjoyed* it. Father had loved his work too. Was I destined to be like him, even if I didn't want to be?

A child can never escape her father, the fortune-teller had said.

The sun sank over the horizon, meaning darkness would fall before I reached Ballentyne. I started to walk faster, but I couldn't outrun my thoughts. There were times when I could almost feel Father in my head. I'd read enough research papers on genetics to know that a child naturally took on the properties of a parent. Even personality. Even an inclination toward madness. Is that what the fortune-teller had meant? Maybe there was no use fighting who one was— and I was inescapably a Moreau.

I must have been a mile and a half from the manor when a shriek like a child's cry came from the moors. I froze. My stomach tightened with fear that Hensley or one of the young servants had gotten lost.

Alarmed, I pulled up my heavy winter skirts and trod into the heather toward the sound. The ground, normally frozen, had thawed a few inches and my boots sank into it, threatening to trap me. Crossing the moors was far more difficult than it seemed, each step sucking me down, heather catching me like thorns. The crying got louder. I scrambled up a small hill where the ground was more solid, and overlooked a bog with ice clinging to the edges.

A sheep was trapped up to its neck.

I drew in a sharp breath.

At least it isn't a child, I thought, though that was small comfort: the sheep's desperate bleats still pulled at my heart. Behind me, I could barely make out the road in the twilight. I couldn't afford to stay out here on the moors with night falling. Yet the sheep would drown or freeze if I left it.

I started down the hill. My heart thudded, warning me to hurry. There were so few trees that it took me a precious few minutes to find a branch I could use. I came as close to the bog as I dared. The sheep had stopped struggling and bleated to me mournfully. I laid the tree branch close to give it purchase, but no matter how the sheep bucked, it couldn't get out. I leaned closer, trying to grab hold of its mud-clotted wool. My fingers grazed its neck when the sheep bucked again, and I slipped off the branch, landing shin deep in the bog.

I cried out with the rush of cold. My dress was beyond ruined; Mrs. McKenna would have to cut it up for scraps. But I was in now, and I could reach the sheep. I waded a few steps closer, mud trying to suck me down, and wrapped my arms around the sheep's neck and leg. I pulled, and it bucked in fear, succeeding only in dragging me down deeper with it. Mud crept up my stockings. A jolt of cold ran through me. I tugged my foot, but nothing happened.

Suddenly, I realized I wasn't saving the sheep anymore.

I was just as stuck as it was.

Panic made my pulse race. I let go of the sheep and grabbed onto the tree branch, but it wasn't attached to anything, and I only got stuck further in the muck. The sheep bleated frantically, frightened by my movements, and I sank deeper.

The sun set on the horizon.

I was going to die out here.

I screamed as loudly as I could until my voice was hoarse, until I could see only the horizon in the faint light, until the sheep gave up struggling.

Until a figure appeared on the horizon, as unreal in the twilight as a ghost.

SEVEN

It wasn't until the figure came closer, walking expertly over the moors, that moonlight splashed over it and I recognized the face beneath the hooded cloak.

"Elizabeth!" I screamed.

She approached quickly but carefully, as though she'd spent her entire life learning how to navigate the hidden dangers of a bog—which I suppose she had. She wore a long brown cloak and a traveling gown, stained now with black peat. I didn't notice the rifle in her hand until she was only feet away.

"Stop moving!" she called. "It only makes it worse."

She lay down on the ground and held out the rifle. "Grab hold and don't move. I'll pull you in, but we must go slow."

I curled my fingers on the rifle, heart pounding, fighting the instinct to kick as hard as I could. Inch by inch, she pulled the rifle toward her, giving the mud time to shift and release me. My heavy skirts caught on roots deep in the muddy waters. No matter how she pulled, she couldn't tear me free.

"Your dress is caught," she said. "You'll have to take it off."

I started on the row of buttons down the front of my dress with stiff fingers. Once I struggled out of it, the cold water bit at my skin through my underclothes, but I felt lighter, freer, and it didn't take Elizabeth long to drag me to the bog's edge and pull me from the water. I was slick with mud and shivering uncontrollably. She wrapped her cloak around me as I huddled on the ground, breathing in her rosewater scent.

"My God, Elizabeth, I nearly drowned. . . ."

A shot rang out, and I jerked up with a cry.

The smell of burned gunpowder hung in the air. She'd shot the sheep to put it out of its misery. The poor animal sank into the bog, a part of the moors now.

She wiped the muck from my face. "I heard your screams from the road. Why are you out here alone?"

"I went to Quick for a wedding dress. God, it seems so stupid now. I heard the sheep—"

"Oh, you foolish girl. My carriage is waiting back at the road. Thank goodness I was held up in Liverpool or I'd have missed you completely. Let's get you home before you freeze to death. Valentina knows which herbs to use in a bath to restore circulation." She wrapped an arm around my shoulders and led me along the winding bog paths. It was dark now, clouds hiding the moon, steam rising from the horse's nostrils. She helped me into the carriage.

I sank into the soft seats. "I'd have died if you hadn't come just now."

She leaned forward and rubbed my knee. "We von Steins pride ourselves on good timing."

"Did you discover what the police know? Are they still after us? I read an article that John Radcliffe wrote about the massacre, and it made no mention of us."

She rubbed my freezing hands in hers. "Right now you need to worry about getting warm, not the police. They won't be storming the house tonight, I can promise that." There was a troubled look on her face, though, and she pressed a hand against her coat, retucking a folded piece of paper that had nearly slipped out of her pocket.

We heard Lucy's and Montgomery's voices calling to us a quarter mile away, but it was Balthazar who reached us first. He flung open the carriage door and wrapped his arms around me. Montgomery raced up just behind him.

"Juliet, what happened?"

I couldn't answer. I was shivering too hard.

Montgomery touched my hair, my face, my hands, as though reassuring himself I was intact. There might have been tension between us, but he still loved me.

"Balthazar, my friend," he said, "carry her back to the manor, quick as you can."

I hadn't the strength to object when Balthazar scooped me up, carrying me toward the shining lights. Once inside the house, Mrs. McKenna fawned over me, wrapping me in a blanket and rambling about getting some tea and scones in my stomach. She led me upstairs, where Valentina already had an herbal bath going. Mrs. McKenna helped me strip off my ruined undergarments and ease into the hot water.

"Mrs. McKenna, I can't thank you enough."

"Enough of those formalities, little mouse. You nearly died tonight. Call me McKenna like everyone else does."

The water quickly browned, but I didn't care. I held my breath and slipped under, letting the water work its way through my hair, daring to imagine that it was bog-water instead of a rose-scented bath. What if I *had* died, tonight? It was Edward we were all so worried about, but the truth was, the world wasn't a safe place. Any one of us could vanish from it at any moment.

I jerked upright, coughing out water. Once my head had cleared, I saw that McKenna had left. Elizabeth was in her place at the side of the tub, still in her stained traveling dress, while Valentina packed away the herbs she had brought for my bath.

Elizabeth reached out to pet my head.

"Silly girl. You must take better care of yourself. People will be relying on your judgment. You can't take foolish risks like that if you're to run this place one day."

I twisted to look at her in surprise. Valentina, crouched down to pick up some of her fallen herbs, had paused as well. "What do you mean, run this place?" I asked.

Elizabeth glanced at Valentina hesitantly. There was regret on her face, as though she wished she could take back what she'd said. "Valentina, could you leave us a moment? Afterward, let's talk, you and I."

Valentina stared at Elizabeth, some silent exchange

happening between them that I could not fathom the meaning of, and gathered the rest of the herbs and hurried from the room.

Once we were alone, Elizabeth took a deep breath. "Juliet, the professor and I intended to make you our heir."

My hands nearly slipped on the wet side of the tub. "A ward, yes. But *heir*?"

"Yes. Heir to all of it. The manor. The grounds. Everything we have."

A tin clattered to the floor outside the bathroom, followed by the sound of footsteps running away. Valentina had been listening in the hallway. I started to call after her but Elizabeth shook her head. "Don't. I expect she'll be quite upset. I shouldn't have told you in front of her—I wasn't thinking, and it was cruel of me. Before I left for London, Valentina and I had begun to discuss her taking over one day, if I didn't find a suitable heir in the next few years. But then I discovered the professor had taken you in, and that we're even distantly related." She gave me a kind smile. "Valentina always knew there was a possibility of long-lost family showing up. She'll be disappointed, but there will always be a place for her here, don't fear."

Valentina was the least of my worries. Heir to Ballentyne? It was enough to make my head spin. "But what about Hensley? He's your own son; surely he should inherit it."

A strange look crossed her face. "Hensley—yes. I should have realized you'd meet him. Unfortunately Hensley will never be suited to manage an estate of this size. He has a defect of the brain."

"Oh, how awful. Is that why you didn't tell us about him? Who . . ." I paused. "Who is the father?" It was hardly a polite question, but women like Elizabeth and me had never danced around propriety.

"An American novelist. I went overseas to visit family in eighty-nine and met him. The father doesn't know, which is just as well." She let out a sigh, running her fingers along the towel. "He wasn't a very good novelist."

It felt good to smile, after everything that had happened.

"Well," she said. "It's not every day one narrowly escapes death. Dry off, and give me a moment to speak with Valentina. Then we shall have a proper talk."

WHEN I'D FINALLY SCRUBBED every inch of the bog from under my fingernails and between my toes, I found Elizabeth, Montgomery, and Lucy in the second floor library, seated around the fireplace, chatting in low voices. There was no sign of Valentina—I imagined she was in her room, trying to get over the sting of losing the inheritance. Hensley sat by Elizabeth's feet. I was surprised he was still awake since it had to be past midnight, but he hadn't seen his mother in months and must miss her terribly. It made me even more curious about his brain defect, and if it had to do with his miscolored eye. Elizabeth stroked his hair absently. In turn, he stroked the fur of his pet rat.

My robe rustled as I entered, and Elizabeth gave her crooked smile. "Feeling better?"

"Yes—well, I think so." I glanced toward Hensley, not

sure such young ears should overhear talk of near death and police chases and murder, but he played with his rat silently, ignoring us. "I'm much more worried about what's on that paper you're trying to keep hidden in your coat."

Lucy and Montgomery sat straighter. Elizabeth raised an eyebrow and took out the paper. "You're nothing if not observant, Juliet. I suppose you'd have found out sooner or later." The paper was crumpled and worn, too thick for a letter and the wrong shape. As she unfolded it with her elegant hands, my heart shot to my throat. I knew that lettering across the top.

"A special memorandum poster," she said regretfully. "The kind advertising rewards for escaped criminals and fugitives. In this case, I am dearly sorry to say, it's for you. The police haven't given up the search."

She handed me the paper, which I scanned in one glance. Lucy jumped up to read over my shoulder. My own face looked back at me, an inky portrait done by a police artist who had never seen me. They'd captured my eyes but the jaw was too wide, the brow too heavy, making me look like a degenerate.

I started to feel light-headed. Montgomery took the poster from me. "One thousand pound reward," he read, "for information leading to the capture of Juliet Moreau of London, wanted for murder. Age: Seventeen. Last known residence: Dumbarton Oaks . . ."

The rest of his words faded as my head started throbbing. Lucy put her hands on my shoulders, shaking me back into reason, but it was all I could do to keep breathing.

"This is impossible," Montgomery said, his voice on edge. "They've no way to prove Juliet was responsible for those deaths."

Even though I was.

Lucy had gone white. "It was my father, wasn't it? He told the police."

"No, it wasn't him." I answered in a rush, relieved at least to put her worries to rest. I took out the article and handed it to her. "I found this newspaper article in Quick. He denounces his role in the King's Club and talks about how sad he is you disappeared. He doesn't blame us for what happened, at least not publicly."

Lucy clutched at the newspaper. "He's worried about me?" She sank into the chair, poring over every word of the article.

Elizabeth sighed. "Inspector Newcastle was the one who told the police, I'm afraid. He was taken to the hospital with fatal burns. He died within hours, but not before he recounted what had happened. You killed some very important men, Juliet. Someone associated with them is scouring the country for you, but it doesn't matter. They won't find you as long as you stay hidden here. The police don't know the location of this manor, and don't even know it's in my family. It's under the name of a distant cousin in Germany. It would take them years to go through the paperwork, and they wouldn't even know to look for it."

Elizabeth reached for a bottle of gin on the side table, pouring each of us a glass, but Lucy waved it away, and so did Montgomery. He stood, tucking the poster into his pocket.

"I'm going to show this to Balthazar, but I'd prefer to keep it hidden from the rest of the staff. It's best they don't know our pasts."

He strode out of the room.

Elizabeth drank the gin he'd left behind, and then Lucy's, too. "I know it's a terrible shock," she said, "but I assure you that you're quite safe here. It seems our more pressing concern is Mr. Prince's health. McKenna told me he's still alive, in and out of consciousness, which is a miracle itself. With the amount of arsenic he took, a normal man would be dead in days."

"Yes, about Edward." I exchanged a glance with Lucy and then dropped my voice. "There's something rather pressing we must discuss. He had a moment of lucidity a few nights ago. He told Lucy and me that the Beast was caused by a disease in the brain and was curable if we could drain or transplant the diseased organ." I knit my fingers as I explained the rest of what Edward had said and why we'd kept the information to ourselves.

"We thought with your advanced medical knowledge," Lucy added, "there might be something you can do." The light from the fire illuminated her desperation.

"I see." Elizabeth was quiet, thinking, as the fire crackled and popped. Hensley crawled along the floor by Elizabeth's feet, laying out bits of dried cheese for his rat. The rat tried to scurry away and Hensley grabbed it hard, hugging it to his chest, stroking it fiercely.

"Don't run away," he whispered. "It isn't safe."

Elizabeth murmured something in his ear about giving

his pet some bread to calm it down, and Hensley relented and handed her the rat. She quickly slipped it into her pocket, which she buttoned closed, but I couldn't help but notice the rat wasn't moving. I dared not ask her about it now, though, with so much hanging in the balance for Edward.

Elizabeth let out a deep sigh.

"I can tell how hopeful you both are about this new development, but I'm afraid I shall have to be the bearer of bad news. Organ transplantations are possible, in some cases. I transplanted a liver, and I've heard of it done with lungs and kidneys, even a heart once—they kept the blood flowing during the procedure with artificial pumps. However, the brain is central to life. If the spinal column or cranial complex is severed or even badly damaged, death is immediate. There would be no way to perform a brain transplant on a living person. It's a paradoxical situation, you see. The procedure might cure him, but he would have to be dead for us to perform it."

The fire crackled more, as the hope slowly drained out of Lucy's face. Her bottom lip started to tremble.

"I can make his days as pleasant and comfortable as possible," Elizabeth said softly. "That's all, I'm afraid. If he is to defeat the Beast, he will have to do it on his own."

"But he isn't strong enough on his own!" Lucy cried. She pushed off from the sofa, tears streaking down her face, and ran out of the room. I stood to go after her but stopped. What could I possibly say to her to make things better?

Elizabeth picked up a sleepy Hensley in her arms. It was hard to reconcile the two sides of her—I had always thought of her as a brilliant and cold surgeon, not unlike my father. Now I saw her as a mother, too.

I swallowed. "How do you do it?" I asked quietly. She cocked her head in question. I explained, "How do you ignore the voices in your head? The ones that won't let you just be happy. The ones that want more out of life. More like what men are free to do—study what they want, go where they want, *be* who they want."

Her smile was rather tight. She held up the glass as Hensley fell asleep on her shoulder. "I drown them in gin, but I'd be no kind of guardian if I recommended *that*."

EIGHT

Days passed, and Edward's fever still didn't break.

We moved about the manor like unquiet ghosts. McKenna tried to brighten our gloom with talk of the wedding. She sent the girls out to prune the flowering trees in the garden so the spring would be full of new growth, and prepared entrees for us to sample for the wedding feast, but it was increasingly impossible to ignore the feverish moans coming from Edward's room. Lucy attended to his bedside day and night.

"You're going to make yourself sick," I told her one morning. "Take a break. Let me watch him."

"Your bedside manner is deplorable." She tried unsuccessfully to feed him broth. "You'd poke and prod him so much, he'd never want to get better."

She tried to feed him more broth, but he turned his head, eyes glassy and unfocused, and mumbled something incomprehensible. Sometimes he seemed to be aware of who we were, and in the next moment he'd push the bowl away and shudder.

"It's getting worse," she muttered, mopping up the spilled broth. "No matter what Elizabeth said, I can't help but think . . ." Her voice trailed off as she caught sight of something over my shoulder. "Goodness, do you see that? It looks like the moors are on fire!"

I whirled toward the windows, where the blackness was broken by huge flames in the lower fields. I pressed my face against the glass.

"Montgomery!" I called. "Balthazar, hurry!"

They soon appeared, and I pointed beyond the window. "The fields are on fire," I gasped. "Stay with Edward. I'll find Elizabeth and warn her." I turned to go.

"Juliet, wait." Montgomery's voice was steady and calm, almost light. "It's just a bonfire. Look."

I squinted into the darkness. He was right—it was a controlled blaze in the lower field. I let out the tension in one long breath.

"It's the festival of Twelfth Night," Montgomery explained. "It's a pagan holiday in this area. Carlyle told me about it while I was helping him chop firewood yesterday. The highlanders celebrate it out here, where no preachers are around to tell them not to."

The flames rose higher, crackling with sparks. Now I could make out clusters of people around the bonfire, some of them dancing. My heart lurched. With Edward so ill, it had been a long time since we'd all laughed and danced, that carefree.

"The whole household must be down there," I said. "No wonder it's quiet as a church around here."

Lucy *tsk*ed as she squinted toward the fire, exhaustion written in her features. "To think they didn't invite us."

"They probably thought we wouldn't approve of a pagan festival," I said. "We being such civilized city folk and all."

Lucy rolled her eyes.

Balthazar turned to Montgomery, fingers knit together. "I've never seen a festival before." He paused and sniffed the air. "Roast pig with honey. Oh, Sharkey loves roast pig. Might we go?"

Montgomery seemed amused. "Certainly you may go, Balthazar, and I've no doubt Sharkey would be welcome, too."

Balthazar grinned and started to straighten his shirt, but his fingers were too clumsy. Lucy adjusted his collar and refastened his top button, dusting off his shoulders. "There now. All the ladies will want to dance with you."

His face fell. "I don't know how to dance."

"Can't dance!" she said. "Well, Montgomery, you'd best go and teach him. And you should go, too, Juliet, or else one of those girls is going to try to steal him from you."

"Only if you come as well," I said to her.

She jerked her head toward the bed. "I can't leave Edward."

"McKenna can watch Edward—it's only for a few hours. Come on, we all need a bit of fun."

She bit her lip in indecision, but then her stomach

grumbled. "Roast pig, did you say?"

I grinned and grabbed her hand, pulling her downstairs and into the night. A gust of cold bit at our legs and I shrieked and pulled her across the fields toward the warmth of the fire. For a few hundred feet we were caught between the house and the bonfire with the stars overhead, and a sudden bolt of joy seized me. After days closed up in such a stuffy manor, my soul yearned for a moment of life. For an instant I loved it here, far from the rest of the world, in a place so wild and free.

The field was full of people, most of them strangers and performers traveling the winter fair circuit, but I recognized the servant girls and a few familiar faces from Quick. The fiddler was the tavern owner. He tipped his hat to us as one of the girls, Lily, passed us a tankard of warm cider. A belch came from the direction of the performers. With a start, I realized it came from the same old woman from the inn on the road to Inverness. I looked more closely at her companions and recognized the thin leader of the carnival troupe, acting out a play that seemed to involve a donkey. There was no sign of the fortune-teller.

I shivered at the memory. *A child can never escape her father.*

Was it chance that brought them to this particular festival, out of all the Twelfth Night celebrations happening in the north? The coincidence left me uneasy, but then Montgomery and Balthazar caught up to us, legs damp from the dew, and Sharkey trotted up to the fire trying to catch flames in his teeth. I relaxed. They were festival performers, after all, and this was a festival. Why should I be surprised to find them here?

I spotted Elizabeth through the flames. She wore a heavy fur stole out of the pages of a Viking history book, and with her hair down she looked like one of the fairy folk, strong and beautiful. No wonder she had left the city, when here she was queen.

"I didn't think you'd join us," she said as she walked around the fire, "or else I'd have invited you myself."

"Well, don't tell the vicar we're here," I said. "He'd never agree to preside over the wedding of two heathens."

She smiled. "He's over there." She pointed her chin to a group of old men on the far side of the bonfire who were drinking in a very ungodly way. "He brought the ale."

The night passed amid music and laughter, and I was able to let go of my worry over Edward, if only for a few stolen moments. Lucy disappeared for a while, playing games with the younger girls beneath the stars, and after some time I went looking for her. One of the servants pointed me in the direction of the carnival troupe's temporary camp at the edge of the field. I walked through the high grass, hugging my coat tight, and eventually found her by a wood-and-silk tent. A dark-skinned man was reading her palm, muttering words that made her eyes go wide.

It was the fortune-teller.

He kissed Lucy teasingly on the hand. She laughed just as her eyes met mine. "Juliet! I've just had my fortune read. I'm going to marry a count. Doesn't that sound divine?" She grabbed my hand, tugging me toward him. "It's your turn."

The fortune-teller didn't flinch, nor show any sign of recognition, and my uneasy feeling returned.

"Your hands are freezing," I said to Lucy. "Wait for me by the bonfire. I'll be along in a moment."

She grinned and skipped back to the rest of the merriment, leaving us alone. The night was heavy around us.

"It's you," I said. "From the inn."

He reached out to take my hand in answer, his mouth curling in a mysterious smile. A shiver ran down the length of my back.

"You have the hands of a surgeon, pretty girl," he said, laying out my palm atop his own. "Do you have the mind of one, too?"

I flinched at the mention of surgeons. "Lucy's been telling you about me, has she? Well, it's hardly fair that you know so much about me, yet you've never even told me your name."

"Jack Serra," he answered, giving a dramatic bow.

"It's rather odd that this is the second time our paths have crossed. Are you following me?"

He let out a burst of laughter. "We travel the winter fair circuit. It's the same path year after year."

I glanced in the direction of the bonfire, whose music and laughter felt a million miles away. I could barely make out Montgomery by the fiddlers, trying to teach Balthazar to dance.

"I'd like to know the rest of my fortune. You started to tell me at the inn but never finished."

He cocked his head. "Fortunes can't be rushed."

My heart started pounding harder—why was he able to read so much about me in a single look? Was it foolish to be here, when I knew there was no science to fortunes? Soft voices came from the woods, where a man and woman—two of the carnival performers—came back to camp with their arms around each other. My face flushed to think about what they must have been doing in those woods.

Jack Serra traced a long finger down my palm.

"A child can never escape her father," he said, repeating his words from before. "You told me your father is dead, and yet you follow me to a cold field away from your friends because he isn't dead to you at all, is he? His spirit lives on."

"I don't believe in ghosts," I said, though my voice shook.

He scoffed. "Ghosts? Neither do I. Far scarier to know we carry the ghosts of our parents within us. Every decision we make, every mistake we make, is them working through us. One's father is like the stream, from which comes the river. The river cannot set its own path. The stream runs downhill and so the river does, too. They both end in the same place—the ocean."

Around his neck he wore at least twenty charms on twisted leather thongs. He removed one now and pressed it into my palm, a small iron charm in the shape of swirling lines like a river.

I stared at the charm, transfixed. "The ocean? Is that a symbol for madness?"

He smiled. "The ocean is merely the ocean. As far as symbols, it is what you yourself make of it." He placed the charm around my neck, letting it fall against my chest, where it glistened in the moonlight like real water.

"I don't understand. You're saying it's useless for me to try to change course?"

Amusement flickered in his eyes. He extended a hand toward the bonfire. "Your friends will miss you, pretty girl, if you do not join them soon."

I had so many more questions to ask of him. A voice in the back of my head told me fortunes weren't real, yet I was desperate enough to believe anything. But Jack Serra only held his hand up, a clear direction that it was time for me to leave.

I left, hiding the charm beneath my dress, and returned to the bright lights of the bonfire. I took a few deep breaths, reminding myself that fortunes weren't real and that he was only a charlatan after a few coins—never mind that he hadn't asked for payment.

Across the fire, Lucy had taken over teaching Balthazar a dance step, with Montgomery following along to offer Balthazar tips. Balthazar stepped on his toe, but he just laughed and clapped him on the back. I couldn't help but smile. Such a good heart, and still the most handsome man I'd ever seen. I hoped more than anything that one day, after we were married, there would be no more secrets or tension between the two of us.

One of the older girls, Moira, approached him shyly and tugged on his sleeve to get his attention. He leaned down so she could whisper something in his ear.

"They want him to dance with them," a voice said next to me.

Valentina stood at my side, wearing a dress with long sleeves, a Woodbine cigarette between her fingers. I stiffened, wondering if she hated me for being named heir. Her gloves were gone now, and I had a closer look at her pale hand. No one could naturally have skin such a different shade from the rest of her body. I surreptitiously looked for signs of bleaching, but there were no discolorations. Her fingers were delicate and petite—too petite, in fact, for someone of her stature.

Curiosity shivered up my spine.

She took a puff of the Woodbine. Her sleeve fell back, revealing a glimpse of puckered flesh. A scar. A terrible idea entered my head. Could her hand not be her own hand at all—but someone else's? Elizabeth said she had performed transplants. . . .

"After all, there aren't many young men out here," Valentina continued, pointing to the girls dancing with Montgomery.

I cleared my throat, barely able to tear my eyes away from her wrist. "Why is that, exactly? The lack of male staff, I mean."

"I doubt there's anything intentional to it. Elizabeth has a reputation for being able to cure ailments and illnesses, but only women are brave enough to come. The men think she's a witch. All except old Carlyle. He wouldn't believe in witches if one sat on his head."

She tapped the ashes from her Woodbine cigarette, and my eyes lingered on her sleeve. "What type of ailments, exactly?" I pressed.

She smiled knowingly. "Rare illnesses. Even—some-times—missing limbs."

Curiosity blazed in me, and I forgot my distrust of her. My eyes were riveted to her hand, so small and white. I said hesitantly, "If you'll forgive me, I can't help but notice your hand is a peculiar color and shape compared to the rest of your arm."

She laughed, deep and rich. "Miss Moreau, you're practically drooling. You must have the heart of a scientist. No wonder Elizabeth made you her *heir*."

Her voice hardened around this last word, and uneas-iness curled in my insides. Elizabeth had told me that she spoke to Valentina about the situation and that Valentina bore me no ill will, but her resentment now seemed as thick as smoke. Was I the only one who could see it? Per-haps she was different when she was around Elizabeth, trying to win her favor. She had no reason to win mine. Quite the opposite.

Valentina took another long puff on the cigarette. "When you first came here, I thought there must be some-thing remarkable about you for Elizabeth to choose you, but for the life of me, I haven't seen it. You haven't expressed an ounce of interest in the management of the manor. You haven't visited the outer fields, nor sat in on my educational sessions with the younger girls, nor gone with Carlyle on one of his supply runs. So tell me, why do you even wish to be the mistress of Ballentyne?"

My jaw dropped at the directness of her questions.

She put out the cigarette abruptly. "As I suspected,

you *don't* even want it. It's fallen into your lap like a pretty new toy, and just like any spoiled girl, you take it without knowing what a rare gift it is. But Ballentyne is no toy, Miss Moreau. It's a sanctuary. These girls have no place else to go. Elizabeth has dedicated her life to it, and so has McKenna, and so have I. If you aren't ready to make that same commitment, then you should go. Ballentyne has no room for spoiled girls who only care for pretty toys. The best thing you could do for the manor would be to leave."

She dug her heel harder into the cigarette.

Anger flared in me. She didn't understand that I had bigger worries than an inheritance that wouldn't take effect for decades. My palm began to tingle with the urge to connect it with her cheek, until I felt a cool hand on my arm.

"Come, Juliet!" Lucy pulled me away, tankard of ale in hand. "We're dancing!"

I'd never been so relieved to end a conversation, though my blood still boiled. It wasn't until we held hands and she spun me around the fire, amid the other couples, that I started to calm down. We circled around Balthazar and the little girl with the limp. Then around Montgomery and Elizabeth. I couldn't stop throwing uneasy glances back toward Valentina. She'd lit another cigarette and puffed it calmly, staring at me. I wondered if Elizabeth truly had replaced her hands. Fingers that weren't her own, skin that had belonged to another girl. A dead girl, surely. The possibilities made my heart beat wildly. What other secrets was Elizabeth keeping?

We looped around the other couples, Lucy laughing,

the carnival troupe mixing with the servants and the townspeople from Quick. I didn't see the fortune-teller in the crowd, and I was relieved. The fiddler shouted a call and we switched partners. Montgomery grabbed me, to the dismay of the other girls, and pulled me into a Scottish reel. Sharkey wound between our feet, threatening to trip us, but Montgomery only laughed and pulled me closer to the fire. Sweat broke out on my brow. With the stars overhead, the fiddler, and the good company, the night seemed unreal.

After another dance, I let Montgomery go. "The girls will murder me if I don't share you," I said by way of explanation, and was able to slip away. I found Elizabeth presiding by the fire over the manor's residents making merry in the moonlight.

"Elizabeth, there's something I must ask you about. It's Valentina."

Elizabeth raised an eyebrow. "Is she being harsh with you over the inheritance? I thought I noticed a rather heated conversation between you two. She has a hot temper, but only on the surface. Give her a few days to cool, and she'll come around. She loves this place too much not to find a way to get along with its future mistress."

"It isn't just the inheritance. It's her hands. She usually wears gloves but—"

A small voice behind us interrupted. "Mother," Hensley said, tugging on her fur mantle.

"Just a moment, darling," she said, her eyes still on me. "Her hands? Ah, I think I understand where this is going. Juliet, you've no idea the medical advancements I've made out here—"

"Mother," he said again.

"And the electricity from the windmill is only the start. Next year I plan on—"

"Mother!" he interrupted, more insistently.

"Oh, what is so important, love?" She turned to him and drew in a sharp breath. Still dizzy from the ale and the late hour, I didn't yet understand what had made her go silent. The fiddler stopped playing abruptly, and a few of the girls gasped.

"Mother, I had an accident."

From somewhere behind me, a girl screamed. I recognized the voice as Lucy's, but I couldn't tear my eyes away from Hensley. My vision kept spinning and spinning, telling me what I was seeing couldn't possibly be true. Bile started to rise in my throat.

A tree branch as thick as my wrist stuck straight through Hensley's chest. It dragged on the ground behind him, bursting out of his small chest with a ragged end seeping blood too slowly. A coldness crept up my legs.

No one could survive an injury like that and still walk.

No one who was alive, at least.

NINE

ELIZABETH GRABBED HENSLEY, FRANTICALLY whispering reassur-ances in his ear. With a single swift tug Carlyle pulled the tree branch through Hensley's body, and they carried him to the manor while the rest of us stood dumbstruck.

"Did you see that?" Lucy whispered, lips turning blue. She started to slump, and Balthazar caught her before she passed out.

"Take her to the manor," I said, a hand on my head to steady my own dizziness. "Stay with her, Balthazar, in case she wakes up."

He nodded, seemingly the only one not upset that we'd witnessed the impossible, and carried her in the direction of the house. Around the bonfire, the music had stopped. The fire crackled, but no one moved. I could tell by the servants' faces that they already knew about Hensley's condition. As did the villagers of Quick, even the carnival troupe. We were the only ones not included in the secret.

What in God's name was going on?

Across the fire, Valentina smoked calmly on her cigarette. This must have been what she'd alluded to with regard to Elizabeth's medical achievements—that Elizabeth had gone beyond mere science and lied about losing her ancestor's research. As if sensing my thoughts, Valentina's eyes met mine and she smirked.

She hates me. I could feel it in my bones. *She hates that I'm Elizabeth's heir and she's not. That isn't something one can get over easily.*

Montgomery grabbed my wrist and started to drag me across the field toward the house.

"Slow down!" I yelled. "What are you doing?"

"We're leaving this place. I knew there was something wrong from the first night."

"*Leave?* We can't leave! What about Edward?"

His pace didn't slow as we approached the lights of the manor. A light shone in a high room of the south tower, which was always locked. It had to be a laboratory. Elizabeth was probably up there now operating on Hensley.

Montgomery paused at the front door, one hand on the iron knob. "You saw that child. He wasn't human, at least not anymore."

"We need to give Elizabeth a chance to explain."

"Explain *what*? She lied to us. Victor Frankenstein's science was never lost. She must have been practicing it in secret. On a child, no less."

Footsteps came from the gravel courtyard behind us, where Valentina and the younger girls were also headed toward the manor. I grabbed his shirt collar. "We should talk about this in private. Come on."

We hurried into the house and up the stairs to the privacy of my bedroom. The vision of Hensley's one white eye reflected in the space behind my eyelids. Had he died as a boy, and Elizabeth brought him back? Was he stitched together like Valentina's hands? No wonder he wasn't suitable to be her heir.

I took a deep breath. Elizabeth wasn't mad, not like my father. She wasn't ambitious like him. So why had she done it?

"It all makes sense now." Montgomery paced in front of my bedroom windows. "The little girl's limp. Carlyle's missing ear. Do you know what happened that day you went to Quick with Lucy?"

After I nearly died in the bog, the reason Montgomery had wanted me out of the house had been the last thing on my mind, but now my curiosity flickered back to life. "You investigated, didn't you? What did you find?"

"Nothing, and not for lack of trying. Valentina was my shadow all day. She wouldn't let me out of her sight for fear of what I'd find hidden away. The servants must be practically prisoners here, or else they're all mad, letting Elizabeth experiment on them. We should leave before they decide we've seen too much and stop us. We can take Edward in the carriage. Lucy shouldn't be hard to convince as long as Edward's with us, and Balthazar will go where I go."

"Where *would* we go? The police are all over the

country looking for us. Every road, every port, every train station, just waiting to drag us back to London."

"We'll hide out until this is all over. I know how to live in the wild."

"The *wild*? It's wintertime. Can you imagine Lucy in the forest, living off berries?"

He rubbed a hand over his face. "I don't care how dangerous it is out there, it's safer than within these walls."

I shook my head. "No. Elizabeth would never hurt us. She risked her life to keep us safe from the police. Do you really think she'd suddenly turn into a villain because we learned her secret? She knows our secrets, too, Montgomery, and they're just as scandalous."

He stopped pacing, his blond hair lose and wild in his face. "All we did was perform surgery on animals. We didn't bring anyone back from the dead. That goes against nature, Juliet. It's playing God."

"Playing God is *exactly* what Father did!"

"Yes, and you killed your father because of it. You killed three members of the King's Club for the same reason. Why are you so willing to believe Elizabeth is any different from them? You're the one always insisting women can be just as ruthless as men."

I paced the opposite side of the room, chewing on the inside of my cheek until I tasted blood. "It isn't because she's a woman," I said. "It's because . . ."

It's because she's like me.

I stopped pacing, chilled by my own thoughts. "Elizabeth isn't going to trap us here because of what we saw. If we hear her out and you still think leaving is best, then we'll go. Agreed?"

I could tell by the tense set to his shoulders that if it were up to him we'd be in the carriage right now, tearing wildly into the night, leaving the truth far behind. But no one could run from the truth forever.

"Just promise me it won't be like last time," he whispered. "No more unnatural science. No more playing God, not even when there's a chance the ends could justify the means."

I took a step back. Maybe it was my conversation with Jack Serra earlier, but Father was so freshly in my mind he might as well have been standing in the room with us.

"Do you truly have so little faith in me that you think I would become a monster like Father was?" I asked.

I didn't tell him that it was a fear I'd had myself.

"Of course not." His face had softened. "That was never what I meant."

We stood like that for a while, the two of us alone with the wind howling outside. At last, Montgomery took my hands.

"Sometimes you do remind me of your father," he said gently, "but I didn't mean that you're destined to go mad like him. You come from *two* parents, you know. For all your father's faults, there are your mother's strengths. She was such a kind woman, don't you remember?"

I flinched as though pricked with a needle, and all worries about Hensley, and Elizabeth's experimentation, and even Edward vanished. *My mother.* I could picture her if

I closed my eyes. High cheekbones flushed with warmth and perfectly pinned dark hair as she sang church hymns. The opposite to my father's cold countenance. When I was little, she had dedicated her life to helping others. On winter Sundays after church, Mother stayed behind with the Ladies' Auxiliary to knit socks for the inmates at Bryson Prison. I'd once asked her why she never knit a pair for me, and she'd taken me to Whitechapel and pointed out the vagrants with frostbitten toes. It was the first time I understood what wealth meant, and how devastating it would be if we ever lost it.

I stared at Montgomery, transfixed, our earlier argument forgotten. "Do you really think I could take after her instead of my father?" I couldn't keep the hope from my voice. It was a possibility that had never occurred to me before. I flexed my cold fingers, feeling warmth flooding into them for the first time in what felt like years.

His expression softened. "You already do take after her. You just can't see it."

I looked down at my hands' slender tapering and pale color. Why hadn't I noticed before how identical they were to my mother's? How much of me besides that was like her, that I'd ignored all this time? Father's shadow stretched so long that it had hidden any other paths I might have in life.

"Juliet, promise me you'll think more about being like her. Especially in light of what we've seen tonight. It worries me, you being in a house full of experimentation."

My mother had her faults, but she'd loved me. She'd

taken care of me. She'd obeyed Scripture and visited orphans and knit socks for prisoners and never once crossed the line into immoral science.

I took a deep breath. Yes, my mother's blood was also in my veins. She would help ground me as we faced whatever Elizabeth was doing in that tower laboratory.

"I promise."

TEN

ELIZABETH REMAINED LOCKED IN the tower with Hensley all that night and into the next day. Montgomery and I waited for her to emerge, watching from the window at the far end of the hallway as the sun came up and then started to sink again. I couldn't stop thinking about my mother and the possibility of following her path instead of Father's. Memories of her filled the hours while we waited: Mother helping me decorate the Christmas tree, giving me my first pair of dancing slippers, reading me stories at night.

At last, the door creaked open.

I jumped up, brushing the hair out of my eyes. Elizabeth stood in the doorway, wiping her hands on a towel. She wore the green dress from the night before, but without the grand fur cloak she looked less like Queen of the Fairies and more like a worried mother.

"I expected you'd want some answers," she said. McKenna appeared in the doorway behind her, a basket of bloody clothes in her arms, and started down the stairs.

She paused when she reached me.

"Keep an open mind, little mouse," she said. "This is a peaceful house. None of us, the mistress included, have a cruel bone in our bodies." She looked at the floor and hurried down the hallway.

The line of electric lights winding up the stone stairs flickered.

"How is Hensley?" I asked quietly.

Elizabeth smiled. "He'll be causing trouble again in a few days, no doubt."

Montgomery folded his arms across his chest. "We need to know the truth about him."

"Yes—well, it seems you shall have it, whether I wish to tell you or not." She sighed, coming down the stairs. "Let's talk in the observatory. I'm exhausted, and the stars always have a way of putting me to sleep. Come."

I didn't bother to mention that dusk was only now falling, and the stars weren't out yet. She led us down the stairs and through winding hallways that all looked the same, then back up another set of stairs with a new runner and freshly polished brass sconces. The observatory was a tall room with a glass ceiling in the northern tower. The collection of astronomical equipment was impressive: heavy silver sextants, a telescope, a library full of star charts. Elizabeth walked over to a globe of the constellations and swung it open to reveal a hidden compartment.

She took out a bottle of *Les Étoiles* gin and three glasses.

"*Les Étoiles*," she said, holding up the bottle wryly. "It's French for 'the stars.' I told you they always put me to sleep."

Montgomery sat on a wooden stool, and I settled into a leather chair and looked out at the setting sun beyond the observation window. Elizabeth sat across from me, sipping her gin. She'd removed her apron and gloves, but she'd missed a small streak of dried blood on her chin.

"You lied to us," Montgomery said, "about Frankenstein's science being lost."

Elizabeth shifted. "I swore an oath never to tell, and I didn't see any reason why you should need to find out, at least not right away. If your friend Mr. Prince had never poisoned himself, my family's history never would have come up in that carriage ride from London. Raising the dead? Who in their right minds would ever think it possible?"

"Did the professor know?" I asked.

"Yes. All the von Steins have known. The third lord of Ballentyne had a daughter who gave birth to Victor Frankenstein's bastard child in 1786. She helped him with his research and understood how to replicate the procedures, but after he died, she knew it had to be kept secret." She tapped a finger against the gin glass. "When I told you earlier that Frankenstein's journals had been lost, that wasn't exactly the truth. I have them, and I keep them well hidden. They're called the Origin Journals."

"And what do they contain?"

"Everything one would need to re-create Frankenstein's work. Instructions on the reanimation procedure detailed enough that even the most basic surgeon would be able to follow them. The knowledge has been passed down to all our family as guardians."

"For what purpose?" Montgomery said.

"The power to defeat death isn't something that one stumbles upon every day. There might come a time when it's needed. An epidemic in which so many lives are lost that it's necessary to keep the population stable, or a great leader struck down before his time. We have strict rules for when the science may be used. A code. It's called the Oath of Perpetual Anatomy. In one hundred eleven years we've never met the criteria."

My voice felt hoarse. "But you broke the rules when you brought back Hensley."

She laughed, dry and brittle, and picked up her glass. "I thought you might have figured it out by now, Juliet." She took a sip. "Hensley isn't my son. He was the professor's little boy."

A gasp caught in my throat. Memories of the professor's dust-covered nursery came to me: the old toys, the child-sized bed, the portrait on the wall. *"Thomas?"*

Elizabeth nodded. "Hensley was his middle name. I told you, when we were leaving London, that the professor had strayed dangerously close to the line into immoral science. In fact, he crossed it. Thomas took ill and died so suddenly, and the professor's wife not a week later. The professor went a bit mad with grief. He brought his son's body here to Ballentyne and reanimated him."

The feeling had drained from my feet, and yet my heart kept beating faster and faster. They had truly achieved it. Defeated death. Not even my father had dreamed of such lofty achievements.

"He knew it was a mistake right away," Elizabeth continued. "But he could hardly undo it and kill his son all over again. Nor could he bring a dead little boy back to London."

"So he left Hensley in your care?"

She gave me an odd look. "I'm merely the most recent mistress of Ballentyne to care for him. Hensley was born six years before *I* was. He's forty-one years old, though neither his mind nor his body have aged."

I slumped in the chair, stunned. The things it meant for the world . . . A cure for plagues. Eternal life. She was right—it was wonderful and terrible at once, and so easily abused.

Montgomery leaned forward. "Did the King's Club know about this?"

"A few of the elite members suspected, which is why they sent men like Isambard Lessing around to question us. But it was never more than rumors. If they knew the truth . . ." She shuddered. "They wouldn't adhere to the oath, I can promise you that. They'd bring back anyone who might serve their ambitions."

"Well, we needn't worry about them," I said. "With their leaders dead, the rest of the King's Club members have scattered just as we predicted. John Radcliffe's letter in the newspaper proved that."

Montgomery flexed his knuckles. "Perhaps, but there are other associations in other cities, in other countries. There's no shortage of unscrupulous men and women who would exploit Frankenstein's science, if they knew about it.

That science is too dangerous to exist. It should be burned."

"Absolutely not," Elizabeth said, her eyes flaring. "We've kept the secret for six generations. It's perfectly safe."

"The servants know," Montgomery pointed out.

"You needn't worry about them. They're entirely loyal to me. That's what giving people body parts they've lost will do. I've operated on all of them, except for McKenna—but Ballentyne is in her bones. Her family's been the primary caretakers of the estate for generations; I couldn't possibly manage this place without her. Most of the work I've done on the others is beneath their clothes where you can't see, or the odd eye or tongue that you probably haven't noticed. They'll go to their graves with the secret and would give their lives to protect Ballentyne."

I thought of Valentina's hateful glare at the bonfire. Was it possible her anger came, not from jealousy, but from a fear that I was a threat to the carefully constructed secrets that the manor held?

Outside, clouds rolled in, bathing the moors in shadows. Night had fallen, but there were no stars. So remote. A person could lose herself here.

A flash of white near the door caught my eye, and I turned just in time to see dark curls and a white nightdress disappear around the corner. *Lucy.* She must have slipped away from Balthazar. How much had she overheard?

I glanced at Elizabeth, but she was pacing by the desk, running her fingers along the row of dusty books, too lost in her thoughts to have noticed our eavesdropper.

"You said you were one in a long line of Ballentyne mistresses to uphold the Oath of Perpetual Anatomy," Montgomery said. "You have no natural children of your own, so I can't help but wonder if your decision to name Juliet as your heir has anything to do with the Oath."

I nearly choked on my gin. I'd never assumed the inheritance was anything other than the house, but one look at Elizabeth's face told me Montgomery's guess was correct.

"It's true," Elizabeth said. "I hadn't intended to talk to you about this so soon, but after the professor died, I became the last one with this knowledge. If anything happens to me, a century's worth of secrets will be lost. I've already named you heir to Ballentyne, Juliet—the buildings and the land. It is my intention to make you heir to its secrets, too. To teach you Perpetual Anatomy."

Montgomery's hand clamped onto mine. "She's promised never to delve into that sort of science."

I tossed him an uncertain look. "He's right," I said slowly. "I promised to put all that behind me."

Elizabeth gave me a sharp look. "Promised whom? You're the type of girl who makes her own decisions. Besides, it's what the professor wanted. It's the reason he took you in."

I shook my head, confused. "No it isn't. He took me in because he felt guilty that he couldn't save my father. He wanted to give me a chance at a normal life."

A pitying look came over her face, and I realized how naive I had been. "That isn't entirely true, I'm afraid. He took you in because I've no children of my own. We needed someone younger to pass the information along to. Someone who had the intelligence to understand how the science worked, and an open mind. Someone who wouldn't run away screaming. He heard how you slit Dr. Hastings's tendon and thought you might be a good candidate."

I closed my eyes. It was cold, and yet sweat beaded my brow. I could still remember the day, nearly a year ago, when the professor came to get me out of jail and told me he was making me his legal ward.

Why are you doing this? I had asked him.

Because I failed to stop your father until it was too late, he'd said. *It isn't too late for you, Miss Moreau, not yet.*

"You were exactly what we were looking for," Elizabeth said. Hope, mixed with motherly affection, filled her voice. "It doesn't mean he didn't love you like a daughter, or that I don't think of you as family as well. That's why the von Steins have kept the secret for so long: because we're family, and family makes us strong. We take care of each other, Juliet." She paused. "I've taken care of you, even at great risk."

Montgomery's hand squeezed mine hard. "Because you want something from her," he argued.

"No. Because I want to *give* her something. Knowledge. Trust. Family—one that won't disappoint her."

I looked down at Montgomery's hand over mine, afraid to speak. I *had* promised him. But that had been before I'd known there was an oath, and a code of conduct, and that such science was even possible.

Which meant more—keeping a promise, or a chance to achieve great things?

I stood before the temptation grew too strong. "I'm not like my father. You're wrong if you think I am." I signaled to Montgomery that it was time to leave, but she grabbed my arm. I looked at her hand with its long and nimble fingers. A surgeon's fingers.

Just like mine.

"I'm not mad," she continued. "I've no desire to play God. The secrets I've sworn to keep have the power to save the world. There couldn't be any reason more noble."

I closed my eyes. Noble? Could my attraction to these darker sides of science actually have some *noble* ramifications? My heart thumped harder than it ever had. By my side, Montgomery took a step closer.

Elizabeth grabbed the book off her desk and handed it to me. "Take this. It's the biography of the first Lord Ballentyne, who built this place. Before you make a decision, read this so you at least know what you would be walking away from." She gave me a hard look. "Read it tonight."

I took it from her, a bit shaken. Montgomery and I returned to our adjoining rooms, where I told him I needed a few hours alone to think. As soon as I closed the door to my bedroom, I opened the book. A piece of paper with Elizabeth's hurried writing on it fluttered to the ground. She must have scrawled it while Montgomery and I had been distracted by Lucy eavesdropping.

Montgomery is a good man, but he'll never understand why women like us do what we must do, her message said. *If you want to know the real truth, I will teach you everything.*

A shiver ran through me. I balled the paper and tossed it into the fire so no one would ever find it. I glanced at the door to Montgomery's room, hating to keep secrets from him, but knowing that as important as promises were, sometimes my curiosity was just too strong.

ELEVEN

A FEW MINUTES LATER, as Elizabeth's note burned to ash, pounding sounded at my door. When I twisted the knob and peeked out, Lucy burst through the doorway.

"Can you believe it?" Her cheeks burned with excitement. "Reanimation, Juliet. It's incredible!"

I sank onto the bed, wishing I could have just a few moments alone with my thoughts.

"I know," I whispered.

"For a hundred years they've had this power and only used it once, on a silly little boy. Think of all the people they could have brought back: Beethoven, Darwin, Charles Dickens—"

"It's a dangerous science," I cut in, my voice harsher than it should be. "The von Steins are right to keep it secret."

The excitement fell from her face, just for a second, and then flared to life again. "But don't you see what this means? It solves the paradoxical situation that Elizabeth was telling us about, that in order to cure Edward we would first have to kill him." A madness shone in her eyes as her voice dropped. "It's possible now. Death doesn't have to be the end anymore."

I stepped back. "What exactly are you suggesting?"

She came close enough that I could smell feverish sweat on her. "You *know* what I'm suggesting, Juliet. We make certain Edward dies, then perform the operation to cut out the diseased part of his brain and bring him back to life. He'll be entirely cured."

I took another step away from her until the cold glass of my bedroom window bit at my back and I could go no farther. I pressed a hand to my spinning head. Lucy usually talked about lace patterns and French powder, not experimentation on the dead. This wild-eyed girl in my room felt like a stranger.

I took a deep breath. "It's impossible."

"Is it?" she hissed. "Elizabeth has her oath, but we could find a way to convince her to help. We'd just have to drain the diseased portion of Edward's brain of the infection, cutting it out if we have to, making sure the Beast is gone for good, and then bring Edward back to life. We've given him a chance to fight it on his own and he's losing. He *needs* our help."

"We would have to kill him, Lucy," I shot back. "Are you prepared to do that?"

Her cheeks burned, but her eyes were even more aflame. She grabbed my arm hard enough that her fingernails dug into my skin.

"Not me," she said. "You'd do it."

I ripped my arm away from her, breathing heavily, and paced in front of the window. "I'm not going to kill Edward! Murder isn't some lark. It isn't a decision made lightly."

Her eyes burned feverishly bright. "You killed Inspector Newcastle lightly enough. You killed your father easily enough."

I gasped at her accusation. This wasn't a stranger. It was Lucy, my best friend, who had a good heart but wasn't seeing reason right now.

"Go to bed," I said. "In the morning you'll see how insane this plan is of yours, and you'll thank me for putting an end to it right here."

I opened the door, but she didn't make a move toward it. The light in her eyes burned colder now.

"I never thought I'd see the day when Juliet Moreau was too weak willed to do whatever it took to save a friend's life," she said. "Even if it meant ending it first."

She slammed the door behind her.

I forced myself not to go after her. It was better this way. She was mad with grief and didn't realize how insane it sounded to kill Edward so that we could cure him and bring him back.

Could we even do it? Could *I*?

I CRAWLED INTO BED, exhausted. It was dark outside, those witching hours between midnight and dawn when anything seemed possible and the idea of bringing a dead friend back to life was no more strange than rigging a remote manor with electric lights. If one was possible, why not the other?

Montgomery would tell me that I should stay far away from anything resembling Father's dark science. He would remind me that I had another path open for me: my mother's.

I closed my eyes, trying hard to picture her face, and a memory came from when I was seven years old and my parents took me to a carnival at Vauxhall Gardens. There were performing horses. Chinese jugglers. Ventriloquists. Mother had fanned herself with playbills and teased Father that he was going to run away with the bearded lady. Father swore that he'd never love a woman with more facial hair than himself, and she had laughed.

"Come with me to the music hall, Juliet," Mother had said. "They're playing Vivaldi on dueling pianos."

Father scoffed. "Vivaldi, that repetitive hack? I'm off to see the monstrosities, myself. The Dog-faced Boy. Hairy Mary from Borneo." He paused, as if for the first time noticing how I hung on his every word. "Would you like to come?"

My heart had soared. It was the first time he'd invited me to do something, just him and me.

But for the life of me, I couldn't remember which one I had chosen: my mother and her piano music, or my father and his freakish science. In my head there was only a blank. Why couldn't I recall?

I buried my head in my pillow. Now the past was hidden from me, just like my future. And the future seemed so terribly important in light of Lucy's plan. Which was worse—letting Edward succumb to the Beast, or going against God—and Montgomery—to tear his body apart and stitch it back together again?

I tossed and turned in bed for hours, trying to foresee the future, before I remembered that I knew someone who specialized in precisely that.

I THREW OFF THE covers, the smell of caramel apples from my childhood memory lingering in the back of my head. It was still dark outside, with only a faint glow on the horizon to tell me that dawn was coming. I dressed quickly and hurried through the sleeping house. I ran through the fields. The carnival troupe had camped out in the fields since the Twelfth Night bonfire the night before last, and I half feared they would be gone, but their tents loomed beneath the dying stars. As I approached, darkness hid the stains and tears in the tents' fabric, and it looked like a fairy village, magical and forgotten by time.

A voice came from behind me.

"It isn't good to ramble at night. It betrays a wandering spirit."

I turned to find Jack Serra silhouetted in the moonlight, skin so dark I couldn't read the expression on his face. I stood straighter. "That's ironic, coming from a member of a wandering troupe."

"There's method to our wandering," he said. "I wonder if there is to yours, Miss Moreau."

I wrapped my arms tightly across my chest, against

both the cold and his probing question. He came closer and lifted the flap of the tent. Inside, a lantern glowed softly, showing a tidy bed and a neatly stacked pile of clothes. I hesitated to enter a strange man's tent, but he seemed to read my mind and only laughed. "You've nothing to fear from me, pretty girl. You can trust me. Isn't that why you came tonight?"

I gave him a hard look. "Can you read minds now, too, fortune-teller?"

"I can read your face. That's enough. Now, come in."

I followed him inside, where he motioned to a stool. The tent was warmer than I'd expected, but I didn't unclench my arms from across my chest.

"You never finished telling me what my fortune means." I paused to take out the water charm I still wore around my neck. "About a child being like a river headed for the ocean. Finish it, please. I'll pay you however much you want."

I held out my palm flat, insistently, but he didn't take it.

"I didn't think you were the superstitious type," he said.

"It seems I have a much more open mind these days. And you know so much about me that I'd like to hear what you have to say." In the lantern light, it was plain to see that my hand was shaking. What must he think of me, coming out here alone in the early morning, demanding a fortune? If he judged me, however, his face showed nothing. He just took my hand in his warm one.

"You want me to tell you something to reassure you," he said, his dark brown eyes mirroring my own. "You have a decision to make, and you want me to make it for you, but that isn't how this works."

My lips had gone dry in the cold air. "Please. I need help."

"Fate is a tricky concept. Where I am from, people do not linger over the future. They live in the moment. If they are hungry, they eat. If they are tired, they sleep. The only things that dictate their lives are the earth and the seasons and their own instincts."

"And yet you read fortunes for a living."

His mouth curled in a half smile. "I left my people for a reason." He pressed my hand reassuringly before releasing it. "The river can be good, pretty girl. It can bring water to the thirsty and carry travelers to better lands. It can be cruel, too. An angry river can tear down whatever gets in its way."

"Then you're saying I have a choice?" There was hope in my voice. "I can choose whether to be helpful or to be destructive?" It was like Montgomery kept insisting, that it was up to me to choose to be either like my mother or my father.

But he looked at me with pity, as if all my hopefulness was but silly dreams. "The river always runs downhill, pretty girl. Always."

His words turned my insides cold.

"So I can't change who I am?" On impulse I reached out and grabbed his hand, squeezing it tight. "Just tell me, please! No more riddles. Am I destined to be like my father? I need to know. I have a choice to make—a friend is ill and I have the power to save him, but only if I follow my father's footsteps. I swore I wouldn't. What do I do?"

Sounds came from beyond the tent. The rustle of fabric, a man's yawn, pots and pans banging together. The other members of the troupe were waking.

"You should go," he said.

"Please!" My fingernails dug into his palm. "I don't know how you know so much about me, and I don't care. I'll believe that magic is real, if you want. Just help me."

He paused, staring down at my hand clutching his. I would have given anything to see what was going through his mind in that moment.

"To make the right decision you must understand both paths before you," he said quietly. "You must know your demons before you know whether to follow them."

I sat back on the stool, considering his words. *Know my demons.* In the flickering light of his lantern, it made more sense than anything else. Before I could begin to consider Lucy's plan, I needed to know if it was even possible to cure Edward through death and bring him back to life. Only Elizabeth could help me to know those particular demons, and she had already made me the offer.

"Think about my words very carefully," he said.

I nodded, as the sound of more pots and pans came

from outside. "Thank you," I said, and hid the charm back under my dress.

It wasn't until I was back in the field, running toward the manor as dawn broke, that I realized he hadn't looked at the lines in my palm even once.

TWELVE

THE FOLLOWING NIGHT, AFTER the household had gone to bed, I stood at the base of the southern tower stairs that led to Elizabeth's laboratory. Faint beams of light came through the cracks in the door, drawing me toward it like a moth to a flame.

A hand sank onto my shoulder and I jumped. Elizabeth leaned over my shoulder, smelling of roses. "I see you got my note. Does that mean you've decided to learn my secrets?"

I gave a nod I hoped looked confident.

She smiled. "Good. Come with me."

She led me up the steps, but to my surprise we stopped at a door one floor below the laboratory. She opened it to reveal a round chamber with simple wooden furniture, lit by a fading lantern. A girl woke and rubbed the sleep from her eyes.

"Is his sleep troubled again tonight, Lily?" Elizabeth asked.

"Not tonight, mistress."

"Good. You can return to your bedroom. I'll watch him the rest of the night."

Lily gathered up her half-finished needlepoint and left the room quietly. Elizabeth held a finger to her lips and motioned me to follow her. The hearth was cold and the room seemed little more than a cell, until I tripped over a small object and looked down at a wooden duck on a string.

Elizabeth pulled back a heavy curtain to reveal a small bed where Hensley slept soundly. She knelt by the bed, petting his head.

"Sit," she whispered to me, and motioned to the floor next to her.

I knelt cautiously as Elizabeth straightened Hensley's collar. "He only has nightmares after an operation. Normally he can sleep through anything. I suppose that's a benefit of knowing you cannot die."

I bit my lip, both unnerved and drawn to the sleeping boy. Part of me knew I shouldn't even be here, listening to her explanations. But another part of me was fiercely curious.

I eased slightly closer. "He can't die at all?"

"Very few things could kill him. Fire, for one. Everything else I can stitch back together and he's good as new."

"How does his body work?"

"Just as yours and mine does, only stronger. Even at his small size, he has the strength of three men." She unbuttoned his tiny shirt carefully so as not to wake him. At least three dozen scars ran across his chest, a puzzle of flesh and black stitching, a record of more than thirty years of wounds that had been healed by Elizabeth and the professor.

My stomach tightened even as my curiosity flared.

"He doesn't feel pain," Elizabeth whispered, staring at the scars with a fascination that mirrored my own. "If he's injured, he knows I can always fix him again. It makes him much bolder than a normal child."

She led me to a small locked doorway that she opened with a key around her neck. It was a storage room crowded with old trunks and toys and, to my surprise, an entire wall of cages with dozens of white rats.

"So many?" I asked. "I thought he only had one rat."

"Yes. Well, he thinks there's only one, too." She dropped a hand into her apron pocket. "He's very gentle with them—most of the time. Sometimes he doesn't understand his own strength and kills one by accident." She withdrew her hand from her apron pocket, her fingers wrapped around the body of the rat Hensley had been playing with the night I'd nearly drowned in the bog. My throat tightened at the memory.

"The night you returned to Ballentyne," I whispered. "He suffocated it while we were all in the library, didn't he? I told myself I must have imagined it."

Elizabeth nodded. "He didn't mean to. I always take them from him before he realizes what he's done. I throw them out on the moors. It keeps the foxes from going after our chickens." She gazed down at the dead rat. "With all the commotion, I haven't yet had the chance. I've kept this one in my laboratory."

"So he doesn't know he's killing them?"

"No." She sighed, rubbing the sides of her head. "It's better to keep him in the dark. He doesn't grow or age, but his body deteriorates over time and his brain doesn't work as well as it should anymore. He's growing unpredictable. I fear what he might do if he knew his beloved pet was only one of many he himself had killed and I'd replaced."

I shuddered at the thought.

"Better the rats than the girls," Elizabeth said. "He's fond of them as well, and he could hurt them just as easily without meaning to. The rats give him something to focus his attention on."

I hugged my arms across my chest. If Montgomery were here, he'd tell me to leave right now.

But Montgomery wasn't here.

"Would you like to hear the story of Victor Frankenstein?" She stared at the dead rat in her hand, then smiled tightly. "The legends are true, but they don't tell the full story. He was nineteen when he began his research, just a few years older than you are now. His family was Genevese. Very modern thinkers. They sent him to Ingolstadt for a scientific education, but his mother passed away of scarlet fever before he left. He was devastated. He became obsessed with the idea of defeating death. Creating humans who would never die."

She paused, stroking the dead rat's fur.

"The creature he made was . . . well, not far off from the thing described in legends. Eight feet tall with yellow skin and a lumbering gait. Some versions of the legend say the creature lacked the gift of intelligence and speech, but that wasn't true. He was quite smart." She paused. "I think, if the creature had been a mindless thing, the past would have turned out differently."

The rats kept crawling over one another, their little pink noses sniffing our strange smells, but Elizabeth paid them no heed. "Victor ran away, terrified by what he'd done. He thought the creature would die of exposure, but like Hensley, it didn't feel heat or cold. It needed food, but not much. It had the strength to break through locked doors. It lived, and it went out into the world. Eventually Victor left to hunt it down. Neither of them was heard from again."

"And this is the science you want to teach me?"

"Only the daughter of Henri Moreau could understand how important it is."

"I'm also the daughter of Evelyn Chastain, and she'd faint at the very mention of Frankenstein's monster. Why are you so certain I take after Father, and not her?"

She raised an eyebrow. I thought she might speak, but instead she took an apron off a hook near the door and handed it to me.

"Put that on, and we shall see which parent you take after most. Consider this your first lesson: Always wear an apron you don't mind getting dirty. *Very* dirty."

THIRTEEN

"YOU ASKED ME ABOUT Valentina's hands," Elizabeth said as she led me up the rest of the steps to the locked door at the top. "She came to us two years ago nearly dead from blood loss. She'd traveled a long way, following a rumor among itinerant performers that I could restore missing limbs. She'd lost her hands in a wood-chopping accident and brought them with her in a wicker basket, but I couldn't use them. They'd been too badly damaged. I threw them out to the foxes."

"Where did you find her current hands?" I asked, following her up the stairs.

"There's a monastery outside of Quick. They have a graveyard that serves the entire region. It's where I get most of my raw supplies."

Raw supplies? I thought. *More like body parts.*

"The death rate this far north is abysmally high," she continued. "I had the corpses of three girls her same age to choose from. One was very recent, died in childbirth; it made the transplant easier. I would have liked to find a corpse more her natural coloration, but there aren't many Romany in these parts. She didn't mind. She was so thankful to have the use of her hands again that she dedicated her life to Ballentyne. I can hardly recall how we managed before she arrived. She's teaching the girls astronomy and philosophy in addition to needlepoint. They might be milkmaids by trade, but that doesn't mean they can't also be well educated."

My head spun with questions. Did the monks know Elizabeth took the bodies, or did she grave rob them late at night? She probably sent Carlyle to do the dirty work, except now he was getting on in age. Maybe that was why she'd been so kind to Balthazar, wanting him to fill Igor's role as her laboratory assistant.

I followed her up the tower with nervous steps. Each stair took me closer to secrets I'd wished to know ever since I was a little girl peering through the keyhole of Father's laboratory. Elizabeth slid her key in the lock but paused.

"Once we go in here, Juliet, there's no going back. I'll ask you one more time. Are you certain you wish to learn all of this?"

I pressed a hand against Jack Serra's water charm beneath my dress, reminding myself that I had to learn my demons before deciding to follow them or not. Technically, I was also staying true to my promise to Montgomery; I wasn't *following* my father's footsteps. I was only standing in the door and peering down that path to see where it led.

A tremor of excitement ran through me. "Yes."

She opened the door. My greedy eyes took in everything at once: the roundness of the tower walls, which gave the feeling of a giant stone womb; wooden shelves and cupboards; books and papers stacked in piles that were tidy but didn't have my father's rigid adherence to order. In fact, nothing about the room brought to mind my father's cold and sterile laboratory. This space had the touch of a woman, from the apron hanging on a peg to a kettle and cup of tea that must have long since gone cold. There was even a little painting on the wall, done with childish inaccuracy, signed by Hensley. The only thing at all similar was the operating table in the middle: the same leather manacles, the same sawdust underneath to draw the blood, now fresh and unsullied.

She lit a lantern. "What's going through your mind?"

The room was warm, with the windows shuttered against the winter wind. Cozy almost, not unlike my attic apartment in London. I had the urge to wrap a threadbare quilt around my shoulders and curl up in my old rocking chair by the fire.

"It feels more comfortable than I'd expected."

"Good."

She closed the door behind me and locked it, then returned to the table, where she carefully laid out the body of Hensley's white rat. My eyes scanned its tiny feet, the ropelike naked tail. Its fur was matted around its neck in a very revealing way.

"Hensley means to be protective, but he doesn't know his own strength. Instead of throwing this one out for the foxes, I thought it might prove . . . educational."

Her eyes darted to the metal pole coming down from

the spired roof, and I realized it was the reverse end of a lightning rod. It connected to wires designed to hook onto a cadaver's body.

"We're going to reanimate it?" I couldn't keep the thrill from my voice.

She laid out the rat, gathering several vials and surgical tools from the various cabinets around the room. "No," she said, flicking her eyes toward me. "*I'm* going to reanimate it. You're going to observe and not touch anything. It isn't a complicated procedure, but it's a dangerous one, even with a subject so small. Now fetch that clamp, will you?"

I handed her the metal clamp, and she used it to secure several metal wires to the end of the lightning rod, then attached them to sections of the rat. Next, she inserted a syringe of murky liquid into its heart. I took in every detail with wide eyes. It wasn't unlike my own plan for awakening the water-tank creatures: the principle difference being, of course, that those creatures had been alive in a state of stasis, and this rat was quite dead.

Anticipation rushed up my throat, and I had to bite the inside of my cheek. I was going to watch the impossible happen. Death, defeated.

"But it isn't raining anymore," I said. "There won't be any lightning."

"The windmill provides enough power to reanimate small creatures," she said. "Rats, rabbits, birds. When I reattach a human's limb, it also requires a small jolt of electricity to stimulate the dormant nerves. I've performed such minor procedures dozens of times. The lightning rod . . .

well, there's only one time when we would need that much power all at once."

I dropped my voice. "For a body, you mean. An entire human."

"Yes. The rod hasn't been used since the professor brought Hensley back to life thirty-five years ago."

I watched as she finished connecting the wires. After years of studying science out of books, I itched to do the work myself. I had to clasp my hands together.

She glanced up at me. "You might wish to cover your ears. They scream when they come back to life. Even the rats."

I didn't move. I couldn't. My every muscle was riveted to that little dead body on the table. Elizabeth went to the wall, where a lever and dial were attached to the electrical wiring from the windmill outside. "I warned you," she said.

She flipped the lever.

The entire room hummed in a soft vibration, like crackling in the air before lightning strikes. I could feel electricity in the wires and in the metal inlay of the table. For a few breathless moments, nothing happened. I didn't take my eyes from the rat. Such white fur, motionless now. Such black eyes, dulled with death.

Would it be very different with a human subject? Humans shared the same basic neurological systems with animals, after all. The same major nerves and synapses. It was how my father had been able to twist animals into creatures that walked and talked.

A spark snapped, and I jerked. Sweat broke out on my

forehead as though Father was peering over my shoulder.

Elizabeth adjusted the dial, and electricity popped again on the wires connected to the rat. Movement caught my eye—just a flinch. If I'd blinked, I would have missed it. But there was no mistaking what I had seen. *There*—it came again. The rat's little paw, curling with the pulses of electricity. Suddenly I wasn't in the tower at all. I was back in King's College with Lucy, watching students vivisecting an unanesthetized rabbit. Its back leg had twitched just like the rat's. Only back then my body had shaken with rage, not thrill. Those boys had been torturing that rabbit, ending its life slowly and painfully. Now, before my very eyes, Elizabeth was doing the exact opposite. Bringing a creature back to life. Righting its wrongful death. If there was pain involved—well, what was pain, in the face of new life?

Its body was warming, twitching back to life as the electrical currents jolted the heart. Elizabeth cranked the dial once more and the entire rat convulsed.

Its scream was far too human for something so small. I flinched but didn't cover my ears. I *wanted* to hear that scream. I liked it. It was the scream of life fighting back into the world, the scream of the impossible finding a voice, the scream of death's last stand before being banished back into the shadows.

Elizabeth lowered the lever, and the crackling in the air faded. She came to the table, where we watched the rat twitching back to life. Gently, she removed the wires and withdrew the needle from the creature's heart. A tiny drop of crimson marred the rat's perfect white fur.

Blood.

Or rather, life.

The rat suddenly scrambled to its stomach, eyes blinking, nose twitching, both panic and lethargy present in its jerky movements. I reached out to touch the soft fur. Beneath my fingers I could feel its heart fluttering out of control, the warm blood flowing through stiff capillaries. We could give Hensley back the rat and he'd never know the difference. Or maybe I'd ask Elizabeth if I could keep it as a pet. A reminder of the awe-inspiring possibilities of science and a promise to myself that I would be bringing such creatures back to life—not like those medical students.

I pressed my hand over Jack Serra's charm. He had told me to know my demons, and now I did, in the form of a white rat with a twitching pink nose. I knew reanimation was possible. The science behind the procedure was sophisticated, its execution simple. With time and research, I felt confident I could replicate it. Lucy's plan to bring Edward back didn't seem so mad anymore. In fact, it was starting to feel heartless *not* to do it.

Just as the Beast had said, science was in my blood. For all of my mother's goodness, my father's love of science pulsed harder in my veins. In London I'd feared I'd crossed that line and become too much like him. Now, looking at the rat, I *knew*. The Beast was right, just as Jack Serra was right. The river always flowed downhill. There was no point in trying to escape from the inevitable.

Elizabeth gently took the rat from me and placed it in

a glass tank along with a cotton ball that smelled of alcohol and something bitter. Anesthesia. She closed the lid on the tank, and it hit me.

"Chloroform?" I said. "That will kill it!"

"I know," she said calmly.

"But you just brought it back to life."

"To teach you." Her hand remained firmly on the lid. "I did this procedure for you, not the rat. Let this be your second lesson tonight. Nothing comes back from the dead unchanged. You've seen the effect it has had on Hensley. This rat would have been stronger than other rats, its behavior unpredictable. If I'd returned it to the cage with the others, it might have killed them all without even meaning to."

I shook my head. This information was unwelcome. We could cure Edward of the Beast, but would there be other, more dangerous, side effects?

"You don't know that. I could have kept it on its own in a cage and fed it myself."

Her cold eyes didn't waver, and more doubt sank into me.

"We don't do this to make pets," she said. "We don't do it to bring those we love back. There are rules, Juliet. A code. Until you promise to me that you would never use this science for anything other than the rules, you will only watch me do it. When I'm certain your ethics are above reproach, then I'll let you be the one to pull the lever."

I swallowed, watching the rat twitch inside the glass

cage once, twice, and then stop. I closed my eyes.

"You're right. I'm sorry. I promise."

I wasn't sure if it was a lie or not. I wasn't sure of anything anymore.

I took off the apron and walked down the tower's spiral stairs in a daze. I needed fresh air and time to think. I went outside into the dark night and walked the gardens beneath a moonless sky. At night, everything took on a different appearance. I had explored Ballentyne's gardens in the daylight and found them to be an overgrown tangle of vines, but now the shapes loomed like ghosts.

If Edward died, bringing him back was possible—but at what risk?

The Beast had claimed to love me at the same time his claws had dug into my shoulder deeply enough to draw blood. A deranged, twisted obsession. Would it be any different after the procedure? A terrible image flickered in my mind of Edward, brought back from the dead, hugging Lucy with such unnatural strength that he suffocated her just as Hensley did with his beloved rats.

While my wandering feet took me through the gardens back toward Ballentyne, I noticed a light blazing on the front steps, moving back and forth. It was McKenna, dressed in a man's sweater, holding a torch and pacing from one end to the other. She must have realized I'd slipped out of the house and was looking for me.

I hurried back toward the house.

"McKenna," I said, breathing hard as I climbed the steps. "I'm sorry I wandered off. It was selfish of me."

To my surprise, her worry didn't fade. She barely glanced at me.

"Wandered off? Hush, little mouse. You'd hardly be the first. Half of my girls here spend hours wandering the grounds." Her voice was soft, but her eyes were troubled as they scanned the moors, her fingers working anxiously.

I pulled my sweater closer. "Who are you looking for, then?"

"It's Valentina. She was supposed to wake me at midnight; we do the week's baking in the wee hours of Saturday mornings. But she didn't. There's no sign of her, not since yesterday. Her bedroom door is locked and she has the only key."

"Why would she run off?"

McKenna sighed with worry. "The mistress trusts Valentina, but if you ask me, there's always been something off about that girl. Don't get me wrong; she cares about this place. But there's a darkness in her she's never been able to shake. I worry that darkness has come to haunt her."

A shiver ran through me, and McKenna hugged her arms as well.

"Perhaps it's come to haunt all of us," she whispered.

FOURTEEN

WE WAITED ALL DAY for Valentina to reappear, but there was no sign of her. By the following night even Elizabeth was worried enough to stop our Perpetual Anatomy lessons until she was found. The entire household mounted a search for her. I took the south garden, afraid to venture anywhere near the bogs.

"Valentina!" I called, but there was no answer.

After another hour, nearly frozen to death, I stomped back to the stairs, where McKenna and Elizabeth kept watch. McKenna handed me a cup of hot cider.

"Any news of her?" I asked.

McKenna shook her head, lips stitched together in worry. "No, though Moira admitted she heard Valentina crying a few nights ago when she found out you'd been named heir, Miss Moreau. None of us have ever seen Valentina cry, not once."

"You think she ran off because of me?" My stomach twisted with guilt. Did Valentina truly care that much about the manor? Perhaps when we found her, we could put aside our differences and come to an understanding. She could be my advisor, like McKenna was to Elizabeth. I'd own the manor, but she'd be the heart of it.

McKenna hugged her arms tightly. "Don't blame yourself, little mouse. Let's just hope she turns up soon."

The front door creaked open slowly, and a little face with mismatched eyes peered out. Hensley. He caught sight of Elizabeth and slipped his hand in hers. A white rat perched on his shoulder, nose sniffing the cold air. I exchanged a glance with Elizabeth.

"Can't you sleep, darling?" Elizabeth asked.

"I want Lily to read me a story."

"Lily's busy right now, my dear. All the girls are. Someone's gone missing and everyone's out searching. You'll have to wait for a story, I'm afraid."

He looked up at her with that one white eye, then out to the moors. "Who went missing, Mother?"

"Valentina."

He knit his face together in confusion. "She isn't missing."

Elizabeth frowned. "What do you mean?"

He huffed, petting the rat extra hard. "I don't want to talk about her. I want a story!"

Elizabeth and McKenna exchanged a worried look, and I knelt down to face him. "Hensley, I shall read you a story if you like, but first tell us what happened to Valentina."

"She went away. I saw her packing."

"But her room is locked. How did you see?"

He gave an exasperated sigh. "I saw it from the narrow rooms."

Elizabeth let out a small sound of surprise, then turned to me. "That's what he calls the passageways. But there aren't any passageways in the servants' wing, are there, McKenna?"

The old housekeeper ran a wrinkled hand through her hair, trying to think. "I can't rightly say, mistress. The passages were mapped in 1772, but the papers are so old and damaged they're practically useless. If there are any passages there, they can't be but a few feet high, with that sloping attic. I daresay Hensley or one of the little girls are the only ones who could fit through them."

"And you, Juliet," Elizabeth said, seizing me on the arm. "You can bend like a reed. You take the passageways and see if you can unlock the door from within. We'll wait outside her bedroom in the hallway. Hensley, can you show Miss Juliet where you saw Valentina go? And then she'll read you a story, my darling."

His little hand, stronger than I expected, grabbed my wrist. "Come, Miss Juliet. I'll show you the narrow rooms."

"Be careful!" McKenna called. "Remember the passages are dangerous!"

I could scarcely catch my breath before he tugged me back into the manor and through the hallways to the kitchen pantry. He twisted a hidden latch beneath the pickled beets and swung open the door, taking out a candle and match from his pocket. He crawled on hands and knees, with the rat settled on his shoulder. He stroked it with one finger and then looked at me very solemnly.

"Stay close, Miss Juliet, and you won't die."

THE LORD WHO HAD built Ballentyne Manor might have been mad, but he had been a genius when it came to engineering. As I followed Hensley through the walls, crawling over stone floors and through spiderweb-covered tunnels, I marveled at the clever architecture that made the passageways possible: hidden rooms under staircases, secret doors built into the wood paneling. I quickly learned what McKenna meant about the dangers: twice we passed wooden beams fitted with metal spikes, rusty now with disuse, that I imagined were some sort of trap.

"Do you have all the narrow rooms mapped in your head, Hensley?" I peered down a side hallway. "Where does this way lead?"

He spun on me and grabbed my arm, making me jump. He pointed half a pace in front of me, where I'd very nearly stepped. A chasm gaped. I cried out and scrambled backward. It would have been a three-story fall.

"Yes, miss," he said calmly. "I know everything about the narrow rooms."

My heart was still racing as he led me up a stone staircase as narrow as my shoulders and back down another one I had to stoop to pass through.

"Hensley, slow down!" I clambered over some ancient brick ductwork. He tossed a grin over his shoulder but didn't slow. I caught up to him at last, and he pointed to a metal grate that was dusty with soot except for a single clean patch. It must have been recently used. I fumbled with the grate until I found a small panel that slid open. Flames roared on the other side. I jumped back in shock.

Hensley snickered. "It's the fireplace in the library."

I peered through again, and realized the grate looked out from the rear of the fireplace into the stately library, empty now, with a few open books resting on the green velvet couches. He pointed to the passageway's floor, which I could make out in the firelight. There were footprints slightly larger than mine in the dust.

"Are those Valentina's?" I asked.

He nodded and then tugged on my dress. "This way."

He darted down another turn in the maze of passages, and I gave up on trying to memorize the map. I followed him, letting my fingers trail on the walls, hoping not to get snagged by one of those rusty metal spikes. Even with the traps, I had to marvel at the wonderful strangeness of it all. Lucy and I would have adored playing hide-and-seek in passageways like this, when we were his age.

We ran by another door with a light glowing behind it and I paused. "Which room is this?"

"Your friend in the chains. He used to say your name in his sleep. Now he calls for Miss Lucy. She visits him late at night even though he's sick and never knows she's there. She stole the key from Valentina."

I started. Had Hensley been spying on all of us? But then I disregarded my worry. He was only a child, and surely it was just innocent fun. I followed him down a passageway so narrow I had to twist to pass, then up a set of stairs, and at last he pointed to another metal grate. I slid the viewing panel back, peeking within, and found a plain wooden room with a metal bed and dresser. A servant's room, one of the bigger ones with windows on two sides. Clothing was strewn about haphazardly. One long white glove rested on the floor.

"This is Valentina's room?" I asked.

He nodded.

I pushed on the latch until it opened. The hinges had to be ancient but didn't groan as I opened them—they'd been freshly oiled. Valentina must have been more familiar with the passageways than she let on.

I crawled through the small fireplace and came out into her bedroom. Hensley followed me in, dusting off his little hands. There was a half-open trunk in the corner filled with belongings. I took a step toward it. At the same time, the bedroom doorknob jiggled from the other side, and I jumped.

"Juliet?" Montgomery's voice came from the far side of the door. "Did you make it inside?"

"Yes," I called back, and tried the door. "I'm with Hensley. I can't unlock the door from this side either without a key."

"Carlyle's here. We're going to remove the hinges. Do you see any sign of what happened to her?"

I glanced back at the trunk, taking another step closer. Hensley wandered to the side table and opened a box that let out the rich tobacco smell of her Woodbine cigarettes.

"When did you last see her, Hensley?" I asked as I knelt next to the trunk.

"After dinner night before last. She was angry, and I was worried she'd hurt my rat so I hid from her. She was writing in a book. And crying. And saying words Mother says we mustn't say."

The trunk held all manner of strange belongings a maid shouldn't have, even one with as high a position as Valentina. A holster for a pistol—though the firearm itself was missing. Dozens of leather coin sacks, also now empty of money.

At the door, hinges groaned as Montgomery and Carlyle tried to remove them with a screwdriver.

"There," Hensley said, pointing into the trunk. "That's the book she was always writing in."

I took out a small leather-bound book. A journal, though a handful of pages had been ripped out. The few that remained were dated months ago, and chronicled Valentina's progress at educating the younger girls and some of her plans for improving the efficiency of various projects. And then the rest of the pages were torn out in an abrupt fury. I checked the date of the last entry: the day before I arrived at Ballentyne.

"Hensley," I called, feeling uneasy, "check the fireplace, will you? See if you can tell if any papers have been burned."

He poked his little fingers eagerly through the ash and came back with a few curled edges of charred paper that matched the rest of the journal. "Just a few scraps. All the bits with writing burned."

I ran my lip between the hard edges of my teeth,

thinking. I flipped back to the last page of the journal, and then the fresh one after that part she'd ripped out. In the light from the window, I could make out faint grooves. When I ran my fingers over them, I got an idea.

"Hensley, fetch some charcoal from the fireplace." I hurried to the desk, where I snatched up a thin piece of paper and laid it over the blank journal page. Hensley handed me a piece of broken charcoal, and I started running the flat edge along the paper. "Have you ever taken a rubbing of a grave-stone?" I asked him. "The charcoal will mark the paper but leave a blank where the lettering is. I think we can use the same principle here."

He watched as, like magic, an imprint of her last words appeared on the paper. Valentina had clearly been writing furiously, because the letters had gone through sev-eral pages. This resulted in a jumble of random words that at first made no sense.

4 Whitehall Place . . .

. . . can't run a manor . . .

. . . Juliet Moreau will ruin everything.

Seeing the scribbled imprint of my own name, written even harder than the rest, stilled my heart.

"What's this, miss?"

Hensley had drifted back to the box of cigarettes, bored already with my work, and had unearthed a worn piece of paper that had been hidden there. There was something strangely familiar about the folds, and I pulled it open.

My face drained of color.

It was the special memorandum poster announcing a

reward for my capture. The one Montgomery had carefully hidden. Valentina must have stolen it.

In that instant, the poster, and the address, and the scribbled writing all made sense. Before I could get a word out, the door swung open as Carlyle pushed it free of its hinges. Hensley leaped back, pressing his rat tightly to his chest to protect it.

I looked up and met Montgomery's eyes through the broken door. He darted into the room.

"What is it?"

I held up the poster. "Valentina must have found this last night. I think she's going to the police in London. There's an address written in her journal—she burned the pages, but I made a rubbing. I think it's Scotland Yard. She's going to turn us in."

I held out the poster with my own inky face looking back.

He ripped the memorandum from my hand. "The hell she is. She won't make it as far as Edinburgh before I get my hands on her."

FIFTEEN

"I CAN TRACK HER," Montgomery said. I could barely keep up with him as he stormed down the main staircase. "I tracked every beast on your father's island, and they were far more stealthy than a twenty-year-old maid. Balthazar will come with me. His nose is better than the keenest hunting dog's."

"Wait!" Hensley jogged down the stairs behind us, clutching his rat impossibly tight, with Carlyle following at a distance. "You promised me a story!"

Montgomery paused just long enough to give me a look that said we couldn't be slowed down by such nonsense. I ran back up the stairs to pat Hensley on the head. "I shall tell you one, I promise, but not right now." I spotted Lily and Moira at the bottom of the stairs, come to look for us, and pushed him in their direction. "Lily has a story for you, I'm certain."

He narrowed his eyes, his face turning angry red. He might have the strength of three men, but he was still just a headstrong little boy, and I could hardly be bothered with reading stories now. I caught up with Montgomery in the foyer as he was breaking open the manor's rifle cabinet.

Elizabeth heard the noise and ran in, with Balthazar and Lucy just behind her.

"Balthazar," Montgomery said, "hurry out to the barn. Tell me if any of the carriages are gone."

"Are you mad?" Elizabeth said, watching Balthazar leave. "Don't you think that's the first thing we checked, when she went missing? And what on earth do you need a gun for?"

"We broke into Valentina's room," I explained. "We found evidence that she's planning on turning us in to the police at Scotland Yard."

Elizabeth's face went slack. "Valentina? I'd never have imagined her capable of this."

I held out the notebook. "Her journal. I made a rubbing of some pages she ripped out. From what I can tell, she didn't trust me to run Ballentyne and thought turning me in to Scotland Yard would get me out of the way."

Elizabeth let out a curse as she unfolded the poster I'd tucked into the journal. The front door slammed as Balthazar lumbered back inside.

"The hackney coach is missing," he said. "Someone had covered blocks of hay with a tarpaulin to disguise the theft. The horses are out to pasture, but I didn't see the bay mare anywhere. She's the only one big enough to pull the coach."

Montgomery scoffed. "The hackney coach? She can't go more than a few miles an hour in that thing, especially with just the mare. Why would she risk it?"

"It's the easiest to drive," Elizabeth said. "And Valentina wasn't good with the horses."

"Well, that's fortunate for us," Montgomery said. "We'll take the pony trap. It's twice as fast, especially with the dapple stallion. She has a day on us, but she's going slow."

He started for the coatrack by the door, pulling on his oilskin jacket. I took a rifle out of the cabinet. He gave me a sharp look, and I gave him one right back.

"I'm coming with you. Don't try to talk me out of it. I don't weigh enough to slow down the pony trap and I'm a good shot."

He sighed. "As if there was any use in trying to stop you. Come on, then."

We raced out into the night with the rifles. The others followed. Even Lucy threw on a coat and came out.

"You should stay here, Lucy," Montgomery said. "Someone has to watch over Edward."

Her eyes met mine and I remembered how we had last left things: her storming out of my room, furious that I was going to let Edward suffer. I hadn't dared to tell her about my late-night lessons with Elizabeth and that I was actually considering her plan. I wasn't ready to give her that much hope, not yet.

"Lucy, come here a moment." I signaled for her to follow me into the tack room. I dropped my voice. "I know you're still angry with me."

She wrung her hands. "Yes, I am. But I love you, too, angry or not. I'm afraid of what will happen if you find Valentina."

"She's no match for us," I reassured her. "It's important that you stay here and watch over Edward. Keep him chained tight, and maintain a close eye on him. We'll talk more about our previous conversation when I return."

She was so distraught, I wasn't even sure she heard what I said. I squeezed her arm. "I'll be back soon, I promise."

Her eyes were watery, but she nodded. When we returned to the barn, Balthazar was already hitching the dapple stallion to the pony trap. Elizabeth threw several thick tartan blankets into the back. "It'll dip below freezing tonight. Stay under those blankets and take sips of this to keep yourselves warm." She pressed a flask into my hand.

McKenna came forward, wringing her hands. "Such a lonely girl, she was. I know it's terrible that she plans on turning you in, but I'd hate to see harm come to her, just the same."

"We won't hurt her," I said. "We just have to stop her from going to the police."

"It's time, Juliet." Montgomery reached down a hand to pull me into the back of the pony trap. It was a tight fit between the three of us. Balthazar wrapped an arm around my back to hold me close.

"Lean toward me, miss. I'll keep you warm."

Montgomery snapped the reins, and the stallion took off. Lucy ran out of the barn, her fair skin flashing in the moonlight.

"Be careful!" she called.

"You, too!" I called back. For a second, I wondered if I was making a terrible mistake by leaving. Lucy had had such a wild look in her eye when she'd devised that plan to murder Edward and reanimate him. Which was the greater danger, I wondered—Valentina going to the police, or leaving Lucy alone with Edward?

Montgomery cracked the reins again, and the pony trap leaped into the night. In the lighter carriage, with only three of us, we tore down the path to Quick at twice the speed as our ride in.

"We'll have to ride all day to catch up to her," Montgomery said, "but with the hackney coach, she'll be forced to stay on the main roads. Try to rest while you still can."

WE RODE INTO THE dawn and out of it again. The morning and early afternoon passed amid endless roads that all looked identical, with the frost-coated heather reaching out of the land like crystal skeletons. McKenna had packed us a small bag of scones and apples, which we ate on the way so we wouldn't have to stop more than necessary. Montgomery had immediately identified the hackney coach's tracks in the muddy roads.

"Her horse is getting tired," he said, examining the tracks. "Another hour or two and we might catch sight of her. If anyone's going to prison, it's her, for stealing Elizabeth's property. Not you."

My stomach tightened. Prison. I thought again of those socks my mother had knit for the prisoners in winter so they wouldn't get frostbitten. Would Mother have chased down a girl who just wanted the best for the manor? Balthazar's head turned, blinking in the cold. Frost had formed on his long eyelashes.

"What's that, miss?" he asked.

"Nothing," I said, not realizing I had spoken aloud. "I was just thinking of my mother. I wish you'd had a chance to know her, Balthazar. She was a kind woman."

Montgomery nodded beneath the wide brim of his hat. "When my own mother died, she took me aside after the funeral and said I would always have a place with the Moreau family. Beautiful and thoughtful. Just like you, Juliet." Something caught his attention on the road ahead, and he frowned. "That's odd. The main road to London continues to the left, but Valentina's tracks go to the right." He stopped the pony trap at the fork in the road. "It leads through Kielder Forest toward Brampton. Nowhere of significance."

"Are you certain you're following the right tracks?" I asked.

"As certain as I can be." He cracked the reins, steering the horse in the direction of Kielder Forest.

Trees started to rise on either side, a dense forest filled with shadows. The ground was frozen solid, and we couldn't make out her wheel tracks. I bit my lip, hoping that Montgomery's skill as a tracker wouldn't lead us astray.

After ten minutes of riding through the forest Balthazar sat up, on alert. "Ahead. I can smell the horse."

Soon Montgomery and I made out the black dot on the horizon that Balthazar had sensed with his keen nose. Montgomery whipped the stallion faster.

"That's Ballentyne's hackney coach, all right," Montgomery said. "She's driving it like a madwoman. If she hasn't yet spotted us, she will soon, but it doesn't matter. There's nowhere for her to go with the trees on either side. I'll try to ride alongside her and knock her off the road. Juliet, keep that rifle ready, just in case."

"I promised not to hurt her."

"*I* didn't," he said.

He cracked the whip again and we gained more ground. Her coach bumped and jerked over holes in the road, moving so fast I expected it to tip at any moment.

"Get ready," Montgomery said.

The road turned sharply ahead, hiding her from view for a few seconds. When we rounded the bend, suddenly she wasn't there.

"Blast and damn!" Montgomery cursed.

I sat up, heart pounding. "There! She turned and drove deeper into the forest. There are pathways just wide enough for her to pass."

"She's mad," Montgomery said. "The coach will never make it through those woods."

He tugged on the reins as hard as he could to direct the stallion in between the trees. The pony trap bumped over roots and dips so hard, I had to hold on to the sides of the trap to keep from getting thrown out.

"Ride alongside her, if you can!" I yelled.

"The path isn't wide enough," Montgomery answered. Soon we were close enough that I could see her dark hair whipping in the wind.

"Valentina, stop the coach!" I yelled. She tossed me a look of pure hatred before we were separated by a stand of trees. Balthazar had to duck to narrowly avoid a low branch.

We passed the trees and I could see her again. "Valentina, stop and we can talk about this."

"*I* wanted Ballentyne!" she yelled. "I planned for years to get into Elizabeth's good graces. I was fifteen years old, an orphan, when I first overheard actors talking about her at a fair. A woman who lived as free as a man, and could perform miracles without witchcraft, and who would teach girls anything they wanted to know—but only girls with deformities. I knew that was the life I wanted. I did *whatever* I had to." She held up one of her hands, gloveless despite the cold, so porcelain white against the dark skin of her wrist. Bile rose up my throat as I started to comprehend what she was saying.

"Don't you understand, you spoiled girl? I cut off *my own hands* to gain admittance to Ballentyne. I did the left one myself, paid a man to do the other." She whipped the horse harder. "I sacrificed everything; then you came along and ruined it!"

"It wasn't my fault!" I yelled back.

"Yes it is, and I'll see you in jail for it!"

I shrieked as another tree blocked our path, and Montgomery narrowly steered us out of the way. Valentina wasn't as lucky, nor was she as good a driver. She saw the tree too late. Her horse leaped out of the way, but the back of the lumbering coach clipped it, and a wheel spun off. The entire hackney coach went smashing to the ground, freeing the horse, which took off wildly into the trees with half the harness still around its neck. The rest of the carriage went hurtling at incredible speed. Screams filled the air—Valentina's and my own, as I watched in horror.

Her coach slammed into another tree. The rear end tipped over, flipping once, then twice. The sound of splintering wood ricocheted through the forest. I gasped. Time seemed to move too fast. There was nothing any of us could do to stop it. I caught a glimpse of her dark hair as she was thrown from the coach, her porcelain white hands desperately reaching for something to stop her but finding nothing.

The coach shattered against a tree.

I knew I'd hear the echo of that crash for years to come.

SIXTEEN

MONTGOMERY DREW THE CARRIAGE up sharply and the three of us jumped out. We tore over twisting roots to reach Valentina's coach. It was on its side, nearly unrecognizable in its destruction. I was the first to hear Valentina moan.

"She's here!"

I raced around the wreckage, tripping on a shattered strut, and stopped short at the sight. I cupped my hand over my mouth to stifle a gasp. The driver's portion of the coach had been torn completely off and now lay across Valentina's middle.

"Balthazar," I called. "I need you!"

I knelt in the wreckage, tossing off the scraps of wood that were light enough for me to lift. Her hair streaked her face, and when I brushed it back, it caught on a line of blood seeping from her mouth. She coughed, and more blood came. I glanced at the beam pinning her down—right across her essential organs. Balthazar and Montgomery came stomping through the wreckage behind me.

"Hold on," I said. "We're going to try to get you free."

"Juliet Moreau," Valentina whispered angrily, voice barely a sound. "Just a spoiled girl with her pretty toys, who cares nothing for anything or anyone else."

"Shh," I said, and signaled to Balthazar. "Over here. Can you lift this beam?"

"Aye, miss." He wrapped his big hands around the end, then strained with all his strength to lift it off Valentina. She moaned painfully as more blood poured from her mouth. Balthazar tossed the beam to the side.

"Montgomery," I said, kneeling next to her again, "is there anything you can do?"

He bent next to her but didn't bother to inspect her wounds. He grabbed her shoulder instead. "Where were you going?" he demanded. "You veered off the road to London. If not to Scotland Yard, where?"

"Montgomery, she's dying!"

He ignored me and fixated on Valentina instead, but she just coughed more blood, and then let out a joyless laugh. "You might have stopped me, but I'm not alone. Someone is very desperate to find you, Miss Moreau. All of you."

"Who were you going to meet with?" Montgomery demanded.

She convulsed once, twice, her lips stained with blood, and then she sagged against the wreckage.

I put a hand over my mouth. "She's dead."

Balthazar removed his cap out of respect. Montgomery leaned over, letting his loose hair hide his face, and then he took a deep breath and tossed his hair back. He started going through her dress pockets.

"Montgomery, must you do that?"

"She was planning on meeting with someone. We need to know who. She was going to have you arrested, Juliet, so don't spare her any sympathy."

He dug through her coat pockets and came up with nothing, then picked up a leather satchel strapped across her chest. He freed the strap with his knife and pulled out a handful of telegrams.

"Let me see those," I said.

There was a blank where a telegraph operator would normally type the address of the sender; Valentina must have sent it from Quick but specified that she wanted her location kept confidential.

Her first telegram read:

> *RESPONDING TO SPECIAL MEMORANDUM*
> *KNOW WHEREABOUTS OF JULIET MOREAU*
> *INQUIRING ABOUT REWARD*

I felt a burst of panic. She'd already contacted Scotland Yard? I hurried to read the next few telegrams.

> *REWARD £10,000*
> *PRIVATE INVESTIGATION DO NOT GO TO THE POLICE*
> *WHERE IS YOUR LOCATION*

I paused. A private investigation led by someone who didn't want the police involved? That was even more frightening. Who would want to find us without the police's knowledge?

Valentina's response read:

YOUR IDENTITY IS ANONYMOUS
SO IS MINE
WANT TO MEET TO DISCUSS TRADE

The final telegram read:

MEET AT STONEWALL INN NEAR INVERNESS
ON THE EVE OF SAINT TIMOTHY'S DAY

"What do they say?" Montgomery asked.

"It isn't the police looking for us, at least not in any official capacity," I said in confusion. "But that doesn't make sense—the police were looking for us at the inn."

Montgomery studied the telegrams. "Perhaps someone is paying off a few officers. Running their own investigation outside of official police business. But who? We killed all the King's Club members who would have attempted any kind of retribution."

"We must have overlooked someone," I said. "Or perhaps a member of Dr. Hastings's family."

A crow cawed overhead and I jumped.

"We have to go to that inn near Inverness," Montgomery said. "We have to know who she was meeting. It's never going to end, not unless we know who's behind this search." He looked up at the sky, where the sun was getting low. "It will be another few hours to Inverness. If we don't leave now, her contact might leave."

"What about her body?" Balthazar asked. "It isn't right to leave it here."

"I know, my friend," Montgomery said. "The Christian thing to do would be to bury it, but I'm not feeling very Christian at the moment, and time is running out. We can say a prayer for her on the road."

Balthazar whined low in his throat, unhappy to leave her body amid the crows, but he followed Montgomery obediently back to our pony trap.

I rested a hand on Balthazar's shoulder. "Someone will find her horse," I said softly. "They'll follow its tracks back here and give her a proper burial."

Montgomery cracked the reins. I looked overhead, where the sun was murky behind a film of thin winter clouds. A gust of cold wind chilled me and I took a swig of the brandy Elizabeth had given me. It sat in my belly, stickily warm, like a sense of foreboding.

Who were we going to encounter at that inn, I wondered, and why were they so desperate to find me?

INVERNESS WAS A MODERN industrial city, dirtier than London and substantially colder. The pony trap must have made for an odd sight, but no one spared us a glance as they huddled in their coats, hurrying home to supper. We stopped to ask directions and learned the Stonewall Inn was the city's grandest hotel. As we pulled up and saw the palatial inn's lights, my sense of foreboding grew.

"Whoever her contact is, he must have plenty of money to stay here," I said.

"I should imagine so," Montgomery said. "If they are paying off Scotland Yard, that doesn't come cheap."

We climbed out of the pony trap in an alleyway between two millinery shops. "We'll have to be cautious," Montgomery said. "They're sure to recognize you if they see you, Juliet, and chances are our mysterious pursuer knows my identity as well. Perhaps even Balthazar's."

I peeked around the edge of the shop at the gentlemen and ladies climbing out of their carriages in front of the inn. All of them were dressed in finery, a stark contrast to our drab northern clothes. "I have an idea," I said. "There's more than one way to blend in. Balthazar, you stay here with the horse and be ready to make our escape. Montgomery, come with me."

We silently climbed the inn's garden gate and slipped into the hotel's rear entrance, where grocers were unloading boxes of cabbages. I signaled for Montgomery to pick up a box so it looked like we belonged there. We entered the kitchen, which was in the midst of hectic preparations for the feast of St. Timothy. That was fortunate for us—no one gave us a second glance.

I tugged my hair lose from its chignon and pulled it back into a loose braid, then tapped the shoulder of the youngest-looking kitchen girl. "I'm supposed to start today, but they haven't given me my uniform yet."

The girl barely glanced at me as she strained under a heavy dish. "Second door there," she said, jerking her chin toward a hallway. "And hurry, we need all the help we can get."

I grabbed Montgomery and pulled him down the hallway into the linen room. He already wore dark pants, so all he needed was a crisp white serving shirt and an apron. I changed into a kitchen maid's dress.

"Trust me, this will work," I said, fumbling with the apron ties. "I spent years as a maid. No one makes eye contact with you. You might as well not even exist."

"You don't have to tell me," Montgomery said, turning me around to finish doing up the buttons of my dress. "I recall quite well what it felt like to be a servant." He spun me back around, and in the cramped room we were only inches apart. His hands lingered on my waist. "I remember wishing desperately that you would look at me. Speak to me."

I swallowed, suddenly very aware of his proximity. There had been a distance between us ever since the King's Club massacre, a tension that ate away at my insides like hunger. But beneath it all, I still loved him fiercely. "I did speak to you."

"Only because you were lonely for a playmate. Or to ask me to make a fire in your bedroom hearth."

I slid my arms around his neck, looking him fully in the eye. "Well, I see you now," I said softly. "I'd like to spend the rest of my life looking at you. And from now on, I'll make the fires."

He kissed me. It was quick, before anyone might walk in, and it made me believe that somehow we'd work out all our differences. He tucked a strand of hair behind my ear. "Be careful tonight, Juliet."

"You too."

I opened the closet door and we snuck back into the kitchen. Maids were carrying rows of identical serving trays, and I picked one up. Montgomery joined a group of male attendants preparing to serve the wine. We gave each other one last look before the doors opened and we filed into the dining hall.

After the blazing lights of the kitchen, I wasn't prepared for the abrupt shift to dim candle lighting, quiet music from a string quartet, and the soft chatter of the upper classes. For a moment I felt torn between the various stations in life I had held—I'd been born into this world of wealth only to have it torn away and been left as a maid.

To be honest, I wasn't certain which I preferred.

I glanced at the line of male attendants across the room. Montgomery was taller than the others by a few inches, and his long hair stood out even swept back, but I doubted any of the diners noticed since they were so caught up in their own trivialities.

The girl at my rear jostled me, and I realized I was staring. I followed behind the two girls ladling soup into china bowls and set down a dinner roll with silver tongs. I kept my head down so the strands of hair that had slipped out of my braid would partially hide my face, but tried my hardest to search the room for familiar faces. The man or men searching for me had to be in this room somewhere.

My group of serving girls moved to the next table,

where Montgomery was serving wine counterclockwise to us. I caught his eye as we passed.

"See anything?" I whispered.

"Not yet. Check the empty seats—they'll have saved a seat for Valentina."

I nodded and we continued serving in opposite directions. I had no idea who I was looking for. What if it was a family member of Dr. Hastings, furious at me for killing the man? Or someone who knew I was related to the Wolf of Whitechapel's killing spree across London?

I was so lost in my thoughts that I bumped into the maid in front of me and accidentally dropped my roll. I gasped as it landed in the lap of a black-haired young gentleman. The other maids froze.

"Terribly sorry, sir," I stammered, and reached down with my tongs to pick up the roll.

He gave me a disgusted look, shaking out his napkin angrily. "I thought the Stonewall had a higher standard for quality," he said, and the rest of his dinner party laughed.

It was then that I noticed the empty seat at his table. I went stiff.

Across the table, a man was staring directly at me. An older man with white hair and pale blue eyes. A man I'd thought about only in passing ever since leaving London.

Mr. John Radcliffe, financial backer for the King's Club, and my father's former colleague.

Lucy's father.

SEVENTEEN

I DROPPED THE BASKET of rolls. The other girls shrieked as I pushed past them, running for the door back into the kitchen. I looked frantically for Montgomery. In the commotion, he was heading back to the kitchen, too.

I burst through the door, found Montgomery, and pulled him into the closet.

"The man pursuing us," I gasped. "It's Radcliffe. I thought he was just a banker, easily swayed by the others. That article he wrote for the newspaper claimed he'd repented of his connections with the King's Club."

"He must have written that article hoping that we'd see it," Montgomery said, "and that it would throw us off his track. It worked, didn't it? Whatever he's planning, we've underestimated him. We've got to get out of here."

I peeked into the kitchen, which was especially hectic after the incident.

"There's no sign of Radcliffe yet," I whispered. "We don't know if he's alone or has a team of men with him. He could have men already stationed at each of the doors."

Montgomery studied the chaos in the kitchen. "He hasn't sounded any kind of alarm, or announced that there are fugitives loose in the building, so he must want to keep it quiet."

"Why is he after us? Is this is all about Lucy? He said in the article how sick with worry he and her mother are."

Montgomery raised an eyebrow. "How many times did your own father manipulate your love for him to get what he wanted? I'd wager whatever he wants, he's only using Lucy to get it. Look—the back door!" It was wide open for more vegetable vendors to carry their wares in. "I say we make a run for it. Get back to Balthazar in the carriage and try to lose Radcliffe that way."

"God, I hope this works," I said, and took a deep breath.

"Now!" he whispered.

We shoved open the closet door, running as fast as we could through the kitchen, trying not to knock over the cooks at the oven or the men carrying crates of vegetables. There were yells of surprise—if Radcliffe didn't know where we'd hidden before, he certainly would now.

Montgomery and I burst through the back door into the frigid night air, away from the commotion in the kitchen. "This way!" Montgomery called, and I ran after him. I tore off my apron, letting it fly behind me.

At the same time, a police alarm cranked to life down the street.

"So much for not sounding the alarm," I muttered.

The sound of footsteps came behind us but I didn't

dare look back, not once, as we ran through the inn's gardens and the maze of alleyways behind the fine shops. My eyes watered in the freezing air. At last we rounded a corner, where Balthazar waited with the carriage ahead.

"Ready the horse," Montgomery called. "We're leaving!"

A shot rang toward us, and Montgomery cried out.

I skidded to a stop. The sound tore into me as though *I'd* been the one hit. I whirled around. Blood poured out of Montgomery's shoulder. A startled-looking officer with a shaking pistol stood a block away, no doubt summoned by the alarm.

"Balthazar, Montgomery's been shot!" I yelled.

Balthazar steadied his rifle toward the officer, who leaped back to take cover behind a shop. It gave me just enough time to help Montgomery stumble to the pony trap. Balthazar tossed me the rifle while he took up the reins.

"Go!" I cried. Balthazar whipped the horse, which tore into the narrow streets while Montgomery winced with pain. I remembered our quick, stolen kiss in the closet. I wasn't ready for that to be the last.

The trap jostled as we rode onto uneven pavement, and I clutched the rifle harder. The world rushed by, flashes of store awnings and church doors and holiday wreaths. The fog was so thick I could barely make out anything but the buildings on either side of us.

"Are they following us?" I called.

"No, miss," Balthazar said. "I would smell their horses."

It was a small relief, with Montgomery bleeding.

"It's only my shoulder," he mumbled, eyes shut in pain. "I'll be fine."

"You've been shot!"

"It's hardly the first time."

Balthazar jerked the trap down a side road, then another. We left the city with no sign of Radcliffe in pursuit, but Balthazar wove in and out of small hamlets to throw them off, just in case. As night grew I was vaguely aware of the view changing from city to villages to endless moors, though my attention was far more on Montgomery. Under Balthazar's lead the horse calmed to a quick but steady speed, and I did what I could to tend to the wound, then stroked Montgomery's head.

"Another few hours," I said. "We'll be there by morning. Just hold on. I think we got away."

"We have to get back to Ballentyne." Montgomery coughed. "He won't find us there."

"Are you sure? The Radcliffe family has lots of connections and resources."

"So does the von Stein family. He didn't find us before and he won't now. Ballentyne Manor isn't even in Elizabeth's name. Valentina was the only way he might have discovered our whereabouts, but she certainly isn't going to tell him now." He placed a hand over mine, too weak to squeeze it for reassurance. "The rest of Elizabeth's servants are loyal. As long as we remain at Ballentyne, we'll be safe."

I bit my lip, watching the moors pass. "I don't understand what he wants from us. He doesn't care about the science; he was only after the profitability. Now that the science is gone, there's no money to be made from it."

Montgomery clutched his shoulder. "You did murder three of his colleagues."

I stared at him. "You think this is about revenge?" It hadn't ever occurred to me that Radcliffe had considered Dr. Hastings, Isambard Lessing, and Inspector Newcastle anything other than business associates. But there had been that photograph of them as young men in the hallway of King's College. They had known each other for decades. Had they been close associates? Even confidants? *Friends?*

"It's the only thing I can fathom," Montgomery said. "We could discuss it with Lucy. She knows him better than anyone."

"She's been so distraught over Edward that any more bad news will crush her." I let out a frustrated sigh. "I suppose it doesn't matter what he wants, does it? As long as we stay at Ballentyne, he won't find us. Maybe Lucy doesn't even need to know he's the one after us."

As the sun rose, Quick appeared on the horizon, and I knew we were getting close. I'd never been so relieved to see the familiar shape of Ballentyne. Elizabeth would tend to Montgomery. We'd be safe, once more, within those walls. In a way, it felt like coming home.

Balthazar pulled the pony trap as close to the front as he could and leaped out to help me carry Montgomery to the front door. It was strange that Lucy and Elizabeth weren't already rushing out the front door to help us. Surely they'd been keeping a lookout. But the house was eerily quiet as I pounded on the door.

"Elizabeth!" I yelled. "It's me. Montgomery's wounded!"

Montgomery winced in pain. Still, no one came to the door.

"They must be awake by now," I said. "Where would they have gone?"

I pounded on the door harder, and to my surprise it gave an inch. Unlocked. Fear crept up my back as I pushed the groaning hinges open another inch, just wide enough to peer within.

"Juliet, wait," Montgomery said. "Something's wrong. Let Balthazar go first."

Balthazar pushed open the door, taking a few steps inside. "Hello?" he called.

The only response was silence. He poked his head out again.

"Stay here, miss. I'm going to check the kitchen and upstairs bedrooms."

I nodded, pacing slightly, not sure if I should worry more about Montgomery's labored breathing or the fact that the entire household seemed to have vanished. We waited twenty minutes, then thirty, and still there was no sign of Balthazar.

"I can't stand this," I said. "Something must have happened to him. I'm going in."

Montgomery shot me a look. "Like hell you are."

"You aren't exactly in a position to stop me. Stay here and try not to freeze."

I went to the pony trap and took out a blanket and

two rifles. I pushed one into Montgomery's hand and then cracked the other one to make certain it was loaded. I took a deep breath and stepped into the foyer.

My boots echoed on the stone floors. The electric lights weren't working, and the grand fire looked as though it had been out for hours. When I pressed my hand against it, the ashes were cold. I dusted off my hand, heart pounding in my ears, as I headed for the stairs to the second floor with only the mottled light of day through the windows to light my way.

I was halfway up the stairs when a pot dropped in the kitchen, and I whirled around.

"Balthazar?" I called. "Is that you?"

I slowly descended the stairs, crossing the foyer to the rear hallway that led to the kitchen. I kept the rifle cocked and aimed in front of me, though without the electric lights, it was black as night. I could make out only the shadows of doorways off the hall until I entered the kitchen, where a few small windows let in shadowy light.

A small pot rested on the floor.

"Balthazar?" I called again, trying to keep my voice from shaking.

I felt a presence behind me. Heard the scuff of a boot. Startled, I tried to turn, but strong hands were on me too fast, tearing the rifle out of my arms. The smell of woodsmoke and meat clogged my throat.

"Hello, my love."

The hands turned me around, and I was looking at

Edward, but it wasn't Edward at all. The features were the same, his body hadn't swelled in size, and yet every part of me knew it was the Beast.

"Did you miss me?" he said with a sly smile.

EIGHTEEN

"Don't look quite the same, do I?" he added at my shocked silence. "We've finally melded, Edward and I. He won physically, but I won mentally. My mind in his body—a bit of a sacrifice, but nothing I can't work with."

A thousand fears flowed into my chest. Somehow, the Beast had defeated Edward. He'd won possession of Edward's body and broken free of his chains and, for all I knew, had slaughtered Lucy and the rest of the household. Sweat broke out on my forehead. I knew I should fear him, and I did—but I also felt a terrible kinship.

You and I, the Beast had once said, *are more alike than you want to believe.*

"How did you break the chains?" I whispered, taking a step back, but the kitchen table prevented me from going any farther.

His yellow eyes reflected in the low light—the only part of him that hadn't belonged to Edward. "I didn't have to. Lucy unlocked them. She was convinced Edward was still in here, but I had long ago won the battle. It was easy to pose as him, delirious and weak. She planned to slit his throat, reassuring him the entire time it would be only temporary and the mistress of this house would bring him back to life. A neat trick, I must say. But she couldn't bring herself to kill him. Such a naive soul." He took a step closer. "That's when I dropped the pretense and made myself known."

Fury flooded my veins. "What did you do with her?"

He clutched the rifle so casually. "It's sweet how much you care about your friend."

He was taunting me now, and it made my blood boil. "Where is she, and Elizabeth, and Balthazar?"

"That lumbering puppy should have smelled me a mile away. I suppose he was too distracted by his master bleeding out on the front porch." He leaned toward me, bracing either arm on the table at my side. "Oh yes, I've a keen nose, too."

"Where are they?" I demanded.

He was only inches away now, close enough for me to feel the heat coming from his skin. I had always expected the Beast to be cold, but he was burning up with fury, just like I was.

"Don't worry about them, my love."

"Stop calling me that! You aren't even a true person. Edward told us that you're a manifestation of a disease, a strain of rabies and malaria and damaged animal organs. You're a virus attacking a host. You can't live on your own because you were never real!"

His yellow eyes flashed like I'd slapped him.

"Disease?" he whispered. "Yes, it's true. Perhaps I am

born of disease, but what are you born of, Juliet? My perverse nature may be physical, whereas yours is psychological—but no less potent. At least my identity is based in the flesh. Yours is nothing more than ideas your father put in your mind." He cocked his head. "Has Montgomery told you the secret he's been keeping from you all these years?"

I clenched my jaw, trying to withhold my fury.

"Ah, he hasn't. I didn't think you'd be standing here if he had."

"If you know it, just tell me," I snapped. "Stop toying with me."

"But that's what I do, my love. Cat and mouse. Predator and prey." He straightened, the rifle still in one hand. "Unfortunately, I'm growing tired of games. They are childish things, and we are both adults, are we not?" He leaned in, his lips only a breath away from my jaw, and fear knifed in my stomach.

"I saw Montgomery in your father's laboratory," he whispered in my ear. "He didn't know I was watching. He burned an entire file along with a letter. I only saw the first line. *To my daughter*, it said. *It's time for you to know the truth.*"

I drew in a sharp breath. Montgomery had burned a letter that my father had written to me? What had it said, and what was in those files? I'd never felt so confused.

"You're lying," I said. "Just like you always are. Tell me where Lucy and Elizabeth are."

"I could take you to them, but I'm not sure you would like it. Did you know there's a cellar here filled with corpses? Makes me wonder what exactly the mistress has been getting up to—she might be a woman after my own heart. In any case, there was plenty of room for more bodies."

For a moment, the world seemed to stop. I blinked, replaying his words back through my head, refusing to believe them. Had he *killed* them?

"No!" I hurled myself at him, clawing his face, but he caught my wrists and laughed low in his throat.

"Don't act so surprised." He fought me off easily, then took my hands in his, pulling me into a waltz around the room. "Remember when we kissed beneath the mistletoe at the ball in London? How badly I wanted to dance with you then. Now we can forever. This house can be ours, our private escape from the world."

"You're mad!" I yelled. "I'll kill you if you've hurt them!"

"You can certainly try."

My heart was pounding, telling me to get away from him, but he was too strong. I balled my fists, ready to tear him apart with whatever I could get my hands on in McKenna's kitchen. The iron skillet. A rolling pin. I just had to get close enough to the cabinets.

A gunshot blasted through the kitchen.

The Beast went stiff. I screamed in shock and pushed away from him as his dark blood splattered onto my dress. The floor was already slick with drops of blood. He lunged for me, but I ducked his hand.

"Juliet!" Montgomery slumped in the doorway, holding a rifle. "This way—run!"

I shoved at the Beast, who clawed at me with his

fingernails. With a growl, I dug my fingers into the mess of his shoulder where the rifle blast had hit. He roared, and I was able to shove him to the ground, tripping over him in my heavy skirts, and race toward the door.

"Outside," I said. "We can lose him in the gardens."

"The wind is too strong. It will carry our scent."

Angry cries came from the kitchen, amid the clashing of pots and pans. I cringed; all I wanted to do was pull myself into a ball and hide from the world.

"Over here," a small voice said.

I whipped my head around the vast foyer but saw no one. Had someone survived the Beast's wrath? Montgomery pointed to the dusty tapestries flanking the grand fireplace. One of the tapestries ruffled, and a little face stared out at us. One milky white eye, the other dark brown.

"Hensley!" I helped Montgomery hobble to the tapestry. It hid a wooden panel that slid open to admit us to the secret passageways. I lifted my skirts to climb in and tried to help Montgomery, but he was too heavy. To my surprise, Hensley—though he barely came up to Montgomery's ribs—easily lifted him over the panel and into the tunnel. I slid the panel closed, and we were bathed in darkness.

"This way" came Hensley's disembodied voice.

"Hensley, are you alone? Is anyone else alive?"

"Shh," he said. "That creature will hear us. He doesn't know about the narrow rooms."

He moved almost too fast for us to follow. My thoughts were in a daze as I stumbled over loose bricks. How could I kill the Beast with Montgomery wounded and only a little boy to help? If I offered to stay with the Beast, waltz with him like a madwoman around the kitchen, would he let Montgomery go?

Hensley hurried down a flight of narrow stairs that Montgomery struggled with.

"Hensley?" I called, loud as I dared. "Hensley, wait for us!"

At the bottom of the stairs, I stumbled into a sudden brick wall that marked the end of the passageway. No call answered mine.

"Blast, we've lost him," I said.

A squeak came from the darkness, though whether it was a child or rat or rusty hinge, I wasn't sure. My heart leaped at the sound. I felt the wall until my fingers grazed a narrow opening, too low and narrow for Montgomery's wide shoulders.

"You can make it if you lie on your stomach," Montgomery said. "Leave me here. I have the rifle. You heard Hensley—the Beast doesn't know about the passages."

I shook my head fiercely. "I don't want to leave you."

"You must."

I kissed him, trying to convey my love, ignoring what the Beast had said about the secret he was keeping. Then I crawled through the passageway on hands and knees. More sounds came from someplace ahead of me, a sort of scratching that stilled my breath. Was this one of mad Lord Ballentyne's traps? I couldn't turn around now, even if I wanted to. I crawled faster, desperate to fill my lungs with air. At last I reached a small door at the end. My hand searched for a handle, a knob, but there was nothing but the smooth end to the tunnel. I pounded on it. Shoved it with my shoulder. Called for someone to help me get out.

Suddenly the door was flung open. Light stung my eyes. Strong hands pulled me from the damp tunnel. I coughed for air, blinked furiously as a frigid cold bit into my skin.

I recoiled, fearing the Beast, but no yellow eyes met mine. Beneath me was a familiar stone floor, bodies wrapped in white sheets stretched out on benches, a cross in the wall: I was in the cellar chapel. Holding on to me was a girl with dark hair and eyes as blue as my own.

"Lucy!" Relief flooded me. Behind her stood Elizabeth and McKenna and all the servant girls huddled together for warmth, and Balthazar pacing near the door.

"Juliet!" Lucy said. "Balthazar told us what happened. We feared the Beast had gotten you."

"I thought he'd gotten you! He practically told me he slaughtered you all!" I hugged her close.

"He was toying with you," Lucy said, holding me tight. "He locked us down here this morning after he'd frightened us all he could and grew bored. Where's Montgomery?"

"Safe, for now. He's in the passageways, but he was shot. He'll need medical attention soon." I looked around the room, frowning. "Where's Hensley?"

A deep wrinkle creased Elizabeth's forehead. "You saw him? He's been missing this entire time. Just before the Beast awoke, I'd denied him a second helping of pudding and he flew into a rage and vanished." She tugged on her sleeves, and I saw angry blue welts there. My heart leaped to my throat—suffocating rats was bad enough, but he even hurt Elizabeth?

"He helped Montgomery and me escape the Beast, but then he vanished."

Elizabeth nodded. "Good. He'll be safer than any of us. You should go back into the walls as well, Juliet. The Beast will no doubt come down to check on us soon, and he can't find you here."

"If I may, miss," Balthazar said to me, knitting his hands together, "I believe I know how you might throw him off. If you can convince him you've left the manor for the moors, he'll leave the house and you can pass safely through the passageways and perhaps help these ladies and girls get out as well."

Elizabeth considered this. "That's not a bad idea. If we could get outside, there's a hidden cellar in the barn where Lord Ballentyne stored his winter ale. We'd be safe there, with the animals to mask our scent."

I hugged my arms for warmth, thinking through their words. We didn't have much to work with. Montgomery was wounded. Hensley was missing again, and judging by the bruises on Elizabeth's wrist, he was growing more unpredictable.

As I wracked my brain, footsteps sounded on the stairs outside the door.

Lucy whirled on me. "The Beast. Hurry, Juliet, into the walls!"

"There isn't time," Elizabeth said. Her eyes fell on

one of the white funeral sheets and she picked it up. "Under here. Lie next to the body. The smell of decay will hide your scent."

I sank to the floor, crawling under the sheet, trying to ignore the rigidly cold body at my side. There was a distinct odor, but it wasn't the sweet headiness of decaying flesh, more like ice and blood. Elizabeth smoothed the sheet over me just as I heard the chapel's heavy door swing open.

Footsteps approached slowly.

NINETEEN

I CLAMPED A HAND over my mouth. I could hear people breathing, a few of the younger girls crying, and heavy, deliberate footsteps. I kept waiting for the telltale *tap-tap-tap* of the Beast's claws on the stone floor, but none came. Were his claws gone completely? I wondered what exactly had happened within that body. The Beast had won, but not without a cost.

"Well, well," his voice came as his footsteps wove in and out among his captives. "How are we doing down here? Haven't frozen to death yet? Pity."

"You can't keep us down here forever," Elizabeth said. "Not if you like living in this house. You'll need someone to keep the electricity running and to feed the animals."

"The animals?" He laughed, dry and brittle. "You should be far more concerned with your own fate, mistress. Now tell me, have you had any secret visitors?"

From the corner of my eye I could see the person whose funeral shroud I was sharing: a girl a little younger than me with wild red hair and freckles. The cold had frozen her eyelids open and iced over the corneas. There was dried blood on her lips. I squeezed my eyes shut.

"Visitors?" Elizabeth said. "There's just the one door, and you have the only key." She paused for drama's sake. "Why, has someone come? It isn't Juliet and Montgomery, is it?"

"Quiet, woman," the Beast snapped. "Your only concern should be trying not to starve down here."

"That's just it," Elizabeth said boldly. "We might starve, but you might, too. Let a few of my girls free, just to work in the kitchen. They can make enough food to keep us all alive, including you." For a moment there was silence, and I was desperate to know what was happening. "Come now," she entreated. "What was your plan—slaughtering the lambs in the barn and eating them raw? Not much of a proper meal. Wouldn't you rather have roasted chops with a rosemary glaze, and buttered potatoes on the side? McKenna makes the most succulent lamb chops, I can assure you."

I wondered if Elizabeth had noticed the same thing I had—that the Beast was more human than he had been before. Roasted potatoes would never have appealed to him previously. It wasn't just the lack of claws, but the fact that he'd kept Elizabeth and the others imprisoned instead of killing them. Could he have found a bit of humanity? Could he possibly be reasoned with?

"An interesting proposal, mistress." I could practically hear his mouth watering. "But I don't know your servants, and therefore I don't trust them. I shall take someone of my own choosing."

His boots whirled, and then a startled cry came from one of the girls—only this cry I recognized.

"Lucy," he said, low and seductive. "You've always been in love with Edward, haven't you? He's gone, but we do bear a striking resemblance. You can take care of *me* now. Come." She shrieked as he dragged her toward the door. "I hope you know your way around a kitchen."

The door slammed closed, and the massive lock clicked. It was but another moment before Elizabeth threw back the sheet. I jolted upright, away from the redheaded girl's body, gasping for fresh air. I scrambled to the far end of the room, putting as much distance as I could between me and the bodies.

"He took Lucy," Elizabeth said.

"I know." I pressed a hand against my head, trying to think. "She won't be safe for long, not once he realizes she doesn't know the first thing about cooking. He might turn on her—any of us—at any moment. I don't care that he doesn't look like a monster anymore. He is one, at heart." I squeezed my fist hard enough that my nails dug into my palm.

Elizabeth opened the secret door into the passageway and drew a key from a hidden pocket in her petticoats. "I've kept this from the Beast. It's the key to my laboratory. You'll find all manner of instruments there that can be used as weapons. If the passageways lead there, I've never known about it, so you'll have to enter the main part of the house."

She went to McKenna and returned with a small sewing kit that she pressed into my hand as well. "For Montgomery."

"Thank you. I'll be back for you all as soon as I can."

I started to crawl back into the narrow passageway, but Elizabeth touched my back. "Wait, Juliet. If you see Hensley, please tell him to be careful. But also—be careful yourself. The Beast isn't the only unpredictable one." Her hand drifted to her bruised wrist. "Like most children, Hensley is subject to wild changes in moods over nothing. But unlike most children, he has unnatural strength. He doesn't always realize when he hurts those he loves."

I swallowed uneasily. "I understand."

I crawled back through the tunnel until it opened more, and in the light from the wall seams I was able to retrace my own dusty footprints from earlier.

"Montgomery?" I whispered as loud as I dared.

"Here" came a faint call.

I crawled faster until I found him. He'd moved into an alcove protected from view, leaving a trail of small dots of blood. I touched his hair, his face, his arms, to reassure myself he was safe.

"Take this," I said, pressing the sewing kit into his hands. "Elizabeth gave it to me for your shoulder."

"Elizabeth! She's alive?"

"All of them are. The Beast locked them in the cellar." I paused. "He's different, Montgomery. He melded with Edward. He's more human than he was before."

In the shadows, I couldn't make out Montgomery's

face. "Does that change anything?"

I balled my fists. There were times for mercy, but this wasn't one of them. "No. He took Lucy. If I don't stop him, there's no telling what he'll do to her. Besides, it isn't just Lucy I'm worried about. We need to get everyone out of the house, so that you and I can face the Beast on our own. Balthazar came up with an idea. If one of us could lure him out of the house, the other could lead the servant girls to safety using the passageways." I frowned down at his wounds. "I'm afraid you can't do either, though."

"It's my shoulder that was hit, not my legs," he said. "I can walk. I'll stitch the wound myself and then sneak out of the house and set the goats loose. The Beast will smell them and come outside to investigate. That should give you time."

I nodded, thinking. "We'll need a signal for you to know everyone is safe and it's time to lure the Beast back into the house." I tapped my fingers anxiously against the wall. "The windmill. I'll stain the sheets a different color for the signal."

"That will work. Once you've gotten everyone to safety, promise me you'll stay near Balthazar. He'll keep you safe." He took my hand.

I intertwined my fingers with his. Who would keep *him* safe, I wondered?

"Go on," he said softly. "They need you. But Juliet . . ." He pulled me closer. "Be careful." He pressed his lips to mine, and I longed to hold on to him forever. Neither of us was blameless. We both had sins to atone for. And yet my love for him didn't diminish.

He broke the kiss. "Go."

I crawled between the walls, up ancient stone foundations, past another alcove where I found a narrow ladder. It led to a trapdoor that opened into a dark room smelling of animals: fur and feces and straw. It was the secret room where Elizabeth kept the rats. I dusted off my hands as the rats squeaked softly, most likely thinking I was Elizabeth with their daily meal.

"Shh," I whispered to them. "You'll give me away."

I took a deep breath. I had only to run through Hensley's room and climb the spiral staircase and I'd be in the laboratory. I closed my eyes to listen for footsteps. There was nothing save the usual creaking of the house and my own ragged breathing.

It was now or never.

I darted through his room and up the stairs as quickly as I could, clutching Elizabeth's key, afraid the Beast was right behind me. I threw myself at the laboratory door, unlocking it and then slamming it behind me. My breath came shallow. Had I closed it too loudly? I went to the window. The sun was high now. These winter days were far too short. There was no sign of Montgomery or the Beast, but the goats were loose in the front yard. Montgomery must have succeeded in his half of the plan.

I turned to the laboratory cabinets. Bone saws, surgical knives, scalpels. I snatched up a wicker basket and filled it with anything sharp. My hands wrapped around the instruments like old friends. Any of them, used properly, could yield a deadly blow. In a drawer, I even found a small silver pistol. That went into the basket as well.

I felt far more confident as I left the laboratory. I retraced my footsteps through the passageways, avoiding Lord Ballentyne's ancient traps, and peeked through the spy holes until I found the kitchen. There was Lucy, standing alone by the oven with one of McKenna's recipe books, looking completely lost.

"Lucy," I whispered through the spy hole. "Over here."

The panel opened wide enough for me to reach my hand out. She shrieked at the sight of a disembodied hand reaching through the wall, but then raced over.

"Juliet," she whispered. "You gave me a fright!"

"The Beast hasn't come back, has he?"

"I heard the front door slam about twenty minutes ago—I think he went outside. He left me here to make a feast but took away all the knives and anything sharp. How am I to peel the potatoes? I barely know what a raw potato looks like!"

"I have a plan. I found weapons in the laboratory, so I'll arm everyone in the cellar for their safety, and then set them free while the Beast is distracted. Once I give the signal, Montgomery will lure him back to the house. Balthazar and I will be waiting for him. As soon as you hear any commotion, you must hide. There's a trapdoor to the passageways in the pickling room. Hide just behind the trapdoor and wait for me to come get you—don't venture deeper into the passageways unless you want to stumble down one of mad Lord Ballentyne's traps. And take this." I passed her one of the surgical knives through the spy hole.

She took the blade with as much dread as if she were handling one of Hensley's pet rats. Her face twisted in anguish.

"It's all my fault, isn't it? I was a fool to unchain him, but he was so convincing, and he looked just like Edward. I realized too late that he'd tricked me. I had a knife—not so different from this one. I was going to slice Edward's throat so that Elizabeth would bring him back cured, but I couldn't do it."

I squeezed her hand through the wall. "Be thankful, Lucy. Killing easily is not a trait one should ever desire. Besides, he would have gotten free one way or another. This confrontation was inevitable."

She studied her reflection in the gleaming knife blade. "If I get another chance, I won't make the same mistake again."

Dread filled me. I didn't want to leave her in that big empty kitchen, when the Beast might return at any moment. And yet Montgomery couldn't hold him back forever.

"Just remember, no matter what he looks like, it isn't Edward anymore." I gave her hand one more squeeze, then closed the panel, plunging my world back into darkness.

TWENTY

MOVING THROUGH THE PASSAGEWAYS was starting to feel like second nature. I could see why Hensley liked them. Once I learned to navigate the jagged nails and the uneven stairs, they felt so removed from the rest of the world that anything seemed possible.

I reached the trapdoor to the chapel and knocked out a quick melody I knew Balthazar would recognize: "Winter's Tale," the song my mother used to sing. Sure enough, the door swung open and his wonderfully ugly face looked back at me.

"We have to move fast." I pulled out the basket of weapons and handed them out to the staff. For the littlest girls, scalpels—the small blades would make them feel safe, but they wouldn't hurt themselves accidentally. For McKenna and Elizabeth, the largest of the surgical knives. Elizabeth took one look at hers and shook her head, reaching in the basket instead for a heavy metal clamp.

"I prefer my weapons blunt and powerful," she said.

"Did you find Miss Lucy?" Balthazar asked, folding his lips in concern.

"She's in the kitchen. I've instructed her where to hide once things get dangerous. Now, I'm going to lead you all to an outside door, where you can make it to the barn. Balthazar, I want you to take the rear, just in case . . ." I paused, looking at the impossibly narrow opening of the passageway. He'd never fit. "Well, dash it all. You'll have to stay here. Montgomery or I will come to unlock the cellar door as soon as we can."

He scratched the back of his head. "I don't like it, miss. You and Montgomery up there on your own against that creature."

I gave him a smile, trying to look brave, but something about Balthazar always crumbled the walls around my heart. I leaned over and gave him a kiss on the cheek. "I learned a thing or two on the island. I can sneak around this manor without the Beast hearing a single peep. We'll see you soon."

I crawled through first, with Moira behind me, and the younger girls behind her, and Elizabeth and McKenna at the end.

"Follow my path exactly," I said to the girls. "Don't touch the walls, if you can avoid them—there are loose nails. And don't veer off to the sides—there are some tunnels that plunge down into nothing." In the near darkness, I could make out their eyes, wide and frightened. "Let's go," I said.

We crawled as quickly as the younger girls could. My heart pounded in fear over what might be happening outside: if the Beast had discovered Montgomery, or worse, had already come back inside. What would he do if he discovered the chapel empty save Balthazar? Could Balthazar defeat him alone?

I touched my dress pocket, where the silver pistol dragged against the ground. If I got the chance to take a shot, I couldn't afford to miss.

The line of women continued through the walls, down a precarious ladder, and into the sewer system, where we were finally able to stand. Light winked around the corners of a square grate that I kicked open with Elizabeth's help. Fresh air poured in. It was freezing outside, but after being trapped in the frigid cellar, the touch of sunlight was heavenly.

I climbed through the grate, jumping down on the other side. I scanned the southern gardens and moors beyond but saw no movement. Wherever Montgomery had led the Beast, it seemed to have worked.

"All right," I said. "Pass the girls to me, Elizabeth."

They crawled through, one at a time, dusting off their clothes.

"We can take it from here," Elizabeth said. "Do what you must, but be careful."

"I will."

She and McKenna led the girls to the barn, where they disappeared one by one inside. Now that they were safe, I hurried to the windmill, which was spinning briskly in the midday breeze, and climbed the ladder attached to the side of the building. Reaching into my basket, I took out four vials of Elizabeth's beetroot iodine solution and, as each white sheet passed, splashed it with the dark red liquid. When I gazed up at them, the white sails looked streaked with blood. An unsettling signal, but an effective one.

I left the basket, taking only the knife tucked in my boot and the silver pistol, and went to the front door, pacing, shading my eyes to search the moors for any sign of Montgomery. There were few hours of daylight left. We had to confront the Beast before night fell; with the electricity cut off in the manor, only the Beast, with his superior animal vision, would be able to see.

In another second, my signal worked. Montgomery appeared around the side of the house, running as fast as he could without jarring his wounded shoulder. "Get inside. He's right behind me!"

I threw open the main door. The Beast rounded the corner behind him, twenty feet away, lumbering as if he wasn't used to his restrictive human body. Fury gleamed in his eyes.

"Hurry!" I called to Montgomery.

He took the steps two at a time, wincing at the pain in his shoulder. I squeezed the doorknob harder, urging him on. At last he reached the doorway and I slammed the door and locked it. Half a breath later, the Beast collided into the other side of the door, growling with frustration.

"There's more than one way inside!" he bellowed through the thick wood.

I ran to Montgomery, touching his shoulder. "Are you hurt?"

"He caught me once, but without the claws he wasn't as powerful."

"It won't take him long to break through a window," I said. "Everyone's safe in the barn, except for Balthazar. He's still in the cellar. Go fetch him, and I'll check on Lucy. We'll meet back here."

As he stumbled off toward the cellar, I paused long enough to take the pistol out of my pocket and make sure it was loaded, then headed for the kitchen. It was empty save the vat of untouched potatoes and a dozen overturned pots and pans on the floor—Lucy must have set them out as a trap to announce if someone was coming.

"Lucy?" I called, but heard nothing in return. I threw open the door to the pickling closet. "Lucy, are you there?"

The sound of shattering glass came from some unseen room, and I jerked upright. It had to be the Beast breaking into the house, which meant I didn't have much time. I crawled on one hand and my knees to the trapdoor, knocking on it frantically.

"Lucy, answer me!"

There was still no response, and I felt paralyzed. Where would she have gone?

Two hands suddenly grabbed my ankles, dragging me out of the closet with terrifying strength. I screamed, clawing at the floor for grip, but my fingernails tore uselessly on the tile. As soon as we were back in the kitchen, I was released abruptly.

I scrambled onto my back.

The Beast stared at me.

His face was just as mercurial and mysterious as ever. He was made with Montgomery's blood, though I had never seen any similarities in their features. Now, however, there *was* an echo. It wasn't the shape of his nose or the spacing of his ears, but a depth to his eyes that looked so much like Montgomery's, just for a flash, that I nearly forgot who I was looking at.

I fumbled for the pistol and aimed it at him. "Don't come any closer."

He cocked his head, unconcerned. A strange voice whispered in the back of my head that he'd never looked more human before.

"Why aren't you attacking?" I demanded.

"Why aren't you?" he countered.

I aimed the gun at him again. This was just another game to him—show a well-calculated flash of humanity, confuse me, then once I started questioning myself he'd tear me to pieces. I clenched my jaw. I aimed the pistol between his eyes, at the diseased brain that was his origin. At only ten feet, I couldn't miss. And yet my finger wouldn't pull that trigger.

"Well?" He even moved a step closer to make my aim better. "Now that you're faced with killing me, it isn't so appealing, is it? Because without me, there's nothing darker than your own heart. I've always been more ruthless than you. Without me, you'll be left to stare at your own capacity for evil."

"Stop talking," I hissed, cocking the pistol. I urged my finger to shoot. *He's toying with you. He'd say anything to make you spare his life.*

And yet try as I might, I couldn't pull that trigger. In

some terrible way, I agreed with part of what he said. Having the Beast meant I wasn't the most violent person in the room, nor the darkest. Besides, it was Edward's face looking at me, and a little bit of Montgomery's as well, and even a bit of my own.

"You can't do it, can you?" There was a ring of sympathy to his voice that had never been there before.

Suddenly, one of the cabinets flew open, and Lucy sprang down, the surgical knife gripped tightly in her hand. At last I understood why the pots and pans were on the floor—she'd emptied the cabinet as a place to hide.

She hurled herself at the Beast. "Maybe she can't, but I can."

TWENTY-ONE

LUCY DUG THE BLADE into the side of the Beast's neck before he could react. I froze. This was Lucy, who was afraid of practically everything, who had never so much as smashed a spider under her shoe.

"I should have done that the first time!" she yelled.

She drove the blade deeper into his neck, letting his blood spill out onto the floor, but he overpowered her. I screamed as he pulled away, wrenching the knife from her, letting it clatter to the floor.

At the same time, Montgomery and Balthazar appeared in the kitchen doorway with rifles. Shock flickered over Montgomery's face but died quickly: he was a trained hunter, and it didn't take him but a second to raise the rifle.

The Beast clamped a hand over the bleeding wound on his neck, stumbling out of the kitchen's rear exit toward the winter garden. Balthazar lumbered after him, while Montgomery knelt by my side.

"Are you hurt?" he asked.

I shook my head. "Hurry. If he goes back outside, he might find the girls."

A bellow sounded from the direction of the winter garden, interrupting me, and we all jerked our heads around.

"That was Balthazar!" Lucy gasped.

The three of us raced toward the winter garden. Visions flashed in my head of terrible things: the Beast with a knife through Balthazar's gut, carving him up like his victims in London.

Montgomery made it to the winter garden first and stopped short. I caught up to him and my hand shot to my mouth.

"Dear God."

Balthazar stood by the side of the glass-enclosed garden between the white statuary of a deer and a fox. He was perfectly unharmed, though I'd never seen such a look of shock on his face. He let out another bellow—not one of pain, but of fear.

In the center of the room, within a growing pool of blood, lay the Beast. I didn't need to see his face to know he was dead. I'd seen enough dead bodies in my day to recognize a chest that didn't rise for breath, limbs that sagged lifelessly.

Behind him, standing perfectly still, was Hensley. His hands were covered in blood up to the elbow, bits of blood and flesh splattered across his face and high-collared shirt. In his hands he clutched the Beast's heart, red and dripping.

He looked at us calmly, then wiped the back of one hand over his blood-splattered cheek. "I was tired of him,"

Hensley said. "He wasn't much fun."

He dropped the heart to the floor, where it splashed in the puddle of blood.

A shiver of terror ran up my spine, vertebra by vertebra. I had thought there couldn't be a creature more dangerous than the Beast, and yet now he lay dead at my feet, defeated so easily by a little boy who had died three times over. When I glanced at Montgomery and Lucy, they were both as white faced as I was.

Hensley turned to me.

"*Now* can I have a story?"

I watched the sun fall on Ballentyne from the windows of the library, where I sat on the green velvet couch, still dressed in my bloodstained clothes, reading to Hensley from a book of Scottish folktales. My hands were unsteady as I turned the pages, and my voice shook. Montgomery sat across from me with the silver pistol hidden under his coat, aimed at Hensley should his mood suddenly shift.

I finished the story, and Hensley burrowed closer to me with sleepy eyes. "Another one, please."

I glanced at Montgomery, who nodded solemnly. I kept reading. After his startling display of violence, we had decided to do whatever Hensley asked while the others ran outside to fetch Elizabeth. I wasn't quite sure what to make of the little boy nestled at my side. It was hard to imagine him capable of such violence while he was listening to bed-time stories.

Footsteps sounded at the door and Elizabeth rushed

in, panic on her face—Lucy must have told her what happened. Moira was right behind her. Elizabeth swept into the room and pulled Hensley into her arms.

"Enough stories, darling," she said, trying to keep her voice light. "Look at you—dirty through and through. Moira will give you a bath and then read all the stories you like."

She passed the sleepy boy, even now nodding off and rubbing his eyes with little fists, into Moira's arms. Only once they were gone, and the library door was closed and locked, did I let out a ragged breath.

"Blast it all, Elizabeth, you didn't tell us he was *that* dangerous."

She gave me a hard stare. "He saved your lives, didn't he?"

"You didn't see the look on his face! He killed the Beast on a lark because he was bored with him. He ripped his heart out of his chest like he was pulling weeds."

Elizabeth pulled at her collar, pacing. "He doesn't ever do it from malice. He'd never hurt any of us intentionally."

"As long as we do what he wants," I said. "What if we refuse to play games and read him stories?" My gaze dropped to the ring of bruises around her wrist, and she tugged on her sleeve anxiously.

"I've managed him for fifteen years," she said. "I can keep him under control now. I'll have two girls watch him at all times. In the meantime, I sent Lily to clean up the kitchen and winter garden and to attend to the Beast's body. You should all change clothes. You're covered in blood."

Lucy looked down at her dress as if only just realizing

this. "I want to help," she said in a shaky voice. "With the body. That was Edward once, and the least I can do for him is take care of him now."

She started for the door.

"Wait," Elizabeth said, and Lucy paused. "There's something else we need to discuss, and you're an important part of it, Lucy." She turned to Montgomery and me. "When the Beast locked us in the cellar, Balthazar told me what happened when you pursued Valentina."

I exchanged a glance with Montgomery. "Her death was an accident. We didn't kill her."

"I believe you," Elizabeth said. "Her death is unfortunate—she was an essential part of this place. We shall notify the younger girls in due time, but at the moment I'm more concerned with Mr. Radcliffe. Balthazar told me he's the one who's been looking for you. Are you positive he didn't follow you back here?"

"Beyond a doubt," Montgomery said. "Balthazar would have smelled horses following us. We'll have to avoid any cities for a few months, maybe even a year or two, but that's a small price to pay for our safety."

Lucy had flinched at the sound of her father's name. "*Papa* is the one after us?"

I cast her a worried look. "Oh, Lucy, I'm sorry. I hadn't wanted you to find out. Don't worry, we were able to lose him in Inverness. The manor's location is still secret."

"B . . . but the article Papa wrote in the newspaper," Lucy stammered. "He said he repented his association with the King's Club. He said it was all a mistake on his part."

"We think he was just trying to clear his name and cast off any suspicion about his true intentions," Montgomery said.

"His true intentions?" Her face had gone quite white.

"Retaliation, we think. For killing his colleagues."

"But what about the part where he said he and Mother were worried about me? Couldn't that be why he's after us, to find me?"

"I don't think so," I said softly. "I can't imagine it was anything other than a ruse to draw you out and lead him to us. I'm sorry. I know what it feels like. My father used my affections for him as well."

Lucy hugged her arms over her bloody dress as though she refused to believe it. "So they don't care about me at all?" She dragged a hand through her wild hair and started for the hall in a daze, choking out a sob. I went after her, but Montgomery shook his head.

"Give her some time. It's a lot to take in."

Elizabeth reached for the bottle of gin, hands shaking slightly, pouring herself a glass. "The poor girl." She took a sip, closing her eyes, leaning one hand against the wooden bookshelves. "And I still can't believe Valentina would turn on you like that. I thought I knew her better. We shall have to hold a funeral for her, regardless. For the Beast as well, I suppose, even if he was a monster."

"No," I said. "We'll mourn Edward's passing, not the Beast's. It was Edward we all cared about, particularly Lucy. You saw how distraught she was just now. . . ." I paused, head cocked toward the door where Lucy had disappeared. She had been upset over the news of her father's pursuit, yes, but she hadn't actually said a word about Edward. It felt strange, given how in love with Edward she had been, that she wasn't mourning his death more.

An itch tickled behind my left ear, the start of an idea. Or rather, a suspicion.

Lucy had wanted Edward dead all along so we could cure him through reanimation. She'd admitted to unfastening the chains and planning to slit his throat while he was sleeping. That was all before the Beast's wild rampage, of course, but the fact was, she had achieved what she'd set out to do.

Edward was dead—just as she'd wanted.

Was it possible that she still held on to some desire to bring him back?

I shook myself out of such dark thoughts. No, of course Lucy wouldn't be thinking of such extreme possibilities. Why was *I* even thinking of them?

"As far as Radcliffe goes," Elizabeth said, "I know a bit about him, and he isn't a man who gives up easily. My guess is that he'll only expand his search now with renewed vigor. We should send someone to look into what he's planning and make sure he doesn't discover our location." She glanced out the window, toward the south fields where we'd held the Twelfth Night bonfire. "I suggest we send Jack Serra. He has a talent for slipping in and out of the shadows. His troupe left a few days ago, but they can't be further than Galspie. Carlyle can send him a message."

Montgomery frowned. "Jack Serra?"

"He's one of the carnival performers," Elizabeth explained. "You must not have met him at the bonfire. Troupes like his are always on the move this time of year. He'll be able to enter London unnoticed to spy on Radcliffe."

Montgomery and I exchanged a glance, and he nodded. "Then send him, with our thanks."

Elizabeth stood. "I should check on Hensley. For the love of God, take a bath, both of you. Get a meal, and then a good night's sleep." She opened the door, then paused. "I am sorry about Edward." She cleared her throat. "And I know this sounds a bit petty right now, but the dressmaker in Quick sent several pairs of shoes for you to try on, Juliet, to go with the dress she's making. I'll have them brought to you tomorrow."

She left, and I squeezed my eyes shut.

A wedding, and a funeral, and my best friend's father scouring the country to hunt us down for vengeance.

"I thought life at Ballentyne would be simple," I said.

Montgomery came over and pressed a kiss against my temple. "It will be. But not yet."

TWENTY-TWO

OVER THE NEXT FEW days, a despondency fell over the house. The servants were used to strange experimentations—they bore the scars of Elizabeth's surgery themselves—but nothing could have prepared them for the Beast. I tried to explain that two souls had shared his body, one evil and one kind, but they hadn't known Edward like I had.

Montgomery avoided dealing with Edward's death by throwing himself into work: the pony trap strut had broken on our ride back from Inverness, and he pounded away at it with hammers and nails until his hands bled. Lucy also went about her work as though his death hadn't affected her, nannying the younger girls and helping Balthazar with his reading. I watched her closely for signs of mourning but saw none, and it only made me more uneasy.

We held a small funeral service in the cellar chapel. McKenna came out of kindness, wearing her thick rubber boots, hovering in the doorway as if she was afraid her presence might disturb us. We formed a loose circle around the shrouded body. Elizabeth had performed small repairs on the cadaver to make it presentable: stitched up wounds, replaced the heart in his chest cavity. Lucy picked at her fingernails. I would have expected her to be hysterical, but her eyes weren't even red.

Balthazar drew something from his vest pocket and set it on Edward's shrouded chest. A paper flower, clumsily made, but sweet and childlike.

"That's lovely," I said.

"The carnival folk taught me how to make it."

I looked back at the paper flower in surprise. Leave it to Balthazar to make friends with drunken transients and shysters. McKenna produced a Bible and Balthazar offered to recite some passages, thumbing through the delicate pages with big graceless fingers but reading with a steady voice.

"'Help us find peace in the knowledge of your loving mercy,'" he read, finger tracing the words. "'Give us light to guide us out of our darkness.'"

What's wrong with the darkness? the Beast's voice echoed in my head. *Without darkness, there is no light. Without me, there's no Edward. Without your father, there's no you.*

A shiver ran through me.

After the funeral, I paced the house restlessly until everyone had gone to bed, and then knocked on Montgomery's door. He was in bed, reading by the light of a candle, but one look at my face and he closed the book.

"Juliet. What's wrong?"

I pinched the bridge of my nose as I sat on the edge of his bed. "Listening to Balthazar read at the funeral today got me thinking. Father could have saved Edward, I know it. I didn't tell you this, but I had my fortune read by the fortune-teller, Jack Serra. He said I was destined to follow Father's footsteps. I think . . . maybe he was right. If I had, I could have saved Edward, too."

I turned, afraid my confession would only drive Montgomery further away. But instead he smoothed my hair back gently. "Just a fortune, that's all. You know how those carnival types work. Say something vague and let you impose your own meaning on it."

"Yes, I know, but that's just it. Magic fortune or not, Father *means* something to me. I can't deny it. It wasn't until the end that he went mad. Before that he was rather brilliant."

Montgomery's strong hands tucked back a loose strand of my hair. "I remember. I loved him too, you know. But he was also a monster."

"Do you think . . ." My voice caught. "Do you think I'm a monster, too?"

"Of course not," he whispered. "I haven't agreed with all your decisions, but I wouldn't be engaged to you if I thought that."

"Bringing the creatures to life, letting them slaughter those men . . ." My voice dropped even lower. "I *enjoyed* it, Montgomery. The justice of it. The power of it."

His hands paused. Though my father had raised him to be his successor, Montgomery had managed to resist the temptation to follow in my father's footsteps.

I hadn't been that strong.

"I suspected you did," he said quietly. "That's what scared me most." His hand absently rubbed against the scar on his fingertip. It was where my father had taken the blood to make Edward.

"I'm sorry," I whispered. "I'm sorry for what I did at King's College, and I'm sorry for what happened to Edward. I know you're grieving, too. You and Edward never had a chance to be brothers."

He looked at me in surprise. I'm not certain he had ever really let himself feel sorrow. When his friend Alice had been murdered on Father's island, he'd been furious. Now he was trying to take care of me, but I wasn't the only one hurting.

He glanced down at his fingertip.

His hair looked nearly gold in the candlelight. I couldn't help but touch it. What were a few secrets, when death was always just one step away?

"I love you," I whispered. "I'm sorry for what I've done. I'm sorry for all the fighting and arguments."

I touched Montgomery's cheek, feeling the hard ridge of bone there. Hard to believe the boy I loved was, at the core of it, nothing more than skin and blood and a beating heart. The sounds of the house around us were as loud as my own beating heart: rain on the windows, joints settling. His eyes sank closed. "I love you, too."

I leaned in to kiss him. His hand, big and heavy, found the smooth silk shift around my waist. Each time we kissed felt different. New. We still had so much to learn about each other, for better or worse, and I wanted to spend a lifetime finding out.

"I was so afraid the Beast would kill you," Montgomery whispered against my cheek. "I never should have let you out of my sight."

My fingers smoothed over his bare chest. His tan had faded over the past weeks, but the story of the island was written in each scar and scratch on his skin. One day, after all this was over, the scars would be nothing but memories we could chose to forget.

He pulled my hair lose from its braid and ran his fingers through it.

"I can take care of myself," I said. "I know how to use a knife and a pistol. You won't lose me."

He paused, meeting my eyes. "There is more than one way to lose you."

Voices whispered to me of the King's Club's laboratory in London: how I'd brought the water-tank creatures back to life with a determination bordering on madness, and how I'd felt that same thrill in Elizabeth's operating room with the reanimated rat. Had Montgomery known about the bond I'd felt with the Beast? Did he know that at the last moment I hadn't been able to pull the trigger?

I kissed him again. Not slowly this time. His hand found the curve of my waist, bunching the fabric. His other hand pushed the hem up to graze my knee. Ripples of electricity ran through me. My mind turned to things I'd only dared dream about late at night.

"So much death," he said. "All I could think about during the funeral was that any of us could be next." He swallowed hard, and when he spoke next, his words were in a rush. "Let's not wait until the spring, Juliet. I've wanted to marry you since I first saw you in London, standing in my room at the Blue Boar Inn, pummeling Balthazar with biscuits. Marry me sooner. Next week. It can be a small ceremony. Whatever you want."

My hand went slack against his chest. "Next week?"

"With lives like ours, who knows what tomorrow will bring. We have to take happiness when we can." He paused. "That is, unless you've changed your mind."

My heart softened. "I haven't."

I looked down at the silver ring around my fourth finger. There was still so much Montgomery and I needed to work out before our relationship would be sound. The secrets that both of us kept, the madness that overtook me at the King's Club massacre . . . and yet what was more important, our love for each other or our secrets?

I twisted the ring. "Next week, then."

He kissed the ring on my finger. A grin cracked his face. "Then in a few short days, you shall be Mrs. Montgomery James."

His eyes scoured my body, lingering on my bare shoulder. Tomorrow we would announce the wedding and shed some happiness on the gloomy household. Beyond that the future was far too uncertain, but at least Montgomery and I would face it together.

TWENTY-THREE

Elizabeth's attention was consumed over the next day with watching Hensley for signs that he was growing more violent. His body didn't age, but it did deteriorate. Elizabeth admitted she had already replaced his failing liver twice and his heart once. Now it was his brain that concerned us—the flesh might be breaking down and making him act irrationally. After the Beast, the last thing we needed was another madman.

The only piece of brightness in our lives was the impending wedding. No one was more excited than McKenna to hear of the change in date, and she flew into a flurry of preparations, telling the girls to search the moors for any pretty greenery, spending the morning baking us sample cakes.

"I took the liberty of picking my three favorite recipes," she said. "Not to mention the three with ingredients we can get this time of year. Go on, now. Tell me which you'd prefer for the big day."

Ever since Edward's funeral my heart had felt as though it was missing a small piece, but for her sake I picked up the fork and tried the chocolate cake. To her credit, it was delicious. I took a bite of the other two as well. When I met Montgomery's eyes over the cakes, I smiled for the first time in days.

"Oh, this shall be such a happy day for the manor, after poor Mr. Prince's death, and Valentina's as well." McKenna chattered on like a mother hen. "No one has been wed on the grounds since Elizabeth's mother some forty years ago. I was just a girl, not much older than Moira is now. A duke from London came to give the bride away. He was a distant uncle. He brought with him the most beautiful horses any of us had ever seen." She rambled to herself, thinking back on fonder days.

An idea seized me as I thought about her words. "If you'll excuse me, I have an errand to run."

Before they could answer, I grabbed another bite of cake and ate it while I ran outside and crossed the courtyard.

"Balthazar?" I stuck my head in the barn. "Are you in here?"

The sound of a mumbled song came from the tack room. "A Winter's Tale," my mother's song. Balthazar came out with a curved shepherd's staff, pausing his tune when he saw me, flushing with guilt.

"Hello, miss. Pardon my singing—I know it's a time of mourning, but the goats so like music." He scratched behind a goat's ear. "It's good to see you out of the house in the fresh air. After the funeral I was afraid you and Miss Lucy would stay hidden away for days."

"I suppose life at the manor must continue, whether Edward is here or not." I watched him scoop some feed for Carlyle's donkey. "It's good of you to help with the animals."

"I don't mind. I like to stay busy. And the little girls don't much like getting their hands dirty, except Moira. She likes the horses. Especially that big bay one." To my surprise, he handed me a bundle of dried-out carrots. "You could help, miss. If life at the manor continues, that means you must as well."

We crossed into the barnyard, where a light rain settled into our clothes. Balthazar smelled musty, like Sharkey after he'd been tromping through the dew-heavy moors. It was a smell I'd come to love.

"That's actually why I'm here. About trying to move on after Edward. Can I ask you a favor, Balthazar?"

"Yes, miss."

"It's Lucy. She puts on a brave face, but I know Edward's death must be destroying her inside. She's so fond of you that I wonder if you might keep an eye out for her. Try to get her outside to breathe some fresh air, maybe help you teach Sharkey some tricks."

He straightened at this, proud. "Of course, miss." We reached the hutches, and I held the first one open as Balthazar set down one of the shriveled carrots, prodding it toward the nervous rabbit. "There now, little fellow. A special treat."

We moved to the next hutch and Balthazar used his same gentle manner. It occurred to me how different he was with animals than Hensley was. Hensley thought he cared for his pet rats, not realizing he was strangling them with his affection. Balthazar, however, knew exactly what great strength he had, and knew how to be gentle.

We finished feeding the rabbits, and Balthazar tipped his hat and started back for the barn.

"Wait, Balthazar! That isn't the main reason I wanted to talk to you." Rain came harder outside, and we took shelter in the barn's eaves. I brushed the moisture from my face. "Montgomery and I have decided not to wait until the spring to marry. We're going to marry next week. A small ceremony. Just the residents of the manor."

His eyes went wide. Before I could react, he pulled me into the warmth of his arms. His comforting musty smell let loose a flood of emotions, and I leaned into him, closing my eyes, wishing this moment could last.

"I'm glad, miss. This is a very good thing."

"I have another favor to ask of you. It's tradition for the bride's father to give her away." I swallowed the rush of emotion in my throat. "I'd like you to do the honors."

His brown eyes went wide. He shuffled a bit, rubbing the back of his neck. "*Me*, miss?"

"My father's gone and I've no family, so I'd like a good friend to give me away."

His face broke in a wide grin. He pulled me into another hug that felt warm against the cold. I wrapped my arms around him. I held goodness in my hands, his thick muscles beneath my fingers, his shaggy-dog smell beneath my face. Not everything created in a laboratory had to be an abomination.

Sometimes, it could be a friend.

I lost track of how much time I stayed with Balthazar in the barn, helping him clean, thinking about the wedding, while Sharkey slept on the wooden steps to the loft. It was a peaceful time—until I saw Balthazar's back go ramrod straight. A low growl came from his throat.

I turned to find Hensley standing perfectly still in the entryway, alone, petting his white rat.

Alarm shot through me. Where was Elizabeth? Where were the girls who were supposed to be watching him? He stared at us blankly with that eerie white eye. I was about to reach for the knife in my boot when Lily rushed up behind him.

"There you are!" She tried to sound playful, but there was fear in her voice. "Remember, Hensley, you aren't to run off by yourself anymore. You frightened Moira—"

"Moira told me I must take a nap. I didn't want to."

"Yes, but you forget how strong you are. You accidentally hurt her."

He shrugged. "Mother will fix her. Mother can fix anything."

I met Lily's eyes over his head and read fear there.

"Balthazar, perhaps you can help Lily take Hensley back to the manor?" I asked. "I'll check on Moira. Is she all right?"

"I think so, miss," Lily said. "The mistress is with her now in the tower."

I spared no time hurrying back to the manor and up the spiral steps.

"Elizabeth?" I knocked at the door to her laboratory.

Low voices came from inside, then the sound of footsteps. The heavy wooden door cracked open. Elizabeth's face relaxed when she saw it was me.

"Juliet. I'm just finishing up with Moira. She and Hensley got into a tiff. Come in."

A tiff?

I stepped inside, closing the door behind me. Moira sat on the operating table with her back to me, hands folded neatly in her lap. My eyes immediately went to the bare skin of her hands, her ears, her bare feet, deeply curious to know what body part Hensley had damaged. A broken finger? A bruised throat? As I came around the table, Moira turned her head to look at me, and I stifled a gasp.

Her right eye, usually a deep green, was gone now. Only a gaping hole looked back at me.

"Boo," she said, lurching toward me.

I jumped back with a shriek, and her face broke into a grin.

"My God," I breathed. "Are you all right?"

She shrugged, unconcerned, though her fingers were clenched tightly. "Will be soon enough," she explained. "Elizabeth gave me medicine for the pain. I was fighting to get Hensley in bed. He lashed out. I stumbled back and hit my face on the edge of the bed."

Elizabeth gave me a knowing look. "Before you say anything, I already know that he's getting more unpredictable. I'm going to speak to Carlyle about fashioning a room with bars in the cellar, something like what you did to cage the Beast. Perhaps after all this wedding madness is over, you and Montgomery can help him draw up the plans." In her right hand, Elizabeth held a round object in a sterile cloth. It was one of the cadaver eyes. I watched in fascination as Elizabeth reattached the ocular vein and gently pressed the eye into the socket.

Moira pressed her hand against her eye, waited a few breaths, and then opened it. Dark green, a nearly perfect match. She blinked a few times and smiled at me. The deformed face from before was once more that of a pretty, freckle-faced girl.

She climbed off the table.

"Thank you, mistress."

Elizabeth scribbled a few notations about the procedure in her medical journal, nodding. "You're quite welcome. Don't worry; it won't happen again. I'll look after him myself from now on and ask McKenna to give you a different task. Just remember to take it easy until the sedation wears off. Don't want you putting your eye out again because you aren't walking straight."

Moira scampered down the tower steps. Elizabeth took a cloth and started cleaning her tools. Her shoulders were tense, no doubt with worry over Hensley's worsening condition. I recognized the clamp she held as the same one she'd chosen on the day the Beast had attacked. Now all those instruments were back on the wall, everything tidied, as though nothing at all had changed. And yet Edward's body was in the cellar, cold and preserved, along with all the others. I shivered.

She followed my line of sight. "A scalpel is still

missing," she observed. "One of the little girls must have gotten careless. We should keep an eye out for it." She finished cleaning the room, wiping down the operating table, disposing of Moira's damaged eye in the same airtight glass container that held Hensley's dead rats. An image flashed in my head of the foxes swallowing the eye whole.

She removed her apron and smoothed her dress. "I'm glad you're getting married sooner. All the festivities will be a pleasant distraction for Hensley, until we can get that cell in the basement built."

I fiddled with the ring on my finger, and she noticed.

"Are you nervous?" When I didn't answer, she added, "It's natural to feel anxious before one's wedding. I attended your parents' wedding, you know. I haven't thought about that day in years." She leaned back on the counter. "Your mother was nervous. She was almost as young as you are now, and I thought her foolish for tying herself to a man at such a young age, even a man as intriguing as your father. He was quite the catch back then. Handsome, clever, wealthy. And your mother was the most beautiful girl of the season." Elizabeth sighed. "She was so caught up in his charm that she hadn't taken the time to get to know him. It's different with you and Montgomery. I can tell it's a deeper love."

I swallowed and looked down at my clasped hands. *Did I truly know Montgomery?*

Elizabeth sensed the sudden change in my mood and rested a hand on my forehead. "You aren't feeling ill, are you? Don't tell me you've started wearing one of those dreadful corsets again."

"It isn't that." Did I dare tell Elizabeth that there were secrets between Montgomery and me? About the mysterious letter he'd burned? About how I'd reanimated a rat and told him nothing?

"I'm worried about Radcliffe," I said, though that wasn't entirely the truth. "I fear he'll have a surprise up his sleeve, something we haven't thought of. It bothers me that we haven't heard from Jack Serra since you sent him to London. It's been over a week." I took a deep breath, toying with a scalpel on the wall. "Perhaps we're foolish to hold a wedding during such a time."

She came around the table. "We would hear from Jack this soon only if it was bad news. I assure you, there's no way Radcliffe can trace this place to us. No one in London knows this manor is in my family. Besides, even if he did discover your whereabouts, this place is a fortress. The original structure was attacked by Vikings in the tenth century, and then by marauders in 1790, and revolutionaries in 1880. It's never been breached." She squeezed my arms. "Or is it something else you're worried about, perhaps the wedding *night*?"

My cheeks burned crimson.

She gave her crooked smile. "I might not be married but I'm no saint when it comes to the bedroom. If you need any advice, I hope you'll come to me."

"I don't," I said quickly. "Need any advice, I mean. I'm more worried because it's been months since life has been normal for any of us. I was starting to think I was cursed, and so was anyone I tied myself to. That this wedding will only end in tragedy." I looked down again, feeling foolish to hear my own fears spoken aloud.

She patted my arm. "Oh, I doubt that. I haven't told you about Victor Frankenstein's wedding night, have I? It was here in this very house. He was to wed his cousin Elizabeth, my namesake, but it never happened. He had promised his creation he would create a female like him—a reanimated bride—but at the last moment changed his mind and destroyed the body. The creature was furious, so he took away Victor's bride in return. He murdered her only moments before the wedding, here in this same room."

My eyes went wide. "How awful!"

She gave me a crooked smile. "Indeed. Whatever happens on Friday, it can't be as bad as that, can it?"

"I suppose not." I toyed with my engagement ring, still uneasy.

"Blast," she said. "I've gone and been too morbid again. I forget not everyone has spent their lives with the ghosts of my ancestors. Don't worry, my dear. Radcliffe can't reach the house. I'll get Hensley under control. No one's going to be murdered on your wedding night." She handed me the jar of dead rats and Moira's unblinking eye. "Now be a dear and throw these out for the foxes before dinner."

TWENTY-FOUR

IT WAS MESSY WORK, disposing of dead animals and leftover body parts. I followed the path behind the manor as it meandered among the sulfurous bogs. Night was falling, and my stomach grumbled with hunger despite the morbid contents of the glass jar.

A flash of orange-red darted between two bushes. I stopped. A fox's keen black eyes watched me through the branches. Deciding I was far enough away from the house, I emptied the jar's contents on the ground, then stepped back to watch the foxes make dinner out of Moira's eye. Something crunched under my boot and I looked down to find a bone, long ago picked clean. It was part of a human hand. The wrist bone had been cut unevenly, as though someone had almost changed their mind halfway through the job.

Was it the bleached bones of Valentina's hands that she had cut off herself and brought with her in a basket? She had wanted ownership of this manor so desperately that she'd crippled herself for a chance at ingratiating herself to Elizabeth. And I had sauntered in and been named heir without even wanting it. Was it right that I got everything so easily while Valentina met such a terrible end?

I looked at my own hands, thinking of my mother. If she were here, she would tell me that this was a sign. I shouldn't just accept being the heir to Ballentyne lightly—I should embrace it and work as hard as Valentina would have, educating the girls and making improvements to the house.

I turned back to the building looming in the twilight. Lights were just coming on as the servants prepared dinner.

Anyone would want to oversee such a place, and yet I felt only hollowness in my chest. I wished Jack Serra were back, with his cryptic predictions.

Was running Ballentyne truly my fate?

A fox yipped behind me, reminding me that I was alone and that night was falling. I wrapped my sweater tightly and jogged back to the manor just in time to change clothes and get ready for dinner with the staff. Elizabeth had decided to forgo tradition and let the servant girls dine with us at the grand table. I loved having them there. They drilled me with questions about the wedding: what type of flowers I liked and what my dress looked like and if they could try it on when it arrived and pretend they were to be brides as well.

Lucy's seat, however, remained empty.

Halfway through dinner, I leaned toward Montgomery. "Do you know where she is?"

"Balthazar said she isn't feeling well and decided to skip dinner."

After the meal, I wrapped some cold chicken in a napkin to take to her room, but when I opened the door, no one was there.

A strange feeling trickled down my back. Lucy had been acting odd since Edward's death, first slaughtering the Beast with that wild look in her eye, now throwing herself so fully into work. Thinking back on it, it didn't make sense. Lucy hated work. And she wasn't the type to fall so deeply in love as she had with Edward, only to watch dry-eyed at his funeral.

Maybe my worries were more than just suspicions.

I hurried down the hall, peeking in keyholes, not finding her anywhere. I went to Elizabeth's laboratory, but it was locked and I knew Lucy didn't have a key. I scoured the observatory and the winter garden, and finally went down to the cellar.

I found her there. She was leaning over Edward's body, head bent in prayer. My heart faltered for a moment. This must be where she was disappearing to when she'd been claiming to work or to be ill. She came here to mourn in private, so she could appear strong in public. My heart ached; I'd do anything to take away her pain.

"Lucy," I whispered.

She jerked upright, breathing hard in the cold air. "Juliet! Are you trying to make me die from shock?"

I took another step closer. A book was open on the floor. I had assumed it was a prayer book, but on closer inspection I saw anatomical drawings. She scrambled to shut the book and pick up various instruments, including the missing scalpel from Elizabeth's laboratory.

"Lucy, what are you doing?" My voice was harder now.

Her face went white. She tried to block Edward's body from my view, and alarm bells went off in my head. I pushed past her and stopped short.

It wasn't Edward.

It was the body of one of the vagrants, a boy about Edward's height and age. The shroud had been drawn back to reveal his bare chest, which was marked in dotted lines following the anatomy book. A line of cut flesh ran down his center. There was little blood—the body was too cold. The cut line was unsteady and imprecise, made with hands that had never done such work before and were hesitant to try.

I lost the feeling in my fingertips. "Lucy, what have you done?"

She jumped up and pressed her hand over my mouth as though she feared I might scream. "Shh, Juliet," she whispered, face even whiter. "I was just . . . I thought I might try . . ."

She was normally so good at lying. I'd seen her lie effortlessly to suitors and to her own parents. But now she stared at me, blood drained from her cheeks, without a single explanation as to why she was cutting open a stranger's body with a stolen scalpel.

"Blast," she cursed, dropping her hand. "Don't tell anyone. Not Montgomery. Certainly not Elizabeth."

I looked around at the other bodies, noticed some of the other sheets disturbed, a few drops of congealed blood on the floor. This clearly wasn't the first time she'd come down here with the scalpel and an anatomy book. And there was only one reason why she'd do something so gruesome: she was trying to teach herself basic surgery by practicing on the vagrants' bodies. All in an effort to bring Edward back.

"Lucy, you can't mutilate strangers, even if they're dead!" I hissed, low and frantic. "Have you gone mad?"

"It's the only way!" she pleaded. "You refused to help me, and Elizabeth has that oath of hers, and I know Montgomery wouldn't do it. I don't understand how you all can just let Edward's body rest down here, knowing there's a cure. He's dead now—there are no more hurdles. No questions of morality. We could bring him back, Juliet."

"No questions of morality?" I pressed my hand to Jack Serra's charm beneath my dress. I had gotten to know my demons and been tempted to bring Edward back, but that was before I'd witnessed Hensley's horrible show of violence. "What about Hensley? You've seen him. He's hardly a normal child. There's no telling if the procedure would even work, but if it did, who's to say Edward wouldn't be like Hensley, his mind as simple as a child's but his body able to kill so easily?"

"It isn't the same thing at all," she argued. "Hensley died and was reanimated as a child, so of course his mind stayed the same. Edward's an adult. And besides, the professor was distraught when he brought Hensley back, so it's only natural that he made mistakes."

"And you think *you* wouldn't make mistakes? Lucy,

you've never done any of this before! This is highly skilled science. Only trained surgeons could perform such a procedure."

"I don't know what else to do!" She collapsed on one of the benches near Edward, burying her head in her hands. "I know I don't have the skill, but I can't sit around giggling about your wedding while the boy *I* wished to marry someday is dead. He could be back with us, Juliet. Cured of the Beast. How can you say you don't want that?"

I stared at her in the flickering electric lights, afraid of the look in her eyes, and even more afraid of how much sense she was making. Had I been heartless not even to consider bringing Edward back? What a fool I'd been, planning my own wedding, acting as though everything was fine and we'd all have a grand future together, when one of us was gone.

I sank onto the bench opposite her. Edward's body lay between us, still shrouded, with Balthazar's paper flower resting on the center of his chest. I dared to let myself peel back the shroud to get one final look at him.

His face was so familiar it made my chest ache. He'd survived days alone at sea. He'd survived the fire in my father's burning island compound. He'd even survived an attempt to poison himself. He'd escaped death so many times that it didn't feel real to see him like this, cold and lifeless.

I studied the lines of his face, trying to read his fortune, just like Jack Serra had read mine. The water charm felt heavy around my neck.

Lucy would never have the skill to bring Edward back, no matter how many bodies she practiced on, but *I* might. I had watched Elizabeth reanimate the rat, and the procedure was well documented in Frankenstein's Origin Journals. I'd have to practice on other creatures first of course—Lucy had been smart on that count. I could start with the dead rats, then move to one of these cadavers. I wouldn't bring it fully back—that would be too dangerous. But I could hook the body up to the machines, test the procedure out, and make certain I understood how the operation worked. As to fixing Edward's broken body—repairing his heart, swapping out the diseased part of his brain, sewing back the incision mark across his throat—I had seen the medical notations Elizabeth made on all of her transplants. I'd watched her transplant Moira's new eye. If I could get those notes, and the Origin Journals, I could study them.

It was possible—quite possible—that I could reanimate Edward.

I stood abruptly, scared even by how far I had let my own fantasies unfurl.

Lucy looked at me with wide eyes. "You're considering it, aren't you?"

I grabbed the anatomy book and the scalpel, wrapped both in a sheet, and hugged the bundle to my chest. I shook my head a little too hard. "No, Lucy. I couldn't go against Elizabeth's wishes. This is her house."

"But you could do it, couldn't you?"

I recognized that feverish look in her eye because it matched my own. Just like my father's voice, urging me to do something remarkable instead of living a quiet life.

This is how you shall be exceptional, my father's voice said. *By defeating death to save a life.*

I hurried from the cellar, afraid to face Lucy any longer. Upstairs I nearly collided with Montgomery in the kitchen. He frowned at the bundle clutched in my arms.

"Is everything all right?" he asked.

I glanced at the table where the samples for our wedding cakes still rested, minus a few bites. They had tasted delicious at the time, but now all that seemed foolish.

"I think I might have caught whatever Lucy's sick with." It wasn't a lie. My stomach threatened to turn at the sugary smell of the cakes. I hurried upstairs to my bedroom, where I twisted the key in the lock and let the bundle fall onto the floor.

The scalpel fell out, still caked with dried blood.

The idea had already taken hold of me, and it wasn't as easy to dig it back out again. It was as addicting as a drug, beautiful and promising and so, so dangerous that I hesitated to even look at it directly. It was an idea that could change everything.

Already my fingers were itching to try. Isn't this what I'd been craving, deep down where I didn't want to admit it? Since I'd first learned about Frankenstein's science, since I'd first seen Hensley brought back to life. My father's spirit was in my veins, urging me to do this. Suddenly the memory of the carnival I'd attended when I was a little girl returned to me: flashes of a man with skin like scales and a little boy with black fur covering his face. I'd gone to the freak show tent with my father. He'd given me a caramel apple and explained the monstrosities' various afflictions.

No matter how much Montgomery pushed me to be like my mother, he was wrong. Only my father's legacy could guide me now. Father had created man out of animal, but he'd never conquered death before. I *could*.

I took out Jack Serra's water charm. Perhaps this was what his cryptic fortune meant: a stream and a river are made of the same substance, and yet the river has the potential to be so much stronger. The river *always* surpassed the stream—just as I would surpass my father. Only I'd use his science for good.

I closed my eyes, squeezing the charm. I felt like it was giving me permission, even pushing me toward fulfilling my fate.

I snuck up to Lucy's room and knocked quietly. In the low light of a few flickering candles, our eyes met.

"I'll do it," I said. "I'll bring him back."

She threw her arms around me so tightly I could hardly breathe. "I knew I could count on you to see reason."

TWENTY-FIVE

THE DAY OF MY wedding approached, and yet I could think of little else but bringing Edward back. All I had needed was permission, and that's what decoding Jack Serra's fortune had given me. I knew what Montgomery would say if I told him—that fortunes were only a way for us to impose our hearts' own desires—but so be it. If this was my heart's true desire, I couldn't deny it any longer.

Lucy conspired to help me sneak away from wedding planning whenever I could, tiptoeing into the hidden alcoves in the walls and reading by candlelight every book I found in the library on anatomy and galvanism, though I already knew most of the information by heart. It was the Origin Journals I needed, the ones Elizabeth kept hidden.

"I know this is probably silly," I told Elizabeth after dinner, dropping my voice conspiratorially. "But Balthazar was telling me about some old journals he'd found while tidying up the manor. Said there was quite a bit of German in them. I know you keep the Origin Journals well hidden, but I thought you might want to make certain he hadn't accidentally found them."

Her eyes went wide for an instant; then she dismissed the notion with a wave. "He must have stumbled upon other old volumes. Lord knows there's no shortage of dusty books around here."

But there was uncertainty in her eyes, just as I knew there would be. That night, after the household went to bed, I crawled into the passages and peeked through all the spy holes until I found her in her bedroom. She climbed silently up the stairs to her observatory. I followed in the walls and watched through a small hole. She went to the globe with the hidden compartment where she kept her *Les Étoiles* gin, knelt down, and opened the bottom half—a second hidden compartment.

She took out three dusty leather-bound books, checked them quickly to make certain no one had touched them, and then stowed them away again. As soon as she left, I crawled through a trapdoor and took them. I stayed awake all night reading over them in fascination and copying important sections, then replaced them in the morning so they wouldn't be missed.

"I've learned all I can from the books," I told Lucy. "Elizabeth's going to Quick tonight to telegraph Jack Serra in London to see if he's discovered anything. Come with me to the laboratory after everyone's gone to bed. It's time for us to practice."

She pressed a hand to her mouth, whether to hold in fear or excitement, I couldn't tell. I imagined that, like me, she felt a combination of the two. All through dinner I could scarcely keep my hands from twitching, thinking about working the controls of the machine in Elizabeth's laboratory. It wasn't storming, so I'd have to reanimate something small, like a bird or a small mammal, that wouldn't require lightning.

Once everyone had gone to bed, I left my room quietly and was accosted by Lucy—she'd been waiting for me on pins and needles. We tiptoed to the south tower and up the winding stairs.

"Don't touch anything," I whispered to her. "We can't give Elizabeth any suspicions that we've been here. Stand next to the table and wait for me to tell you what to do."

She nodded and I unlocked the door. We closed the curtains, using only shaded candles so any girls wandering outside wouldn't see a light on in the tower. The laboratory was just as I'd remembered, tidy and comfortable. Lucy held the candles up to the row of surgical instruments, the flame reflecting both in their metal blades and in her wide eyes.

"I can't believe she's operated on *all* the servants," Lucy said. "They seem so normal."

"They are normal," I answered. "They're just people who needed a little help beyond the realm of conventional medicine. They aren't like father's creations. Besides, you like Balthazar, and he's as abnormal as they come."

She reached out to touch a pair of clamps but paused, remembering my instructions. "Balthazar's different. No one in the world could dislike him, even if they tried."

I went to the glass jar. As I suspected, the latest of

Hensley's victims were there: three rats to chose from. I smelled them to see which was the freshest, and gently probed their bones to determine which had been suffocated, which would be far easier to reanimate. The ones he had crushed to death would require intricate bone setting that would take too long.

I found a good specimen and set it on the table. Lucy made a face.

"You like Edward, too," I reminded her. "He's also one of Father's creations."

She lifted a shoulder in a helpless shrug. "I don't care how he was made, or how I was made, or how the trees outside were made. All that matters is what we are now. In Edward's case, what he'll be once we cure him of the Beast."

I pointed to the lever attached to the windmill controls. "On my mark, give that a solid pull."

I delicately laid the rat on the table and hooked up the various wires. At its slight weight, how easy it would be to smother it all over again. I wondered if such thoughts had ever crossed Father's mind as he worked. Did he smooth his hands over the puma's matted fur before he shaved it off? Had he marveled at a tiny eyelid, a little claw, and felt wonder at the natural world before he tried to bend it to his own will?

"It's your lucky day, little rat," I said softly.

I signaled to Lucy, and she pulled the lever.

THAT NIGHT, LONG AFTER we had carefully cleaned Elizabeth's laboratory of any signs of our presence, Lucy and I huddled in my bed under the blanket with the live rat. It was incredible to see a creature that only hours ago was a lifeless cadaver now sniffing at the corn kernels we left for it. Even Lucy, who hated rats, seemed enchanted.

As I watched Lucy play with it, my thoughts turned to my parents.

Perhaps Father's madness had always been a part of him, but it hadn't fully manifested until he'd left London for the island. I remembered him so clearly back then, at fancy dinners and garden parties and lectures in our salon. He'd been determined, but not mad. There had been one party in particular, summertime in the back garden, when Montgomery and I had played hide-and-seek among the azaleas. We'd heard angry voices and peeked out from the branches to see Father arguing with one of his students. I'd never seen him so cross: red face, eyes glassy, a string of expletives that made Montgomery reach over to cover my ears. Mother had come and whispered soothing words into Father's ear. The anger had melted off his face. Mother had such a calming influence on him, once upon a time. If only she could have maintained that influence on him, maybe everything would have been different.

I sighed, holding out a finger to pet the rat.

"We can't keep it," I told Lucy. "If we let it run wild, Sharkey or one of the barn cats will kill it."

"What do we do, then? Return it to the cage with the others?"

"I suppose. Elizabeth warned me that reanimated

creatures might have unnatural strength like Hensley, but it's just a rat, and it seems perfectly normal."

A knock came at the door and we froze. I threw off the covers to find daylight streaming through the windows. Morning had come sooner than I'd realized.

"Miss Juliet?" Moira's voice came from the other side of the door. "You might want to come downstairs. A package just arrived from Quick."

I sat up. "Just one moment!" I signaled frantically for Lucy to hide the rat. She looked around the room desperately, until she kicked the lid off a hatbox and shoved it inside.

I opened the door. "A package?"

Moira grinned. "It's your wedding dress, miss."

I sucked in a breath. Wedding dress? God, the wedding was tomorrow and I hadn't even bothered to try on those pairs of shoes yet. Guilt washed over me that I'd forgotten about it. Two little girls were with her, smiling widely. She motioned to them apologetically. "They're dying to see it, miss. Haven't ever seen a proper bride's dress before."

The innocent look on their faces made me feel guilty all over again. I forced a smile. "Then let's take a look, shall we?"

I tossed one glance back at Lucy before the girls grabbed my hands and led me to the library, where Elizabeth and McKenna stood around the big mahogany table. A package tied with ribbon sat in the middle.

"The dressmaker just delivered it," McKenna said, "Oh, do open it. We're all dying to see."

It felt surreal to tug on that bow, slide the ribbon off. The little girls crowded around the table, eyes big and wide. I opened the box, fighting through crumpled tissue paper the dressmaker had used to pack the dress. I folded back the paper gently, and the girls gasped.

"Oh, Juliet, it's beautiful," Elizabeth said.

I stared down at the satin dress that Lucy had helped me design. My heart beat a little faster. It wasn't really so bad that I was lying to Montgomery; I did want to marry him, and it would be a grand occasion. We had a lifetime ahead of us to come to terms with any secrets from our past—or our present.

"You will be the most beautiful bride!" the smallest girl said.

I gave her a sincere grin.

"Here, girls," I said, holding up the dress. "Why don't you try it on? Lily, Moira, it won't be but slightly too big on you."

Smiles broke out across all their faces. Lily picked up the dress with the utmost care, and they hurried from the room amid giggles. Tissue paper covered the floor. I shoved it back in the box and sank into a chair.

McKenna went to the window and pulled back the curtain with a frown.

"Looks like another storm is setting in. Let's keep our fingers crossed it comes and goes before tomorrow afternoon. Rain at a wedding—oh, I couldn't bear it."

"I'm sure it will stop," Elizabeth said, giving me a smile. "Anyway, a misty day can be perfectly romantic."

I smiled in return, torn between how kind they were being to me and the fact that I was lying to them all.

TWENTY-SIX

THAT EVENING I OPENED the hatbox and took one last look at the rat.

"Time to take you home, little fellow." I slid open the back panel of the armoire that led into the passageways in the walls. I climbed into the tight space, finding my way by candlelight to the secret storage room next to Hensley's chambers. I let the rat into the cage, observing it carefully for fear it might be stronger and unpredictable as Elizabeth had warned, but it acted just like the others. If it hadn't been for the tiny burn mark on its side where the electricity had singed its fur, it would be totally indistinguishable from the others. I bade it good evening and crawled back inside the walls.

I didn't return to my room straightaway. The manor was different seen through the cracks in the passageways. Timeless. Without the electric lights I could imagine it was a hundred years ago, and Victor Frankenstein was up in that tower with a lightning rod and a bone saw. If I closed my eyes, I could almost hear the sound of scalpel on flesh.

I stopped and leaned against a dusty wall of the passageway to brush away cobwebs on my dress. A thin beam of light shone from a horizontal crack in the wall. I squinted to peer through. It was Balthazar's bedroom. He sat in the rocking chair by the fireplace with Sharkey asleep in his lap and a book in his hands. He traced the lines of text with his thick finger, soundlessly mouthing the words to himself.

I felt bad for spying on him and started to leave, but I tripped on one of Lord Ballentyne's uneven brick traps. I cursed before I could stop myself, and when I looked back through the crack, Balthazar was sniffing the air.

"Miss Juliet," he said calmly. "I can smell you in the wall. Is something wrong?"

"Blast," I muttered to myself, then pressed my mouth to the crack. "No, Balthazar, everything's fine."

"It isn't, miss. If you forgive me, I can smell that you're lying. A body produces different scents when one isn't telling the truth." He was already out of the chair and had swung opened a hinged section of the wall that served as a hidden door into the passageways. He stuck his head in, sniffing again, and sneezed at all the dust. "Come in, miss. You'll scrape yourself up in there. It isn't safe."

"Oh, that's really fine, I was just . . ." *Sneaking through the walls after secretly bringing a rat back to life?* "Well, all right." I paused. "Is it really true that you can smell a lie?"

"Yes, miss. When Montgomery and I were traveling the world, we developed a signal, because there were plenty of men who wanted to cheat us. I'd tap my nose once for truth and twice for a lie."

I climbed into the cozy warmth of his bedroom and shook the dust off my dress. Sharkey wagged his tail. Balthazar offered me the rocking chair, but I sat on the rug instead and pulled Sharkey into my lap, scratching behind his ears.

"How did you know there was a passageway behind that wall?" I asked. "Could you smell that, too?"

"Aye, miss," Balthazar said gruffly, sitting in the rocking chair. "I can smell Master Hensley. Always prowling around in there."

"You don't care for him, do you? I suppose he is a bit unnatural." I paused as Balthazar scratched his nose with a thick finger—a nose that betrayed his ursine origin. I cleared my throat. "Not that there's anything wrong with being unnatural, of course."

"He doesn't smell right," Balthazar said, casting a wary look at the wall. "Mistress Elizabeth asks me to help her in her laboratory sometimes, but I don't care for it. It makes me uneasy."

"Then why do you do it?"

He scratched his nose again, thinking. "She's the mistress. She's the law. I must obey her the same as I must obey Montgomery, the same as I obeyed your father." He raised a hand and let it fall helplessly. I had never quite put it together before, but now Balthazar's constant obedience made sense. He was part dog, after all, and well trained to be loyal to anyone he viewed as a master. Faintly, I wondered if that included me.

"What are you reading?" I asked, hoping to change the subject away from experimentation.

He held up the book. "Aristotle. I like the messages he talks about. I wanted to reflect on the duties you've asked of me for your wedding day tomorrow. I pray that I'll do a good job."

I smiled. "I'm positive you will. How did you learn about Aristotle?"

He ran his hand along the spine of the book. "I started reading it on your father's island."

Just the mention of my father's island sent a shiver down my back. I hugged my arms around my knees. "I don't recall seeing Aristotle on Father's bookshelves. There was only a handful of books there, most of them Shakespeare."

"He had more in the laboratory," Balthazar said. "There was a room off the back filled with books and old paperwork."

A curious tickle whispered in the back of my head. I'd been so captivated by Elizabeth's science and my impending wedding that the Beast's warning had been the furthest thing in my mind, present but set aside like needlework I'd always intended to come back to and had then forgotten about. *Ask Montgomery about your father's laboratory files on the island,* he had said. *About the ones you* didn't *see. He burned a file along with a letter.*

"You didn't ever see a letter my father wrote to me that Montgomery burned, did you?"

Balthazar gave a heavy shake of his head, distracted by a torn page in the book he was trying to glue back together with a gooey lick of saliva.

"What exactly was in those files in the second room?"
I pressed.

The sharp tone in my voice caught Balthazar's attention. He looked up with his heavy jowls, between me and
Sharkey, and scratched his nose. "Files, miss? What files?"

"You just said there was a second room filled with
files." He scratched his nose harder, a sure sign he was
hiding the truth. "Balthazar, I know there's something
Montgomery isn't telling me. Something he's lying about."

His big eyes went wide. He said nothing.

I studied him closely, the way he fidgeted with the
book, shifting uncomfortably beneath my scrutiny. He
started rocking in the chair, almost imperceptibly at first.
Back and forth, back and forth.

"Balthazar, why did Montgomery burn a letter? What
was in it?"

His lips folded together nervously, and he rocked
harder. I'd seen Balthazar rock that way only once before, on
the *Curitiba* when I had asked him about my father. His eyes
had glazed over. I'd get no answer out of him now.

I sighed and stood, heading for the main door back
into the manor's hallway. I was done with secrets and passageways, at least for tonight. I had a wedding to think about.

"Good night, Balthazar," I said, and closed the door
behind me. Thunder shook the windows outside the hallway, and I pushed the curtain back. Lightning crashed.

Looks like another storm is setting in, McKenna had said.

Lightning—we needed it in order to bring a human
body back to life. There was no telling when another storm

would come, or how much longer Edward's body would stay preserved down there in the cellar.

Whatever Montgomery was hiding, was it worse than what I was hiding from him?

I went to Lucy's door and knocked quietly. "If we're going to bring Edward back," I told her, "it has to be tonight."

ONCE THE STAFF HAD gone to bed, we crept downstairs. The basement was flooded from all the rain. Water seeped in from the stone walls, filling the low-lit hallways with the sound of dripping and the smell of damp. Luckily the chapel was built on slightly higher ground, so the stone floor—and the bodies—remained dry.

Lucy made a face and lifted her skirts, checking each step carefully. Inside the chapel, we set down the lantern and looked at the dozen bodies. Lucy pulled the sheet back from Edward's face.

"Do you think he'll remember what it was like to be dead?" There was a ring of excitement in her voice that I hadn't heard in weeks.

"I suppose we will have a good many questions to ask him, when he wakes. Now, if we're going to cut out Edward's diseased posterior lobe, we have to hurry. I'm getting married tomorrow, after all. We'll need a replacement brain from one of these bodies. The cadaver should be in good condition. Male and around his age, if possible."

Lucy drew back another sheet and grimaced. "What about this one?"

I glanced at the corpse of a young man who seemed

healthy enough—present condition excluded, of course—with gangly long arms and legs that draped off the end of the bench.

"Goodness, he must be seven feet tall. But he looks healthy enough. Help me carry him."

Lucy took the lantern in one hand and picked up the man's feet with the other, while I wrapped my arms under his shoulders. The body had a distinct odor—a sterile coldness not so different from the damp stone walls. A trace of soap from his shirt lingered and reminded me that he had been a person with hopes and dreams that had ended far too young.

Lucy grunted as she lifted the man's feet. "Is he filled with bricks?" she muttered.

"Bodies feel heavier when they're stiff."

She let his feet fall back to the bench. "I'm not going to ask how you know that. What do we do? We can't possibly carry him on our own."

I pulled a bone saw from my satchel and held it up to the glinting light. "We only need his head."

"Juliet, no!"

I gave her a hard look as I knelt by the man's chest, steadying the bone saw on his neck. "It isn't going to kill him again," I muttered, and threw my weight behind the saw.

It was grisly work, but at least his body was frozen, so there was little blood. Lucy fetched a pumpkin from McKenna's pantry to place under the sheet so no one would notice a headless body anytime soon.

I stowed the head in my satchel, taking extra care not

to damage the top of the spinal column. Lucy shivered and wrapped her arms across her chest as she turned to Edward's body.

"What about Edward? We can't very well cut *him* into pieces to carry up to the laboratory."

I clenched my jaw. If we were going to bring him back, it had to be tonight, while there was ample lightning. We needed someone's help, but I didn't dare go to Montgomery or Carlyle, and the female servants weren't any stronger than Lucy or I.

At last, I let out a frustrated groan, knowing I only had one choice.

"Wait here," I muttered, hating myself for what I was about to do. "I'll be back in a moment."

I hurried up the stairs into the main section of the house, staying close to the walls where the floorboards squeaked less. I knocked gently on the same door I had so recently left from.

Balthazar opened it, dressed now in his striped blue pajamas, with Sharkey wagging his tail at his heels.

I couldn't bring myself to look into his eyes. I whispered, "You said you felt compelled to obey Elizabeth, because she was the law. Does that extend to me as well, as the doctor's daughter?"

"Oh, yes, miss," he answered. "I've always striven to obey your law as well."

I took a deep breath, hating myself even more. Balthazar deserved more respect than I was about to give him, and yet I was desperate. "Then come with me. I need your help with something. I fear you aren't going to like it, and I'm sorry for making you do it. Regardless, you must keep it secret from everyone, even Montgomery."

His face fell, and it nearly broke my heart. Father had been cruel, but I never had been. Not until that moment.

"I'm sorry, Balthazar," I whispered. "But you really must come with me. It's time for you to fill the role of Igor Zagoskin."

TWENTY-SEVEN

THAT NIGHT, THE WORLD seemed bathed in blood.

With Balthazar's help, we carried Edward's body up the spiral stairs to Elizabeth's laboratory. He said nothing as he carried Edward, and his silence tortured me with guilt all the more.

"Truly, Balthazar, I wouldn't ask you to do this unless I had no choice."

He laid out Edward's body on the operating table and didn't speak.

His sullen obedience gnawed at me like a rat's teeth. Of course Balthazar would feel like what we were doing was wrong. If Father had bothered with an ounce of kindness, used anesthesia, taken care with his patients, then Balthazar might feel entirely differently. He might have even supported his work wholeheartedly.

He whined low in his throat, the strongest objection his sense of loyalty would allow him to make.

I closed my eyes. "You can wait outside, Balthazar. You don't have to watch."

"But we might need him," Lucy whispered.

I shook my head. "We've already asked too much of him. Balthazar, please just keep watch and let us know if anyone's coming."

He gave me one long forlorn look, but there was a flicker of devotion there, too. Even after everything I'd made him do, he still saw me as his beloved master. It only made my heart ache more.

As soon as Lucy and I were alone, I opened the gash in Edward's chest cavity and began to suture together the severed veins and arteries of his heart.

"Victor Frankenstein first arrived at the idea of reanimation by watching lightning," I told her as I worked. "Elizabeth told me the story once. A sheep had died in a bog, much like the night I was nearly drowned. It was storming at the time. Lightning struck a tree and carried an electric current through the bog water. The jolt restarted the sheep's circulatory system. Victor witnessed the entire thing."

I finished repairing Edward's heart, then took out the vagrant's severed head and placed it on the table. I picked up the bone saw.

"Victor was entranced," I continued, trying to keep Lucy focused on anything other than the fact that I was sawing a stranger's head in two. "He started to replicate the effect of the lightning on small animals using the lightning rod. Then he discovered he could combine reanimation with surgery and build a human from disparate body parts. That led him to master organ transplantation. That's why Elizabeth is so good at it, from studying his notes." With a final heave I sawed clean through the man's skull to expose the delicate brain. I set down the bone saw and wiped my brow. "She's transplanted nearly every organ and body part, but never a brain. She never had the chance, because it requires both bodies to be deceased and she's bound by her oath. One can't go severing spinal columns while one's patient is still alive."

"No." Lucy grimaced. "I don't suppose so."

I inserted forceps into the skull cavity and stretched back the bone, then used a scalpel to carefully remove the posterior lobe, severing the blood vessels and connective tissue, and setting it carefully on the table.

"When you switch this portion of the brain out with Edward's," Lucy asked hesitantly, "it won't change him, will it? His personality, I mean."

I prodded the posterior lobe gently, measuring the connective tissues to ensure a proper transplant. "No, it won't. Remember how Edward told us about the 'reptile brain'? I did more research on it. They call the posterior lobe that because it controls our most animalistic instincts, like impulse control and sexual drive and the voices that tell us we're hungry or thirsty. It doesn't store any memory or intelligence or personality; those reside in the front and center lobes of the brain, which will remain intact in Edward's head. So the Edward we know should remain, but the Beast will be gone."

She stared at the brain in morbid fascination.

I pointed to Edward. "I need you to help me prop his torso so I can access the back of his head." Lightning crashed outside, shaking the windowpane. Lucy's head whipped toward the windows. "We should hurry," I added, "while there's still a storm."

We moved faster, propping his body up, as I marked off measurements on the back of his neck. I selected a scalpel and carefully cut into the base of his head. Blood seeped out over my white apron—Edward hadn't been dead as long as the other cadavers. I didn't bother to wipe it away. The anticipation was almost too much to bear. Would he truly sit up again? Sip tea and read Shakespeare and play backgammon as terribly as he always had?

"Is he supposed to bleed like that?"

Reason snapped back into me as Lucy nodded toward the blood dripping down the back of Edward's neck.

"I injected him with an anticoagulant," I explained. "It will make him bleed profusely, but it will also help bind the reattachments. You can help. Take that rag and mop it up."

She hurried to dab the blood away with a clean cloth, exposing the smooth white of the bone beneath. His skull. I made an incision just below the occiput, four inches in diameter, and exposed the pink tissue of his brain. So simple, and yet so complex.

I pressed the scalpel to the base of the brain and cut.

My stomach lurched in response. Before, when I had watched Elizabeth work on Moira's eye, I had wanted to be the one holding that blade. I had wanted to cut apart the essence of a human and stitch one back up again—and now I was.

"Keep holding his body steady," I said. "And hand me that larger scalpel."

I knew every fold of skin, every joint and artery. I'd memorized human anatomy on pages in a book, and I felt it beneath my own fingers. Lucy handed me the scalpel and took a small step back. My fingers were shaking, but I took a deep breath and thought of my father's steady hands, and mine stilled.

"My God," Lucy said, watching with rapt attention. "You really were born for this."

Pride, mixed with shock, laced her breathless words. I wondered what it must feel like to have a parent who supported one's desires and talents. If only Father had taught me alongside Montgomery. I could have made him proud.

"Yes, now the carotid artery . . . I need to sever the connective tissue. . . ." I already knew the procedure by heart. In another few cuts, the posterior lobe was exposed. A sharp, rotten smell emanated from it, and I nearly dropped my scalpel in revulsion. Edward's reptile brain was swollen to the size of a rotten and bloated tomato. Deep lines of black marred the purple surface. The tissue looked thin and waxy, and thick yellow pus seeped out of a tear.

Lucy gagged at the rotten-egg smell. "How foul!"

"Indeed. There's the problem," I pressed a hand over my own nose as I pointed the sharp end of a scalpel toward the ganglia. "See the connective tissue? It's diseased. The jackal organs my father used were diseased from rabies, and it combined with the malaria from Montgomery's blood."

My eyes followed the pus dripping down the side. I was looking at the Beast in his most animalistic, physical sense. I knew disease and cancers could result in modified brain activity. This swollen, diseased organ had gone one step further: created an entire second self within Edward, not only toyed with his personality, his temperament, but also changed him on even a physical level.

The sterile cloth lay on the table; I wrapped it around my nose and mouth to stanch the smell before pressing the scalpel into the base of the medulla. The sharp point sank into it like butter. White-yellow pus foamed out. Lucy gagged and turned away, but I kept cutting. In another few incisions, I had freed the diseased organ. With hands slick with pus and blood, I unscrewed the lid of a glass jar and dumped the organ inside, sealing away the terrible stench.

In the jar, the organ looked so small. Could an entire personality truly be reduced to pus and flesh in a glass jar? Loss and longing pulled at my gut. The Beast had been a monster. He'd been a murderer. And yet on some terrible, deep level, he had been the only one to understand me.

"Juliet," Lucy said, pulling me from my past. "The rain is letting up. The storm won't last forever."

I flicked a glance at her: dark hair twisted back tight, streaks of blood on her cheek and staining her hands. Such an innocent face, but she wasn't innocent any longer. What happened in this room would change her forever.

I jerked my chin toward the metal table. "The manacles. Help me secure him in place."

She picked up one heavy leather cuff, dusty with disuse. "Is that really necessary?"

"You've seen Hensley's strength. We aren't taking any chances until we're certain he's not dangerous."

The sight of a gaping hole in the back of Edward's head made her uneasy, but she strapped him to the table while I sutured the vagrant's healthy posterior lobe to Edward's brain stem, wired the vertebra and bone back together, and bandaged his head.

"That's the worst of it over now," I said as I reached for the complicated system of wires. "This part is far less bloody. It's just like we did with the rat." Her eyes watched in wonder as I attached the electrical nodes to the key neurological points on his body: the sciatic nerve, the base of the spinal cord, the nerves in his wrists. We soaked two sponges in a brine solution and pressed them to the sides of his head. Outside, thunder clapped. It seemed the heavens were as anxious to witness the impossible as we were.

I finished with the wires and then went to the cabinet and opened the drawer. I took out the silver pistol.

"We can't take any chances," I said. "On my signal, pull the lever, just like before." Her hand rested on the lever, her eyes on the storm outside. Wind blew the window open and rain pelted in, stinging both of our faces.

Time seemed to slow. I took in the room in flashes: Edward, cold and dead on the table, Lucy with wild eyes awaiting the storm, the pistol in my own numb hand. The hair slowly rose on the back of my neck. Tingles began along the nerves running up the backs of my legs.

"Now!" A bolt of lightning struck the rod, and Lucy threw down the lever. Sparks flashed from equipment that hadn't felt such direct voltage in forty years. Lucy remained steady, but her eyes were on fire. My breath came fast as pulses of sheer electricity ran down the lightning rod, into the wires, into Edward's flesh. I could imagine them finding the web of nerves, connecting synapses, traveling from the extremities to the core to the heart to the head, waking everything with a jolt.

More lightning crashed outside, with the sound of a tree falling somewhere. I became aware of a pounding at the door downstairs; no—the door to the laboratory. Balthazar was knocking. He had heard me screaming, but I couldn't stop. Couldn't make it to the door. Couldn't even keep a hold of the pistol in my hand.

"Turn it off!" I shouted at last, and Lucy complied.

The equipment powered down with snapping wires, with the smells of burned flesh and ozone in the air. Lucy slumped against the table, spent. I forced my fingers to wake up and curl around the pistol. I raised it on instinct toward the body on the table.

More pounding came at the door, followed by Balthazar's frantic voice asking if we were all right.

"Yes!" I called back in a shaking voice. "We're fine!"

"Juliet, look," Lucy whispered, and I whipped around. I pointed the shaking end of the pistol at Edward's chest. Almost imperceptibly, his chest was rising and falling. He was breathing. His wrist pulsed within the manacle.

"It worked," she breathed. "We did it."

I stumbled forward, clutching the table. Below us, Edward's eyes slowly, impossibly, opened. Swirls of green and brown, hazy now.

He blinked.

TWENTY-EIGHT

"EDWARD!" LUCY RUSHED TOWARD his side, but I dug my fingers into her arm to hold her back.

"Wait." I pressed the pistol into Lucy's hands. "Keep this aimed on him until I tell you it's safe."

Edward blinked again, moaning, his eyes glassy and unfocused. I took a cautious step closer, and then another, as a bolt of lightning lit the night sky outside.

"Edward?" I reached out trembling fingers to touch him. "Can you hear me?"

He mumbled a few incoherent words and shut his eyes. I let my fingers slide over his forehead. Cold, but alive. Blood pulsed beneath the sheen of sweat on his skin. I was at a loss for words. We had done it. Defeated death.

"I should check his heartbeat and breathing," I said, still dazed. "Make sure everything is working."

I went through the motions I knew by heart, monitoring his pulse, taking his temperature, utterly amazed to see his body working. I pressed the silver end of the stethoscope against his pale skin and listened to his beating heart. What a difference a single day could make. Yesterday Edward was a cold body in the cellar, and now I was feeling his breath against my cheek.

Had I changed as well, in a single day?

"His pulse is a little slow, but still in the range of normal circulatory function."

"But is he *himself*?" Lucy asked, clutching the pistol.

I lifted his eyelids one at a time. Even when the Beast had taken on a more human body, his eyes had still glowed a golden yellow. As I peered into Edward's glassy eyes, they were an earthy brown the color of peat. Relief overcame me like a warm bath. He mumbled a few incoherent words and I caught a sniff of his breath: unwashed teeth and day-old bread. Unpleasant, but very human.

A relieved laugh slipped from my lips. "It's him."

Lucy let the pistol tumble from her hand and threw her arms around him, sobbing, petting his hair, speaking as incoherently as he was. I watched the reunion with a mixture of awe and gratitude. Why had I ever doubted this was the right thing to do? Edward was one of us, and he'd sacrificed himself for us, and now we'd repaid that favor. At long last I had made up for Father's cruelty in making him.

It occurred to me that now I could always keep the ones I loved safe. No matter what happened, accident or illness or violence, death wasn't the end anymore. I could bring Lucy back, or Elizabeth, or Balthazar, if anything happened to them. Tomorrow I would marry Montgomery, and we truly could have a lifetime together—many lifetimes—safe from the fears that one of us might die young.

Lightning crashed outside. The electricity flickered and dimmed, then abruptly cut off. Lucy gasped in the sudden dark.

"The candle—I left one on the cabinet," she said.

I lit it quickly, letting the light spill out over the wires and switches rigged into the walls of the laboratory. "This is where Elizabeth controls all the electrical systems," I said. "She'll be here soon to repair it. We need to clear out quickly before she comes."

"I don't think he can walk yet," Lucy said.

I bit my lip. I'd poured all my energy into reaching this point; I hadn't actually thought past it to what we'd do with him afterward.

"Help me with the manacles." By the light of the single candle, Lucy and I unfastened the shackles and dressed him quickly. His unfocused eyes moved back and forth in their sockets; his forehead was damp and feverish. While Lucy did up the buttons on his shirt, I cleaned the laboratory of signs of our presence as best I could, swept up the blood-soaked sawdust and tossed it out the window along with the poor vagrant's empty skull, and wiped down the knives and instruments.

I opened the door. Balthazar stood on the other side in his blue-striped pajamas. When he gazed beyond me at Edward moaning on the table, he whimpered.

"My friend," I said, "I need your help once more to carry Edward downstairs. But I won't command you to do it this time. I was wrong to before. This time I'm asking, as a favor to me. You can say no."

He rocked back and forth in indecision, until Edward moaned again. "I shall, miss, but only because Master Edward needs me." He paused, kneading his fingers together. "Though if I'm free to say no, am I also free to make a request?"

"Of course."

"Tell Montgomery about this. Or allow me to tell him. It isn't right, keeping it from him."

Edward moaned again, and Lucy gave me a look that said we dared not wait much longer.

"I will," I blurted out to Balthazar, a little desperately. "I promise. Only give Edward some time to heal. I'll tell Montgomery after the wedding. Is that good enough?"

He nodded. "Yes, miss." He lumbered into the room and picked up Edward with gentle care.

"Take him to my bedroom," I said in a rush. "There's a dressing screen with a chaise longue. We'll keep him there until he's fully conscious, then move him somewhere more permanent until we can figure out how to tell everyone about him."

Lucy and I followed Balthazar down the winding staircase and through the halls as he carried Edward. For once, I was thankful for the poor electricity that let us sneak through the halls under cover of darkness. At last we made it to my room.

"Thank you," I whispered to Balthazar.

He paused before leaving. "Just remember your promise. It isn't good to keep secrets, miss."

When he was gone, Lucy helped me lay Edward down

in the chaise longue behind the screen. He reached a hand up, combing it through his sweaty hair, his eyes still glassy.

"Juliet?" he mumbled.

I knelt at his side, wiping the sweat from his too-cold skin. "Yes, it's me. You've undergone an extensive medical procedure and you're recovering."

"I died," he said. "I think . . . I died."

I glanced at Lucy. I hadn't thought through how to explain to him what we had done.

A knock came at the adjoining door, soft at first, and Lucy and I both froze.

"Juliet?" It was Montgomery. "Are you awake? I thought I heard you walking around."

Eyes wide in terror, I thrust the cloth into Lucy's hand and signaled for her to keep Edward quiet. I hurried to the adjoining door, trying to think straight.

"Montgomery?" I said through the door.

"I can't sleep. Stay with me tonight—I want to wake up with you on our wedding day."

My wedding. Tomorrow. I looked back at the dressing screen, where I could barely make out Lucy and Edward. I'd tell Montgomery about Edward eventually, as I'd promised, once he regained his strength and things had settled down. It would be a shock, but Montgomery would understand in time. He'd even be delighted to have Edward back—surely.

But I didn't dare tell him tonight.

"I think . . . that's bad luck, isn't it?" I said. "To see the bride on her wedding day."

"It isn't yet midnight," his voice came. "There's no rule about not seeing the bride the day before." His voice was so light and playful, in stark contrast to the procedure we had just wrought in Elizabeth's laboratory.

I glanced back at the dressing screen, where Lucy was dabbing at Edward's forehead as he tried to sit up.

"One kiss," I said, and twisted the key in the lock, swinging open the door and stepping into his room quickly. If he sensed how nervous I was, he must have attributed it to wedding jitters.

He stepped close, sliding a hand behind my back. "One kiss," he murmured, "For tonight, that is. Tomorrow, after the wedding . . ."

He nearly growled as he pressed his lips to mine. I could feel his heart pounding beneath his thin shirt, and it made my own flare to life. Tomorrow I'd marry the boy I'd known forever. Edward wouldn't be able to attend the wedding, but it would be enough to know he was alive, returned to us, completely healed.

Montgomery pulled back, one corner of his mouth hitched in a grin. He looked so very young then, and more handsome than I'd ever seen him. "Your hands are shaking."

"I'm . . . just nervous about tomorrow. That I'll trip walking up the aisle."

"If you do, I'll be there to help you up."

He kissed me again, more passionately this time, his hands drifting farther down my dress to settle on my hips. The clock on his mantel struck midnight, and I managed to pull myself away. I gave him a smile that I hoped appeared coy.

"*Now* it's bad luck," I said, and returned to my room. I twisted the key in the lock and leaned my head against the door.

Lucy was watching me, dabbing at Edward's brow. I took a deep breath and released it slowly.

"We have to get him out of here," I said. "We must find a secret place for him to stay tomorrow, and for a few days after while he heals. We could put him in Valentina's room. No one's been in there since she died."

Edward moaned again, his body jerky as though he was still getting used to it. He kept rubbing the bandages on the back of his head where I'd replaced his posterior lobe.

"Do we dare leave him alone during the ceremony?" Lucy asked.

I sighed. "Let's get him to Valentina's room first, and then we'll figure it out."

We struggled to help him stand. He seemed to have regained some strength, but his steps were unnatural and robotic.

I took a deep breath. I only needed to keep him secret until after the wedding. I wasn't going to suffer the same curse as Victor Frankenstein—there wouldn't be any tragedies on my wedding day, not after Montgomery and I had suffered so much already, only to find a safe haven here.

From today forward, I told myself, *things are going to start going right for all of us.*

TWENTY-NINE

I SLEPT LITTLE THAT night. Lucy and I had spent hours with Edward in Valentina's room, monitoring his breathing and pulse, trying to communicate with him, though his eyes and hands moved strangely, as though there was some disconnect between them and his brain. He fell asleep at last, and in his sleep looked so startlingly human—so perfect—that it stole my breath. Lucy pushed back the curtains as the first tinges of dawn appeared on the horizon.

"Go to bed, Juliet," she said. "I'll stay with Edward. You should get a few hours of sleep. You'll need it. It's your wedding day."

It felt unreal. I left her with the silver pistol, only as a precaution. Edward had been jerky and confused since reanimation, but not violent. Now, as I gazed at Edward sleeping quietly in Valentina's bed, I couldn't believe the Beast had ever even existed.

We're more alike than you want to admit, he had once whispered.

I shivered with the memory. *Not anymore,* I told myself.

I collapsed on my bed, thoroughly exhausted by the procedure. My fingers ached in a delicious way, and I stretched and popped my knuckles as I'd seen farmers do after a hard day's work threshing. As I drifted off, I wondered if Father had fallen asleep at night this satisfied. I doubted he had. After all, he'd never accomplished his goal to create the perfect creature.

I had.

In the morning, I woke to knocking. My first thoughts flew to Edward upstairs in the attic, and I scrambled out of bed and threw open the door, only to find a half dozen excited faces staring at me. Lily and Moira and the little girls crowded into my room, grinning from ear to ear.

"Today is your wedding!" they squealed, bustling into the room with combs and soaps and piles of ivory ribbon and lace. I watched them in a daze, a hand to my head, trying to calm my racing heart.

"How wonderful of you all to come help me," I said, in an attempt to pass off my shock as jitters. "I just . . . need to check on something for a moment. I'll be right back."

I gazed in the direction of the stairs leading to Valentina's room, but Moira clucked her tongue and shook her head. "Oh, no, no running off for you today. McKenna wants to hold the ceremony right at sunset, when the moors are at their prettiest, and you've slept so late we don't have much time to get you ready." She looked over my bare feet and frowned. "First things first: a bath!"

I protested, desperate to slip upstairs for just a peek to make sure everything was all right with Edward, but they wouldn't hear of it. They dunked me in steaming water, scrubbed me with rose-scented soap, and slathered my hair with precious oils, only to dry me off and check my fingernails and do it all over again. By the time we finished in the bath, my skin was the consistency of a prune and my stomach was rumbling.

Back in my room, Lily threw open the curtains and started to air out the corset and underclothes I would wear beneath my wedding dress.

"Look at that sun," she said, even though the sky was mottled with clouds. "I told you the storm would break, eh? But the vicar sent a note he can't make it. Had too much to drink last night, the rumor is."

"McKenna's offered to take his place presiding over the ceremony," Moira added while raking her fingernails through my hair. "She can forge the vicar's signature to all the official documents. It won't be the first time, and he won't mind."

The girls spent the next hour toying with my curls and rubbing lotions into my hands and face, peppering me with compliments about what a beautiful bride I would be and speculating who would be next. Lily voted for Lucy, and Moira thought McKenna and Carlyle would discover they'd been passionately in love for years. When I suggested Elizabeth might marry, they only burst into laughter.

"Speaking of Lucy," I said, managing to extricate

myself from their primping, "I haven't seen her yet today. I really should go find her."

"She came down for breakfast," Lily said. "Grabbed the entire basket of scones and ran back upstairs. Said she shouldn't be disturbed."

It wasn't until McKenna called the younger girls down to help with the cooking that I was able to give Moira and Lily the slip and race up to the attic.

I knocked on Valentina's door. "Lucy," I whispered. "It's me. How is he?"

She threw the door open and looked both ways to make sure I was alone, then pulled me into the room. Her entire face glowed as radiantly as mine, and she hadn't used a single salve. It was amazing how sheer joy could transform a person.

"Ask him yourself," she said with a grin.

EDWARD COULDN'T STOP STARING at his hands.

Lucy had helped him move from the bed to a reclining chair by the windows, and he sat upright as casually as any gentleman, though his skin was still clammy, and his muscles trembled as he took a glass of water that Lucy offered him. He drank it greedily.

"I keep expecting the claws," he said in a rusty voice, clearing his throat. He held out his hand, flexing his fingers. "Even when I was in control of my body, I could still feel them. Now they're just . . . gone."

His brown eyes met mine. Not even a hint of gold in them.

"*He's* gone too," he added. "The Beast. I could always feel him before. Now there's nothing."

Lucy took the glass from him. He looked over with a smile and rested his hand over hers. "Lucy explained to me the basics of the procedure you performed, but I still have questions."

"And I'll answer them all," I said. "But you should rest first. You've been through so much."

He flexed his hands again, marveling at them. "All I've wanted is to be a normal person with a normal life. I didn't know I just had to die first."

I smiled. Even brought back from the dead, Edward had a sense of humor. Lucy grinned as well.

"As far as I'm concerned, you're quite normal now," I said. "Your breathing is slower, as is the rate of your blinks, but it's nothing to be concerned about. Hensley's levels are slower, too."

"Hensley?" Edward asked.

"Oh—I forgot. You never met him." I tactfully avoided mentioning that Hensley was the one who had ripped out the Beast's heart. "Hensley is the professor's son. You'll meet him soon enough; he likes to crawl around in the walls and play with rats. He's like you—brought back."

Edward's eyebrows raised. "There are more like me?"

"Only the two of you."

His dark eyes shifted to mine. "Where's Montgomery? He helped with the procedure, I imagine. I should very much like to thank him."

Lucy and I exchanged a look, and when I didn't answer

straightaway, he guessed the truth. "He doesn't know, does he? That's why you have me hidden away up here."

I leaned forward to take his clammy hand in my own freshly washed one. "Lucy and I brought you back ourselves. We'll tell Montgomery soon, and he'll be delighted. Today, though . . ." I glanced at Lucy again. Right now, Montgomery would be dressing in his suit, perhaps sharing a drink with Balthazar to calm his nerves. "Let me worry about what Montgomery thinks. You worry about getting used to being alive again. Now, open your mouth. I want to run a few more tests."

I prodded Edward with a metal tongue depressor, then checked inside his ears and nose, and jotted everything down in a notebook at my side. On something of a whim, I handed him the tongue depressor. "Take this. See if you can bend it."

He raised an eyebrow. "It's made of steel."

"Humor me."

He took the metal depressor in both hands and gave it a slight jerk, no more effort than breaking a matchstick, but it bent like it was hinged in the middle. I stifled a gasp.

"Unnatural strength. I'm not surprised. All humans have powerful latent strength, but normal bodies are conditioned to respect limits so we don't harm ourselves. Because of your condition, you can't harm yourself, so your body doesn't register those usual warnings."

"Can't harm myself?" he asked, confused. "I thought I was normal now." His dark eyes found mine. From the day he'd washed up on the *Curitiba*, all Edward had ever wanted was a normal life.

"You're better than normal now," Lucy said tactfully. "You can't die."

This news made him stand up anxiously, but the effort was too much and he had to sit back down. "How do you know this?"

"Hensley is the same way," I explained.

He rubbed a hand over his face. There was a heaviness to the lines around his eyes and mouth that hadn't always been there. I could imagine a small part of what he was going through—when I'd cured myself in London, the wracking pain in my joints was gone overnight. My hands—like Edward's now—were mercifully still. Cured. And yet the Beast had seen straight through my supposed cure.

"Lucy, could you give us a moment alone?"

She hesitated only a second. "Of course." She left the room, closing the door behind her.

Maybe the serum cured your physical afflictions, the Beast had said, *but it didn't cure the illness of your soul.*

"I can't imagine what you feel like," I said softly. "But I hope you don't hate me for bringing you back."

He looked up from his hands. "Hate? No, I could never hate you. I know my feelings for you were rash when we first met. I had only been alive a few months, and you were the most beautiful thing I'd ever seen. It's taken some time to understand what loving a person truly means." His head turned in the direction Lucy had gone. "Sometimes it must grow. And sometimes it's quieter, less expected, not like how they describe in books."

He turned back to me, looking more serious. "I'm grateful you've given me a second chance, though I'll always be an experiment, won't I? An aberration. Something made in a laboratory."

I knew what it meant to be an aberration, but I'd never longed for a normal life like Edward had. I'd dreamed of an exceptional life for as long as I could remember. Ambitious, just like Father.

"Can I ask you a question?" I drummed my fingers nervously against my knees. He nodded. "After the Beast took over your body, he told me that I should be wary of Montgomery. That he had burned some files and a letter that my father had written to me." I swallowed. "Do you know what he meant?"

Edward rubbed his eyes. "I'm afraid I don't. When you cut the Beast out of my head, you cut out his memories, too. I might have known once, but not any longer."

I let out a heavy breath. "I shouldn't have even asked."

"Montgomery is a good man, Juliet." I looked up in surprise, and the corner of Edward's mouth pulled back in a smile, though the movement seemed to pain him. "Even if he did try to kill me a time or two. I know he was only defending you. He and I have had our differences, but I can recognize a good heart when I see it, and if my blood had to come from anyone, I'm glad it was from him. If Montgomery is keeping secrets from you, it's for a good reason."

I spun the ring on my finger slowly. "The reason I must keep you secret today—it's because Montgomery and I are getting married. After the ceremony, once things have calmed down and we are certain you're well, I shall tell him everything."

Edward nodded slowly at the mention of my wedding, unsurprised, and I wondered if Lucy had already told him or if he simply was too exhausted for strong reactions. He had loved me passionately once, but that time had slipped away sometime between his death and rebirth.

"I'm glad," he said. "You deserve to be happy."

I paused. "So do you."

Lucy opened the door, peeking her head in and giving me a smile. "All the girls are downstairs looking for you, Juliet. It's time to put on your dress."

THIRTY

I HAD NEVER BEEN the sort of girl who dreamed of her wedding day. Instead, I had spent my childhood poring over biology books and stealing glimpses through the keyhole into my father's laboratory. Marriage had felt so far off back then. The only man in my life who mattered had been my father.

I sat alone at the vanity table in my bedroom, looking in the mirror, a bouquet of dusky dried heather from Valentina's herb collection at my side. The girls had rubbed rouge on my cheeks and powdered my entire face and pulled my hair up in a formal Highland twist.

A knock came at the door.

I nearly dropped the heather. "Come in."

Elizabeth stepped into the room. She'd changed out of the simple muslin dresses she wore most days into one of her silk gowns from London. She sat beside me on the dressing bench and fixed a loose pin in my hair. I wondered what my mother would have thought of me. Had she ever imagined my wedding day? If she were here, would she hold me tight and tell me she was proud of the woman I'd become?

"There now." Elizabeth smoothed down a curl. "You look lovely."

I touched the dried bouquet of heather delicately. There had been a man once—one of Mother's clients—who bought her a china set with a heather pattern. I must have been thirteen years old at the time. Mother loved fine china, but she'd sold the set to buy me an elegant dress.

There's only one way out of this life for you, Juliet, she had said. *In a few years you'll need to find a respectable young man. Wealthy. From a good family. Charm him, make him fall in love with you, and never, ever tell him who you really are.*

Montgomery wasn't from a respectable family, nor was he wealthy. But he loved me despite my faults, and I loved him despite his.

Elizabeth helped me undo the ties of my robe and carefully slipped the dress over my head. I'd expected it to be stiff with newness, but it was soft as silk. As Elizabeth knelt to adjust the hem, a stray pin from the bouquet stuck my finger and a bead of blood appeared. My strength wavered. Was love enough? What would Montgomery do when he discovered Edward hiding away in the attic?

"Are you nervous?" Elizabeth asked.

"Yes, a bit," I confessed. "It's difficult to know what the future will hold."

She gave me a sympathetic smile. "Whatever comes, you'll weather it. Besides, whatever happens can't be as bad as poor Victor Frankenstein's wedding night, can it? There's only room enough in this house for one cursed wedding tale.

I promise you—no murders, no attacks, no monsters lurking in the shadows. Now smile, and marry that man."

I took a deep breath and nodded. Elizabeth squeezed my hand. The door opened and Balthazar stuck his head in. He wore an old black sash tied around his neck in a bow, since all of the formal wear was too small for him.

He stood at attention. "We're ready, miss."

BALTHAZAR LED ME DOWN the stairs. With my arm in his, we stepped out of the glass-encased winter solarium into the south garden, where the servants gathered around an altar of winter greenery. Montgomery stood at the front. His hair was combed back, his hands clasped in front of him. As far back as I could remember, he had always been in my life. Now he always would be.

I had taken him for granted back when I'd been a foolish girl in awe of my father, but I wasn't foolish anymore. I was keeping Edward secret from him, but he was keeping secrets, too. In time, everything would come out, and we would lay ourselves bare and make amends. We had years for that.

I took another step, the lace hem sweeping the ground. Lily and Moira whispered to each other about how lovely my dress was. I spotted little Annabelle in the back, standing on tiptoe to see until Carlyle picked her up and set her on his shoulder.

I squeezed Balthazar's arm. "I'm sorry again about last night. I hope you can forgive me. There's no one I'd rather give me away than you."

"It's all right, miss," he said somberly. "Just remember your promise. After the wedding, you must tell him."

He stood straighter, taking his duties seriously. I was in awe of him. No human could forgive and forget so easily.

Lucy stood to the side of the wedding party, dressed in a purple gown with Edward's pocket watch glinting around her neck, no longer a sign of his death but of his life. She caught my eye and gave me a reassuring smile to say that everything was all right with him, and then raised a fiddle and started playing a reel. I had forgotten she could play. The music was beautiful. Overhead, the sinking sun found breaks in the clouds and cast a golden-colored light over the wedding party. Balthazar led me toward the altar.

"Montgomery says we shall live here, at the estate," Balthazar whispered to me. "He said this will be our home forever."

My stomach clenched. It reminded me of when I'd fled Father's island, when I'd known we had to leave Balthazar behind even though it broke my heart. I squeezed his arm harder, reassuring myself that I'd never have to make a choice that difficult again. "Of course we shall."

He grinned, and we walked the rest of the way to the wedding party. Balthazar patted my arm and then moved to stand next to Lucy. She gave his hand a squeeze, and he beamed.

Montgomery came to stand beside me. I could feel his presence like warm sunshine, my mind racing to take all this in, the flowers and the clouds overhead and his hands clasped behind his back.

"Dearly beloved," McKenna began.

She continued through prayers I'd heard at the few weddings I'd attended when I was younger. I didn't care about the words, the same words spoken at all weddings. What I cared about was capturing the parts of today that wouldn't last forever in the pages of a book: the rolling moors behind us, the single strand of hair that fell into Montgomery's eyes, the anxious way his fingers flexed, betraying his excitement. Lucy holding Balthazar's hand. Sharkey sitting at Moira's feet with a bit of twine fastened to his leather collar as a leash. The wind still carried the smell of the storm, and it blew harder, ruffling my dress and making the windmill churn fast. I wanted to remember every moment. Most of all, I wanted to remember Montgomery.

I reached out to hold his hand. I knew it was untraditional for the bride and groom to touch during the ceremony, but we'd given up formalities long ago.

McKenna asked for the ring, and we made our promises to each other, and Montgomery slipped the ring over my finger.

"You may kiss the bride," she said.

Montgomery placed a chaste kiss on my lips that lit a fire within me. I fought the urge to throw my arms around him and never let go.

"I'm sorry this wedding has to come at so difficult a time," he whispered. "So soon after Edward's funeral. But I love you, and I always will."

I tried to show no reaction; for all I knew, Edward might be in the attic even now, looking down on us. I glanced that way but the sun was reflecting on the upper windowpanes, obscuring whatever was behind them. I told myself it was a good thing—Edward was back with us, and in time perhaps he and Lucy would be standing where I was now, the past forgotten, and the four of us could share in the management of Ballentyne.

Before I could answer, Lucy struck up a tune on the fiddle and the servants cheered. The little girls wrapped their arms around themselves for warmth, and Elizabeth herded everyone toward the glass-enclosed winter garden, where McKenna was waiting to serve cake. The coming darkness brought with it a chilling breeze, but I didn't care. Today only one thing mattered.

"I love you," I whispered to Montgomery.

He grinned, but a tug on my dress caught my attention, and I looked down to find Hensley in a tidy little suit with a rat perched on his shoulder, that one milky white eye seemingly staring into nothing. A coldness crept up my bare arms at the memory of him holding the Beast's heart in his bloodred hands, staring at me the same way.

"What is it, Hensley?" I asked as calmly as I could, though my heartbeat sped. Montgomery was gone from my side; two of the little girls had pulled him into a dance.

"You're keeping a man secret in the attic," he said, and blinked solemnly.

THIRTY-ONE

MY HEAD WHIRLED AROUND to Montgomery, making sure he was out of earshot. I looked for Lucy but she was gone, probably to check on Edward's recovery.

"I've been watching through the walls," Hensley added. "He's the same man who was scaring everyone before. You brought him back to life. You weren't supposed to do that."

My heart pounded harder. He couldn't tell Montgomery about Edward, not today. I couldn't shatter this one day of happiness with such shocking news.

"Come with me." I led him away from the group and knelt down, hoping that if anyone caught sight of us, they would think it merely a sweet scene of the bride playing with a child on her wedding day.

"I know it looks like the same scary man, but it isn't," I said in a rush. "The man in the attic is good. He's a dear friend, and he's recovering from having been very ill. For now, let's keep it a secret, what do you say? Like a game between the two of us."

I could feel panic creeping further into my skin. Hensley was unpredictable and dangerous. There was no telling what he might do or say.

"Mother says we can't ever bring them back. Bad things will happen." He spun his head in Elizabeth's direction. He had a cold look in his eye. "I should tell her what you've done."

He started toward her, and I pounced on him. "No! No, listen to me, nothing bad will happen. The ones brought back from death aren't anything to worry about. *You're* fine, aren't you? You only meant to kill that Beast because he was harming us, right?"

I knew that wasn't true, but I hoped it might sway him.

He seemed to be wavering but then started for Elizabeth again. I grabbed his little wrist. "Wait," I said, a little desperately. "I'll tell you a secret, but you have to promise not to tell your mother. I can prove that the man in the attic isn't a threat. I did the same procedure on your rat here, and it's perfectly normal, isn't it?"

He frowned, head twisting toward the rat on his shoulder. "My pet?"

I swallowed, speaking in a rush. "You're quite strong for a little boy, and sometimes you crush them without knowing it. Your mother throws them out and replaces them, but this one I brought back to life. And he's good, isn't he? He's a sweet little pet. Aren't you glad he's back? For me, it's the same with Edward. Everyone will be glad he's back, in time."

Hensley's jaw tightened. I had never been able to read the expression on his face. Even when he had killed the Beast with his own hands, he had barely flinched. His hand slowly reached up to clutch the rat. God, how I wished I could read what that little boy was thinking.

"There is more than one rat?" Hensley asked slowly.

"Yes. It's true. Now you have a secret and so do I. If you keep mine about the man hiding in the attic, just for a few more days, I'll read you all the stories you want." I swallowed, worried. "Do you agree?"

He didn't answer. He stared at me blankly and then stomped off toward the house. I uneasily watched him go. At least Lucy was watching out for Edward—Hensley surely wouldn't do anything drastic like try to pull his heart out again. I'd read him a story later, and with luck he'd forget all about it.

Montgomery grabbed my hand, pulling me from my thoughts, and led me into a spin with the other dancers. I leaned in to him, breathing in his smell, memorizing it, trying not to worry about Hensley. Just one day of happiness, that's all I wanted.

I hugged Montgomery closer. We had a wedding party to celebrate, and then the wedding night.

THE STORM STRUCK AS night fell. Everyone crowded into the glass-enclosed winter garden to stay out of the rain, and in the jumble Montgomery and I were able to sneak away to be alone. Laughing, we climbed through the portrait in the library and followed the wall passages to the upstairs closet, where we spilled out in the empty hallway next to my bedroom door.

The laughter faded on my lips as other feelings grew: nervousness, excitement, apprehension. The only man I'd been with was Edward, and that night hadn't been about love. It had been about loneliness and desperation and trying to pretend I wasn't slipping, when I'd already slipped too far.

Montgomery pulled me close. He was my tether to the real world, not the other, darker one that had called to me so many times before. I closed my eyes and tried not to think about my unsettling meeting with Hensley.

"Juliet James," he whispered against my cheek. "How do you feel, knowing you'll never be a Moreau again?"

"I suppose I haven't given it much thought." A cold feeling ran up my spine like drips of ice water. No longer a Moreau? Was it really so simple as a name changed on paper, my father's to my husband's? Was Juliet James a different girl—a normal girl? I looked at my hands, scrubbed clean now, the gold ring glinting on my fourth finger. One nail was jagged.

"Come with me," Montgomery whispered, leading me to the bedroom door. He wrapped me in his arms, and the kiss felt so natural and so right that I was hardly aware of who was shutting the door, who was dragging whom toward the bed. Cracks in the windows let in hints of cold winter wind. Montgomery reached for the row of buttons down the back of my dress.

"Wait," I whispered, unable to shake the unsettled feeling. "There's just one thing I must do first."

He raised an eyebrow. "One moment, and not a second more."

I pressed a kiss to his cheek, and then went to my own bedroom. I kicked my wedding shoes off and tiptoed to the doorway, then down the hall and up the stairs, fighting with my heavy dress, to the attic. No matter how I'd tried, I couldn't forget Hensley's words at the wedding. I wanted just to see Edward to make certain Hensley hadn't done something rash. Night had fallen, and the windows were black beyond, showing me my reflection. With all the rouge and fancy hairdressings, I scarcely recognized myself.

There was a photograph taken once of my mother when I was a baby. She wasn't much older than I was now. It seemed to be my mother looking back at me, and at first the sight was startling, but then I felt comforted. Montgomery had been right. She'd been with me all along, a quieter memory than that of my father, but still there. Only now was I starting to realize it.

I hurried the rest of the way down the hall and rapped on Valentina's door. There was no answer, so I twisted the knob and peeked within.

A single candle flickered on the bedside table. Lucy and Edward lay on the bed, fast asleep with exhaustion. They were fully clothed, though her dress strap had fallen from her shoulder, and his shirt was unbuttoned at the top. She had an arm wrapped across his chest and he, in turn, had buried his face against her shoulder.

It was a sweet, simple scene. Edward sighed in his sleep and pulled her closer, just like any couple in any bed in the world.

I glanced at the fireplace that held the trapdoor to the

passageways. Tomorrow I'd board it up with nails so Hensley couldn't get inside—just in case. And besides, I'd tell Montgomery about Edward soon enough, and then we'd all tell Elizabeth together. She wouldn't be happy, but what choice did she have but to accept it? She had accepted Hensley. In time, she'd come to accept Edward.

Feeling deeply contented, I eased the door closed so as not to wake them. Was there anything in the world better than a husband waiting for me downstairs, and my two best friends healthy and falling in love upstairs?

I tiptoed back to my room and sprayed some perfume over my shoulders to justify my absence, and then knocked on Montgomery's door.

When he opened it, he pulled me inside. "That was two moments. Are you trying to torture me?"

"Perhaps," I whispered. "Now, kiss me."

He was all too happy to oblige. His hands found the row of buttons down my back and he undid them gracelessly, anxious to feel my skin beneath. Once his fingers brushed the scar that ran the length of my back, I moved his hands away and slid the straps off my shoulders, shedding the lace and pearl buttons, stripping down to my undergarments with the ivory ribbons, a thin chemise and corset and petticoats that stretched to just below my knees.

"I've never seen anything more beautiful," he said. I turned around so he could unhook the corset, which he let fall to the floor. He tugged loose the tie around his neck, threw it on the pile along with his black jacket, and dragged the shirt over his head.

"Are you sure you're ready?" he asked.

I silenced him with a finger over his lips. "You're the one who wanted to wait. Not me."

With something like a growl, he wrapped an arm around my back, pulling me into a soft kiss, and then it wasn't so soft anymore, and my thoughts were lost amid the sounds of wind pushing at the window. Making love wasn't like it had been with Edward. That had been rushed, hungry. Being with Montgomery was nothing *but* love. Victor Frankenstein's wedding night might have ended with tragedy, but history wasn't always doomed to repeat itself. Sometimes, things could go right.

We fell asleep, arms intertwined, to the sounds of the windmill churning outside. Even in sleep, I didn't want to let him go. I dreamed of us together in my house on Belgrave Square with children of our own and hallways that always smelled of fresh roses. I dreamed that one day, years from now, it would be safe for us to leave Ballentyne and we'd travel to Paris and New York and Rome.

As I fell deeper into sleep, a different scent reached my nose. Montgomery's arm suddenly tightened around me, shaking me until I blinked fully awake.

"Do you smell smoke?" he asked, just as screams rang out from beyond the walls.

THIRTY-TWO

WE THREW ON CLOTHES and raced through the dark hallways toward the sound of the screaming. I nearly slipped on the stairs before Montgomery caught me with quick instincts. Smoke. Screams. It was still night out, but just barely. What had happened? Had lightning struck the house?

We reached the foyer and spun, trying to find the source of the screams. Footsteps came from the kitchen, where Lily appeared straining under a bucket of water, still dressed in her nightclothes, her eyes glassy with fear.

"It's the south tower, miss!" she cried.

The laboratory. We raced up the stairs, but a door flung open, startling us. Moira stumbled out of Hensley's bedroom with smoke billowing behind her. She leaned against the wall, coughing.

"What's happened?" I said.

She let out a wail, and a terrible dread twisted inside me. Hensley's bedroom. The secret room of rats that I'd told him about last night.

No, no, no . . .

"Is anyone hurt?" Montgomery asked, but I just squeezed my eyes closed. I'd have done anything not to face that room, afraid of what we'd find, and my own role in it.

Moira cried harder. "It's the mistress," she choked. "And Hensley too . . ."

I opened my eyes and took a shaky breath. We pushed into Hensley's chambers, and I froze.

I had expected a raging fire. Charred furniture. Every scrap destroyed.

But everything was exactly as I'd last seen it, untouched by flame, save the smoke stains on the ceiling. They came from the secret room where Elizabeth kept Hensley's rats. The door was cracked open.

"There." My voice was faint, as I pointed toward the secret room. "In there."

Montgomery threw open the door. His face went white. "My God." He tried to block the sight from me. "It must have been an accident. I'm so sorry. Tonight, of all nights . . ."

My head started spinning. Everything felt surreal. "Let me through," I said, though my own voice sounded distant. "I need to see."

"You shouldn't," he said, but it was too late, as I pushed past him. My breath caught, as the lingering smell of smoke hung in the air. The fire had died out. The rats' cage was completely burned—as were the two human bodies in the center of the room.

They were charred beyond recognition, and yet there

was no mistaking them. A woman and a little boy. Elizabeth and Hensley.

Both dead.

My stomach clenched. I doubled over and emptied my stomach onto the floor, again and again. The smoke came from them. Loose rats crawled through their ash—their flesh and blood. I coughed and gagged, but couldn't get the taste of smoke from my throat.

"Murdered," Montgomery murmured, and then went rigid. "It must be Radcliffe. He must be here!" He ran to the door. "Moira, fetch Balthazar. Sound the alarm. Radcliffe has found us—"

"No." I interrupted him. "No, it wasn't Radcliffe."

My eyes fell on another small body in the ashes, this one charred but not burned. One of the white rats. A terrible certainty grew as I knelt down and recognized the wounds on its side, made from the procedure to reanimate it.

This was the rat I'd brought back. I had only just told Hensley about it. I had thought the reanimated rat was harmless, and perhaps it was.

But Hensley wasn't.

"Jack Serra would have alerted us if Radcliffe knew our location," I whispered, eyes still squeezed tight. I forced myself to stand straight. "It wasn't an accident, either. Hensley did it." Moira let out a strangled gasp. "He killed her—look at the way her neck is broken. The same way he strangled the rats." Guilt flooded me so hard I could barely stand. I'd been so desperate when I'd told Hensley the truth about the rats. I should have known better after he'd killed the Beast, and after those bruises on Elizabeth's wrist. He must have flown into a rage and killed her, then killed himself when he realized what he'd done.

I sank to my knees, burying my face in my hands. Montgomery stared at the bodies with wide eyes, the idea horrifying. I sank against the wall as a harsh, mad laugh bubbled out of me. "History did repeat itself," I coughed. "A cursed wedding night. Oh God, just like Victor Frankenstein's."

Montgomery's brow wrinkled, but before I could explain, Lucy crashed through the doorway in her nightclothes, Balthazar right behind her.

"I smelled smoke . . . ," she said, and then froze.

Balthazar took one look at the rats crawling around the charred bodies and wrapped her in his arms, squeezed her tight.

"Don't let her see," I said. "Take her away from here, Balthazar."

Lucy sobbed as Balthazar carried her back toward the stairs. Lily came in with the bucket of water but let it fall when she saw the scene. Frigid water soaked into my slippers.

"Oh God," she whispered, and sank onto Hensley's bed.

I took a shaky step closer to the charred bodies, nothing more than ash and bone now. As I knelt, my skirt brushed Elizabeth's leg, which fell away into black ash. I pulled my hand back, afraid of crumbling their charred bodies any more.

"She gave us everything," I said.

"She did," Montgomery agreed. "She gave *you*

everything. Which means you're the mistress of Ballentyne now." He looked back at Hensley's bedroom, where McKenna held two girls pressed into her skirt to spare them the awful sight. "They'll be looking to you now for guidance."

I looked at him helplessly. "Me, guide them?" I dropped my voice to a hushed whisper. "I practically killed their mistress with my own hands, Montgomery. Last night I told Hensley about the rats. That's what threw him into a rage."

He hesitated for a moment, but then shook his head and smoothed down my hair to calm me. "He was unpredictable. He'd hurt her before. There's no telling what might have set him off, today or a month from now. All that matters now is the room full of girls who need you."

I looked back through the doorway. Moira let out another sob and McKenna pulled her close, rubbing her back. Over the girl's shoulder, the old housekeeper's wrinkled eyes met mine. Waiting for me. Waiting for my leadership.

I stood, fighting the urge to dust the black ash from my hands and my dress. Outside, dawn was breaking.

"Moira, Lily, take the little girls back to their bedrooms," I said, barely recognizing the sound of my own voice.

"And the ashes, miss?" McKenna asked quietly.

I looked at the wet ash on my hands. I wouldn't ask McKenna to clean up the ashes of her own beloved mistress. "Fetch me a pail," I said. "I'll handle it."

McKenna raised an eyebrow but muttered something to one of the younger girls, who scampered off to fetch a pail. The rest of them, wiping their eyes, hurried away with fearful energy. After a few minutes, only Montgomery and I remained.

"I can't do this," I whispered. "Elizabeth was their leader. The staff obeyed her. She knew everything about this house and how to run it and keep it safe. I can't do it on my own."

"You're not on your own," he said.

I paced, feeling the warning swell of panic as the truth of this situation crashed down upon me. "They loved her. They would do anything for her. She gave them *hands*, Montgomery. Hands and feet and eyes and organs. What can I give them?"

"They didn't love her because she was a brilliant surgeon. They loved her because she was kind and generous and strong." He came forward, rubbing my arms. "Just like you are. She made you her heir for a reason, Juliet. She trusted you, and so will they."

"Trusted me?" I said. "She shouldn't have. I'll only make a mess of everything, like I did before."

"That's not true." I leaned into him, closing my eyes, wishing we weren't standing in their very ashes. The weight of this burden placed on my shoulders was crushing. I wasn't sure I even wanted to be the heir of Ballentyne, and now I was its mistress.

A metal clang came from the door, and when I looked up, a pail rested there with a brush, but the girl had left. I drew a little of Elizabeth's spirit into my lungs, picked up the pail, and knelt in the ashes. Montgomery joined me. Together, we spent the morning erasing all evidence that Elizabeth and Hensley had ever existed. We carried the ashes outside, where we cast them to the wind. We'd have to have a funeral soon—the staff would want to say their good-byes. But I couldn't bear to go through a proper ceremony just yet. Not so soon after the professor's death. Not after Edward's.

Not after my father's.

From the edge of the moors, beneath the midday sun, Ballentyne looked like one of the ancient castles of legends. It was a sanctuary, not just for me but for the girls, who had all come seeking Elizabeth's healing skills. If more came, would I take up her scalpel and continue her work?

I glanced out of the corner of my eye at Montgomery. Secrets had caused this tragedy: Elizabeth keeping the rats secret from Hensley. Me keeping Edward secret from Montgomery. We were married now, and I was tired of secrets.

"There's something I must tell you. It's part of the reason Hensley was so upset. It's about Edward, and something I've done—"

"Hold on." His attention was focused on the tree-lined road cutting through the moors. "Someone's coming."

My head jerked toward the road. A single rider on a thin old horse emerged from the trees, approaching the manor slowly. Alarm overcame me. A stranger, now? Was it a girl seeking healing—or one of Radcliffe's spies?

"Come on," I said, resolving to tell him about Edward as soon as I could, as we hurried toward the stranger. He wore a heavy cloak that obscured his face. He stopped the horse as we ran down the road.

Montgomery flexed his hands. I realized we had no pistols, no knives. Whoever he was, he'd arrived at the moment we were at our most vulnerable.

"Show yourself," Montgomery ordered.

The man slowly pulled his hood back. I tensed my hands as well, ready to fight if necessary, or run back to the manor to sound the alarm. But as soon as I saw his dark skin and darker eyes, I relaxed.

"Jack Serra," I said. "I was afraid you were one of Radcliffe's men." As relieved as I was to see a familiar face, worry stirred. Elizabeth had sent Jack to spy on Radcliffe and report back. What if he'd come to tell us that Radcliffe had discovered our location?

Montgomery was strangely tense at my side, staring with uneasiness at Jack Serra, and I remembered that they'd never met when the carnival troupe had come before.

"It's all right," I said. "He's the spy Elizabeth sent to London. A friend."

"I know damn well who he is." Montgomery's expression shifted to one of complete distrust. I wrapped my arms across my chest, feeling suddenly very cold, and took a step away from Jack. Had I been wrong to trust him? Had I made a terrible mistake in telling him so much about us all?

Jack Serra's face hitched back in a cryptic smile. "Montgomery. Hello."

Montgomery didn't blink. "What are you doing here, Ajax?"

THIRTY-THREE

AJAX?

The name conjured the image of Father's island. The last time I'd seen Ajax—Jaguar, he'd called himself then—he was nearly regressed into a jungle cat, walking on all fours, covered in thick yellow and black fur, unable to speak.

Jack Serra was *Ajax*—one of my father's creations?

Thunder cracked in distant skies as rain fell on the moors. Montgomery reached for his pistol.

"You won't be needing that, brother," Ajax said. "I've come to help, not to harm." He whistled behind him, and the rest of his carnival troupe appeared from amid the trees, some on horses, some on foot, all wearing heavy cloaks that hid their satin performing clothes. I recognized the old man among them who I'd mistakenly thought was their leader, as well as the belching old woman. "As has my troupe. You're going to need us."

A door slammed in the courtyard. Lucy came out with Balthazar behind her, hurrying toward the commotion.

I couldn't tear my eyes off the bones and planes of his face. I felt a fool for not recognizing him earlier, but how would I have known what he looked like in his fully developed state? Montgomery had never said that when Ajax had been a man, he'd had black skin and a mysterious smile. Montgomery had only ever said that he was one of Moreau's best creations, able to pass for a human nearly as well as Edward.

Now that I looked at Jack more closely, it all made sense. That strange feeling I'd had that I knew him and that he knew me. He *did* know me, and it had nothing to do with premonitions and fortune-telling. We had spoken together on the island. He had led me through the jungle to safety. He had looked into my eyes and silently begged me to open the locked laboratory door so he could kill my father.

Jack glanced at me as if sensing my thoughts. His brown eyes flashed with gold flecks and my breath caught. His eyes hadn't changed.

Lucy and Balthazar reached us. "The fortune-teller," she said in surprise, and then caught sight of the rest of his troupe. "You've all come back."

Montgomery frowned. "Fortune-teller?"

I leaned in to explain. "He's been posing as a fortune-teller. He and his troupe were at the inn on the road to Inverness, and they performed at the Twelfth Night festival." I turned to Jack Serra. "Why did you hide yourself from Montgomery all those times?"

"He would have recognized me. As it happened, I had my own business to attend to first, and it required anonymity." His eyes settled on Balthazar. "Balthazar knew who I was, but you know your place in the pack, don't you, brother? I told him to keep my identity secret, and he had no choice but to obey."

I glanced at Balthazar, who was hanging his head guiltily. It seemed I wasn't the only one taking advantage of Balthazar's animal nature.

Clouds had rolled in; the rain started to fall, though no one moved.

"I don't understand," Lucy said, her eyes trained on Jack. "You mean you're a . . . a creation? Like Balthazar? And Edward?"

"Indeed I am, Miss Radcliffe."

"Who brought you back to your human form?" she asked.

"I did," Montgomery answered, to my surprise. "After you left the island, Juliet, it was chaos. The beast-men went feral, and Edward's other half had escaped. I needed help, so I went to Ajax. I begged him to let me restore him to human form to help me hunt for Edward. He agreed, and we left the island together. He, Balthazar, and I." He swallowed, and a look of both hurt and distrust crossed his face. "But Ajax disappeared in the deserts of southern Morocco. We didn't hear any word of him since then, until this moment." He met Jack's eyes. "I trusted you with my life, yet you abandoned us."

"I've always been a friend to you," Ajax said. "But not a servant. I obey only myself."

"Why come back, then?" Montgomery asked. "If it's the human experience you're after, you could be in France, or Australia, or you could have stayed in the desert."

Jack pointed straight at me. "I'm here because of her."

All eyes turned to me and I shifted nervously, wiping the rain off of my face.

"The doctor's daughter," Jack continued. "I made it my mission to end the doctor's work, but his ruthlessness found a home in her. I needed to be certain she chose a different path in life."

My lips parted. The fortunes, those cryptic words about my father and my fate—they were all part of a calculated plan to learn if I was as cruel-hearted as my father. I winced, pressing a hand over the charm he had given me.

"And what if I do choose my father's path?" I asked hotly. "Would you kill me like you killed him?"

"Yes." The directness of his answer was like a slap in the face. Montgomery drew his pistol and I took a quick step back, but then Jack's eyes softened. "But you aren't like him. I learned that the day you came to my tent in the fields. It wasn't your own fate you were most worried about, but that of your sick friend. Henri Moreau never once cared about anyone but himself. He turned to darkness for his own selfish reasons. You were drawn to the darkness, but that wasn't what made up your mind. It was the hope of saving a friend's life." He paused. "You can be ruthless, pretty girl, but not cruel. Determined, but not mad."

"So you've decided not to kill me, and to help me instead?"

He nodded. "It seemed a fair trade."

Montgomery muttered a curse as I stared at Jack blankly. Should I be furious that he'd lied to me, judged me, and nearly murdered me? Or should I be thankful that he'd changed his mind?

It was all too incredible just to believe he was even *here*, amid his ragtag group in stained satin clothes and heavy cloaks. A new worry twisted my gut. "The rest of your troupe. Are they my father's creations, too?"

The thin man with the potbelly gut cackled, and the old woman let out a snort.

Jack smiled. "No, but we are all misfits on the edge of the world, and that is enough to bring us together."

I pressed a hand against my head. I was still reeling from Elizabeth's sudden death, and from the fact that I still hadn't told Montgomery about Edward hiding in the attic, and from the fact that Ajax had nearly killed me.

"Why return now?" Montgomery asked.

"To help you, as I said. Elizabeth asked me to locate John Radcliffe and determine if he was a threat. My troupe has been following him over half the country as he's searched for you. He's been paying off the police. Working both with them and behind their backs." His troupe's faces grew serious, as did his own. "You're going to need our help, Miss Moreau. He has learned your location, and as we speak he's on his way with two dozen paid soldiers."

The air vanished from my lungs. Lucy let out a gasp.

"That's impossible," Montgomery said. "Elizabeth kept the manor's location secret, and he didn't follow us. I made certain of that."

Jack signaled to the old woman, who took a rumpled piece of paper out of her pocket and handed it to Montgomery.

"It's a letter, written to Mrs. Margaret Radcliffe," Jack explained. "John Radcliffe's wife. It was delivered a week ago." He paused. "Written by Radcliffe's daughter. It gives away the location of this manor."

Radcliffe's *daughter*?

We all whirled on Lucy, and her lips fell open in shock. She took a step backward. "No! I would never do that!"

"It has your signature," Montgomery said, holding up the letter like an accusation.

"I *did* write a letter," she said, looking pale. "That part is true. After that article Papa wrote in the newspaper about how sick with grief he and Mama were, I couldn't bear to let her worry about me. I wrote a letter to her explaining that I was safe. I sent it from Quick, but I didn't include a return address, I promise. I certainly didn't say we were hiding in northern Scotland!"

Jack glanced at the old woman. "Genevieve posed as a wealthy dowager and was invited to their home. She was able to sneak away and found the letter in Mr. Radcliffe's study. In it, Miss Radcliffe references an obscure type of heather that only grows near Quick. Radcliffe was able to use this information to locate Ballentyne in the tax records and draw a link to Elizabeth von Stein's family."

Lucy stifled a gasp. "Oh God, Juliet, you have to believe me. I was just telling Mama how pretty the moors were. I didn't want her to worry about me. I would never have revealed our location, not in a million years."

"I believe you," I said quietly. "But it doesn't change the fact that he knows." I turned to Jack. "Where is he now?"

"When we left them, they were preparing to leave Inverness. I took the liberty of opening the levees between here and the village to flood the road behind us. That will slow them down, but not for long. The moors will drain soon enough, or they'll find some way past the floodwaters. You haven't much time, Miss Moreau. Where is Elizabeth von Stein?"

A silence fell over our small group.

"She died," Montgomery answered at last. "Last night. There was a fire in the southern tower. Hensley is gone as well. Juliet's the mistress now."

No emotion showed on Jack's face. He was as unflinching about death as Valentina had been on our first night here, telling me about the vagrants' bodies in the cellar. Was he just used to death? Or was he one of that particular rare breed of person, like my father, who felt so little, one wondered if they felt anything at all?

"I hope you have a plan, Miss Moreau," Jack said. "Radcliffe is heavily armed, and he's planning on storming Ballentyne and killing anyone who gets in his way."

"All this effort, just in the name of retribution?" I asked in a faint voice.

"If it's retribution, then he is determined to get it, and a bloody one at that. Either you can flee, or you can stay and make a stand. We shall help you in whichever course you choose. I advise you to give both options careful thought, but think quickly. He could be here as soon as the day after tomorrow."

THAT NIGHT, AFTER JACK and his troupe made camp in the lower fields, Lucy found me sitting on the manor's cold front steps, huddled in a tartan blanket, staring at the deep puddles collecting in the courtyard since Jack had broken the levees. She sat beside me and pulled the corner of the tartan around her own shoulders, too.

"I can't apologize enough," she said. "I feel awful for writing that stupid letter. I didn't think any harm would come of it."

"I know, Lucy."

"And now Papa's on his way here. It feels like something out of a nightmare. I keep clinging to some desperate hope he's just worried about me, but I know that you must be right. He probably put that article in the newspaper hoping I'd come across it and contact them. It wouldn't be the first time he's taken advantage of my affections for my mother."

I wrapped an arm around the small of her back. If there was one thing I understood, it was manipulative fathers.

"What will we do?" she whispered. "Shall we stay here and take our chances, or flee?"

The night was too quiet, as though it also waited for my answer. My first impulse had been to flee. We could keep heading north, hoping the cold and desolation would dissuade Radcliffe, or we could try to find a new place to hide. But I had no other contacts in Scotland except for Elizabeth, and I dared not trust anyone else with our secrets. The possibilities had been eating away at me like a snake consuming its own tail, pointless and never-ending.

"We could flee," I said, taking my time to think it through, "but that would only buy us a few more weeks at most. Without the safety of Ballentyne we'd be vulnerable on the road, with no place to go but inns and abandoned barns. It wouldn't be long before someone recognized me from the poster, or else saw Balthazar and started asking questions. Besides, I fear what might happen to the servants if your father arrives and finds us missing. He might torture them to see where we've gone."

She was very quiet. "So we stay?"

I took another deep breath. Staying went against everything that came naturally to me. On my father's island, when I'd discovered the terrible crimes he was committing in his laboratory, I had run. After I'd maimed Dr. Hastings and the police had come after me, I'd run, too. It seemed no matter what danger I faced, my instinct was to flee, and yet fleeing hadn't solved any of those problems. They'd all come back, one by one, to haunt me.

There was no escaping one's fate.

"I don't think we have much of a choice," I said, tightening my fingers in the blanket, and with it my resolve. "I've been running for so long—from the police and from my father and now from yours. If it's ever going to end, then I think we must face it, and I think it must be here, where we at least have a fighting chance." I pulled the tartan closer. "I'll have to talk it through with Montgomery and McKenna to make certain they agree. I don't know if the staff will trust me like they did Elizabeth. And I can't imagine telling them tomorrow—just one day after her death—that an army is bearing down on us, and I expect them to stay and fight." I shook my head. "I can't ask that of them."

"You saved them from the Beast. They'll remember that."

"I didn't save them. Hensley stopped the Beast, and now we don't even have him." I sighed, burying my head in my hands. "As unpredictable as he was, Hensley would have been a great asset. Your father would never suspect a child of such unnatural strength."

Lucy rubbed my back, pulling the tartan tighter around both of us.

"Hensley wasn't the only one with extraordinary strength," she said softly, and our eyes met in the twilight. "I think it's time we told everyone about Edward."

THIRTY-FOUR

It wasn't yet dawn when I went to the kitchen, after dressing in one of Elizabeth's tailored dresses. All my dresses were those of a young woman, with ruffles and lace, and I wasn't that type of girl any longer.

I found a grieving McKenna already awake and tinkering in the kitchen. Her eyes were rimmed in red, though she pretended she hadn't been crying. She jumped up when she saw me.

"Miss Juliet! I thought I'd seen a ghost with you in the mistress's dress." She motioned to the bread almost apologetically. "Just heating up the bits left over from yesterday's feast for breakfast. Didn't have the heart to cook a full meal, not after last night." She turned away, fiddling with the oven so I wouldn't see her tears. "You and I should sit down and discuss the running of the manor. I've kept meticulous ledgers over the years, just like my mother and grandmother. I'll help get you on your feet, and the staff will be calling you 'Mistress' in no time."

I touched her shoulder gently. "McKenna, I know everyone is mourning Elizabeth and Hensley, but there's something else I must discuss with the staff. As soon as Carlyle and the girls have finished their morning chores, have them meet me in the library. Send someone to the lower field to fetch Jack Serra's carnival troupe as well. They arrived late last night and are camped there."

Her eyes went wide for an instant, but she nodded, drying her hands on her apron. I went upstairs to the attic, where I found Lucy coming out the door. She closed it gently.

"Did you tell Edward that your father is on his way?" I said.

She nodded. "Yes, and about the deaths last night. He's feeling much stronger. He can help us."

"I'm gathering the staff later this morning—be ready to bring him downstairs, but wait for my signal."

A few hours later, I paused just outside the open library doorway. I could hear the somber voices of the girls inside, gathered and awaiting me. One of them was still sobbing over the tragedy. Pity twisted at my heart. They were my responsibility now. I had never wanted to be a mother, and yet now I had six young girls and Lily and Moira, all of them looking to me for guidance.

I leaned against the doorway, trying to steady my breath.

A gentle hand brushed my back.

Montgomery was dressed in the dark work trousers and faded shirt that he had worn so often on the island. My heart pounded to see him like this, so wild, looking just like he had when I'd first fallen in love with him.

"McKenna told me you'd gathered everyone," he said. "I assume you're going to tell them about Radcliffe. Have you decided what to do?"

I nodded. Part of me wanted to tell Montgomery about Edward in private, but I forced myself to wait. He might try to convince me not to tell the others, but we needed Edward too much. I couldn't afford to have Montgomery contradict me.

I clutched his arm on impulse. "Whatever happens, please trust me," I said. "If I've ever kept secrets from you, it's because I had no choice. Marrying you was the best thing I've ever done."

He leaned in and placed a kiss on the center of my forehead. "I would follow you to the ends of the earth if you asked. They will, too."

We entered the library and all eyes turned to me. Lily and Moira sat on opposite sofas, each with a girl in her lap, and the rest of the girls sat cross-legged on the rug, corralled in by McKenna and Carlyle. Jack Serra and a handful of his troupe hung about in the back, blending into the shadows. The girls' faces were splotchy from crying, but their round eyes found mine almost beseechingly, and I realized how desperate they were for a leader.

"Listen to Miss Juliet, girls," McKenna prodded gently. "She's your mistress now."

"Is this about a funeral for the mistress and Master Hensley?" Lily asked, hugging the girl in her lap.

"No," I stammered, and then touched Jack's charm

beneath my dress, centering myself. "There will be a funeral, but not today. I encourage you all to find time to say your own prayers of farewell to them both; I know how much they meant to you, and when we are able to, we will commemorate this tragedy with all the respect they deserve."

The little girls just stared with wide eyes, but Moira and Lily exchanged a troubled glance with McKenna.

I looked at Montgomery, and he gave me a slight nod of encouragement.

"I'm afraid Ballentyne is facing a new danger," I said. "A gentleman by the name of John Radcliffe is on his way here from London, as we speak. I have reason to believe he intends my friends and me harm, as well as anyone we are associated with." I motioned to the carnival troupe in the back. "Jack Serra and his men have been spying on him. They've reported that he has plans to attack this household. We believe he's seeking retribution for the deaths of several of his associates. It's true that we're responsible for those deaths, but we didn't have a choice. They intended to release deadly creatures in a public square that would have killed hundreds of people." I paused long enough to take a deep breath. "Our best option is to fight him off. We'll have to strengthen the defenses and gather as many weapons as we can. I won't ask anyone to stay; I don't want to put anyone in harm's way, and we shall hide the younger girls in the barn just as we did with the Beast. Lucy shall stay with them. This man, Radcliffe, is her father. It will be better this way, so she won't have to face him."

An image flashed in my head. I pictured the red door to my own father's island laboratory, the doorknob under my hand, Jaguar slinking along the shadows ready to tear him apart if I would only twist that knob.

Through the crowd, my eyes met Jack Serra's. No, I would not force Lucy to make the same impossible choices I had.

"Just this one man, mistress?" Moira said. "How can a single man harm Ballentyne?"

"He has two dozen men with him," Jack answered from the rear of the room. "And horses and weaponry. It's a small private army."

The girls were quiet. One of them let out another sob and it pierced my heart, so soon after the tragedy of having lost Elizabeth.

"Two dozen men?" Carlyle grunted. "They'll slaughter us."

"Not if we're strategic," Montgomery countered. "If you chose to stay, we can station those of you who know how to fire a rifle on the higher floors to give you an advantage. You'll be protected by the windowsills."

"*Assuming* we'll help," Carlyle said, and McKenna shot him a look.

"I can only speak for myself," she said. "I'm an old woman, and I've sworn my life to Ballentyne, as have most of us. I'll stay and do what I can, but without the little girls that only leaves seven of us, counting Lily and Moira, and your friend Mr. Balthazar. Those aren't well-matched numbers, mistress."

"Eight of us," I said, shifting a nervous glance to Montgomery. "There are eight of us."

His brow furrowed in confusion, and I went to the door.

"Lucy," I called. "Bring him in."

Two sets of footsteps sounded outside. She came in a bit shyly, dressed in a simple gown, and extended her hand toward the hallway.

"Come on," she said softly.

Edward stepped into the library. His hair was freshly trimmed, the sallowness to his skin all but gone, and he was dressed in a charcoal suit that hid the slight bit of trouble he had walking.

"Hello," he said quietly.

Montgomery leaped off the desk and drew his pistol, aiming at Edward's head. The girls let out squeals of fear—the last they'd seen of him had been the Beast wearing Edward's body like a disguise.

"Montgomery, stop!" I yelled, throwing myself between them. "I told you to trust me! That goes for all of you. I'm the mistress now, and I promise you this man is no danger. It looks like the monster who locked us in the cellar, but it isn't. This man's name is Edward Prince. He's a good man. A friend of ours who was sick, but he's better now. He died when Hensley killed the Beast, but we've brought him back, just like Hensley. He's strong, and he can't be easily killed. He can help us defeat Radcliffe."

I took a deep breath. Montgomery's pistol was still aimed in Edward's direction. Even standing between them, I knew he could make the shot if he wanted to. I grabbed the barrel of the pistol and pointed it toward the ground.

"Montgomery, it's *Edward*."

He stared incredulously, the pistol still clenched tightly. "I don't believe it," he murmured.

Lucy took Edward's hand in hers as a sign of solidarity, holding it tight, and he leaned into her slightly. McKenna cleared her throat and took a step forward.

"Mistress Juliet, with all due respect to your friend, Hensley wasn't right in the head. What happened after your wedding only proved that. How can we be certain he won't fly into a similar rage?"

"Hensley had a child's mind," I countered. "And it had deteriorated over four decades. Edward is as healthy as he was before he died, and he's trustworthy. The Beast is gone."

Montgomery slowly holstered his pistol, as if the shock had only just worn off him. He gave me a hard look. "Juliet. We need to talk. In private."

He grabbed my arm and dragged me into the hall. Apprehension made my heart beat faster. This was the moment when I would find out which was stronger: the bonds of marriage or the betrayal of having kept such a secret. He didn't stop until we were downstairs in the alcove by the grand fireplace, far from prying ears. His blue eyes searched mine. "Have you gone mad?"

I pulled away, feeling guilty and stung all at once. "He isn't dangerous anymore. We cured him by cutting out the diseased portion of his brain that manifested as the Beast. The conditions in the cellar kept his body in pristine condition, so there hasn't been any deterioration. I've monitored him carefully. The Beast is gone."

"But he'll deteriorate over time."

"Then we'll worry about that in forty or fifty years. Not today."

Montgomery paced back and forth in front of the hearth, a bead of sweat dripping down his face. "How did you convince Elizabeth to do such a thing?"

"I didn't convince her. She never knew. I did the procedure, with Lucy's help, and Balthazar's."

He stared at me in shock. After everything we'd been through, he still didn't understand the level of skill—and determination—I had.

"*You* brought him back?" He shook his head. "That's impossible. And I refuse to believe that Balthazar helped you. He'd never approve of that sort of work, and he'd have told me right away."

"You know how he is with authority; he'll obey if he thinks you're the law. I convinced him I had more authority in this house than you did, and that he could never tell you. Be mad at me if you must, but not him. He made me promise to tell you the truth after the wedding. And now I am."

He paced harder, dragging a hand through his loose hair. I feared he'd stomp back upstairs and put a bullet in Edward's head at any moment.

"We need Edward," I reasoned. "Hensley was nearly indestructible, and I'm almost certain it's the same with

Edward. I know you don't like the science I used, but it might save the life of everyone in this manor." An idea latched into my brain like a fever. It started as a small ache but it spread rapidly, an infection taking over my every thought, until I felt my mind was on fire. "We could even create more like him. There are a dozen bodies in the cellar and more in the monastery's cemetery. We could bring them all back. An army of indestructible men fighting on our side. Radcliffe wouldn't stand a chance."

Montgomery's jaw tightened. For a flash, there was fear in his eyes. It was the same look he'd given me in London when I'd proposed bringing the water-tank creatures back to life.

He leaned in, the fire throwing shadows over his face. "Don't even think such things, Juliet."

I took a step away from him, pacing just out of his reach. "Why not? They'd be loyal to me, even more loyal than the servants are to Elizabeth. She only gave them back their hands or eyesight; I'd be giving them back their lives. It would be like the beast-men. Like Father. . . ."

Montgomery slammed his hand against the mantel loud enough to rattle the hanging portraits. "Your *father*?" Something dark crossed his face. "I thought you were done trying to be like your father. It's your mother you should aspire toward. She never would have done such an ungodly thing. She wouldn't have brought Edward back, and she certainly wouldn't be talking about creating an undead army."

I threw up my hands. "Maybe I'm *not* like her! You've been trying to steer my future toward her, but I can't help what I am. It's always been inevitable, don't you see? Father's inheritance is stronger. I've never had a choice, not really. It's in my blood. I can't fight who I am."

"You don't even know who you are!"

His hand dug into the wooden mantel above the fire so hard that his knuckles went white. I froze, surprised by his words. He stopped, too. Regret crossed his face and he turned away, but not before I saw panic there, too.

"What do you mean by that?" I asked.

I could tell by the set of his mouth that he was about to dismiss his words as nonsense fueled by anger. But then he looked at me—*really* looked at me—and something broke in his face. "It's never going to stop, is it?" he said more to himself than to me. "You think you're fated to be like him. You think it's genetics and prophecy both." He cursed softly under his breath.

Worry started to pull at me. "Montgomery . . ."

"I never wanted to tell you this, Juliet. I've tried so hard to protect you from the truth."

I forgot about Radcliffe, and the servants, and my plans to reanimate an army of dead, as a thousand little claws of fear dug into me. It felt just like that terrible day on the island when I had opened Father's files and found my own name written there, among his other creations all named after Shakespearean characters: Balthazar, Ajax, Cymbeline, Juliet.

Ask him about your father's laboratory files on the island, the Beast had said. *About the ones you didn't see.*

I shook my head a little too hard. "If you're trying to

say I'm one of Father's creations, I don't believe it. He gave me a few organs from a deer, that's all. I'm human."

Montgomery's face softened. "I know that." His voice was so gentle that I knew that whatever he would say next was going to break my heart. "You're right—you aren't one of his creations. You were born to your mother, just as he said. The only difference is . . ." He swallowed, slow and reluctantly. "He isn't your father."

The flames in the fireplace stopped. The drafts ruffling the tapestries froze. The entire world ceased in its orbit for the space of just a few words.

"What did you say?" I whispered.

THIRTY-FIVE

"HENRI MOREAU ISN'T YOUR father," Montgomery said, more emphatically. "I've known it since we were little. He kept the paper records locked away, even on the island. He told me himself once, after you'd tried to sneak into his laboratory on Belgrave Square. That's why he never wanted to teach you his research, Juliet—not because you were female, but because you weren't *his*."

I pressed a hand to my head. "That's impossible."

"He raised you as his own. He could have left you and your mother, but he didn't."

I leaned against the wall with the feeling that my blood was moving in fits and starts through my veins. *Moreau* blood. It had always been his blood in my veins, guiding me, leading me. Hadn't it?

"I don't understand," I stammered.

"Your mother had an affair." His words came like a crash of thunder. "I'm sorry to be the one to tell you, but your mother wasn't the pious woman you thought she was.

She had affairs since long before you were born, many with the same men she later went on to be a mistress to—".

"No!" I slapped my hands over my ears. It was difficult enough to process that my father wasn't really my father, but that my mother wasn't the pious woman I remembered? "That's not true. *You're* the one who keeps reminding me what a good woman she was!"

His open hands pleaded with me. "Your father didn't want you to know the truth. He was afraid you'd turn out like her, so he lied about the type of woman she was, and I did the same, but he changed his mind after you'd arrived on the island. He thought you were old enough to know the truth, so he wrote you a letter I was to give you on the return voyage back to London. He kept the letter in a file in a locked section of his laboratory along with other records that proved your mother's transgressions."

The burned letter.

"The Beast saw you," I said. "He told me you set fire to a letter meant for me, along with secret files you were trying to keep hidden. I didn't know if I could believe him or not, but he wasn't lying, was he?"

Montgomery looked very pale. "No. He wasn't lying."

"But why would you burn them?" Anger started to flood my veins. "That's the truth—*my* truth! You had no right!"

"I didn't want you to know," he said. "I thought if you believed your mother was good, then you might want to be like her and less like your father. All this obsession over being like him, inheriting his madness . . . I wanted you to think there was another option. Even if that other option was a lie." He clenched his jaw. "I grew up without a father. It's terrible not knowing a thing about who you come from. I didn't want you to suffer the same way."

"It's worse to believe the wrong man is one's father!"

He looked down at his hands. "Is it? I don't know anymore. Now I see I shouldn't have lied to you, but it frightened me when you kept insisting you had no choice but to be like Henri Moreau, when you weren't even his child."

I stared at him. The day was getting late. Upstairs the staff was waiting for us, Edward was reacquainting himself with life, and I couldn't bear to think about anything other than my parents.

"Then who *is* my father?" I asked.

Montgomery blinked, like the question had never occurred to him. I continued, "You said there were files on my mother's transgressions. You must have read them. It must have said who my true father is, before you burned it all."

He shook his head. "I didn't read the files. There was talk once about a French diplomat who died years ago. Whoever he was, it doesn't matter. No one of consequence."

I stared at him, feeling like a glass left too long on a burner, heating and glowing and so very, very close to the point of smoldering.

He had destroyed any chance I had of knowing my true parentage.

I went to the front door, throwing it open so I could gulp fresh air and let the afternoon storm clouds shroud me.

The blood in my veins belonged to a stranger I'd never met. The wedding ring on my finger tied me to a liar.

I had been so afraid of revealing my secrets to him; perhaps I should have feared more what he was hiding from me.

I closed my eyes, feeling my whole body shake. Montgomery called my name but I tore outside, down the front step, through the mud and the dark day away from Montgomery, away from the truth, away from the fact that he had lied to me.

I wasn't Henri Moreau's daughter. I wasn't a Moreau at all.

And if I wasn't that, what was I?

WITH A MOONLESS SKY, the entire world looked black. Dusk and night had fallen, and I'd barely noticed as I crashed through the soggy muck away from the road and the manor and the servants depending on me. I didn't want to be found, not now. How could I be found, when my soul was this lost?

My thoughts moved faster than my steps, and I barely paid attention to where I was going. For my entire life, society had defined me by my father—and so had I. I'd blamed all my faults on him: my unnatural curiosity and my inclination toward experimentation and even how easily I was able to kill. I'd also thought of him as my source of strength. All those desperate nights I'd comforted myself with my father's brilliance and determination. I'd structured my entire world around a man who was both a madman and a genius because I thought his spirit lived in my blood.

But I was wrong.

I closed my eyes, collapsing against the skeleton of a tree. I stared at my hands in the moonlight, flexing them, feeling as if I didn't recognize the lines of my own palm. There was no fate there. No fortune. All Jack Serra had read was the desperation in my face.

The tree's bark scraped against my back, but I felt nothing. Memories of my mother looked different now: she had always clutched a Bible, so I'd assumed she was pious. Now that I thought back, *was* she a good person? All those times she came back from church sweaty and flushed, I'd assumed she'd been praying fervently, but it seemed so evident now she'd been with a lover instead. Or those days she was gone knitting socks for the inmates at Bryson Prison. I had never seen her knit at home, not even once. Did she even know how to knit?

Had every memory I had of her been a lie?

I sank into the mud, hugging my knees in tight. I wished I could disappear into the tree, into the soil, into the dark night, until there was nothing of me left. The bog had tried to swallow me once. Maybe I'd made a mistake in not letting it.

A branch snapped and my head jerked up, breath frozen. In my desolation I hadn't thought about the foxes out here on the edge of the forest, winter starved and used to the taste of human flesh from Elizabeth's thrown-out experimentations. Now that the rains were gone, they'd be coming out of hiding, just like Radcliffe.

He might be in Quick even now, stopped only by a

flooded road, hunting us like some famished animal. The household of Ballentyne was resting all its hopes on me.

The branch snapped again, and I bristled. I reached for a fallen limb, tearing off one branch to form a sharp end. Fear clawed at the soft parts of my throat as movement caught my eye in the darkness, and I clutched the branch harder.

Out of the gloom the creature came at me on fast little legs, and I let myself relax. Those short legs and black snout didn't belong to a fox.

"Sharkey," I said, as my little dog ran up to me. I pulled him close, burying my nose in his fur, breathing in that earthy smell I so loved. More footsteps came and another figure loomed in the darkness, this one much too large for a fox, even too large for a man.

"Balthazar, what are you doing out here?" I asked as he entered the clearing and Sharkey ran over to nuzzle his leg.

"Looking for you, miss. Montgomery said you'd run away. Everyone's out searching for you."

He stopped a few feet away, tapped the ground with a foot until he'd found a dry patch, and sat cross-legged across from me. In the darkness he was little more than a voice and a smell of tweed and wet dog, though I knew that with his sight, he could see me perfectly.

I wiped the wet from my eyes. "I can't go back there. I don't belong there."

"You're mistress of Ballentyne."

I barked a cruel laugh. "Elizabeth and the professor only made me their heir because they thought I was my father's daughter. It turns out they were as wrong as I was." I pulled my knees closer. "Did you know?"

"That the doctor wasn't your father? Yes, miss. I knew from the beginning. You didn't smell like him."

Father's smell came back to me, formaldehyde and apricot preserves, but I knew Balthazar spoke of a deeper smell. The scent of family. Henri Moreau must have instructed Balthazar never to tell me the truth, taking advantage of his unwavering obedience just as I had.

"I'm not a Moreau," I said, testing out the words. "I'm a . . . Chastain, I suppose," I said, thinking of my mother's maiden name. "Or rather a James, since I married Montgomery."

So many names, and none of them felt right. They didn't have the right number of syllables or the right feel in my mouth. None of them were *Moreau*.

"It's useless." My voice broke. "I was so certain I knew who I was and who I was supposed to be. I'm not certain of anything now."

My running, sniffling nose was the only sound in the night, save distant moisture dripping from branches and the wind in the moors. Balthazar's joints creaked as he shifted.

"You're Juliet," he said simply.

I looked up at him helplessly. "I don't know who that is."

"Then you'll find out."

I found myself staring at the dark space his voice came from. One thing I'd learned about Balthazar was that even though he was created by my father, he wasn't bound by him. He'd gone from idolizing the man as a god to forming his own thoughts and beliefs and identity. How had a creature made of bits of a dog and a bear already learned so much more about life than I had?

Tears started coming harder. Big, thick ones. Balthazar shuffled closer and wrapped an arm around me, patting me gently. Sharkey nuzzled his snout against my arm. Sitting in the dark forest, I still felt lost, but now there was a light to move slowly toward.

As I squinted, I realized the light wasn't just in my head. It moved through the trees, far off, but silently. My body went rigid as I turned to Balthazar.

"Someone's coming," I whispered.

I pictured Elizabeth's ghost walking through these bogs, just as she had when I'd nearly drowned with that sheep. How I wished she were here now to guide me, as she had then.

Sharkey barked as the light grew closer. I made out Montgomery's guilt-ridden face reflected in the light as he followed the sound of our voices. He stopped.

"Juliet, thank God. I'm sorry."

I wiped the last of the moisture from my eyes. Sharkey nudged himself closer, and I scratched his head as hard as he liked, hoping it would calm me, too.

"You should have told me the truth," I said quietly. I stood, holding Sharkey tightly in my arms. "I'm not that same little girl you used to shelter from the bad things in the world, Montgomery. I'm grown, and I might make mistakes, but I'm capable of taking care of myself—and Ballentyne." I took a deep breath full of the highland mist and looked in the direction of the lights of the house, hoping that was true.

"We'll figure something out," Montgomery said. "Radcliffe won't take Ballentyne."

I squinted toward the house, feeling the cold mist spread over me, listening to the sound of the dripping bogs. "I might have an idea how," I said hesitantly, letting the idea grow, and reached down to cup a handful of water from the closest puddle. "It has to do with Jack Serra flooding the moors."

Montgomery tensed. "You mean to drown Radcliffe and his men?"

I knew he wouldn't like the idea of more bloodshed. Violence wasn't in his nature, but he'd slaughtered the beast-men when he'd been given no choice. We had no choice now, either. I would try to reason with Radcliffe, but if that didn't work, there was no way I was letting him harm a single one of those girls.

I shook my head. "We're going to electrocute them."

THIRTY-SIX

ON THE WALK BACK to Ballentyne I explained my idea.

"Jack Serra—Ajax—flooded the road when he broke the levees to slow down Radcliffe. It flooded the manor's courtyard as well. There must be three inches of water soaking the gravel, deeper in places. The entire manor's wired with electricity. If we can trap Radcliffe and his men in the flooded courtyard and introduce an electric current, it would electrocute anyone touching the water."

For a few moments, Montgomery said nothing. I couldn't tell if he was considering my plan, or if his silence came from disapproval. "That's true," he said at last. "But I think we owe it to Lucy to reason with him first. If we try to negotiate and he is still bent on bringing us harm, then I suppose we haven't many other choices. The problem is that someone would have to connect a metal line to carry the current. There isn't enough rubber in the house to insulate someone's entire body against a current that strong. That person would be electrocuted, too. It's suicide."

I hesitated. "For a normal person, yes. Not for someone who can't die."

Ballentyne blazed in the distance, reflecting in Montgomery's eyes. "You mean Edward."

"Exactly. Elizabeth said the reanimated can't be killed unless their bodies are destroyed beyond repair, which is how Hensley burned to death. A simple electric shock wouldn't hurt Edward any more than the tree branch harmed Hensley. He might need a few small repairs, but he wouldn't die." I paused. "At least, I don't think he would."

"Is this why you brought him back? Because he's useful to you?"

I stopped in the road, and Montgomery stopped as well, as Balthazar and Sharkey continued toward the flooded courtyard. I lowered my voice.

"You make me sound as ruthless as Henri Moreau. I didn't bring Edward back to serve some purpose. He's a person. A friend. I brought him back because he had been wronged, and I had the power to help him. If you died, I'd bring you back as well. Not because I wanted to use you, but because I love you."

His face softened in the light of his lamp. Montgomery had destroyed the truth about my past. About my very identity, even. And yet as I looked into his eyes in the lamplight, I remembered how Henri Moreau had manipulated and abused Montgomery as a child, making him adore Father like a god, only to treat him like a slave. And Montgomery had gone along with it all those years, just for the chance of having a father.

"We're married now," I said. "No more secrets between us. Agreed?"

He held my hand in his, our gold rings glinting beneath the stars. "No more secrets."

By the time we returned to the library, McKenna had put the little girls to bed and was waiting with Carlyle and Jack, and Lucy and Edward, discussing how best to strengthen the front doors against attack.

A floorboard squeaked under my boot and they all turned. Edward stood.

"Montgomery," Edward said. His skin had gained some color, though he still moved with just the slightest bit of stiffness.

Montgomery held up a hand to silence him. "No. Let me speak first. It was wrong of me not to accept that you were back. It caught me by surprise, but I shouldn't have raised my pistol. I've played a hand in my fair share of experimentation, and I'm not one to judge how we are brought into this world, only our nature as we are now." He absently rubbed the scar on his thumb where his blood had been drawn to make Edward. "I'm glad to see you standing here, and I'm proud to call you a brother."

He held out his hand, and after only a slight hesitation Edward stepped forward to take it. Lucy squeezed her pocket watch tight, beaming to see them no longer at odds.

"I suppose, if we're making amends," Edward said in a lighter tone, "I should apologize for all the times I tried to kill you. Don't take it personally."

Montgomery gave the hint of a smile. "As I recall, I also tried to kill you a few times."

"Then we're even."

They broke apart, and I smiled to think of the four of us on friendly terms: no more misunderstandings, no more sickness or anger. Our friendships had even overcome death itself.

Now we just had to overcome Radcliffe.

I went to the windows, looking down on the flooded courtyard and the road beyond. For all I knew, Radcliffe was already in Quick, just waiting for the road to drain. "We don't have much time, and there's much to be done. I have a plan that involves all of you. I want to know your thoughts."

We stayed up until dawn discussing how to prepare for Radcliffe's arrival and the logistics of trapping his men in the courtyard to electrocute them. Montgomery said that he and Balthazar would dig a trench around the rear of the house to force Radcliffe into the courtyard, while Edward and Carlyle reinforced all the doors and ground-floor windows, and Lucy agreed to work with McKenna to stock the barn cellar with supplies to keep the girls warm and well fed during the siege.

Rain fell against the windows. "Let's hope the rain holds until we've prepared the house," I said. "The longer it rains, the longer it will take for the road to drain."

Montgomery squeezed my hand. "We'll be ready for him."

The following day was a flurry of activity. The rain continued, steady and cold, turning the gardens into a soggy mess. We laid out thick wooden planks along the courtyard to walk across as we went about gathering weapons and ammunition. To my surprise, when I handed Lily and Moira each a rifle and started to explain how to fire, they just laughed.

"Mistress, we've been hunting foxes since we were three years old," Moira said, and took the rifle with a well-practiced hand.

By midday, when we took a break to eat some sandwiches McKenna had prepared, the trench was dug and most of the windows were boarded up, and I was starting to feel like we might have a chance after all.

"I've been thinking about the secret passageways," I said. "In case Radcliffe's men do get into the house, the passages could be extremely useful to help us move around unnoticed, but I only know a handful of them."

McKenna arranged the sandwiches, thinking. "I have the previous mistresses' ledgers in my study. One of them tried mapping the passages in the 1770s, though the map's been damaged. Parts aren't readable, but it might be a good place to start."

She fetched the map and brought it back to the library, where Montgomery and I pored over it. "You and I already know how to travel through the passages without getting hurt," he said. "It won't take but a few hours to fill in the blank sections of the map."

Frowning, I looked outside in the direction of Quick. The rain was already lessening, and there was still so much left to do. But the passages could save our lives. "Let's do it, then."

While everyone else continued readying the house,

Montgomery and I went upstairs to the second floor hallway, to a watery portrait I'd never given much thought to before. *Amelia Ballentyne,* read the plaque. Her hair was a fair shade of red, but otherwise she looked very much like Elizabeth: her defiant stance, the crooked smile, the mischievous glisten in her eye.

Montgomery raised his hammer and smashed it into her face.

I flinched as the canvas and wooden frame shattered, reveal the gaping chasm of a secret passageway beyond that had been long sealed away.

"Poor woman," I muttered as he used the hammer to pull away the remaining bits of wood and debris, giving us access. "All this was hers once. She entrusted it to Elizabeth, and now to me. She'd be disappointed if she knew."

Montgomery took my hand before I could continue down that dark line of thought. "You must stop doubting yourself. Come on." We climbed through the broken portrait. The only light came from seams in the walls. Montgomery's presence was nothing more than a shadowy figure until he lit a candle.

"If only Hensley were here," I said, picking my way carefully along the uneven brick floor. "He could have mapped these passageways with his eyes closed." I ducked under a jagged broken post. "I keep thinking that if Elizabeth could have gotten away from him and crawled into these passages, she might have survived."

"It would be a death trap to be caught in here in a fire, with so few exits and so little ventilation." He studied the map. "This way." He turned left and climbed a flight of rickety stairs. We wound around a brick fireplace to continue down the branching hallways. I tried to ignore the thought of the hundreds of spiders that must be there and I didn't see. Montgomery found a crack and peered through.

"What do you see?"

"It's nothing," he said, straightening a little too fast. "We should keep going."

I bent down to look myself and jerked in surprise to find lifeless eyes staring back at me. A deer—one of the white statues from the winter garden. Behind the statuary, Lucy and Edward sat on the wall tucked between the stone fox and stone wolf, speaking in low voices I couldn't make out. Edward's pocket watch glinted in Lucy's hand. She was trying to give it back to him, and he was folding her hand around it, insisting she keep it. His hands stayed wrapped around hers for quite some time, as though he didn't quite want to let go. She suddenly leaned in and kissed him, and his initial surprise gave way to an embrace.

My cheeks went red.

"We should give them their privacy," Montgomery said softly. "Let them have their happiness wherever they can find it. They might not have too many chances once Radcliffe gets here, even if we do manage to defeat him."

"What do you mean?"

He hesitated. "If you or I can't kill Radcliffe ourselves, then Edward stands the greatest chance of . . ." His voice trailed off.

"Of killing the father of the girl he loves," I answered.

Montgomery looked away; the tension was too high, reminding me that I'd as good as killed the man I'd thought was my own father, a man who'd been like a father to him, too.

Montgomery stood up. "Come on. We've faced a lot worse than him. I'm not going to let a banker take us down, army or not."

We kept walking, faster now, but I couldn't shake the thought of Lucy in Edward's arms. I remembered what it had felt like to kiss Edward—wild and passionate. Was it different now, without the Beast? I could never admit it to anyone, but in a way, I missed that dangerous side of him. For a brief period of time, there had been a creature even darker than myself.

I shivered.

"What's wrong?" Montgomery was at my side in an instant.

"Just cobwebs. But look." I pointed ahead, at the gap in the floor I had nearly fallen into my first week at Ballentyne, before Hensley had stopped me. "Another one of Lord Ballentyne's traps. It's three stories up. You'd fall to your death."

Montgomery marked it on the map, and we took our care stepping over it. "Well, there are worse things than death," he said in a tone that was strangely distant.

I cocked an eyebrow. "You mean you'd rather die than be caught by Radcliffe?"

"No." In the faint light, his face twisted with indecision. "I mean that if I don't survive Radcliffe's attack and you do . . ." He paused. "In the forest, you said you would bring me back to life. I don't want you to."

A draft blew through the passageways, making me shiver. "It worked for Edward."

"I don't care if it works or not. I want to know that this life is the only one that matters. When you can never die, do you ever really live?"

I stared at him. "We have the secret to eternal life, and you don't want it?"

"I want only this life. With you."

"But I don't want to lose you." I intertwined my fingers in his, feeling the sturdiness of the ring around his fourth finger.

He pressed his lips to mine, silencing those thoughts. I kissed him harder, twisting my hands in his shirt. There was no telling what would happen when Radcliffe arrived. Like Montgomery said, we had to steal any moments of happiness we could.

"One last battle," Montgomery whispered against my cheek. "One last stand, and then we'll be left to live our lives however we desire."

Here in the darkness and shadows of the hidden passages, I knew I'd never love him more.

I won't let him risk himself, I promised silently. *He wants only one life; then it shall be a long one.*

And as I devised a way to keep him safe from Radcliffe's army, even from his own crazed sense of morality, I kissed him harder. We stayed like that until time didn't exist. As I broke the kiss, resting my head against his shoulder and breathing in his scent, I heard a muffled voice on the other side of the wall. It was calling my name.

"Do you hear that?" I asked.

"It sounds like Lucy."

We hurried to find an exit to the passageways back into the house, and when we finally crawled out of the walls, covered in cobwebs, I heard Lucy frantically calling my name.

She rounded the corner, stopping short when she saw us.

"Juliet!" she cried. "There are lights on the road, coming fast."

I looked at Montgomery in confusion. "But the road is still flooded. The rain hasn't stopped."

She swallowed. "They've found some way around the flooding. They're nearly here."

THIRTY-SEVEN

We RACED OUTSIDE TO the courtyard, where Jack and his troupe were gathered with Balthazar. Lights were just visible through the trees.

Balthazar cocked his head, calculating the distance with his superior hearing. "They are two miles off. On horses and riding fast. Twenty riders."

McKenna must have heard the commotion, because she eased open the kitchen door. A few little girls peeked out from behind her skirt. "I couldn't help but overhear, mistress. Should we take the girls to the barn?"

The little girls squealed with fear. My heart started pounding harder, imagining Radcliffe's horses pawing the ground. *Twenty men.* Even with Jack and his troupe, could a handful of servants defend this place?

McKenna cleared her throat. "What will you have us do, mistress?"

The word cut into me. *Mistress.* That was Elizabeth's title, not mine. That was the title for a leader, for someone who understood strategy and risk and had a grasp on reason. Ever since Montgomery had told me Moreau wasn't my father, I didn't even have a grasp on myself.

Jack Serra took a step forward. "You've proven yourself to me, pretty girl. Now prove yourself to them."

I gave him an unsteady look, but his gaze didn't waver. Maybe I wasn't a monster like Father, but did that make me a leader?

"Lucy, take the little girls to the barn," I said, stumbling over commands that felt foreign on my tongue. "Hide in the underground cellar, and no matter what happens or what you hear, stay there until morning."

Lucy nodded and gathered the girls.

"Wait." Edward took a step toward Lucy. They wouldn't see each other again until the battle was over, I realized. Edward was needed here with us to defend the house, and Lucy was needed in the barn. He brushed her hair back gently, sweeping the line of her cheek with his thumb. "Be safe," he said, then leaned in and whispered a few words I couldn't make out. They weren't meant for my ears, anyway.

Lucy covered her mouth with a hand, stifling emotion, and nodded to whatever he'd whispered. She placed a quick kiss on his cheek, aware of the little girls watching, then herded them through the rain toward the barn.

Lightning flashed in the distance.

I closed my eyes to reaffirm my resolve. "I want everyone safely inside, except for Balthazar and Montgomery. You two will be posted on either side of the gate. Keep hidden and don't show yourselves unless we need to surround them.

McKenna, lead Lily and Moira to the upper windows and take up arms with Carlyle, but don't shoot until I give the signal. I want to hear Radcliffe out first. If I can keep this attack from turning violent, I will."

The servants nodded and hurried upstairs. The rain was coming harder now.

"Jack, I don't want to put your men in any more danger than necessary, but I could use your help. We need people who are physically skilled to climb onto the roof and tear down the wire rigging. Edward knows the full plan—he can explain."

Jack nodded solemnly. "We've performed acrobatics at times. We shall be honored to do so again."

Thunder crackled, strangely long and sustained. I frowned, turning toward the sound, and realized it wasn't thunder at all, but hoofbeats. I made out the light of a half dozen lanterns shining through the trees.

I squeezed Montgomery's hand, hard. "Everyone, get to your posts. They're coming!"

The riders came through the pouring rain with all the force of a train engine. Montgomery and Balthazar had silently slipped into their hidden positions on either side of the entryway into the courtyard, with two rifles each and knives strapped to their chests. From where I stood on the front stairs, letting the rain pummel me, I could just make out the brim of Montgomery's hat. A glance at the windows overhead revealed the tips of rifles at the ready—Carlyle and McKenna and Lily and Moira, ready to follow my orders as they'd once followed Elizabeth's.

I stood alone on the steps as the riders formed a half circle in the courtyard. Five riders, then ten, then twenty, filled the space with steaming horses and rain-slick jackets. I held my head high. The night of the bonfire, Elizabeth had looked so regal and confident. I hoped to summon some of her courage.

The horses stamped in the flooded gravel. The water came up past their hooves, even to their knees in the deeper puddles. Four of the riders held oil-wrapped torches that cast light over the riders' faces and uniforms. Half wore dark blue police slickers, though judging by their unshaven beards and slouched posture, I doubted that a single one of them was an actual officer. The rest of Radcliffe's men didn't even bother with disguises: hulking men with thick beards and worn leather jackets splattered with mud.

Mercenaries for hire, all of them.

One rider came forward through the flooded court-yard, as the others parted to let him pass. He held no torch, but I didn't need one to recognize him. That ramrod-straight back. The eyes so light blue they were almost white. Dark hair the same color as Lucy's.

John Radcliffe.

He seemed taller than I remembered. To me he'd always been a financier, the type who huddled over led-gers and accounts in an office, and I'd hardly cast him a second look when Lucy and I had been friends. Now, he sat atop his horse as though he commanded the night itself. My confidence wavered for a moment. I glanced toward the barn, praying Lucy was tucked safely away with the little girls. At least she was spared having to face her own father.

"Miss Moreau." His voice was deep and just a little bit weary. "I've gone to great expense to find you."

I squeezed my fists together. "Elizabeth von Stein is dead. Ballentyne belongs to me now, and I haven't given permission for you or your men to enter my lands. Leave now and we won't shoot you."

I pointed to the row of rifles in the upper windows aimed in their direction.

A brief ripple of uncertainty ran through the other riders, making the horses snort and paw at the gravel, but Radcliffe didn't flinch. "I don't care if you're mistress of this estate or a maid cleaning my boots. You can see my men are armed as well. We can avoid bloodshed, but that's up to you." He adjusted his horse's reins. "Now, where is Lucy?"

I blinked. Of all the demands I had expected him to make, this hadn't been one of them. I'd told Lucy myself that he was only using her affection to learn my location. Had I been wrong? Was I simply looking at a banker from Belgrave Square who just wanted his daughter back?

From the corner of my eye, I noticed a wire snaking down the southern wall, hidden in the shadows. It came from the window of Elizabeth's laboratory, where a few shadowy hands were lowering it as quickly as possible. There was a flash of green satin, and then a dark-skinned face looking down.

Jack Serra and his troupe, holding up their part of the plan.

I swallowed, trying to regain my confidence. "You forfeited your right to be a father to her when you joined the King's Club. You knew what they were planning, whether you've since renounced them or not. Now, tell me why you've come or get off my land."

A murmur ran through his men, and Radcliffe eyed me closely. "I've already told you, Miss Moreau. I came for my daughter. You made her doubt her own family, put her life at risk, and have her imprisoned here. I've come to take her home."

My confidence vanished. Had I truly been so wrong, all along? Across the courtyard I tried to meet Montgomery's eyes, but he was hidden in the shadows. I was alone. And uncertain. A drowned cat standing in the rain.

"All this is about Lucy?" I stammered. "Twenty armed men?"

Radcliffe raised an eyebrow. "Why did you think I would come, if not for her?"

I swallowed. "We killed Isambard Lessing and Dr. Hastings and Inspector Newcastle. They were friends of yours."

A silence ran through the courtyard as a strange look flickered over Radcliffe's face. To my shock, he let out a deep laugh. "*Revenge?* You think that's why I've spent so much time to discover your location? Miss Moreau, you *are* prone to dramatics. I knew Newcastle a few weeks, nothing more. Lessing was a thief. Dr. Hastings, a cad. Why would I care about the deaths of worthless men?"

My heart pounded harder. I'd been so wrong.

From the far end of the courtyard, I saw a flicker of movement. Balthazar, stepping slightly out of the shadows. He tapped his nose twice slowly. I stared at him, until I remembered our conversation from earlier. Balthazar's keen nose could smell if a man was lying by the odor of his sweat. One tap for truth. Two taps for a lie.

Radcliffe was lying.

Fury swelled in me, along with determination. He wasn't going to make a fool of me, not again. "You've missed your calling," I said. "You should have been an actor, not a banker. I can't imagine that a truly dedicated father would show up at the house that gave his daughter shelter with twenty heavily armed mercenaries and threaten her best friend. I was there for Lucy when you weren't. She was terrified of you when she learned what you were involved with. She hates you. Now tell me why you've really come, or we can end this in bloodshed right now."

For a moment, his face betrayed nothing. Those fair blue eyes seemed as icy as the rest of him. Then, slowly, he signaled his men to lower their arms.

"I wasn't lying, not entirely. I do want Lucy back. She belongs with her family, in London, not living as an outcast up here in the wastelands. But yes, there is another reason I have come. It is a business arrangement that I want, and you see, I won't take no for an answer. They are here to see to that." He signaled to his men.

"What do you want?" I demanded.

"The only thing of value in that house, besides my daughter. Victor Frankenstein's journals. Don't look so shocked—I've known about them for years. Your father was the one who told me about them, in fact. He and Professor von Stein used to be friends. We were all students at the time. He borrowed from Frankenstein's ideas to create his own science. You were his inspiration, Miss Moreau, but Victor Frankenstein's research was the source of his skill." He held out a hand, looking like his patience was growing thin. "Now, hand over the journals and release Lucy back to me, and my men won't slaughter everyone in this house."

I stood straighter. "Lucy isn't going anywhere, and whatever my father told you about Victor Frankenstein's science, he lied. There are no journals. They were long ago destroyed."

He scratched his chin. "Miss Moreau, I've come too far to be lied to now. I have been laying plans to get my hands on those journals for the past ten years. I'm very aware that they exist. In fact, they are the reason I joined the King's Club and pushed for them to seek out your father's research. I knew eventually it would lead to the greatest research of all, the research your father based his own work on—Perpetual Anatomy."

His confidence made my own waver. He wasn't delighting in this, wasn't relishing my fear. He simply wanted something and would stop at nothing. That terrified me most of all.

"Didn't you ever wonder who within the King's Club was devising these complicated plans? It certainly wasn't Hastings, or that ambitious Inspector Newcastle. It was me whispering in their ears. I planned on hiring mercenaries to murder them as soon as we had our hands on your father's research, but I didn't have to. You did my dirty work for me."

Images flashed in my head of that night in the King's Club's smoking room: clawed-out eyes, dead bodies dripping blood. My throat was so dry I could scarcely breathe. "Why is this so important to you? You aren't a scientist."

He gave a mirthless laugh. "Must you really ask an aging man why he seeks immortality? Though my interests are not purely personal. A vast number of people could benefit from a second chance at life. I believe your father's carcass is still buried on that island of his, come to think of it. We made a pact, you know. If one of us were to die, the other would obtain Frankenstein's science and reverse the situation. I'm quite certain that the great Henri Moreau and I could make a fortune off this research. A fortune I shall use to give Lucy every advantage, as she is entitled to. Now tell me which of us is more interested in her happiness."

My hands shook like they belonged to some other body. I tried to reassure myself that his threats were hollow. Father's body would be too decomposed to reanimate, and yet the fear of it, unreasonable as it was, left me so terrified I could hardly find my voice.

"Turn them over and I'll leave peacefully," he said. "Don't, and my men will kill every living thing on the property and tear through the manor until we find the journals ourselves. You're ruthless, Miss Moreau, and so am I. Don't test me."

The tension crackled in the air. From the stone gates behind Radcliffe's men, Balthazar and Montgomery peeked out with their rifles at the ready. Overhead, the servants would be poised to fire. I knew McKenna would be damned before she let the likes of Radcliffe seize the manor that gave them all sanctuary.

It would be a bloodbath—but sometimes blood was the price to pay.

I took a deep breath to give the order to fire. Just before I spoke, movement at the southern tower caught my gaze. A figure was climbing down the electric wire Jack Serra's men had lowered. Edward. I'd never seen him move so fast, even when he'd been the Beast.

I dared a glance back at Radcliffe; he hadn't noticed. A terrible moment of indecision overcame me. Did I let Edward risk it? Or did I give the order to fire?

The windmill spun faster and faster.

A low hum began, and the hair on the back of my neck started to rise. I jerked my head toward the tower window, where I could just make out Jack with his hand on the electrical switch. I couldn't have stopped him now, even if I'd wanted to.

He flipped the switch, and sparks rained down the southern tower.

I screamed. The horses went wild, pawing at the gravel as their riders fought to regain control. Amid all the chaos, Edward threw himself to his knees into the deepest end of the courtyard, and plunged the live wire into the water.

With a terrible crackle and burst of smoke, the electricity spread.

I threw my hands over my ears; men cried out, horses screamed. Not even the rain could clear the air of the smell of burned flesh. When I dared to open my eyes, half of Radcliffe's men were dead, the other half disoriented and dying.

Montgomery and Balthazar still hid in the lee of the stone gate, on pillars that kept them dry and safe.

Edward, however, lay facedown in the water.

He wasn't moving.

"Edward!"

I started toward his body but jerked back as a bullet hit the gravel inches from my foot. It came from Radcliffe. Atop his horse, on the highest ground near the front steps, he hadn't been electrocuted. Through the rain, he aimed his pistol at me again with unwavering determination. I fumbled for the pistol I'd strapped to my leg, but my skirts were soaked and heavy, and I collapsed back onto the wet gravel. He spurred his horse closer.

From the corner of my eye, I saw Montgomery running from his hidden post, rifle aimed at Radcliffe, but I knew he wouldn't make it in time. I stared into the barrel of Radcliffe's gun and saw my future there. Blackness. Death. There'd be no one to bring *me* back.

A volley of gunshots rang out overhead as the servants took aim. With a grunt of pain, Radcliffe clutched his thigh where a bullet had gone clean through. McKenna grinned down at me from the window before reloading. Beside her, Lily and Moira and Carlyle were all raining down bullets on Radcliffe's few remaining men.

I stumbled to my feet, scrambling over the slick gravel onto the stone steps, and took shelter from the gunfire, crouching behind a statue of a lion. My pulse raced as bullets flew around me. One clipped the stairs by my foot. Another chipped the lion's ear. The wooden entrance to the manor was only a few feet away, but I couldn't make it. I'd be exposed for too long.

Carefully, I peeked over the lion statue. As best I could tell, only four of Radcliffe's men had been on ground high enough to survive the electrocution. They'd taken shelter behind the bodies of their comrades' dead horses. Montgomery and Balthazar both crouched by the gate, taking careful aim, narrowly avoiding being shot themselves.

I crawled to the other side of the statue to look for Edward's body. I prayed that he'd awoken and managed to crawl away, yet my heart sank. He still lay facedown in the puddle. Blood trailed in the water from where an errant bullet must have hit him. I bit my lip, willing him to move.

"Get up," I urged. "Prove that you can't be killed that easily."

But he didn't. One of Radcliffe's men caught sight of me and started racing up the steps, knife in one hand.

"*Blast.*" I tore at my skirt to get my pistol out. Finally my fingers found the cold, sturdy handle, and I pulled it free of its holster. I aimed, but panic made my hands tremble, and I missed the man by a few feet. I scrambled to reload, but the gun slipped from my wet fingers and tumbled down the stairs.

I lunged after it. I was exposed, an easy target, but I

had to get that pistol. The officer had his knife at the ready. Another few feet and he'd be on me.

A blur came from the rain, a flash of white shirt and brown wide-brimmed hat that tackled the officer to the ground.

"Montgomery!"

I grabbed my pistol and aimed it at the pair scrapping in the gravel, but I didn't dare shoot for fear of hitting Montgomery by accident. Across the courtyard, Radcliffe's head whirled at my call. A pistol gleamed in his hand as he aimed at the pair, not caring if he accidentally shot his own man.

He fired.

I cried out at the sound. Montgomery jerked upright, tossing the wet hair out of his eyes. For a terrible instant I thought he'd been shot and my heart missed a beat. But then the other man slumped to the ground, blood pouring out of a hole in his back. I let out a ragged cry.

Montgomery hadn't been shot.

My relief was short-lived. Radcliffe took advantage of the chaos to grab the back of Montgomery's shirt and press the pistol against his temple.

"Give the order for your men to cease fire, Miss Moreau." He jerked his chin toward the upper windows. "Or I'll shoot him in the head right now."

"Stop!" I called without hesitation. "McKenna, Carlyle, hold your fire!"

One more errant bullet went off, and then there was silence. Smoke cleared as gunpowder settled, the night air thick with the smell of blood and sulfur and the moans of a few dying men.

"You two," Radcliffe said, nodding to a few of his mercenaries. "Keep your pistols trained on this man. If he moves, shoot him."

Blood pooled from a nick on Montgomery's arm. His blue eyes met mine.

I couldn't let it end like this.

Radcliffe wiped away a line of blood running down his nose, breathing hard. "Tell your staff to throw their weapons down here and come outside."

I clenched my jaw. I might as well be ordering McKenna and the others to commit suicide. "Go to hell," I spat.

"Wait!" McKenna leaned out the upstairs window. "We'll do as you say. I'm sorry, mistress, but it's our duty to protect you as much as this home." She threw down her rifle and I winced. With Edward immobile, she and the others had been our greatest asset. Moira and Lily threw theirs down as well, followed by Carlyle's heavy old Weston. The pistols clattered to the ground, where one of Radcliffe's heavyset mercenaries picked them up.

"You can kill all of us and scour the house," I seethed. "You'll never find those journals."

Radcliffe didn't seem troubled by my threat. The front door groaned open and the servants filed out, defenseless. They lined up under the eave of the door.

Radcliffe's jaw shifted as he looked among them. "Tell Lucy to come out as well. I want to see that she hasn't been harmed."

My stomach twisted. My own father had never shown such concern over me, not even when my life had been in danger. He'd only studied my fear like another one of his twisted experiments.

"She isn't in the house. She's hiding out because she doesn't want to see you. You might as well leave, because you'll never get her or the journals."

"Leave?" His cold countenance was falling, and there was rage beneath it. "Perhaps, after you are dead."

"I'm the only one who's memorized the information. Shoot me, and the knowledge will be lost forever."

Something about my words caught his attention. A strange look gleamed in his pale blue eyes. "You've memorized the science, have you? Suppose I were to kill Montgomery, then. Journals or not, you would have to use Frankenstein's science to bring him back. All I'd have to do was watch over your shoulder. It's your choice how we get there, Miss Moreau, but I assure you we'll reach the same conclusion."

I balled my fist, furious. "It's Mrs. James now. *Not* Moreau."

Radcliffe cocked his gun. "A difference I care nothing about."

Time slowed, my vision becoming a series of flashes as panic took hold of my body. I couldn't let it end like this, and yet I was helpless. There was the pistol in Radcliffe's hand. His finger on the trigger. Montgomery's eyes sinking closed, waiting for the bullet that would take his life.

Out of the fog lurched a figure. It seemed like a ghost at

first, a shadow. I saw a flash of tweed cloak, pale white skin, as the figure threw itself in front of Montgomery's kneeling body.

"Wait!" the figure cried. Only then did I recognize the voice.

Lucy.

The sound of a bullet ripped through the night. It was too late. Radcliffe had already pulled the trigger.

I stumbled back, stunned. Montgomery's eyes flew open at the gunshot. Lucy rolled over, her hood falling back. Dark brown hair not so different from my own spilled out. My throat closed tight.

"Lucy!" I collapsed beside her.

"Papa," she choked as a line of blood appeared at the edge of her lips. I pressed a hand against my mouth, attempting to seal in a scream, but it didn't help. My desperate wail rang out over the moors as I scrambled close to her, touching her face, her hair, her cloak.

"Lucy. God, no!"

But her eyes weren't on me. They were fixed on Radcliffe. His pistol clattered to the ground. His icy facade was gone now, and there was only horror at what he'd done.

"*Lucy?* No . . ."

"Papa." She had to force words out as more blood trickled from her mouth, "I didn't think you would shoot me."

My eyes trailed down her body in horror. Her cloak and dress were already soaked through. The bullet must have hit an artery. Blood was everywhere.

"I didn't know," Radcliffe pleaded. He wasn't the cold

leader of the King's Club now; he was merely a father watching his daughter die. "I didn't see you. Lucy . . ."

Her eyes rolled back in her head. I felt frozen. Another part of me took over, taking in the scene with the objective eyes of a scientist. The line of blood at her mouth. The paleness of her skin. The way her chest had stopped rising and falling.

It was too late.

THIRTY-EIGHT

I PRESSED MY HANDS against the bullet wound as if that could somehow keep the life inside her. Montgomery tore free from the startled men and knelt next to me, feeling her pulse. His movements were skilled, yet there was a dazed look to his eyes.

"She's gone," he said, as if struggling to believe it himself.

I sank back on my heels. I couldn't think. I couldn't breathe. My entire body had gone numb, as if it was my blood dripping out into the mud. *Gone?* The girl I'd grown up with, the only friend who'd stood by me after the scandal, the daughter who'd abandoned her wealthy life for what was right?

"You did this!" Radcliffe hauled me to my feet next to Montgomery. Montgomery stood, too, and Radcliffe's remaining men aimed their rifles at our heads. "It was supposed to be *you* dead, Mr. James. Lucy shouldn't ever have been brought into this!"

"You brought her into this!" I screamed, twisting out

of his hand. "She fled with us to escape *you*!"

He blinked. For a few terrible seconds, none of us spoke. I threw a look to where Edward's body still lay in the puddle. Was he truly gone, like her? Had we lost them both? Had we lost *everything*?

"Leave," I spat at Radcliffe. "Take your men and go. What do a few journals matter when your daughter just died by your own hands?"

He looked at me as if I were some nightmarish specter. He dragged a hand over his mouth, murmuring something to himself, refusing to believe it. "Died?" he said aloud, testing the word. "No."

All his mad plans about acquiring the journals and selling the science seemed like an afterthought now. He turned to the courtyard wall, breathing heavily. In a way, I understood how he felt. My best friend was dead. After that, did anything matter?

"Juliet," Montgomery whispered. "I'm sorry. I don't know what to say."

Radcliffe's men still stood around us with rifles aimed. I could tell Montgomery wanted to fold me into his arms, but we dared not. Radcliffe still faced the wall, arms braced against it, shaking his head back and forth.

I couldn't tear my eyes off Lucy's body. So many people I loved had died. I'd buried too many of them. We'd brought Edward back, but his fate was unknown now. If he lived, I couldn't imagine what he'd do when he learned about Lucy. I looked up at the tower where I'd brought him back at her insistence.

"The tower," I whispered, more to myself than anyone else. "Montgomery, if I could take her to the tower . . ."

"No." Montgomery's eyes flickered with warning. "Don't think like that."

But Radcliffe had turned from the wall and was looking at me with wide eyes. He'd heard me and put together what I meant. "The tower," he repeated, and looked toward the window that showed Elizabeth's equipment. He swallowed. "Elizabeth's laboratory. That's it, isn't it, Miss Moreau? You can bring her back with Frankenstein's science. She doesn't have to stay dead."

"It's impossible," Montgomery said. "It's ungodly."

"I didn't ask you, Mr. James." Radcliffe's light eyes were fixated on mine. "We understand each other, don't we, Miss Moreau? We can both have Lucy back."

My mouth felt dry. I pressed a hand to my head. "I don't know."

"*I* do." He grabbed my arm, dragging me toward the house. "You will bring her back, or I'll slaughter everyone in this household. Bring my daughter's body," he called to his officers. "And keep a gun on Montgomery James. Lock him in the cellar until this is done."

I twisted to look behind me, where one of his men walked Montgomery with his hands clenched behind his head. They dragged us inside the foyer, where the electric lights stung my eyes.

"You there, housekeeper," he ordered McKenna. "Show my associate to the cellar where we can lock up Mr.

James. Miss Moreau, you and I are headed for the tower."

He dragged me toward the stairs, while an officer carried Lucy's lifeless body behind us.

"Juliet, wait," Montgomery called. I paused just long enough to meet his eyes. A million things could be said between us, but he chose only one. "Remember what I told you. You aren't your father's daughter. You choose your own fate."

The words sank into me more deeply with each step toward the tower. The world around me seemed dim despite the electric lights. Only my thoughts blazed. For so long I'd fought against the idea of turning into my father, only to accept it with a feeling of inevitability. Was I now to uproot all my beliefs once more?

I clutched Jack Serra's water charm, wishing for magic when I knew none existed.

We reached the landing, where the portraits of the von Steins and the Ballentynes of old seemed to whisper to me, but what they wanted, I wasn't certain. The only thing I was certain of was Radcliffe's steel grip on my arm, my best friend dead, and Montgomery's final words.

You choose your own fate.

At the top of the stairs, Radcliffe kicked open the laboratory door. The smell of roses met me, and my stomach clenched to think of Elizabeth's and Hensley's ashes on the wind.

"Put Lucy there," Radcliffe ordered his mercenary, nodding toward the surgical table.

He released me, knowing there was nowhere I could run. He started to pull out the books on the laboratory shelves.

"You won't find Frankenstein's journals in here," I said. "Elizabeth hid them. The staff doesn't know where."

He steadied me with a cold look. "I shall make you tell me, Miss Moreau, but you have more important work at the moment." He brushed a hand gently over Lucy's hair. His eyes scanned the tools, the metal trays and utensils. "I trust you have everything you need."

I glanced toward the window desperately, wanting to buy time. "Lightning. I can only perform the procedure if there's a strong enough electric shock."

He pushed back the curtains. "The rain hasn't stopped. It'll only be a matter of time before a storm strikes. That should give you time to ready the body and prepare for the procedure. I'll return soon."

"Wait! I can't do it on my own. I need Montgomery. He's a surgeon."

Radcliffe gave me a withering look. "And so are you."

He slammed the door shut.

I tore a strip of cloth from my dress and plugged the keyhole so the prying eyes of the officer standing guard couldn't see.

A steady *drip drip drip* started behind me, but I didn't dare turn around.

I only stared at that door. Radcliffe wouldn't open it again until he heard Lucy's voice. But if I brought her back, he would know Frankenstein's science was possible. He would tear the house apart until he found the Origin Journals, and he'd sell the research to unscrupulous men who would bring back countless dead bodies, perhaps even Henri Moreau's. And yet this was Lucy. I couldn't imagine life without her. With the exception of Montgomery, she'd been the only person in my life who had stood by me through the scandal. She'd defied her own parents to sneak to the park with me and sip stolen gin and giggle over boys, as though I was just a regular girl. She was my tether to the real world. She was my best friend.

How could I not bring her back?

Slowly, dread tiptoeing up my spine, I turned toward the surgical table. The *drip drip drip* continued. It was blood running off the side of the table, pooling on the stone floor and rolling toward a metal drainage grate. With trembling fingers I peeled back her blood-soaked coat.

The bullet had struck her in the center of the chest, just below the two little freckles she used to think looked like a constellation. It must have grazed the right ventricle of her heart, explaining the profuse bleeding. It would require removing the bullet, stitching up the torn ventricle, setting the broken ribs, and sealing the wound.

All within my skill. It wouldn't take but an hour of careful attention. My fingers already twitched to pick up a scalpel and begin the work that came so naturally.

My feet felt warm, and I looked down to find her blood had seeped into my slippers. I shrieked and kicked off my shoes, throwing them across the room, scrambling back into the corner of the laboratory.

I watched the line of blood slowly weaving among the flagstones toward me.

This wasn't a patient. This wasn't a specimen.

This was Lucy.

I pulled my knees in tight, trying to calm my breath, looking at the pale curve of Lucy's dead hand hanging off the table. Henri Moreau wouldn't have hesitated to reanimate her. If Montgomery hadn't told me the truth, I'd be reaching for the scalpel even now.

But my father wasn't in my blood. He wasn't even my father. He was just a stranger's skeleton on a faraway island. Which left me alone with the body of my best friend and a thousand unanswered questions, but only one mattered:

What should I do?

I glanced again at the scalpel on the floor. A wild idea entered my head. There was one way to spare me this terrible decision. I could take the scalpel, make two quick slits, and let my blood pool on the floor with Lucy's. I could join her in whatever dark place of peace she was in now.

I crawled toward the scalpel slowly, picked it up, and pressed it lightly against my wrist, just to test the feel of it. A person would bleed dry in ten minutes, but lose consciousness in two. Two minutes and it could all be over. Radcliffe wouldn't find the Origin Journals in Elizabeth's secret hiding place. Frankenstein's science would end. Lucy would still be dead, but I'd be with her, at least.

I bit my lip so hard I tasted blood, tart and salty.

Was I ready to die?

With an anguished cry, I threw the scalpel across the

room. I pushed to my feet and paced to the window, throwing it open and breathing in fresh air mixed with rain. In the distance, thunder rumbled.

Below, in the fading light of the house, I could just make out the barn. A lumbering figure moved slowly along the exterior wall of the courtyard. It was Balthazar, who must have snuck away from Radcliffe's men and was now headed to the barn to take over Lucy's role sheltering the little children.

Balthazar hadn't been made with a purpose, but he had found one.

If he could, then maybe I could, too.

I *wasn't* a madman's daughter. I wasn't a Moreau. I wasn't a Ballentyne either, not in my heart. Before, I had feared I'd be left with nothing and no identity, but now I realized that very lack of identity left me stripped free of shackles. For the first time in my life, I could make my own decisions, unbound by the shadow of my father. From now on, every thought, every word, and every decision was my own to make.

Starting now.

I turned to the table. Father wouldn't have hesitated to bring Lucy back, but I wasn't my father, and it was time I started making my own decisions.

IN DEATH, LUCY LOOKED older than seventeen. There was a darkness around her eyes that made me imagine what she'd look like at twenty, thirty, forty. She would have been a good wife and a good mother. Maybe in a different life she'd have married Edward and had children of her own playing Catch the Huntsman in the hedge maze behind her house.

I brushed a strand of dark hair from her face, smoothing the wrinkles from her eyes. Her body still held the lingering warmth of life.

I could give you back that life, I thought. *I have the power.*

It wasn't long ago that Edward had been strapped down to this same table. I'd been so convinced at the time that bringing him back was right. It had been my father's ghost urging me on. Now, no voices whispered in my ear, no urges compelled my hands to act. I took a damp cloth and dabbed away the spots of blood on her face and chest.

"I could give you back your life," I whispered as my voice broke. The cloth shook in my hand as a rise of emotion swelled.

It was time to make the first decision of my life that was truly mine and not influenced by my father. I had the power to cure death, but what had new life brought to Hensley, or Frankenstein's monster, or Edward? Only more pain.

I couldn't shake Montgomery's words that there was only one life, and we must live it well. *When you can never die,* he had said, *do you ever really live?* Lucy's life had been short, but she'd lived it well. She had chosen her own fate, bleak though it was.

I closed my eyes and listened one final time for voices. For my father's, for my mother's, for Elizabeth's. There was only silence, and in that silence, I let my own voice speak.

The whisper was quiet, but it was there.

A tear rolled down the side of my face.

"I could bring you back," I whispered again. "But I won't."

A sob hung in my throat. I leaned over her body on the table, crying against her bloody dress. All these tools and books had held such meaning for me once, when I had yearned for Father's approval. Now I understood that such science never came without a steep cost. Pain. Suffering. Loss.

"I'm so sorry, Lucy. I can't do it. No more experimentation. No more ends justifying the means. No more screams in the night. I'm not like my father."

With a deep breath, I wrapped the coat tightly around Lucy's body, hiding the wounds the best I could, and carefully dragged her body off the table. I set her on the floor, sitting upright with head slumped as though she'd fallen asleep. There was a hard object in her pocket; I took it out.

A matchbox, empty now. She must have taken it to light a small fire in the barn to keep the girls warm overnight.

An idea worked its way into my head. I couldn't get to the Origin Journals, but I could make sure Elizabeth's personal notes and experiments never fell into Radcliffe's hands. I began to open the books with a wild madness. I tore out the pages, crumpling them, stacking volumes. Outside, thunder cracked closer. I studied the coming storm with a grim determination. Lightning could bring a body back, yes—but it could also destroy.

"I'm sorry, Elizabeth," I whispered. "I have to break my promise."

A creak from the eastern wall caught my attention. It came from the drainage grate that emptied Lucy's blood from the room. It must be some of Hensley's rats crawling in the walls. They would burn if they didn't get out in time. My heart pounded, but there was nothing I could do. Their fate was their own.

I poured Elizabeth's vat of sterile alcohol over the books and papers. Four generations of women protecting this knowledge, passing it down, and it would all end tonight. As much as I admired what the von Stein women were trying to do, I no longer agreed with them.

In my careless hurry, alcohol splashed on my dress.

"Blast." A crack of lightning lit up the sky. Any moment lightning would strike the rod and all this would go up in flames—and my soaked dress with it unless I found a way to escape.

I peered out the window, but the four-story fall was too dangerous. That left only the door, which was locked and guarded by one of Radcliffe's armed officers. More scurrying came from the grate, and I thought of those poor rats trapped in the walls. I couldn't save them. I couldn't save Lucy.

I couldn't even save myself.

They say a sort of peace falls over you when you know that you're going to die. I had seen enough people die to know that wasn't true, and yet as I watched the storm grow closer, I did feel a strange calm. It was a letting go of the determination that had kept me alive this far. It was the acknowledgment to Death that he had won, and I was a fool for thinking I could defeat him. I'd cheated him enough for one lifetime.

I sank to my knees in the puddle of blood and alcohol. I'd killed so many people, including the man I thought was my father. If this was the trade I had to make to keep this science lost to time, then I was ready.

Montgomery was right. We only had one life. One chance to make the right choice. And this was mine: to burn with the rest of Ballentyne.

THIRTY-NINE

WITH MY HEAD BURIED in my arms, waiting for the moment when lightning would strike, I didn't notice that the scurrying sounds had changed into footsteps.

"Juliet," came a hushed whisper, "are you there?"

I jerked my head up. Montgomery's voice sounded like a ghost's.

His hands reached out from the grate.

"Montgomery!" I scrambled to the grate, threading my fingers through the bars. "I didn't think there was a passageway to the laboratory."

"I still have the map." He held the crumpled old paper to the light. "Radcliffe's men locked me in the cellar and I managed to make my way into the passages. There were markings on the map that indicated a passage once existed here, but it had been boarded up. I was able to break through. Now we just have to get you out." He tugged on the bars, but they didn't give.

"Listen to me!" I clutched the bars. "There's no time

for that. You have to get out of the walls. Get out of this manor, *now*. Tell all the servants to flee."

Lightning crashed closer this time, and I shrieked. Montgomery at last noticed the bonfire I'd built of books and journals and soaked with alcohol. His eyes went wide. "What have you done, Juliet?"

"What needed to be done," I said. "You were right. The science is too dangerous to exist. Once lightning strikes, the fire will burn the entire house, including Frankenstein's journals."

"Are you mad?" he said. "It'll burn you, too!"

He pulled at the bars, muscles straining. I pushed on his hands, trying to pry them off the bars. "Just leave me. Go!"

A crash came from behind me. I smelled the ozone a second before I saw the spark. The entire room vibrated just as it had before, a humming coming from the metal equipment, and Montgomery grabbed my hand through the grate a second before the lightning rod pulsed.

A spark flashed. The alcohol caught. The room erupted in flames.

I screamed and covered my head with my hands. "Get out of here, Montgomery!"

I tore away from him, scrambling to the far wall as a wave of heat struck me, and threw open the window to let out the billowing black smoke. The servants and Jack Serra's troupe would see it and know to get out of the house, but that still left Montgomery in the walls. He might not get out in time.

"I'm not leaving you here." He pulled on the grate with all his strength, but it was useless. Only Edward might have had the strength, but for all I knew Edward was still unconscious—or worse.

I hugged myself into a ball, terrified of the painful death that would come. A scraping sound came, and incredulously, stone dust crumbled down from around the metal. Before my very eyes, the grate began to tear out of the stone. Montgomery let out a groan, pulling the bars even harder. I blinked in shock. It shouldn't have been possible. I had heard stories of normal humans developing incredible strength in times of crisis, people able to lift huge weights or run for miles with a broken leg. Such strength never came without a cost. Sometimes it could even kill a person.

"Montgomery, stop! You'll hurt yourself!"

But he didn't stop. Muscles straining to the point of giving out, he pulled on the grate until it tore out of the wall with a clatter.

"Climb through!" he yelled.

It took my brain a moment to comprehend that he had actually done it, before I scrambled toward him and crawled through the hole. I collapsed onto a grimy stone floor. It was cool to the touch, covered with dust and cobwebs. Everything was a strange kind of dark, like the world had been cast in shadows. I sat up, struggling for breath.

"You inhaled a lot of smoke," Montgomery said. "It's making you sick."

I clenched my hands over his, squeezing tight. "I told

you to run." I coughed. "To save yourself. It's impossible, what you did."

His fingers brushed back my tangled hair, damp with sweat. "Love can sometimes do the impossible. You're mad if you think I would have left you there to die."

I pressed my lips against his. The sound of fire spreading through the manor roared in the distance, and the stone under our knees was warming, but I needed to feel his lips on mine. If we only had one life, then I wanted to live it right.

Something crashed in the house, jarring us out of the kiss. His arm tightened around my back. The muscles of his biceps shook strangely from the superhuman exertion; I needed to get him out of here and treat him properly before his muscles gave out completely.

"Come on," I said. "We're not out of danger yet."

I grabbed his hand and pulled him away from the burning tower. Smoke was already seeping into the ceiling of the passageway. We moved faster, and I tripped over a brick and fell against the wall, flinching. The dust was disturbed here, and I looked closer at the uneven brick. I'd tripped over it before, with Hensley.

"We're by the library!" I said. "That means this passage leads down to the tunnel that goes outside, the same one I used to escape the Beast."

The roar of the fire was getting louder. It took me back to another time, another fire, one that roared into the island night. Father had died in that one. Maybe I'd die the same way, fated to end up like him.

No, I reminded myself. *We choose our own fate.*

Montgomery coughed. Smoke was so thick that it was hard to make out his face even from a few steps away. We kept low where the air was still breathable and descended stairs, sliding more than climbing, until the temperature lowered. The stone walls here were blessedly cool. Our feet splashed in the flooded basement.

"There it is!" I spotted a low wooden door that led to the outside. But when I turned around, my smile faded. One glance told me Montgomery's superhuman strength was failing. There was only so long a body could do the impossible.

"The south garden is just beyond this door," I urged. "It's jammed—we just have to push through. Don't give up yet, Montgomery."

He nodded. I counted, and on three we both poured the last of our strength into that wooden door. It slid open an inch, then two, and at last wide enough to crawl through.

A cold wind bit at me as rain stung my face and mixed with tears of relief. Montgomery came through the passageway behind me. I clenched my hands in the mud, wanting to collapse into it.

Laughing with exhaustion, I crawled over to him. His hand tightened on mine as his eyes closed. I rested a hand on his chest, enjoying the steady beat of his heart and knowing that everything would at long last be all right.

"We're safe now," I said, brushing the rain from his face. "We made it."

The sound of a boot scuffing came through the rain, and I had just enough strength to look up. Radcliffe's fair blue eyes stared at me. He aimed his pistol at my head.

All the joy drained out of me.

"Miss Moreau. Where, may I ask, is Lucy?"

Anger flooded into me. I pictured Lucy's body in the tower, slumped against the wall as though sleeping. Dead by her own father's hand.

From the other end of the courtyard, a crash came as flames exploded through the upper windows of the tower. Smoke billowed into the dark night sky.

"She's already gone," I said, coughing. "Burned in that fire along with all of Frankenstein's equipment and journals."

Radcliffe's face went slack as he stared at the smoke that consumed his daughter's body. There was loss there that I was sure my father had never felt, and for a moment I felt pity for this man I hated. But then he turned to me with a furious growl.

"Get up!" He dug the pistol against my forehead. When I stumbled, he wrenched me to my feet, digging the pistol in harder.

"Pick him up as well," Radcliffe ordered to two of his men, nodding at Montgomery. Worry spiked in me again. Montgomery was flat in the mud, streaked with rain. Radcliffe's men tried to lift him, but he was much larger than both of them, and they could barely lift his chest. His eyes were closed.

My heartbeat sped. Had he passed out from exhaustion? I looked around the courtyard frantically. There was no sign of the Balthazar or the little girls, so Radcliffe must not have discovered their hiding place. I hadn't seen Jack

Serra and his troupe since they'd lowered the electric wire, but they were nimble acrobats and would be able to escape the burning building. At last I saw McKenna, Carlyle, Lily, and Moira huddled under a tree that gave them little shelter in the rain, guarded by one of Radcliffe's men. That left only Edward, and his body still lay in the same place, faceup in the gravel, blood surrounding him.

Faceup? I thought. *He had landed and been shot facedown.*

My heart beat faster. Was he alive?

This exhilarating thought was met with a crash from the house as part of the roof fell in. The servants shrieked, and even the mercenaries seemed nervous so close to a raging fire. The only one who didn't flinch was Radcliffe.

"There's no point anymore," I said. "The research is gone. You've lost."

A low moan came from the courtyard, and Edward's arm twitched. Radcliffe took notice, just as I did. "Not dead yet?" he called. "I suppose all that's left is to finish the job, since you've made it perfectly clear you aren't willing to bargain, Miss Moreau."

"Don't!" I cried, but Radcliffe's mercenary had a rifle aimed at me.

Radcliffe cocked his pistol, aiming for Edward's head, but then paused. He holstered his firearm and took out a hunting knife instead. "No. A bullet is too easy. I'll cut open his throat so deep not even you could stitch it back, Miss Moreau, and then do the same to everyone else in this household."

He hauled Edward to his feet, the knife glinting at his throat, cutting into the outer layer of skin. My heart beat wildly as a line of blood rolled down his chest. It flowed too freely, not at all like Hensley's had. It made me start. If Edward could bleed like that, could he also die? How much damage could his body take before shutting down completely?

My eyes met Edward's over the glinting knife. Radcliffe didn't know that he was stronger than most, possibly even immortal. Edward raised an eyebrow, asking me a silent question. He could overpower Radcliffe easily, but not before Radcliffe slit his throat.

I shook my head, telling Edward not to try anything.

"Let him go," I said. "Return to London and we'll pretend none of this ever happened."

"I don't give up so easily."

My mind whirled with ideas for how to bring him down. I caught sight of a gleaming metal object—the lightning rod. When the roof had collapsed, it had landed in the center of the courtyard, revealing a jagged end.

I took a step closer to the rod. Edward followed my gaze with understanding.

"There's a problem with your plan," I said slowly, taking another step closer.

Radcliffe moved the knife closer against Edward's neck. Flames burst out of the upper windows, raining glass to the front steps.

"I don't give up so easily either." I lunged for the lightning rod. It was heavier than I'd expected, but that only meant it would kill quicker. I aimed it at Edward's chest, and by extension Radcliffe's chest behind him. "Let him go."

Radcliffe laughed low in his throat. "You really expect me to believe you'd murder your own friend just to kill me, too?"

My eyes met Edward's. Memories flashed in an instant: a curled body in a rocking dinghy, the boy behind the waterfall, the boy who'd fought against the Beast.

"Believe it," I said.

I rammed the rod into Edward's chest with all my strength. He jolted with the shock but didn't cry out. Radcliffe, however, howled with pain. The force pinned them both against the courtyard wall, but I hadn't the strength to push it far enough through Edward's body to entirely pierce Radcliffe's chest.

"Edward," I gasped. "I need your help."

He winced as he gripped the lightning rod, and together we thrust it all the way through his chest. Dark blood seeped from the wound, and alarm again shot through me.

How much blood could he lose and still live?

Radcliffe cried out in anguished pain as the lightning rod went straight through him. His arms went limp, the blade falling from his fingers. At last he was silent.

I picked up his pistol and aimed for the mercenaries who remained, but they were already fleeing the manor, disappearing into the darkness. I knew we wouldn't ever see them again.

I returned to Edward, close enough for his dark blood

to stain my hands. I was terrified to look up, afraid that he'd be dead, and this time I'd have killed him.

But he let out a deep sigh.

"You're alive," I whispered.

He winced, reaching for the lighting rod. I hurried to help him pull it from both Radcliffe's body and his own. Radcliffe's body sagged onto the mud, face in a puddle, no air coming from it.

Dead.

I knelt next to Edward, brushing the hair from his face. He clutched a hand to slow the seeping blood from his chest. "Nothing you can't fix, right?" A small smile played at the corners of his mouth.

I wrapped my arms around him, holding him tight, knowing that soon I'd have to tell him about Lucy. What place was there in the world for a man like him, so unnatural and yet so good?

"Go to him," Edward said, nodding toward Montgomery's unconscious body.

I pulled away, wiping my eyes. Edward gave me a gentle push, and I crawled across the muddy courtyard to where Montgomery lay. The color had drained from his face and arms. I pressed my fingers to his neck, praying to every god I knew that he wouldn't be dead. He couldn't be. Not after everything.

Someone shuffled behind me, and I smelled wet dog. Balthazar crouched next to me. Blood seeped from a gash on his shoulder, but otherwise he seemed unhurt.

"Is he alive, miss?"

Beneath my fingers there was a pulse, and I closed my eyes with gratitude. I braced my arms in the mud, crying freely now.

"Yes," I said. "He'll make it."

Balthazar patted my shoulder, and all the strength ran out of me. I hadn't realized that, like Montgomery, my body had been pushing me beyond what was humanly possible. I slumped to the mud, barely able to keep my eyes open.

"Balthazar, it's still dangerous. The fire—"

He patted my shoulder. "I'll take care of everything, miss. Rest now. It's over."

The final bit of resistance within me let go. *Over.* I let my eyes sink closed, and the last thing I felt was the soft rain against my eyelids.

FORTY

I WOKE AS MORNING broke over the moors.

The last tendrils of smoke streaked across a mottled pink sky. I was lying beneath the open ceiling of the winter garden; though all the glass had shattered, the iron skeleton still stood. I sat up, a thick quilt draped over me, still dazed from smoke poisoning, and took in the other survivors.

Edward had dragged one of the white metal chairs into the grass and sat with his back to me, facing the smoldering house. He rested his elbows on his knees, slightly hunched and stiff. Montgomery, still unconscious but breathing steadily, was laid out on the ground beside me on an old saddle blanket. A bark came at my side, and Sharkey nuzzled against me.

"Good boy," I said, scratching his ear. There was something so simple about petting a dog. Sharkey didn't understand what the burning building meant. Sharkey didn't know that Lucy was dead and the world had turned upside down time and time again.

He lay on the dusty floor, rested his head in my lap.

"I found him in the barn this morning." Balthazar lumbered over, crouching down to scratch Sharkey's back. "The fire didn't spread there. He was sleeping in the straw with the goats."

"So all the servants are safe?"

"Yes, miss."

"How's Montgomery?"

"Still hasn't woken, but the rest is good for him. His body will take some time to recover."

I let my eyes trace over his sleeping form, remembering how he'd torn open the metal grate with his bare hands. It had wrecked his body, but maybe that was a blessing. If he'd been involved in the fight with Radcliffe, there'd be no telling if he'd be alive right now.

"And Edward?"

"He bled and bled," Balthazar said. "I tried to do stitches, but these hands. . . ." He held up his giant fingers and sighed. "I haven't the dexterity. You'll have to do it, miss. I plugged the hole in his chest with straw, and that's held for now. He's like Master Hensley, I think. Not much can kill him."

"No. I don't suppose so." I drew my knees into my chest, taking a deep breath. The air was thick with the smell of smoke. A few lingering fires still crackled in the east wing; we'd probably find burning embers deep in the ruins for days. In the morning light the manor looked like a looming skeleton, all burned wood spines and ragged stone bones. A building that had stood for hundreds of years, against the attack of the Vikings, and had protected a secret that had the potential to change the world.

Now it was nothing but ashes and stone.

"What about Jack Serra and his troupe?" I asked.

Balthazar scratched the back of his neck. "They're gone, miss."

"What do you mean? Where did they go?"

"I can't say, exactly. After the fighting ended, I carried you and Montgomery here and did my best to attend to your injuries. Then I went looking for the carnival troupe but found nothing. They moved on."

"They can't have just left. Jack . . . Ajax . . . he's one of us."

"He *isn't* one of you," Balthazar explained patiently. "He's like me, you know. A creation. His ways aren't the ways of men. He isn't one to stay for good-byes."

It was the first time I'd ever heard Balthazar admit to the truth of what he was. He was so lovably naïve to the ways of the world that at times I had doubted he *did* know what he was.

"What about you?" I asked Balthazar. "Will you go, too?"

His face went very serious. "No, miss. My place is with you and Montgomery, whether I'm one of you or not."

I envied him the certainty that hung in his voice. This man had once been a creation in my father's laboratory, then a dog at Montgomery's heels. Now he was so much more. A savior. A friend. I reached over and squeezed his hand. "You do belong with us."

The wind must have carried the sound of our voices beyond the winter garden, because Edward turned in the chair and came over to us. There was a carefulness in the way he handled himself, one hand pressed against his chest, his movements guarded and slow. I jumped up to help him ease onto a low brick wall. Behind him, the stone statue of a fox watched, unscathed by the fire.

"Are you all right?" I asked.

He winced as he settled on the brick wall. Carefully, he pulled away his hand from his chest, where he'd been clutching a blood-soaked cloth packed with straw. "It doesn't hurt. That's something, at least."

There was a strain to his voice; just because he had survived the metal rod didn't meant it hadn't damaged him. "We'll get you to Quick and stitch you up there. There must be a carriage left that didn't burn." I glanced in the direction of the barn, but the space was empty now where Carlyle's wagon usually resided.

"I can help with that, mistress, if you don't mind."

It was McKenna, making her way across the heather toward us. She wore her boots and a tartan cape and though her gray-streaked hair was a bit wild, it was clear she'd bathed and rested.

"McKenna! You came back."

"Of course, little mouse. Even burned and gone, this is my home. Did you really think I could leave it for long?" She motioned behind her, to where Carlyle was hitching the mule and wagon, staring off at the ruins of his home. "We took the girls to Quick last night and settled them down. I reported the fire to the authorities—said it was caused by an errant spark in the fireplace." Her voice trailed off as her gaze drifted to the courtyard, where the bodies of the dead still lay, starting to bloat beneath the morning sunlight. "There's much work to be done, eh?"

I'd never been so thankful for someone so practical. Her tired face with the laugh-line wrinkles and the shock of white hairs mixed in with the red. Such a quiet woman, but there was strength there. *I couldn't possibly manage this place without her,* Elizabeth had said. Maybe, with McKenna's help, I could be as good a mistress to Ballentyne as Elizabeth had been.

Carlyle came over, a deep frown on his face. He and I had never really gotten on, but he'd been there when I'd needed him, and for that I would be in his eternal debt.

"Came to see if there was anything worth salvaging," Carlyle said, and then nudged Montgomery's unconscious leg with the tip of his boot. "He'll do, for a start."

"Would you mind taking him back to Quick?" I asked. "We can stay at the inn for a few days until he and Edward are both recovered."

"Aye," he said, and signaled to Balthazar. "Help me load 'em up in the wagon, won't you, big fellow?" The two of them placed Montgomery gently on the saddle blanket, and Carlyle took his seat at the front and picked up the reins.

I rested an arm over the wooden wagon bed, brushing Montgomery's hair out of his eyes. "I'll see you soon," I whispered to him. "There are a few things I have to do first."

I gave the signal to Carlyle, who clicked to the mule,

and the wagon rolled off down the muddy road. Baltha-zar and I watched it go. With a deep sigh, Balthazar turned toward the courtyard.

"Lot of bodies, miss," he grunted. "I'd best get started on the graves; the ground is frozen, so I'll have to sink them in the bog."

"I'll help you."

He shook his head. "You inhaled a lot of smoke, miss. You need rest as well. Edward can help; he's strong, even now." He lumbered off.

I faced Ballentyne, watching the smoke rise. The roof of the southern tower had caved in, but the stone bones still stood sentry over the moors. I thought of the winding steps that led to the secrets those rooms once held: Hensley's room with the cages of rats, and above it, the laboratory. All of it now reduced to ashes.

Just like Lucy.

"Parts of the house have burned before," McKenna said, standing beside me. "When my mother was a girl, a fire started in the southern tower and took the entire wing. There'll be demolition to do, plenty of wreckage and clean-ing, but the walls have stood for hundreds of years, and look—they're still standing. We'll rebuild. In a few years it'll be good as new. We can wire electric lights properly, as Elizabeth always wanted. And we can expand the ser-vants' rooms to bring more girls here. So many of them have nowhere else to go, you know. It'll be grand." She clasped her hands. I stared at the wreckage. Whatever lofty vision she saw there, I saw only ashes and smoke.

At my silence, she wrung her hands. "Of course, you're the mistress now. It's entirely your decision how we rebuild. I'd be grateful to offer some advice, just because I've spent my whole life here. Was born in a guest room on the second floor, as a matter of fact. And my mother before me, and her father. This is my home, mistress, but it's your estate. You let me know your plans, and I'll see them carried out."

I squinted at the manor, trying to see the potential there. Elizabeth had entrusted this all to me, along with the secrets the walls held. Ballentyne had been her dream—but was it mine?

"No," I whispered.

McKenna's eyes went wide. "You don't want to rebuild? But mistress, surely you understand—it's useless as ruins. . . ."

"That's not what I meant," I said gently. "I mean *I* don't want to rebuild. Ballentyne has never been my home, not like it was Elizabeth's, and not like it's yours. You should rebuild it, McKenna. I'd like to give it to you. The building—what's left of it—the land, responsibility for the staff."

She stared at me like I was speaking some foreign language, then shook her head emphatically. "I couldn't. Not in a thousand years."

"Why not? Elizabeth told me you knew this place better than she did. She said she couldn't run it without you."

"But it isn't my inheritance," she pressed. "My family's always been the caretakers. The von Stein family has always owned it. It's passed down from generation to generation. I'm not of that family. You are. You're related by marriage."

She wrung her hands harder. My offer truly troubled her.

"Sometimes inheritance has nothing to do with family ties. It's about what's best for Ballentyne, and that's you."

She gaped at me. "Are you certain, miss?"

I thought of Jack Serra, flipping his fortune-telling cards in the light of a lantern, talking to me about finding my fate. I pressed a hand against the charm around my neck. I didn't know what my fate was now, but I knew Ballentyne wasn't it.

"I am." I smiled, looking at the building. Now I was starting to see how it could thrive again, but under McKenna's care. "But first, I need to say my good-byes."

FORTY-ONE

THE RUINS WERE SURROUNDED by a deep quiet. Most of the stone walls still stood, giving the manor its iconic shape. I imagined that from a distance a traveler wouldn't even know it was ruined. It wouldn't be until he came closer and saw the sunlight glinting through gaps in the stone that he'd realize it was only a shell.

Elizabeth. Hensley. Lucy. I wasn't sure I believed in the idea of souls, but if they did exist, I was glad they had such a place to wander.

I traced my fingers along the walls as I entered the gaping hole that had once been the thick front door. Not but a few weeks ago I was knocking on it, desperate for refuge. Had I brought about its destruction the minute I set foot here?

No, I thought as I stepped through the foyer. *The science within these halls was never meant to exist.*

The ancient tapestries had burned, revealing more entrances to the secret passageways. The passages seemed less mysterious with the light of day pouring through the roofless ceiling. I stepped inside, heedless of the soot staining my dress. The rubble shifted and a little pink nose poked out. One of Hensley's white rats, alive and well except for a small burned patch on its tail. I knelt down.

"Come here, little fellow." I held out my hand as Hensley and Elizabeth used to do. But the rat shied away, sensing that I wasn't one of its masters. I didn't mind. I liked thinking that some of the rats had survived the fire. Life still thrived in Ballentyne, even in ruins. Something still remembered Hensley and Elizabeth.

I followed the passageway slowly, having to climb over fallen beams and collapsed walls. McKenna had quite a task ahead of her, but I was confident she'd succeed. I liked thinking of Ballentyne as a sanctuary for girls who didn't have anywhere else to go. When I'd been alone and on my own, I would have loved calling this place home.

But it wasn't my home, not really. Neither was London, which was the site of so much loss, the place where the professor had died and where scandal had befallen my family, and where Lucy's mother waited for a daughter and a husband who would never return.

I closed my eyes, resting my fingers on the walls. When the wind blew, I thought I could smell a little of Lucy's perfume, and it made me miss her all the more.

Was it fair that I survived and she didn't?

If Lucy hadn't died, I imagined, she'd have lived out the rest of her life here, taking care of the girls. Her father was wrong when he said she only cared for dresses and handsome men. She'd loved the girls, and she'd loved me, and she'd loved Edward. She'd cared about us enough to sacrifice her own life for us.

I left the passages and climbed the central staircase up to the ruins of the northern tower. The glass window of the observatory had shattered, littering the charred floor. All that was left of Elizabeth's settee was a broken frame. I remembered her leaning in, her face a mirror to my own, telling me the story of Victor Frankenstein.

I kicked aside some charred furniture until I found her metal globe of the constellations. The wooden stand had burned, and the metal was dented but mostly intact. I ran my fingers along the top portion, where Elizabeth had kept *Les Étoiles* gin.

I opened the secret latch of the globe, but the bottles had shattered and melted. Ruined, like everything else. Then my fingers drifted to the bottom compartment, where she'd stored Ballentyne's biggest secrets.

I glanced over my shoulder, listening for the sounds of footsteps or breathing that would tell me I wasn't alone. But all the paintings and tapestries that hid the secret passages were gone now. I could see everything, even straight to the morning sky. I was alone.

I slid open the metal compartment, breath drawn. Ashes rained out: thick black ones that stained my fingers. They still had the shape of books until I touched them, and they broke apart into dust.

All of Frankenstein's legacy, the Origin Journals, had been destroyed.

I looked at my soot-dark hands. These ashes had been ideas once; they'd given birth to my own father's research, which had given life to Balthazar, and Edward, and even to me.

Even days ago, such a loss might have filled me with melancholy. I knew Henri Moreau's work was wrong, but I'd come to believe in its potential. Now that I knew he wasn't my father, and his genius and madness didn't flow in my veins, the journals seemed distant, like something that belonged to someone else. I let the ashes fall past my fingertips.

I felt anything but sadness. In fact, I'd never felt so alive.

I stood up, dusting my hands off, and left the observatory without looking back. A shattered window in the hallway gave me a glimpse of Edward and Balthazar in the courtyard, loading the mercenaries' and horses' bodies onto a pallet to drag out to the bog. I could still remember how close I was to death that day I nearly drowned with the sheep.

I had escaped those frigid waters. Radcliffe and his men never would.

I spent the rest of the morning checking the rest of the rooms, finding little to salvage save a few pieces of jewelry and coins that had survived in a lockbox in Elizabeth's bedroom that we could use to pay for the inn in Quick and food and transportation. It wasn't until afternoon, when Balthazar and Edward were almost finished with the last of the bodies, that I steeled my strength and went to the southern tower.

I stood at the bottom of the stairs, tracing the crumbled walls. A small line of smoke still drifted out of some pile of rubble, off to the heavens. I took a deep breath and climbed to the laboratory.

The roof was gone, letting light touch every corner. The wooden operating table was only ash. A few glass jars remained, but I threw them out the window, letting them shatter in the rubble below.

I knelt on the floor, where the metal bits of a corset mixed with white pieces of bone. This is where I had left Lucy's body, where I'd decided that she wouldn't have another chance at life. I found a metal pan and gathered her bones carefully, wrapped them in my own shawl.

This isn't good-bye, she had said to me before I left for the island. *I'll see you again.*

I whispered the same to her, telling her that I'd follow her when it was my time. Amid the ashes something metal flashed, and I brushed aside rubble to find Edward's pocket watch, which Lucy had worn around her neck the entire time he'd been dead.

I slid the watch into my pocket. It was time to bury Lucy and leave this place forever.

I took a step back toward the stairs but hesitated, recognizing my own boot print in the ash. It was small, like Elizabeth's, and yet the steps were tight and determined, like Henri Moreau's had been.

I wouldn't follow in Father's footsteps anymore.

I wouldn't follow in Elizabeth's, either.

I walked through the ash. The only footsteps I'd make would be my own.

FORTY-TWO

My last view of Ballentyne was with the sun behind it, the moors in the wind, as I scattered Lucy's ashes in the bog where Edward and Balthazar had buried her father.

"I'll miss you, Lucy," I whispered. "You never gave up on me, or on Edward, or even on your father. We were lucky to have called you a friend."

Balthazar stood solemnly a few steps away, blinking into the fading sun with his Bible folded in his hands, Edward by his side and Sharkey at his feet. At my nod Balthazar opened the pages and read from one of his favorite passages.

"*A good name is better than precious ointment, and the day of death than the day of birth,*" he read, and then closed the Bible. "Miss Lucy was special to me," he added. "She was like a beam of light on the wall you couldn't catch. She never thought about the shadows. I tried to look after her." He took a deep breath. "God will look after her now."

While he said his good-byes to Lucy, I drew the pocket

watch out of my apron and pressed it into Edward's hand. He looked at me in surprise.

"She would have wanted you to have it," I said. "She kept it with her to remember you by. I thought it might remind you of her."

"It will." He slipped it into the shirt pocket over his heart, pressing it once to feel its weight against his chest.

When the three of us had said our good-byes to her, I gathered a handful of dried heather from the barn and tied it with a ribbon, and left it on the corner of the field. We walked along the muddy road, past the oak tree with the lightning scar down the trunk. It was strange to think of Ballentyne empty now, with Carlyle and McKenna and the servants already in Quick. McKenna said the monastery had some spare rooms they could stay in until Ballentyne was livable again, in exchange for help around the monks' farm. Life was already finding its new path for them.

But would it for us?

Montgomery was lying in a bed in Quick, waiting for me. I toyed with my wedding ring, thinking of our future together. The world was ours, now. No fates or inheritances to bind us. No more shadows, no more lurking threats. Maybe Montgomery and I would travel. He knew how to sail, and I'd love to see the lights of Paris. Maybe we'd go to America, where the great redwoods towered. Or maybe we'd settle in Quick, in a little cottage on the edge of town, and take up Elizabeth's role as healer of small things: broken bones, gout, indigestion.

Balthazar paused, looking back down the road in the direction of the manor.

"What is it, Balthazar?"

"Something I forgot to do," he said, shuffling a bit. He cast a worried expression back over his shoulder. "I must go back. Not for long. You don't need to wait for me."

I rested my hand on his shoulder. "We'll see you in Quick tonight?"

He nodded, distracted, and shuffled back down the road at a surprising clip. Sharkey followed at his heels, eternally loyal.

"What do you think that's about?" I asked Edward.

"Who knows," he said. "The man is entitled to his mysteries."

We kept walking as the sun sank lower and the twilight shadows darkened the forest. Ahead, the lights of Quick winked. Another mile and I'd be back with Montgomery.

But it wasn't just Montgomery and me, and the longer Edward and I walked without speaking, the greater that silence became. I cast him a sidelong look, wondering what was going through his head. He had another chance at life now—but without Lucy.

"What will you do now, Edward?" My voice was the kind of quiet saved only for the really important questions in life. "I don't know what Montgomery and I will do, or where we'll go. I think Balthazar will always be with us regardless of where we end up. You're welcome to stay with us, too. You know that, don't you?"

He rubbed the back of his head. He might have been nearly indestructible, but the bloodstain and hole on his shirt were impossible to ignore.

"I'm grateful, I truly am, but we both know my future isn't with you and Montgomery. Nor with Balthazar." The conversation fell back into a thoughtful silence as we continued toward Quick. "I never told you this," he continued, "but Hensley showed me the secret passages."

"He did?"

"He was suspicious of me but intrigued to have someone else like himself. I don't think anyone truly realized how lonely that child was. Not just because he was the only little boy in a house of women, but because life is different when you're like we are. Everything's the same, and yet it's as though you're looking at the world from a distance through a spyglass. It can make a person feel very removed from everyone else." His fingers drifted up to touch the pocket watch in his shirt. "He told me a story about the previous residents of Ballentyne."

I raised my eyebrow. "Victor Frankenstein?"

"Yes, but it wasn't Frankenstein I was interested in. It was his creation. The fate of the monster he made."

"It wasn't a monster," I objected.

Edward shrugged. "Call it whatever you like. The truth is, I'm not so different from him. Created from bits and pieces of man and animal. Brought to life by a madman. Like him, I know what death feels like. How many people can say that?" He looked off to the horizon, where the first buildings of Quick were just visible. "I think with Hensley gone, there must only be me and him in the entire world."

He stopped and wiped his forehead, though there was no sweat on the cold night. I heard a dog barking—the rest of the world was just a few steps away, but I felt caught here on the road between my old life and my future one.

"I'm going to go after him," Edward said. "To the Arctic. He went there because he didn't belong in the realm of men. I feel it, too. I wanted to be human for so long, but that's not what I am. I never have been. It's time I accepted that. It occurs to me that Frankenstein's creation and I, well, we could each use a companion."

I tore my eyes away from the lights of Quick. "That was over a hundred years ago. He might not still exist."

Edward shrugged. "I'd like an adventure."

The dog barked again, closer now, amid the sounds of a door slamming and a couple arguing and the realities of the real world. Edward gave me a smile. "Come on. Montgomery's waiting for us."

MONTGOMERY DIDN'T WAKE UNTIL the morning. I'd spent the night slumped in a chair by his bedside. There was something strange about watching him sleeping. When I still suffered from my illness, it had been me so many times in bed for days with a raging fever. Our roles were reversed now—Montgomery ill and me sitting by his bedside, praying for him to wake safe and sound.

"Juliet."

I jerked awake, disoriented by the sunlight pouring through the window. Montgomery was sitting up in bed, dark circles under his eyes and deep lines in his face.

"Montgomery!" I pushed out of the stiff chair and climbed onto the bed, feeling his forehead, trying to count the pulse on his wrist, but he brushed off my attempts with a laugh.

"I'm fine," he said, though his voice was gravelly with exhaustion.

"You've been asleep for a full day," I said.

He took my hands in his, kissing the palm of each one. "You're safe, and that's all that matters." He squinted around the room. "Where are we?"

"The guest rooms above the tavern in Quick."

"What happened at Ballentyne?"

I swallowed, hating to relive all those terrible memories. "You passed out after you saved me in the passageways. Balthazar dragged you to safety, and we defeated Radcliffe and his men. They're all dead, even Radcliffe, buried in the bog. Edward and Balthazar are fine. And Jack and his troupe . . ." I looked at the lines in my palm. "We wouldn't have made it without them, but they left. Disappeared. They didn't say good-bye."

Montgomery reached past me to the bedside table, picking up a small piece of paper. A card. Bright colors flashed on it.

"That's one of Jack's fortune-telling cards!" I recognized the same bright blue paint, the same lettering. I'd only seen a few cards of his deck before: the Fool, the Emperor. This one was the Lovers, a man and a woman embracing. Someone had taken an ink pen to the woman's fair hair and colored it dark, like mine.

"This wasn't here last night," I said. "I haven't left the room once."

Montgomery's mouth hitched back in a smile. "Well, Ajax is nothing if not clever. He probably left this while you were sleeping."

"Then he's still in Quick?"

Montgomery shook his head. "I doubt it. He's probably long gone."

I ran my finger down the edge of the card. "At least he did say good-bye, after all."

By midday, Montgomery was well enough to dress and go downstairs to the dining room, where we ordered a feast and indulged as though we were just any travelers in any inn in the world. It was a fantasy that was starting to feel real, and I liked it.

When I looked out the dining hall window and saw a familiar figure, I grinned.

"Balthazar's back!" We ran outside to greet him. He held his shepherd's staff in one hand, a lead in the other tied around the neck of the little goat that was always getting away. Sharkey barked when he saw us and ran up to have his head scratched.

"The goats," Balthazar explained, nodding toward the flock that trailed behind him on the road. "No one remembered the goats. We couldn't just leave them."

My smile grew.

Montgomery wrapped an arm around my back and pulled me close, pressing his lips to my hair. "Elizabeth would have been happy to see you smile, so carefree," he said. "Lucy, too."

I brushed back a strand of blond hair that had fallen

into his eyes. "Edward's decided to leave us and go north. I wonder if he'll find what he's looking for."

There was silence for some time, and then Montgomery turned me around, taking my hands. "Did you?"

I thought about my fantasy of the cottage in Quick. Perhaps Balthazar would live in a little house behind ours, where he'd take care of the goats and attend to his spiritual matters. It was a far cry from the grand house on Belgrave Square I'd grown up in, and from the imposing Ballentyne Manor. It reminded me more of my little attic apartment in Shoreditch, where I'd felt so at home. The only thing that had been missing from that life was someone to share it with, but now I had Montgomery.

"Yes," I said, and leaned in to kiss him.

I didn't know exactly where our paths would lead. I might study botany, or animal husbandry, or meteorology, or even take up the piano again. I wasn't sure what I wanted in life, but I knew now that it was my choice, and as I grinned against Montgomery's face, I knew that there really was only one life, and I intended to live mine as richly as any person could.

ACKNOWLEDGMENTS

SO THIS IS WHAT ending a trilogy feels like—satisfying but bittersweet. When I wrote the last page and ended Juliet's story, I was overcome with gratitude that I had the opportunity to share these books, and for everyone who's been a part of that process. Quinlan Lee, you pulled me out of the slush pile all those years ago. Josh and Tracey Adams, you've helped me navigate the uncertain waters of publishing. Kristin Rens, you've taught me so much about writing, editing, and making words come to life. To the rest of the HarperCollins and Balzer + Bray teams, including Caroline Sun, Alison Klapthor, Alison Donalty, Renée Cafiero, Anne Dunn, Judy Levin, Emilie Polster, Stephanie Hoffman, Margot Wood, and Aubry Parks-Fried: I owe you big and shall repay you by 1) naming a future character after you or 2) bringing you moonshine next time I come to New York.

Thanks as well to Megan Miranda and Beth Revis for reading an early version of this book at our Bat Cave retreat, and for the insistence that creepy child characters are never a bad idea. April Tucholke, you've helped me maintain my sanity, ironically by talking about marvelously insane things. Thanks to my friends, family, coworkers, and members of the writing community who have patiently supported me, especially to my parents, Peggy and Tim, my sister, Lena, the Shepherd clan, and my very patient husband,

Jesse. Also, Leila, thanks for letting me borrow your name. Von Stein manor lives! Cue lightning strike!

Thanks lastly to my readers, for going on this journey with me. I hope I've given you some sleepless nights, new ways of thinking about classic science fiction, and a few good hours with books about finding oneself amid the madness.

Read on for a sneak peek at *The Cage*,
the first book in Megan Shepherd's new series.

1

Cora

THERE ARE CERTAIN THINGS the mind cannot comprehend. People fall into the same routines of thinking day after day: toss an apple and it falls to the ground. Pick a flower and it withers. Fall asleep in your bed and wake there the next morning.

But *this*. This was like dropping an apple and having it fall toward the sun.

Cora Mason dug her hands against her temples to steady the churning sea between her ears. She'd woken in a foggy daze minutes ago—or maybe it was hours—in what seemed to be an endless desert. Her bedroom windows were now rust-red dunes rising in hundred-foot swells. Her ceiling was a cloudless sky. Her bedside lamp was a blazing sun searing her skin.

Wherever she was, it definitely wasn't Virginia.

And it wasn't like any desert she'd ever heard of. This wasn't cacti and thirsty clumps of dry grass. This was an impossibly vast smear of red as far as she could see.

Was she dreaming? In dreams, her mouth never felt this dry. When her father had first been elected senator, his security detail had trained Cora and her brother, Charlie, in what to do in the event of a kidnapping—stay in one place, don't fight back, wait for help. But that had been a decade ago. She'd just barely started kindergarten. Did the same logic apply to a sixteen-year-old? There were no footsteps in the sand, no tire tracks, no indication of how she'd even gotten there.

A starburst of pain streaked through her head. She hissed, pressing her temples harder. Only moments ago, she'd been in a car with Charlie, her down-lined parka pulled tight against the cold, cranking the heat as they drove to a ski resort to meet their parents. She'd had her feet on the dash, scrawling lyrics in a notebook.

"What do you think of this line?" she had asked. "'A stranger in my own life, a ghost behind my smile, not at home in paradise, not at home in hell'?"

Charlie had grinned as he took a left into the resort. "Not bad," he'd said, "but a senator's daughter can't sing songs about hell."

Now, surrounded by sand, Cora felt panic clawing up her throat. She was supposed to be in that Jeep. She'd waited nearly two years for this. The four of them together as a family. No more custody battles. No politics and reporters. Just winter in Virginia. Parkas and snow. Her parents waiting with hot chocolate, not a couple anymore, but not bitter enemies either. She and Charlie had been close enough to see the resort over the next rise. Were her parents there, waiting, wondering how she'd vanished? Were they safe?

The breeze stung her eyes, carrying a strange smell—granite and ozone. As she scraped her tongue with her teeth, she could taste the smell in the back of her throat. It triggered another memory. A dream. Hazy images of a man's handsome face—bronzed skin, heavy brows, closed eyes—that danced in the back of her mind like a will-o'-the-wisp. The dream beckoned her, but the more she reached for it, the farther away it floated, always frustratingly out of reach. Was he someone real? Or had she been unconscious for so long that she'd dreamed of an *angel*?

Or ...

Am I dead?

She hugged her legs close. Dead people didn't sweat as much as she was. She was alive; she just had to figure out where. *Stay in one place*, the security guard had taught her. *Wait for help.* But if she stayed, she'd die of thirst or sunburn. She hugged her legs harder, fighting the urge to panic, and remembered the advice her mother had given her when things got too overwhelming.

Count backward. Ten. Nine. Eight ...

She forced herself to her feet. She'd find shade, or water, or some kind of town, and wait there for help.

Seven. Six ...

She started walking. One more step after the last. One more dune after the last.

Panic lingered in her joints, making her feel loose and unhinged, like her legs might walk away from the rest of her body. The blazing sun dried her tears into salty crusts that she tasted each time she licked her lips. She shaded her eyes and squinted upward, hoping for a helicopter, but there was only an eerie quiet.

Where were her kidnappers? What was the point of leaving her in the middle of nowhere?

Five ...

Ahead, the valley floor sloped sharply into a towering dune that was higher than all the others. She blinked up at the wall of sand, her body wobbling as she started to climb. Up, up, crawling more than walking, sliding back one step for every two forward. She brushed sweat off her forehead with her sleeve, then froze.

The clothes she was dressed in weren't her own.

Her down parka and ski boots were gone. She was barefoot, with skinny black jeans and an oversized shirt advertising a band she'd never heard of, with thick black cuffs on each wrist. A *punk* look? She was more lace skirts and cotton dresses. The only concert she'd ever been to was her neighbor's garage band, and she'd left with her hands over her ears after ten minutes.

Now, she ran the tissue-soft fabric between her fingers. A white strap flashed beneath it. She peeked down her collar, and fear bubbled up her throat. Beneath her clothes were a white camisole and white panties. Not hers. Whoever had put her here had first dressed her like a paper doll and then left her for dead. Her stomach lurched at the thought of strangers' hands all over her. But whose hands? Who would do this?

Don't panic. Keep counting. Four . . .

She was unhurt, as far as she could tell, except for the sunburn. But would she stay that way? She needed her father's security guards. Or Charlie. All those years when they were kids, while her dad worked in Washington and her mother slept half the day away, Charlie had looked out for her. He was the one person she could always rely on, if you didn't count Sadie, which you couldn't because she was a dog. He'd told her old episodes of *Twilight Zone* as bedtime stories. He'd taught her where to hide her notebook of song lyrics from their snooping mother. And six months ago, he'd picked her up when she was released from Bay Pines juvenile detention facility. He'd even punched a reporter who shoved a microphone in her face and asked how an upstanding senator's daughter went from straight As to eighteen months for manslaughter.

Three. Two . . .

She pawed for her necklace like a lifeline. It held a charm for each member of her family: a theater mask for her mom; a golf club for her dad; a tiny airplane for Charlie, who wanted to be a pilot. All she'd wanted was for them to be together again, as close as the clinking charms on her necklace. She'd been so near to the resort where they would all sip hot chocolate like a family again—but her fingers grazed only air.

The necklace was gone.

Sweat chilled on the back of her neck. She threw a glance over her shoulder, suddenly overtaken with the feeling that she was being followed. The dunes were empty. Breathing harder, she climbed the final few feet to the top of the highest dune. *Please, let there be a road. A telephone. A donkey.* The only thing she desperately didn't want to see was another dune, and another, and another, stretching forever.

She crested the dune with burning lungs, brushed the sand from her hands, and squeezed her eyes shut. She took a deep breath and finished counting backward.

One.

She opened her eyes.

2

Cora

FROM THIS HIGH, CORA had a 360-degree view. The desert stretched in choppy waves behind her, but to her left was a field of rich black soil, and fruit trees reaching their branches toward the sun, and rows of rainbow-colored vegetables: purple eggplant, yellow squash, red tomatoes, golden corn.

A *farm*?

Cora crumpled to the ground as pain ripped through her skull. She cried out, squeezing her temples. Had she been drugged? Was that what the dream of her beautiful angel had been, a hallucination? She blinked furiously, but the farm didn't go away.

Count backward.

Ten . . .

She forced herself to look to the right and nearly choked. Opposite the farm, a stony outcropping covered with sea-green lichen sloped into a valley of windswept trees. Enormous oaks, and firs, and evergreens; all covered with a dusting of white. Not like the leafless winter forests of Virginia, but an arctic tundra. A cold breeze blew, carrying a snowflake that settled on Cora's sunburned palm. She shoved herself to her feet.

Screw counting.

She shook her hand wildly, pacing. Even more impossible than everything else was the slice of water directly in front of her. Gently lapping waves stretched to an ocean bay that made her stomach plummet like she was sinking. She spit out the phantom taste of salt water. An ocean didn't belong here. *She* didn't belong here.

Sweat poured down her temples, despite the tundra wind. On the far side of the bay, mountains loomed, and even what looked like a cityscape. A desert, a farm, an ocean, a forest—habitats that couldn't exist right next to one another. It had to be a secret government biosphere experiment. Or a rich maniac's whim. Or virtual reality.

The granite-and-ozone smell clogged in her nose, and she steadied herself until the sensation passed. She wasn't a little girl—she could handle this. She *had* to. As her breath slowed, a dark shape appeared at the bottom of the hill, where the ocean lapped against the farm's edge.

If she squinted, the shape looked like a person.

"Hey!" She tumbled down the path. Her feet tangled in the grass underfoot as the trail led between rows of peppers bursting with ripeness.

"Hey! I need help!"

The path gave way to a small beach. The person—a dark-haired girl in a white sundress—must have been panicked, because she was curled in the sand, frozen with fear.

"Hey!" Cora stopped short at the edge of the sea, as black-deep water and reality caught up to her all at once. The girl wasn't curled in panic. Facedown in the surf, hair matted, water billowing around motionless legs.

"Oh, no." Cora squeezed her eyes shut. "Get up. Please."

When she opened her eyes, the girl was still motionless. She forced herself to step into the surf, wincing as it swallowed her ankles, and dropped to her knees. In Bay Pines, one of the delinquents had suffocated herself with a plastic shopping bag. Cora had been writing song lyrics in the hallway as the police wheeled the body away: glassy eyes, blue lips.

Just like this girl.

Except this girl also had angry bruises on her shoulder, like someone had grabbed her. For a few moments, all Cora could hear was blood pulsing through her ears. A tattoo flashed on the girl's neck beneath the bruises, a collection of black dots that meant nothing to Cora and never would, because she could never ask the girl about them. Behind her, the forest was perfectly silent, with only the soft falling snow to tell her that the world hadn't stopped.

She stood. The water seemed colder. Deeper. Maybe those bruises meant the girl had been murdered. Or maybe the girl had drowned trying to escape from someone. Either way, Cora didn't want to be next.

She raced out of the water. *Stay in one place. Don't fight back.* That was the advice she'd gotten as a kindergartener. But how could she stay in one place with a dead body?

Footsteps broke the silence. She whirled, searching the spaces between the trees.

There.

White clothes flashed between the branches. Two legs. A person. Cora's muscles tightened to run—or fight.

A boy trudged out of the forest.

He was about her age. He wore jeans and a rumpled white shirt beneath a leather jacket, looking like he'd stumbled out of a pool hall after a night of loud music and beer. A pair of aviator sunglasses were shoved into his jeans pocket. As out of place as Cora—though he was barefoot, like she was. Cute, in a messy way. His dark hair fell around brown eyes that looked as surprised to see her as she was to see him. For a moment, they only stared.

He broke the tension first. "Aren't you . . ." His words died when he saw the body. "Is she *dead*?"

He took a step forward. Cora scrambled backward, ready to bolt, and he stopped. He popped a knuckle in his left hand. Strong hands, Cora noted. Hands that could have held a girl under water.

"Back up," Cora threatened. "If you touch me, I'll claw your eyes out."

Sure enough, that stopped him. He dragged a hand over his mouth, eyes a little glassy. "Wait. You think *I* killed her?"

"She has bruises on her arm. She struggled with someone."

"It wasn't me! I don't know what's going on, but I didn't kill anyone." He paced to the edge of the surf, where the water brushed his toes—not afraid of the water, like she'd been. "Look, my clothes are dry. If I'd done it, I'd be sopping wet." He rubbed his temples. "She must have fifty pounds on you, so I doubt you killed her, but *someone* did. We should get out of here before they come back. Find a phone or a radio. We can try that barn."

A phone. She longed to hear her father's voice on the other end, telling her that it was all a misunderstanding . . . but a girl was dead. Whoever the girl was, those bruises were more than just a misunderstanding to her.

"I watch TV," Cora said. "I know how this goes. You act all friendly and then strangle me behind the barn. I'm not going anywhere with you."

He rubbed a hand over his face, digging deep into his scalp, as though his head splintered with pain too. "In case you haven't noticed, this isn't TV. There's no one but me and a murderer, so I suggest we help each other."

Cora eyed him warily. Her first day in juvie, a gap-toothed girl had offered her a contraband Coca-Cola—a welcome present, the girl had said, to help her adjust. Two days later, the girl had punched her in the ribs and stolen her sudoku book.

You might have grown up in a rich-girl bubble, the gap-toothed girl had told her, *but in here you have to learn the rules of the real world. First off: never trust a stranger—especially one who comes offering help.*

3

Lucky

AFTER LUCKY WOKE IN a snowdrift with a splitting head-
ache, wearing someone else's clothes and missing his granddad's
watch, he'd narrowed down the possibilities: either he was going
insane, or someone at the mechanic's shop had dropped a wrench
on his head and this was some freakish afterlife. Now, standing
opposite the girl with the wheat-blond hair, he knew.

He was definitely dead. And not just dead—he was in hell.

That was the only way to explain Cora Mason.

It had taken him a few moments to recognize her. Ever since
waking, it had been a challenge just to put one foot in front of the
other, fighting the knife of pain in his head. Then, suddenly, there
was a beautiful girl with hair so light it matched the sand. She
might have been a vision, except visions didn't dress like they were
headed to a rave.

Then she'd looked up, and her features had rearranged themselves, and *shit*—he knew her. The senator's daughter accused of

manslaughter. He'd followed her story for the last two years, surrounded by her painfully pretty face on television, read reports about how the accident tore apart one of the country's top political families.

It had torn him apart too. It didn't matter that he'd never met her. He had been the one responsible for ruining her life. Only two people knew it: he and her dad—a man who made Lucky's fist ache with a desire to punch something.

"Who are you?" she demanded.

He rubbed a hand over his chest, where the guilt was still tender as a sucker punch, even after two years. "Call me Lucky. From a little town in Montana called Whitefish. I woke up in the middle of a snowdrift in that forest a couple hours ago; before that, I was working on the busted throttle lock of my motorcycle. That's all I remember."

He stopped short, swallowing his words, the ache in his head pulsing like a second heartbeat. Memories of home played in the back of his head. His granddad's sun-wrinkled face. The smell of chicken feed. Motor oil slick in the lines of his hand, so hard to wash away. He'd been fixing his motorcycle so he could drive to the army recruiting office in Missoula. *With your grades, college isn't an option,* his school counselor had said, and slid a brochure across the desk: red, white, and blue font commanding him to do the right thing.

It didn't matter if enlisting was the right thing. It mattered that his dad, and his granddad, had sat in that same damn chair and gotten that same damn brochure. It mattered that Afghanistan was a long way from the accident that had left his hand busted, and from his mother's gravestone with the plastic flowers, and from Cora Mason's face in the newspaper.

A wave pulled the girl's body out to sea, and Lucky lurched for it. "Shit. Help me grab her before she floats away. The police will want to check the body."

Cora eyed the water like she'd rather step into quicksand.

"Okay . . . then we'll do Plan B. You stand there and look cute, and *I'll* haul out the dead body."

He approached slowly, giving Cora space as he waded into the surf. He'd never seen a dead body before. Would it be warm? Clammy? The dead girl looked foreign, maybe Middle Eastern, and she had to be close to six feet tall. An old scar marred her chin, in the shape of a lopsided heart.

He cracked the knuckles in his left hand. They were always stiffer when he first woke up.

"You ever done this before?" Cora asked.

"Pulled a dead body out of the ocean? Can't say I have." He grabbed the girl under the arms and hauled her to shore. As soon as he was out of the water, Cora helped. They laid her on the sand, and he did a quick check of the body.

"No wallet. No ID."

The dead girl's dress strap had fallen. Lucky fixed it, wishing his hands weren't shaking. He stood up, dusting sand off his palms like he could wipe away the grit of death, and met Cora's eyes directly for the first time. They were surrounded by dark circles in real life. The photographs in the newspapers hadn't captured that.

"I'm Cora," she said.

Now would be the time to tell her that he knew her name, and a lot more. He could tell her about September 3—the day he'd tried to kill her father. It was two weeks after the accident. He'd broken into his dad's gun safe. He'd driven to an airfield where

Senator Mason's son was learning to fly a Cessna 172. He'd parked the car and told himself he could do it. He had to. His mother was in the grave, and Senator Mason was patting his son on the back. Carefree. Guiltless. He'd tried to open the car door, only to find two men in black suits on either side. They'd dragged him out and taken his gun. Then they'd made him an offer.

"Nice to meet you, Cora." He looked away, wiping his mouth. "I'm going to check the barn for a phone. You should come. We're safer if we stick together."

She glanced behind her toward the cityscape. "Yeah, but . . . don't get too close."

He held up his hands in mock surrender and climbed the path. It wound them through the orchard, where a stream ran between the trees, spreading an eerie calmness through the air. He ducked a hanging apple, and his stomach lurched. How long had it been since he'd eaten?

"So what's your theory?" he asked.

"Theory?" She held her arms tightly across her chest.

"Where we are. How we got here." He paused. He really should tell her about that day in the airfield. But she cast a questioning look at him, all wide blue eyes, and he lost his resolve. "I mean . . . it's snowing fifty feet away, and here it's seventy degrees. There's a desert over that hill that goes on for miles. And I swear that sun hasn't moved since I woke up hours ago. The clothes you're wearing . . . are they yours?"

She brushed the strap of the camisole. "No."

"Same for me. Why would someone change our clothes? And put us in these weird locations?" He raked his nails across his scalp to help him think. "I've been through every possible explanation:

it's a joke. An experiment. But it's too weird, changing our clothes. That takes time and planning. Whoever is doing this is messing with us intentionally. I just can't figure out why."

"I don't *care* why," Cora said. "I just want to go home."

Her voice broke, slicing into Lucky's chest. He stopped. "Hey. It's okay. To be afraid, I mean." He gave her a smile, just a tug of one corner. "I am too."

The barn was just feet away. He started for it, but she grabbed his arm. He flinched, not expecting her touch. Her fingers were smaller than he'd imagined. So fragile. Who would do this to a girl who'd already been through so much?

"Those markings on your neck," she said. "The black dots. What do they mean?"

Lucky blinked. He had no idea what she was talking about, but her eyes dropped to the place just below his left ear. He reached up a hand that brushed hard bumps, like grains of sand embedded in his skin.

He dropped his hand.

For years he'd worn his granddad's watch, even back when the strap had been too big, but it had vanished when he'd woken. He felt lost without its weight.

"I don't know." His eyes went to her neck. "But you have them too."

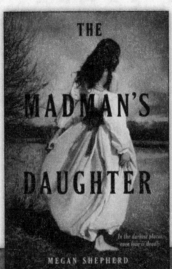